Praise for
Accidentally Dead

"A laugh-out-loud follow-up to *The Accidental Werewolf*, and it's a winner . . . Ms. Cassidy is an up-and-comer in the world of paranormal romance." —*Fresh Fiction*

"An enjoyable, humorous satire that takes a bite out of the vampire romance subgenre . . . Fans will appreciate the nonstop hilarity."
—*Genre Go Round Reviews*

The Accidental Werewolf

"Cassidy, a prolific author of erotica, has ventured into MaryJanice Davidson territory with a humorous, sexy tale." —*Booklist*

"If Bridget Jones became a lycanthrope, she might be Marty. Fun and flirty humor is cleverly interspersed with dramatic mystery and action. It's hard to know which character to love best, though: Keegan or Muffin, the toy poodle that steals more than one scene."
—*The Eternal Night*

"A riot! Marty's internal dialogue will have you howling, and her antics will keep the laughs coming. If you love paranormal with a comedic twist, you'll love this book." —*Romance Junkies*

"A lighthearted romp . . . [An] entertaining tale with an alpha twist." —*Midwest Book Review*

More praise for the novels of Dakota Cassidy

"The fictional equivalent of the little black dress—every reader should have one!"
—Michele Bardsley

"Serious, laugh-out-loud humor with heart, the kind of love story that leaves you rooting for the heroine, sighing for the hero, and looking for your own significant other at the same time."
—Kate Douglas

"Ditzy and daring . . . Pure escapist fun."
—*Romance Reviews Today*

"Dakota Cassidy is going on my must-read list!"
—*Joyfully Reviewed*

"If you're looking for some steamy romance with something that will have you smiling, you have to read [Dakota Cassidy]."
—*The Best Reviews*

kiss & hell

dakota cassidy

BERKLEY SENSATION, NEW YORK

THE BERKLEY PUBLISHING GROUP
Published by the Penguin Group
Penguin Group (USA) Inc.
375 Hudson Street, New York, New York 10014, USA
Penguin Group (Canada), 90 Eglinton Avenue East, Suite 700, Toronto, Ontario M4P 2Y3, Canada
(a division of Pearson Penguin Canada Inc.)
Penguin Books Ltd., 80 Strand, London WC2R 0RL, England
Penguin Group Ireland, 25 St. Stephen's Green, Dublin 2, Ireland (a division of Penguin Books Ltd.)
Penguin Group (Australia), 250 Camberwell Road, Camberwell, Victoria 3124, Australia
(a division of Pearson Australia Group Pty. Ltd.)
Penguin Books India Pvt. Ltd., 11 Community Centre, Panchsheel Park, New Delhi—110 017, India
Penguin Group (NZ), 67 Apollo Drive, Rosedale, North Shore 0632, New Zealand
(a division of Pearson New Zealand Ltd.)
Penguin Books (South Africa) (Pty.) Ltd., 24 Sturdee Avenue, Rosebank, Johannesburg 2196,
South Africa

Penguin Books Ltd., Registered Offices: 80 Strand, London WC2R 0RL, England

This book is an original publication of The Berkley Publishing Group.

This is a work of fiction. Names, characters, places, and incidents either are the product of the author's imagination or are used fictitiously, and any resemblance to actual persons, living or dead, business establishments, events, or locales is entirely coincidental. The publisher does not have any control over and does not assume any responsibility for author or third-party websites or their content.

PRINTING HISTORY
Berkley Sensation trade paperback edition/June 2009

Library of Congress Cataloging-in-Publication Data

Cassidy, Dakota.
    Kiss & hell / Dakota Cassidy.—Berkley Sensation trade paperback ed.
        p. cm.
    ISBN 978-0-425-22785-5
    I. Title.

PS3603.A8685K57 2009
813'.6—dc22   2009004054

PRINTED IN THE UNITED STATES OF AMERICA

10 9 8 7 6 5 4 3 2 1

There are many four-legged pooches to thank for the making of this book. Did you think I was kidding in my bio when I said I had more pets than the local animal shelter?

Ahem . . . with love and eternal gratitude for each toe-licking tickle. All the early morning potty runs (really, thanks, dudes). The überstench-filled doggy breath wakeup calls. The pounces on my stomach to remind me I still have all my girlie innards. The stock I now own in a well-known paper towel brand. The baths I've been forced to take with you against my will. The wayward "chewies" I nearly lost a freakin' eye looking for. The capture and release program invented just for your entertainment when it's time to be brushed and declawed (insert evil laughter here), and the three vacuum cleaners I've clogged and beaten like dead horses.

But mostly for the unconditional love, endless giggles, smiles, cuddles, and utter joy you bring to my life—this is for: Mike, our bladder-impaired, diaper-wearing old man; Mindy, our anxiety-riddled, phobic angel; Milo, the one-eyed wonder; Wenzday, our blind diabetic with an enlarged heart; Gomez, or G-Money, as we fondly call him, our waaaaay overweight "love the one you're with man-tramp," er, precious; and finally, the only damned puppy we own that (so far, cross your fingers for us) we tentatively, and dare I say, hesitantly label "normal," Pebbles.

And to the love of my life, Rob, who never bats an eye when I call him up and ask him how much he loves me—a code question for, "How do you feel about being a daddy to sextuplets?"

Also to Renee George, who helps me plot nearly everything I

write, and Michele Bardsley, who was an enormous help with this, too. Thank you for the eight-hour marathon phone calls when I'm writing in circles and you're following behind me with the shovel, digging me out as I head for China. I treasure your friendships even more than your plotting genius. Cindy Hwang and Leis Pederson, who, as a team, rock. And to the constants in my life—Terri and Elaine Smythe, Jose Lugo, Jaynie Ritchie, Robin, Vicki Burklund, Deidre Knight, Elaine Spencer, Sheri Fogarty, my mom, my "Accidental Fans," the Babes, Michele Hoppe, my überfab test readers Erin and Kaz, the League, the DFW Tea ladies, about a million indy booksellers near and far, and most especially, the people who buy my books.

You guys are a whacked bunch, and that's crazy cool. ☺

Dakota ☺

acknowledgments

To Wikipedia; http://dictionaries.travlang.com; Danny in Germany; Jen B., a real pal and a chemistry genius; Kaz, my Spanish rose; www.imdb.com (really, thank you); www.doggietshirts.com; and www.tshirthell.com. Finally, to my fantabulous readers—do note, any and all mistakes are totally and completely mine.

one

"Boo."

You're kidding, right?

"Uh, nope."

Maybe you should try again—only this time, do it with more feeling.

"Okay. Here goes. Ahem . . . boooooooo."

You're not serious, are you? Like really?

"Completely."

Wow, that's too bad.

"What's too bad?"

That you're not kidding. If the plan was to scare me, here's the thing—your scary skills suck.

"That was rude."

Sometimes the truth is rude.

"Don't you mean the truth hurts?"

That, too. And now it's time for you to go.

Delaney Markham waved a dismissive hand behind her shoulder to shoo away the voice of the ghost she was chatting with in her head—the *male* ghost she was chatting with in her head. Occurrences like this happened more often than not. She was used to surprise visits from the other side—the constant interruptions—and sometimes even the errant, unwanted visitor when she was in the midst of trying to make a buck.

But tonight, she had other things to attend to so her supernatural buddy would just have to hang on to his drawers for a little longer.

Delaney resumed her séance position, latching back onto the hands of the family members who sat on either side of her—armed and ready to contact the dead. "Aunt Gwyneth? Are you here with us?" she asked nothing more than the thin air. The people gathered round her table shifted in their wooden chairs with expectation, the lone candle she'd lit highlighting their faces rife with the fear, expectation, and wonder of the unknown.

She could literally hear them not breathing. Aunt Gwyneth's family was tense with a multitude of emotions—as most were during a séance.

Delaney's wind chimes tinkled appropriately—much the way they always did when a spirit entered her herb store in the East Village of New York. For some reason, the spirits liked to play with the chimes to announce their arrival. The familiar shiver of reverence mingled with otherworldly anticipation raced along her nerve endings, settling deep in her belly. Eight hundred bucks was but a question or two away. The chimes fastened to her ceiling shivered once more.

Ding-dong, spirits calling.

She smiled to herself. Suh-weet. Aunt Gwyneth had arrived.

"Um, look, I said, *boo* as scary as I could. It's all I got."

And apparently, Aunt Gwyneth was keeping some pesky company.

Noted, and didn't we just go over this? Delaney mentally whispered with building irritation to the voice that wouldn't get out of her head. A voice now officially fucking with her much-needed paycheck.

"So why aren't you scared?" the husky, not unpleasant voice queried. His words whistled in her head, swirling in a seductive, siren's call kinda way.

Please. As if. It would take a shitload more than some disembodied voice whispering something as lame as "boo" to scare her. She knew scared—scratch that—she knew shit-in-your-pants, full-on terrified and she wasn't going back. *Because this happens all the time to me. It's what some might say is my calling in life, and after the shit I've seen go down, not much scares me—especially a word as weak as* boo. *And one more time—for the record—I'm busy. Go away. Find another medium to stalk,* she relayed mentally as sternly as she could.

Delaney cleared her throat and turned her attention back to the Dabrowski family and their desperate need to have questions answered by their beloved aunt Gwyneth. She asked once more, "Aunt Gwyneth? Your family is here and they have some questions for you. Come, talk to me." She used her soft, "cajoling the dearly departed" tone to woo Gwyneth into communicating with her.

"Damn right I have some questions," Gwyneth Dabrowski's nephew Irv said, interrupting Delaney's mojo with his gruff impatience. "I wanna know why the hell she left the vacation house at the lake to that fruit Leopold. What kind of a frickin' name is that, anyway? A pansy name, that's what. All playing with roses like they were his friends and doing weird girlie crap all the time. He was the gardener, for Chrissake! The lake house shoulda been mine, the piece of shit!"

Another rustle of chairs and the crinkle of an expensive leather coat greeted Delaney's ears. "Irv! Shut up already, would ya? Didn't

Ms. Markham say we had to be quiet while she called on Aunt Gwyneth so as not to provoke or frighten the dead? Do you really want to piss Gwyneth off in death the way you did when she was alive?" Irv's wife, Edna, chided him with her nasally thick New York accent. "Oy, Irv! You never listen. Now be quiet, and let the lady do what we came here for."

"I hate to interrupt again," the man in her head apologized, "but I just have to know. What's a medium, and why would I want to stalk it?"

Delaney scrunched her eyes shut. This was so not the time to come across a wayward spirit, looking for guidance. Especially when today, of all days, she really needed some moolah. *I'm a medium, and you're interrupting my very carefully planned séance. Now go away. I have rent to pay.*

"That still doesn't explain what a medium is. Do you mean that's your size? Because you don't look like a medium to me. I'd have gone with small."

Delaney suppressed a giggle. At least he was a complimentary spirit. And far too put together for her liking. He didn't seem disoriented on this plane at all . . . *Look, didn't I just say I was busy? You ain't the only freakin' spirit out there, and right now, I'm being paid by a very nice family to contact their dead aunt. You, on the other hand, are what I'd call a freeloader—one of those spirits who think the whole spirit world revolves around just them and they can infiltrate a séance whenever they feel like it. I have some pretty strict rules about that—especially when cash is involved. And seeing as you're one of the rare ghosts who has his wits about him, you get it when I say knock it the fuck off. Go back to wherever you came from and visit me during my normal business hours. Capisce?*

"But you still haven't explained the medium thing to me," whoever pushy was reiterated in a soft but steadily increasing, insistent tone.

Again, you're not listening, and to top things off, you're being exceptionally rude. Now shut up and go away before I, like, send out the spirit world's version of a SWAT team and have your ass dragged off to some alternate dimension.

"You can do that?"

Okay, so no, she couldn't do that. Color her caught. That would be way overstating her importance in the spirit world. Delaney sighed. *Look, do me a solid, okay?*

"A solid . . ."

Yeah, you know, like, a favor?

"Oh. Sure. Whaddya need?"

Wow, again, she couldn't help thinking, he wasn't at all like the typical spirits who darkened her doorstep. He didn't seem even a little confused about where he was, nor did he seem terribly agitated. In fact, his tone was almost too friendly. Which, again, made her suspicious. *You. To. Shut. Up. Now, for the love of all that's holy. Please, before the dogs start to bark and I lose my shot at making some cash.*

"You have dogs?"

Six—all as supernaturally sensitive as I am. If they sense an uninvited presence, one that's hacking me off much like you are, not only am I doomed, but so are your eardrums. Now please, let me finish this up, and then we can connect.

"You have six dogs? *Six?* Doesn't that break some kind of law or at least an ordinance?"

I'm sure it does, but it probably won't be the first law I've broken, or the last. And tell me something?

"What's that?" he rumbled, sort of husky and almost too easygoing for her well-honed, ghostie antenna.

Maybe he was a plant. A shiver raced up her spine. She didn't need this—not when the rent was due. Or maybe he was a dead actor. Dead celebrities loved a captive audience; they had one in her and contacted her often because of it. But he didn't sound at all familiar. Stirring from around the table refocused her on getting rid of this new entity. *Is there a little old lady with you? Dripping diamonds and sapphires and wearing a red sweatsuit with white racing stripes down the arms?*

"Yeah, yeah, there is."

Then tell her front and center. Her family has some questions for her, and I need—

"The money. You said that. Um, she says, and I'm only repeating her words, 'No fucking way.'" He cleared his throat, the sound reverberating in her head. "Sorry, but that's what she said. Word for word. Honest."

His words made Delaney pause because they sounded so sincere. Maybe he'd been a Boy Scout in life. Or a priest. Shit. Priests were always a messy, messy affair when it came to crossing them over to the great beyond. If their deaths involved any kind of religious overtones, or a stall in their faith, they were the hardest to convince they should go into what the living called the light. The light was sort of a sham as far as she was concerned. It wasn't always a light, if what some of the comments she'd heard just before the crossing were accurate.

She well remembered the college football player who'd blown his knee out just before draft picks and had lost his chance to play pro ball. His version of what some would call Heaven was Soldier Field and an endless stretch of green. Then there'd been the rich socialite—her idea of utopia was an upscale mall with row after row of stores like Cartier, Cole Haan, and Tiffany. Apparently, sometimes the light was what you made of it—your love for shopping or your dream of playing football in the NFL come true.

"Didn't I tell ya, Edna?" Irv interrupted Delaney's conversation with the as yet unnamed entity. He let go of Delaney's hand and thwacked the table with his meaty fist.

Edna's row of thick bracelets clanked, jarring Delaney's tenuous at best connection with Aunt Gwyneth as she, too, let go, rearing up in her chair and leaning forward toward Irv. "Tell me *what*, Irv?" Her words were raspy and clearly annoyed.

Irv's wide, bulldoglike face screwed up, adding more wrinkles to his pudgy cheeks. "That this broad was a shyster. A fuckin' fruitcake! I told ya this would never work! But no, ya just had ta throw some cash out the window like I piss it out in the damn toilet every morning to pay for your crazy ideas. This is a load of bullshit, and I want my damned deposit back, you freak!" Irv bellowed.

And Irv's bellowing startled the dogs.

All six.

Which meant there'd be no shutting them up.

Which also meant her landlord, Mr. Li, would be downstairs to hassle her tout de suite.

Because it would remind him she was twenty days overdue with her rent.

Fuckity-fuck-fuck-fuck.

Do you see what you've done? she scolded, channeling the interfering voice in her head and tuning out Irv's angry rants now mixed with the incessant, shrieking yaps of her dogs.

His voice blew through her head, calm like a soft ocean breeze—all reasonable. "Well, that's what Gwyneth said to tell you. I was just doing what you asked. She also said she wouldn't have given Irv the *fucking* house on the lake if they'd peeled her skin off while she was still alive. He's a putz, she says. A no-good, lazy piece of shit—"

Again, shutting up would behoove you right now. Especially if you need my help. I can't concentrate on you and the Dabrowskis all at once. Now let me try to salvage some of this while I can, and you practice waiting your freakin' turn.

"My turn for what?"

She didn't have time to answer him. Irv had popped up, with a squealing, protesting Edna following close behind him. The scrape of his chair against the floor, the stomp of his feet while Edna shot Delaney a look of sympathy, meant game over.

The tinkle of the bell on her front door signaled their raucous, angry exit.

Booyah.

Delaney laid her head on the cool surface of her old wood table, letting her cheek rest against it. She puffed out a sigh of defeat while rolling her forehead over the hard oak. Damn these dumb-ass entities that couldn't be bothered with just a little consideration for a working girl. What about "Get the fuck out of my head" didn't they understand?

Always yammering, day and night, night and day—in her head—in the grocery store—while she was in the bathroom—when she was trying to wax her legs. And always it was at the most inopportune of moments—like the ones that involved freakin' cash.

She didn't hate her gift. There were just times she wished she could put it on mute and finish a whole television program without experiencing other-dimensional difficulties.

The dogs, yipping as though someone was swinging them around by their tails, forced her to act. Placing her hands on the wood, Delaney pushed off to rise from her chair and head to the back of her store where her small apartment was.

"Guys! Shut up!" she yelled to her dogs with frustration. "What do you suppose the Dog Whisperer would say if he could hear how unruly you knuckleheads are? Christ on a cracker! Cesar'd shit a Pit Bull if he could see your behavior. Didn't we just spend a whole

kiss & hell   **9**

weekend learning that *I'm* the leader of the pack, and when I tell you to can it—you can it?"

Five and a half pairs of soulful eyes collectively rolled when she entered her small, makeshift living room as if to say, *Here comes the "I will use the duct tape" speech.* Six bodies in various shapes and sizes lined up on her couch, shaking with anticipation, their tails of various colors wagging. "Don't. Even. Don't you even give me the eye roll, you beasts." She waved a finger under their wet, eager noses. "You know, it just isn't enough that I saved every last one of you from the chopping block in one way or the other, is it? You'd think I'd be due a little grateful, but noooooooooo. We can't have Mommy earning a living or something crazy, now can we? I'm telling you, if you can't all be quiet, I'm not kidding when I say there's a roll of duct tape in your very near futures, and don't think—"

"You really *do* have six dogs," the male voice said matter-of-factly, reentering her head with the ease of applying room-temperature butter to toast.

Now that she and the disembodied voice were alone, Delaney communicated as though he were standing right in front of her—even though he still hadn't made a physical appearance. For some stuck souls, it took time and even some wooing before they'd make themselves visible to her.

Delaney clasped her hands together and cracked her knuckles. "Yep, and thanks to you yakking me up in my head, the dogs heard the commotion from my irate customer, then I went long with the Dabrowskis and pissed off that Irv. He wasn't exactly a believer to begin with, and you showing up didn't help one iota." She made a circle around her face with a finger in the direction the voice had come from. "See this? This is my really tweaked face. I just lost eight hundred bucks because you wouldn't get off my cloud. Now go away and come back tomorrow. I'm too hacked off to ship you off to the other side right now."

"Eight hundred dollars? You charge poor, grieving families eight hundred bucks to contact their dead loved ones?" His voice, silky smooth as it was, held a hint of indignation.

Delaney planted her hands on her hips, the jingle of her bangle bracelets ringing in the small space of her living room/dining room. "Please. Save the righteous indignation. It's not like I can have a real nine-to-five when you bunch keep popping up in my head unannounced. Imagine what it would look like to Wal-Mart shoppers if I greeted not just the living, but the dearly departed, too. Some of you wankers can be really, really pushy when you want something from me. That includes you, pal. I do what I have to do to survive, and as you yourself can see, I'm for real. I really can talk to the dead. It's not something I do often, take money, I mean. But every once in a while, when business is slow in the winter, like now, I do what's necessary to make the rent and pay for my ramen noodles, okay? So don't be a hater."

"Sorry." His contrite mumble echoed in her head.

Delaney groaned, flipping on her lamp with the beaded burgundy shade. It cast a pleasant glow over her very gloomy situation. "Apology accepted. Now go back to wherever you came from until I'm feeling more like making nice. Right now, I just want to relax and watch some TV while I cook up another way to make some cash."

"Can I ask you something?"

Delaney ran a tired hand over her forehead, then yanked out the clip that held her hair up and threw it on the end table. "Like me saying the word *no* has stopped you thus far?"

His chuckle, warm and killa manly, left a slither of a chill riding her spine. "What's 'shipping me off to the other side' mean?"

She ran a hand over each of her dogs' heads lovingly, reaching into the pocket of her floor-length floral skirt and feeding them each a treat. "Uh, you know, up there." She pointed a finger to her water-stained ceiling.

"That's not why I'm here."

Delaney plopped down on her small couch, sending her pack of dogs scattering to either side of her. Her half Chihuahua, half Poodle—her Poo-Chi, as she'd dubbed him when she'd found him in an alleyway by her favorite Indian restaurant—instantly hopped into her lap, making her grunt while he settled in. She chucked him under the chin.

From the size of him now, no one would ever know he'd once been skeletal and starving, scrounging for food in bags of trash. His stout, barrel-chested body had just recently tipped the scales at almost eighteen pounds. Waaayyy overweight for what was a mix of two *toy* breeds. Way. "Dude, that's my ovary you're standing on," she reprimanded with a grunt, but her face settled into a warm smile.

Each dog dutifully took its place beside her while she kicked off her satin slippers, crossing her legs at her ankles. "Again, let me reiterate. I kinda don't care why you're here right now. It's been a long day, I'm wiped, and I just lost eight hundred much-needed bucks. I have six mouths to feed and you blew their kibble for the week because you couldn't wait your turn. That means you've stolen from the poor and now potentially homeless. Nice, very nice. Proud?"

His voice came from behind her now. Right over her shoulder. "You talk about these mutts as if they're your children."

Delaney tilted her head backward, directing her gaze in the direction of his voice somewhere near her window, letting out a gasp-snort. "First of all, watch your tone when it comes to the dogs." Delaney ruffled her one-eyed Shih Tzu–Pomeranian's head when he stuck his face pointedly in hers, scratching him just below his fuzzy, multicolored ear. His one eye bobbled at her with that vacant, indirect stare Shih Tzus were famous for. Poor baby had been destined for the Needle of Nevermore, and all because he had only one eye. The shelter'd said he was unadoptable—Delaney'd swept in and called that notion ridiculous, then adopted him and toyed with the idea of secretly calling him Cyclops, or Cy for short.

"My tone? We're talking mutts here."

Delaney planted a kiss on his muzzle before responding. "They're not mutts. Not to me. They're my babies. Dogs who happened upon some misfortune, but were fortunate enough to find me and my bleeding heart. Second of all, they *are* like my children, bonus being I don't have to pay for college when they grow up, and they can't ask to borrow the car. And it's not like I'm going to have any kids, anyway. You need at least a date for that. And when wet blankets like you show up and rain on my social schedule at all hours of the day and night, demanding my attention, it makes it almost impossible for me to make a love connection. Ya feel me? No one wants to date the crazy chick who talks to herself."

There was no self-pity in her statement. Not even a little. Her life was what it was. There just hadn't been a man she'd come across who was strong enough to handle her otherworldly charms—not so far, anyway. And even if that man never came along, she was good being alone. Well, there was one man in her life who got it. Her brother, Kellen. He didn't share her gift, but he believed. That she had one person in her life who understood was more than most who shared her gift had.

Besides, letting other people become involved with her had some hazardous risks she'd just as soon not take. So she'd stopped taking them.

"I feel like I should apologize again. I didn't mean to insult you and your . . . dogs."

Delaney lifted her head, glaring at her only purebred dog—a

black Dachshund with bladder control issues—who was tugging at his festively decorated dungaree wraparound diaper, trying to yank it off.

She nudged him with a gentle elbow, drawing his soft, doe-brown eyes to hers. "You—knock that off. I can't have you peeing all over the place or Mr. Li will have my head. I did decorate the diaper for you, didn't I? Do you know how many hours I spent with that stupid BeDazzler, hooking you up so you'd have pretty man-panties? Now quit being so ungrateful. And you"—she pointed behind her head at the voice—"*should* feel like apologizing again. You stiffed me out of eight hundred smackers. I don't suppose your bank account's still open on the other side, now is it?"

His silence was palpable, resounding in her head.

She nodded her head, affirming her statement. "Yeah. That's what I thought."

"So you don't date?"

Delaney lifted herself off the couch, heading toward her small, narrow kitchen, six dogs at her heels. She popped her refrigerator door open, rooting around for some leftover Hamburger Helper. "Not since, like, 2005 or so, I think it was. Ira Warstein will never be the same, and I can't say as I blame him. I decided, right then and there, after he'd been cracked in the head by his mother's platter of carefully prepared gefilte fish, that not only did it look outwardly like I had the crazy goin' on, but people were now getting hurt because of me. So end of. I'm just too hard to explain. Conversations like the one we're having, where only I can hear you, harder still."

"You hit him in the head with a platter of fish?"

She waved a hand at the voice, now in the center of her kitchen. "Don't be ridiculous. I would never hit someone with anything, let alone a platter of fish. Our date was rudely interrupted by a very angry ghost who wanted my immediate attention and just couldn't hang on to his britches while I made polite excuses to leave." Delaney turned to stare at the empty spot in the room she'd pinpointed his voice in. "Sound vaguely familiar?"

His tone was sheepish this time. "I'm apologizing again, right?"

She shook her head in a firm no, brushing long strands of her auburn hair from her eyes. "No. You're going away. I already accepted your apology. We're golden."

"But I can't go away."

"Yes, yes, you can. It works like this. You disappear until, like, tomorrow, while I feed the dogs, eat my crappy leftovers, and watch *Ghost Whisperer*." She looked down at the eager puppies who'd gathered at her feet the moment she'd opened the fridge door. "We always watch *Ghost Whisperer*, don't we, babies?" she cooed in a tone reserved just for her animals.

His voice, if not his physical presence, remained firmly rooted to the center of her kitchen. "No, no, I can't go away."

For the love of some meaningful, much-needed quiet time, he'd damned well better. "Hookay. I think we need the big guns here. Are you going to make me sic Darwin on you?"

"Who's Darwin?"

"My dead Rottweiler—he's still with me in spirit, though I can't figure why he won't hit the endless Milk-Bone highway in the sky. We're a work in progress even in death. But that does mean he's with you, too—wherever you are. And I hear his bark is definitely as bad as his bite. So scurry along now before I give him a ghostly ring-a-ling, and he eats your rude, interfering, money-stealing ass."

Five and a half pairs of eyes looked woefully in the direction of the voice, then back at her. Dinner—they wanted some. Delaney sank to her haunches on the floor, digging in her cabinets to find the last of the dry dog food she had.

"So what are the dogs' names?"

Delaney sighed and lifted the half-empty dog food bag to the counter, ignoring the fact that this entity was at least trying to sound interested in her life—the one he'd interrupted so pompously. "Would you get the hell outta my head? You've long surpassed eager, and you're well on your way to bordering obnoxious. I really, really need to lay down some ground rules for you bunch. And it's not that I don't understand that most times you can't control how you pop in and out of my life, but you don't seem to have that particular problem. In fact, you don't seem disoriented at all. And as much as I'd like to delve right into that ghostly oddity of yours, I'm all out of patience. Now, for the love of Casper, go do ghostlike things and come back tomorrow."

"I was just curious."

"I know, and you know what they say about curious."

"I'm already dead. That theory no longer applies," he offered with another chuckle—one that wasn't terribly unpleasant.

She threw her head back, exhaling with a ragged, put-upon sigh. "Dog."

"What?"

"Dog. The dogs' names are Dog."

"All of them?"

Delaney nodded. "Uh-huh. And stop moving around so much, you'll scare dog number three in my adoption lineup." She pointed to her Lhasa Apso–Beagle, who was making continual, frantic circles at what Delaney suspected were the feet of her overbearing entity, attempting to nab and capture her tail. "She has anxiety issues—abandonment—food phobias out the wazoo, et cetera. As neurotic as a dieter around a plate of french fries, my baby is. In essence, your unearthly presence is making her crazy, and if you make her crazy, she'll chew up my carpet. I don't have the money to pay my rent because of you. Do you want me to have to pay for new carpet, too?"

"Why haven't you given them all names? You gave Darwin one."

"Why does that interest you so much?"

"I'm not sure I know."

Delaney pinched the bridge of her nose—tonight was definitely a night for some chamomile tea and a healthy dose of white willow bark. "Okay, Q and A is almost over. This is your last answer. I named Darwin because at the time, I only had one dog's name to remember. I don't know where you come from, or if you come from a family with a lot of siblings, but it's flippin' hard to remember names when a bunch of kids are getting into something and you catch them all at once. My mother used to say she wished she'd named my brother and me Bob, and I understand why now. Anyway, it's harder still to remember the names of six dogs that're all yapping because some rude ghost's entry into your life created chaos. Dog is easy to remember. It gets everyone's attention in an instant, and I didn't have to come up with anything clever like Rutabaga or Petunia. Besides, who could name a dog that wears a diaper BeDazzled in faux rhinestones? There's a lot of pressure involved in that. If I go one name too far south, I'd trash his self-esteem. He's already scarred—I figured I'd leave his dignity intact by not naming him something ludicrous like Fifi. And now"—she glanced at her microwave's clock—"your time is up and my show's almost on. Go. Away."

Blessed silence greeted her.

Score.

Delaney cocked her head but once after she'd finished pouring out six bowls of food, and heard nothing but the sounds of anticipatory, mealtime doggy breathing. She let out a sigh of relief. He'd come back, and when he did, she'd be happy to help. She had to admit, she was curious about his story.

She'd never encountered a ghost who was as oriented on this

plane as this one was. She'd only met one other supernatural entity who was as coherent as this one, and that entity, she'd just as soon forget entirely.

Closing her eyes, Delaney trembled while trying to stave off the dark memory that never failed to leave her weak in the knees with a dry mouth full of cotton balls.

Dog number one, a blind, diabetic, partially deaf, fourteen-year-old surmised mixed breed no one could positively identify—but one which her vet said reminded him of a Chinese Crested disaster waiting to happen—scratched impatiently at her leg. She stooped low, letting him smell her hand before she ran her fingers through the tufts of spiky hair along the top of his scalp. "I know, punkin— you're hungry. Tell me something—do you find it as funny as I do that you can't hear me yell shut up, but you can totally hear me open a bag of dog food from a million miles away? Uncanny, no?"

He burrowed his head in her hand and her heart clenched. They'd been together a long time—almost as long as she and Darwin before he'd left this plane.

Setting down their food bowls, Delaney rinsed their water cooler out and threw the Tupperware filled with leftover Hamburger Helper in the microwave. Checking the time, she encouraged them to chow down. She'd already missed almost ten minutes of *Ghost Whisperer*. "Dogs! Hurry up, would ya? Melinda and her über-hawt hubby await."

Running a tired hand over her scalp, she massaged the back of her neck, heading back to her bedroom, situated just off the kitchen. The only saving grace for today was the anticipation that filled her at the thought of climbing into her king-sized bed. Her one and only luxury—a luxury she'd splurged on at a high-end thrift store so her puppies could sleep with her. Which some might call obsessive, but whatevs.

She was in her tiny adjoining bathroom, pulling on her night-gown, when she heard the sound of voices, familiar as old friends, drift to her ears.

"You know, I've been watching this *Ghost Whisperer*, and I have to tell you, you're nothing like Melinda Gordon. You're kinda cranky. She seems much less irritable than you."

How lovely. He was baaaaack.

Very *Poltergeist*.

"Yeah?" she called out, digging in her hamper for her bathrobe. "Well, that's because her paycheck's a whole lot bigger than mine. Not to mention, she has cuter clothes."

"I'd definitely have to agree that what she puts in those clothes is very cute."

How quaint—even from the grave, men lusted for Jennifer Love Hewitt. She continued rooting in her hamper, hoping against hope he'd go the frig away. Where the hell was her bathrobe? How could she watch *Ghost Whisperer* without her crappy, moth-eaten, comfortable bathrobe? It was what Friday nights were all about at Chez Markham. Her pink bathrobe, a bowl of leftover Thursday night Hamburger Helper, her puppies sprawled out on her bed, and *Ghost Whisperer*. In that particular order, damn it.

Delaney poked a head around the corner of her bathroom to find the voice in her head had become a big man, lying casually in the middle of her bed in a pink-bathrobe-clad lump.

Her pink bathrobe.

Which was now semicovered in puppies.

Light and breezy. That was the goal here. Try not to overreact to his materialization. Or react at all, if it could be helped. Ghosts had uncanny senses, and if their intent was malevolent because of the chaos they were experiencing over being in limbo, you couldn't let 'em see you sweat. It also took a good deal of patience to figure out what they wanted you to do, because most times, they were as confused as you were by their presence. But he'd tried her patience. So if he wanted her help, it was going to be on her terms, and her terms included waiting until she was good and goddamned ready to help him do whatever it was he needed her to do for him. Which was as yet to be determined. He didn't seem terribly needy in the way most spirits were, though. "Pink is so not you," she remarked dryly.

He lifted the collar of her robe with tapered fingers and smiled. "You don't think?"

She shook her head, sticking her hand out. "I don't think. Now give it to me. My Friday night's fucked enough—don't screw with my chi by taking the only thing I have left."

He eyed her warily with indigo blue eyes shielded by square dark-rimmed glasses. "But I'm naked."

"So I'm guessing you died while you were boffing, then?" Most ghosts who showed up in the buff were wonking someone when they kicked the bucket. Definitely a nice way to leave this plane, but not so much if you had unfinished business and had to return.

"What is boffing?"

For real? Her eyebrows shot upward in surprise. "You know . . . uh, having sex."

His full lower lip curled upward. "No. I wasn't having sex when I died."

"Then why are you naked?"

"Had I an explanation, don't you think I'd give you one?"

"The only thing you've given me so far is agita." Delaney crossed her arms over her chest to hide the filmy nightgown she wore.

He grinned again, playfully, as if being stuck between two planes was no big thang. He wasn't even a little frantic, she noted. Absently, he reached out to stroke a random dog's head. "Again, this is me apologizing to you."

"Forget the apologies. How about you explain how you picked

up my bathrobe? Learning to pick up physical matter once you've passed is like a long-term gig. It can take a good while to accomplish."

He shook his head. His neatly groomed, shortly trimmed head of hair, as dark as the night had become, and thick like his stubborn skull, bobbed. "I don't know what you mean. I realized I was naked, and I found something to cover up with—a logical thing to do, seeing as this is our first meeting. Though I have to say, it's a little small." He unsuccessfully tried to tug the two sides of the bathrobe together over his thighs.

His lightly sprinkled with crisp hair thighs—all muscled and lean. Niiiice.

Delaney forced her mouth to close because really, gawking at your spirit was unattractive in a medium. She threw a silent prayer upward that whoever was in charge upstairs might want to consider the long dry spell her love life had been suffering and send in some ugly spirits from here on out. It was only fair . . .

He continued to wait without explanation.

This was turning into a battle of wills, and it was time to raise the white flag. He clearly wasn't leaving, and she clearly was going to miss *Ghost Whisperer* if she didn't acquiesce and figure him out. Treading carefully to the end of the bed, she sat at the very edge, noting he had some weight to him. The dip in the middle of her mattress said so.

Huh. When was the last time she'd encountered a spirit who was solid matter? Or for that matter, one who could pick up solid matter?

Once. Only once and that wasn't up for discussion.

Hell to the no.

The very idea made her shiver and rub her arms with icy hands.

"I don't suppose you have anything else I could wear?" His question rang hopeful, cutting her fears off for the moment.

Cool. Calm. Collected. All soothing *c* words she needed to apply here. Delaney slapped a placid smile on her face. "Forget something to wear. You can have my bathrobe for now. So how about we start at the beginning? I'm Delaney Markham. Your earthly guide to all things crossing over to the other side. I'm here to help you with whatever you need, and while I don't want to grudge about it, you're definitely not going away. So how is it that I can help you? Do you need to clear up an event in your life you left unresolved before you died? Contact a living relative? Make peace with someone? Like maybe a sibling—or a girlfriend? Your parents? College roommate? Dry cleaner? Say something—I'm grasping at straws here."

He cocked his head at her, his sharp jaw lifting, his eyes skeptical behind his square glasses. "You can do all that?"

"I can try."

"Well, thanks, but that's not why I'm here."

Delaney nodded knowingly—she'd seen this a million times before. Now she knew why he was here. "I see. So you don't want to cross over? Is it that you're afraid of retribution for something you did in life? Because if that's the case, rest assured, no worries. You wouldn't have ended up talking to me if you were going somewhere crappy. I only do happy-clappy stuff. And if you're worried about what's on the other side, trust me, I've done a bazillion crossings and I only hear good things about where you land. So how about we problem-solve together, figure out why you're stuck here, and then I can get some friggin' rest. I'm thirty-four. I need rest. The kind of life I lead with you nut jobs inspires wrinkles by the dozens." She winked to show she was teasing.

He peered more closely at her, leaning forward, yet keeping his hand on the belly of dog number six. Her Benji wannabe. He'd make a perfect stand-in for the movie dog if not for the fact that he only had one ear, because he'd been tragically injured in a dogfight, and three legs, because his left front leg had been riddled with gangrene and had to be amputated. "I don't see any wrinkles. You look fine to me."

Delaney rolled her neck from side to side. "Hookay—one more time. First, what's your name? Do you remember it?"

Rolling his tongue along the inside of his cheek, he shot her an indignant glare. Like now he was losing patience with her. "Of course I do."

"Then hit me."

His eyebrows, as dark as his hair, rose, creasing his forehead. "I would never hit you."

Oy. "I mean, tell me what your name is."

"Clyde. Clyde Atwell."

"And you died how, Clyde? Do you remember?"

"Yep."

And he clearly wasn't ready to tell her how he'd died. It was written all over his lean, chiseled, yet oh so serious face. Which meant she might be treading into murky, sensitive waters. "Were the circumstances surrounding your death suspicious?"

"Nope." He crossed his legs at his ankles, brushing a toe against her fingertips.

Delaney snatched them away without thinking. No ghost she knew could touch or be touched . . .

Hoo boy. This wasn't looking like what it had appeared to be just moments ago.

She gulped, the sound almost louder than Melinda Gordon's voice coming from the TV. "So why did you contact me?"

"Well, you're Delaney Markham, right? And this is the East Village, correct?"

"What's that have to do with why you're here?"

"I was told to find a Delaney Markham in the East Village."

"Why?" she squeaked—none too proud of the fact that she had.

He pushed his glasses up on the bridge of his nose. "Because you're sort of supposed to come with me—or I'm supposed to make sure you end up there, anyway."

Her eyes narrowed. "Where?"

"Hell."

Oh.

Well, then.

Yeah, she'd get right on that.

Pack a fucking bag or something.

What did one wear in Hell?

It was hot there—definitely hot.

Thongs, anyone?

two

Oh, this was a bad, bad thing.

As bad as bad could be.

Letting her head hang between her shoulders, Delaney gnawed on the inside of her cheek, wrestling to keep her cool so she could decide what to do next.

Because she had to do something.

If Clyde was what she thought he was, and she was pretty sure he was no floundering ghost, that meant he was possibly demonic. Though the bulk of her spirit encounters were of the ghostly kind, she'd run into a demon from time to time, and mostly, they were fairly easy to expunge.

Well, except one.

Delaney shivered.

So she had two choices. Neither prospect terribly debilitating to him, but they would hopefully stall him until she could call for reinforcements. Yet she experienced a flicker of doubt about her conclusions where this Clyde was concerned. And then she mentally scratched that after but a moment's pause. Of course he was what she thought he was—what other explanation was there for his ability to move, er, wear physical matter?

Clyde slid to the edge of the bed with her, letting his elbows rest on his knees. Their thighs grazed each other's—his muscled and sharply angled, hers fighting to keep a quiver visible from his naked eye.

Her dogs scampered to either side of his broad back, scratching at her worn bathrobe for more of his attention.

Well, well. So much for their otherworldly sensitivity. Clearly, it wasn't just their bodies and psyches that were jacked up—so was their judgment. Which gave her pause. Her babies were very keen to spirits, good, bad, and otherwise. Sometimes they knew shit was going to go down long before she did.

Again, Delaney debated mentally, but only for another nanosecond before she decided her assessment of this situation was right.

Clyde's large hand cupped the back of her Dachshund's head, stroking it with firm fingers. He wiggled his BeDazzled backside in panting appreciation. "So I'm guessing you're angry again?"

She swallowed hard, letting the curtain of her hair cover her face in case she did the unthinkable and gave herself and her plan up. "Nope."

"Really?"

"Really."

"I'm not sure I believe you."

Delaney rolled her eyes upward, forcing her body to remain relaxed. "So now I'm a liar? Already, this early in our relationship, you're calling names?"

"I hate to point out a flaw so harsh this early in our *relationship*, but you're pretty quick to anger."

"No. I'm only easily hacked off if someone's stealing my damned grocery money. Which, P.S., you did. And while we're not pointing out flaws so early in our relationship, I just have to point that out. *You* started this."

She watched the nod of his dark head through the strands of her hair, and it sure looked damned sincere. "True enough, but I did apologize, on several occasions, and I'm still getting the gnashing-your-teeth vibe from you. I hate to beat a dead horse; I'm just trying to express myself honestly here."

Bravo. Score one for the interloper for honesty in the first degree. "Well, then, you suck at reading chicks. I'm definitely not angry. I'm not happy, but I'm not angry."

"That's highly likely."

"What is?"

"That I've read chicks, er, that I've read *you* wrong. In another moment of stark honestly I'll tell you I was never very good with . . . uh . . . chicks."

Delaney fought a snort. He was really quite charming, all things considered. She found it hard to believe he wasn't good with chicks—as brick shithouse as he was and all.

Clyde folded his hands, strong but lean, with fingernails that were well manicured, around his knees. "And now, I suppose we ought to talk about this."

Charming or not—she didn't want him touching her. Delaney slid a little further off the edge of the bed until only one butt cheek clung to the lip of the mattress, her thighs burning and screaming from the strain of keeping up the pretense that she was willing to hear him out—and it hurt every muscle in her body.

So now would be the time to thank God for Pilates.

All that crazy talk of your core strength and such, the crap that had seemed soooo silly while she'd been playing with that dumb-ass piece of blue elastic tangled around her ankles, was actually working in her favor. If she could take action without freaking the dogs out, and without warning, she just might have a chance. The element of surprise was what she needed here.

"So can we talk?"

"Uh-huh. Sure we can talk. You do a lot of that without any help from me—you have an uncanny gift for gab—so go for it. My listening ears are on—wide-open." She didn't lift her head—didn't try to read his face for signs as to why he sounded so calm and reasonable when he'd just told her his intent was to drag her back to Hell.

Delaney knew that threat—it'd been around for fifteen long years. It'd also been reinforced by someone far more frightening than Clyde here.

Though, it wasn't delivered quite the way Clyde had delivered it. It'd been accompanied by a whole lot of maniacally scary roaring—riddled with some serious potty mouth, a couple of screaming balls of fire, and sometimes, when effect was the goal, speaking in tongues. Which could be fabulous to behold if you didn't let it make your panties wad and saw it simply for the supernatural phenom it was.

Far, far more dramatic than Clyde's rather dry, almost cheerful statement.

He sighed rather forlornly. "Explanations are in order about that, or something, I guess."

Something was definitely in order . . . she was so close to being sucked in by his tone, the calm, assured presence he gave off, an aura that literally seeped from his pores, that she found she had to fight the simplicity of his easygoing manner. Too close. "Sure. Explain away."

Delaney felt him change positions on the bed, the dogs following close behind, moving as one teeming swarm with him, begging for more of his attention. "Can you give me just a sec so I'm sure I get it right? This was just sort of sprung on me today, and I want to be one hundred percent accurate when I relay the information I have to you."

Sweat trickled between her breasts, forming beads on her forehead, yet she held her ground while she waited for just the right moment. "You can have all the seconds you need." Her face scrunched up while she fought back a grunt, her toes dug into the thin carpet of her bedroom floor, her arm ached from holding herself two inches above the bed.

The bedspread rustled behind her. Obviously there was some deep thought going down on Clyde's behalf.

And really—why was that? What was all this introspection and getting his explanations right about?

What the fuck kind of demon gave a flying Dutchman about how he was going to explain he was here to collect her for Lucifer?

Because that's what Clyde was—*a demon*.

If she hadn't been sure before, she was now. That she hadn't picked up on that the second he'd entered her head—or even when he'd been able to don something from this plane like a bathrobe— made her want to bang her head against the edge of her dresser until she was unconscious.

Had demons gone to the sensitive side since she'd last encountered them? Last she'd seen a demon, he was anything but warm and squishy, and he sure hadn't given a shit about how he'd presented his very evil wishes.

So huh on that.

And while Clyde was working on his verbal dissertation of wicked intent—she was going to hit it while she could. With the merest of squeaks, Delaney inched from the bed, landing on the foot that hadn't gone numb and ignoring the shot of pain that rippled along her thigh.

She hurled herself at her dresser, blessedly close to the bed,

threw open the top drawer, and let her fingers land on a geometri-
cally shaped piece of glass there, blessed by a holy figure, and
something she should probably think about making a necklace out
of in the very near future.

Whirling around, she held it up under Clyde's nose, her chest
heaving with victory.

His head cocked to the left with obvious confusion. Wherever
he'd chosen his human form from—maybe a magazine or an ad-
vertisement he'd seen hanging in the subway—she had to admit,
he'd done good. He had this mad, sexy, geeky professor appeal.
The glasses he wore screamed pocket protector–wearing president
of his former high school's chess club, and so did his haircut, but
his granite cheekbones, his wide blue eyes with a healthy fringe of
lashes, and his thickly corded neck hollered mancake.

But Delaney knew demons like whores knew a potential john.
Trickery, deceit, lies; whatever it took to weave their deceptive
webs were all familiar traits for a demon. And he was killa good at
the innocent look.

His eyes squinted, drops of water forming in their corners. "Uh,
could you put that down?"

Delaney inhaled a deep gulp of air. "Not on your life, er, unlife."

"But it's making my eyes water."

How entertaining. A pansy-ass, whiny demon. "Boo-hoo."

Clyde stuck a finger beneath the rim of his glasses, rubbing at
his left eye. "What if I said please?"

Her eyes narrowed in his direction, her face screaming disdain.
"I'd laugh and laugh, and then I'd tell you to shove it right up your
demonic ass. I know why you're here and the fuck I'll take this lying down!" She shook the prism under his nose once more with a
frantic flick of her wrist, like she was shaking a saltshaker over a
piece of meat.

Clyde thwapped the air blindly at her hand without success. "I doubt there's much you take lying down, but I have no clue what you mean when you say you won't take whatever it is you're supposedly taking lying down." He paused, dragging his other hand across his temple. "What is that and why's it making my eyes burn?" His face, now a summer radish's shade of red, remained perplexed.

Ahhhh. If he'd been good at playing charming, he was even better at pretending to be a dimwit.

Delaney smiled coquettishly, the upward turn of her lips gleaming with menace. "Oh, stop, already. You know damned well what *this* is and why it's burning your eyes, you ass-licking devil worshipper. Now here's where the bullshit stops and we get down to the business at hand. I want you gone—ASAP. And if you think your eyes burn now, just wait until I get the Morton salt. I've got a box of it, you know—like, a Costco-sized box. Big—*very big*. The shit will fly, and I'll fry you like I'm a short-order cook." She moved in just a bit closer, swishing the prism while she went.

Clyde clenched his perfect white teeth together, his breathing becoming ragged, emphasized by the sharp lift and drop of her pink bathrobe on his shoulders. "I think it's worth mentioning, I've been nothing but nice about this. The least you can do is hear me out."

Delaney drew the prism but a hairsbreadth from his cheek. If she merely grazed him with it, she'd burn him, and, while she was all about ditching this dude, she hated what it took to rid yourself of a demonic presence. It was always so violent, and sometimes very, very messy. She didn't have much experience in it, but if what she'd figured out about him was true, that he was a noob, he shouldn't be too difficult to expel. "I think it's worth mentioning that I've been nothing but nice, too. I did sacrifice *Ghost Whisperer*, not to mention the eight hundred bucks you cost me to hear you out. And I let you nab my favorite Friday night ensemble while

I did it. And now I find you don't need to cross over to anything. Your crossing days are ovah, pal, aren't they?"

Clyde's body grew rigid, patches of ugly crimson scurrying up his long torso while he fought to maintain his human form. "I don't know what crossing over is. I just know I need you to lisss— li—sssssten!" he hissed while the ugly transformation of his real form began to emerge.

But no amount of scales and forked tongues was all that big of a thang for her.

Not a lot, anyway. She'd seen some heinous shit—she'd probably see more before all was said and done.

Delaney moved in just a smidge closer, refusing to acknowledge the pain she knew he was in. "Pay attention, Lucifer lover. The listening part of this conversation is over. It's time for you to go," she whispered with a harsh spit in his face.

"But I can't go."

"But you can, and you will."

"If you'd just—"

"Zip. It."

"But—"

Again she whirled the prism at him. "Pffft! I said shut up and get the fuck out—*nooooow*!" she howled all loud and screechy for effect, fighting a grin.

Clyde backed up, using his arms to push him up over the bed and against the pile of pillows. The veins in his neck popped out, his fingers clenched the sheets with a tight, white-knuckled grip, perspiration began to drench his disappearing, sleekly dark hair. Each word he spoke was from between a locked jaw and clenched teeth. "If you'll just listen to me, I—can—explain," he gritted out, harsh and panting.

"Oh, the hell, you fucking Hades-loving groupie. Now get out!"

The dogs began to whine collectively, yet they didn't move to her aid at the end of the bed, where she was swinging the prism in wild arcs. Instead, they all, every last mutinous one of them, plastered themselves against Clyde's hard body. Her blind dog had managed to stumble nearer to Clyde, burrowing his head against the width of his now scaly chest and whimpering.

Well, that was just fucking that. The Dog Whisperer's book was totally going back to the bookstore. She'd spent twenty bucks on a book that was supposed to inspire obedience, yet her pack had turned on her because of just one brawny man? A demon man at that. Cesar was totally getting hate mail from her—right after she got rid of the demon.

"Delaney—pleassssse, just lissssssten!" he growled with a rasp, a poke of his forked tongue slipping from his lips. Then he doubled over, bending at his lean waist to clutch his abdomen.

His grip on the sheets began to loosen; his hold on this plane began to wan. Which meant he *was* a lesser demon. Any demon worth his weight in fire and brimstone wouldn't be as troubled by a little old prism as Clyde was.

And that gave her an advantage she sorely needed.

Delaney crawled to the very tip of the bed, holding the prism high above her head while the dogs howled their discontent, drowning out the sound of the TV. "Get—out—of—my—house!" she roared. The frustration that had begun to well in her chest over losing her rent, coupled with the incredible disturbance he'd created for a perfectly good Friday night, finally spilled out from her throat in harsh gasps.

Plus, the carrying on made for überdrama and maybe that just might make Clyde understand exactly whom he was fucking with.

Clyde's head arched backward, his lips pulling back from his teeth in a howl of agony as his form shimmered with a quiver and a buzzing sound that made the dogs' frantic squeals escalate zinged through her tiny bedroom.

And then he was gone with nothing but a pink lump of comfy, Friday night bathrobe left in his place.

Jesus Christ in a miniskirt.

She yawned.

What a wuss.

But her thoughts turned to what Clyde had said about taking her back to Hell with him.

Lucifer had promised someday he'd come calling.

Dude obviously didn't front.

The tinkle of the bell on her door had Delaney rushing to the front of her now darkened store so the dogs wouldn't bark. She ran smack into her brother Kellen's solid chest. Delaney gave him a hard hug around his waist, inhaling his scent while the puppies all vied for his attention, jumping and scratching at his ankles and knees.

Kellen kissed the top of her head, tilting her chin upward. His eyes, hazel like hers, held that worried look he always had when it came to Delaney and the supernatural cards she'd been dealt. "You okay?"

She jerked her chin away from his fingers, laying her cheek on his shoulder and letting her nose bury itself in the cool leather of his black jacket. "I'm fine, Kellen," she muttered, her words muffled by his coat. Now that Clyde's dust had settled, she found herself a little worried. Not so much that she was breaking out the Bible and holy water, but enough that she was on alert. "I'm not hurt or anything, but I'm definitely very, very . . . aware."

He set her from him, taking her by the hand and leading her to her couch. "Sit. You want me to make you some of that tea that smells like an elephant's ass? It seems to calm you." Kellen kneeled down in front of her, letting the dogs pile onto his lap.

Delaney chuckled, pulling a pillow to her chest and squeezing it tight while three of the dogs leaped up beside her. "Nah, I'm fine, really. He was a noob, I suspect. Didn't even have the nads to fight off something as lame as a prism. I just figured I'd better give you the heads-up that Lucifer'd sent a calling card." She'd called Kellen as a warning. If strange shit began to happen, it was imperative that he be very careful.

Kellen pinned her with one of his concerned, big brother gazes, jamming his hands into his faded blue jeans. "So let's begin at the beginning. What happened, and are you sure this Clyde's a demon?"

She used the heel of her hand to massage her forehead, trying to ease the headache forming at her temples. "I know demon when I see demon. Well, okay, so at first I didn't know he was a demon. He interrupted me during a séance I was performing. Seemed perfectly harmless, and you know how often that shit goes down with me. Someone's always popping into my head or showing up uninvited. It's the nature of the beast. I tried to get him to wait until I was done with the Dabrowskis, but he just couldn't hold on to his britches. He was typical ghost MO. Pushy, demanding that I stop my world from turning just for him."

"And?"

"And we played the spirit game. Well, again, sort of. I gotta tell you, Kellen, all I kept thinking the entire time I was communicating with him was that he seemed way too oriented on this plane. He wasn't at all confused; nothing he said was mangled or mixed up the way it is for most who're stuck between planes. In fact, we carried on a perfectly normal conversation about the dogs and why they don't have names, yadda, yadda, yadda. I didn't even get the weird goose bump vibe I get when a demon shows up during a crossing. And do you think the medium in me might have found that at least a little out of the ordinary? No, instead the outgoing tard spirit lover in me who just wants world peace reigned supreme. I was all Miss Manners." Of all the stupidity . . . For all the years she'd dealt with the other side, that she hadn't seen the demonic signs Clyde presented left her breathless and none too comfy with her ghostie alarm clock.

One of Kellen's dark eyebrows rose, his brow wrinkling. "So what tipped you off that he was a demon?"

Her lips formed a thin line of anger in hindsight. "That he was able to move physical matter made me suspicious. When I came out of the bathroom, he was wearing my pink bathrobe."

Kellen snorted, his nostrils flaring, his lips flashing an amused smile. "Your bathrobe? Huh. Seems harmless enough. Maybe you're just panicked over nothing. Maybe he's just one of those 'looking for a good time' demons you're always talking about. The ones who just like screwing with people versus possessing them or wreaking havoc."

The inhalation of breath Delaney took shuddered. She shook her head. "Nope. He was very clear. He said I was supposed to come with him to Hell."

Kellen's intake of breath was crisp. "Jesus Christ . . ." he muttered. "So how'd you get rid of him?"

She let go of the pillow and grabbed a dog. While Clyde hadn't been terribly frightening, she had a bad feeling in her gut this was just the beginning of things to come. No demon could just whack you and drag you back to Hell. They had to win you with a contract. It was simple, really. Minions from Hell preyed on the weak. Mostly those who had no sense of self-worth or those whose moral barometers were so skewed that even if a demon didn't come along and strike a bargain with them, most likely they'd end up in Hell all on their own anyway.

Then a contract was drawn up, and typically that contract benefited the contracted for a time, and then—wham—the fine print in that binding contract came along and doused you with a bucket of cold water. Demons were masters of deceit—if you told one you had a headache, he'd offer to fix it, and while you're all thinking aspirin and soothing gel eye packs, he whacks your head off.

"That's the strange part. How I got rid of him, I mean. All it took was me waving a prism that had been blessed under his nose and he was writhing in pain. Which means he's a weak demon—or a new one. So why the fuck would Lucifer send a noob? I'm no lightweight in the spirit world. I know spirits who can protect me—at least for a little while, anyway."

Kellen rose from his place on the floor, heaving her overweight pooch over his shoulder like a toddler, stroking his back. "So you think this has to do with Vincent?"

Delaney hauled her three-legged fur baby up into her lap and held him to her chest, burrowing her face in his neck, gulping to fight back her fears. "Well, when was the last time someone threatened to see me in Hell?"

Kellen's nod was curt as he put the dog back on the floor and scooped up another. "When the shit went down with Vincent." His tone was solemn, much the way it always was when they even vaguely touched upon what had happened just a month shy of fifteen years ago. The day she'd been handed this gift to yammer with people no one else could see but her.

A day so horrible, neither she nor Kellen had been able to take it out of its Pandora's box and discuss it at length. Not in nearly fifteen years.

Her eyes instantly began to water, but she brushed at the corners of them impatiently. "Right. So would you do me a favor tonight?" Under normal circumstances, she wouldn't have been much bothered by the expulsion of a demon. But those were random demons, few and far between. Clyde had been sent for *her*. Of all the demons she'd encountered in fifteen years, no one had ever come with a specific intent like that. So having another presence in the house, for all the good it'd do her, brought reassurance. False, but a modicum of security, anyway.

Kellen pointed to where she sat and grinned that disarming, charming grin that made women want to mother him. "Couch?"

Delaney nodded with a distant smile, pulling the sweater she'd thrown on closer to her chest to thwart the chills racing along her arms. "Hope you packed fresh man-panties. Do you mind?"

He returned her smile and winked. "Only if you promise to let me sleep with the one-eyed monster. There's nothing like waking up to his googly-eyed, vacant stare while he breathes his stench on me."

Delaney held out her hand, and Kellen took it, giving it a supportive squeeze. "Just tonight or at least until I can get in touch with Marcella. I'm not overly worried, because this Clyde was as lame as they get, but just for safety's sake."

Kellen's eyes narrowed, glittering with his dislike for her friend Marcella Acosta. "Was she too busy fighting the bowels of Hell to bother to answer her demon hotline tonight?"

Delaney clucked her tongue in his direction, setting her three-legged wonder aside with a loving pat to the head and rising with a stretch of her arms. "I wouldn't go knocking the only connection I have to all things demonic, were I you, big brother. Marcella's helped me more times than I can count. Do you have any idea the kind of help she can be when a demon possesses a lost spirit and is preventing me from crossing them? Not only that, but she's kept hundreds of those very spirits from making a very bad eternal decision. And you know what I always say—one less freaky-deaky demon in the world is one less future possession in the making. Now get off her ass and lighten up. And no, I couldn't get in touch with her. So lay off already." With a finger, she pointed down at her blind dog, snapping her fingers so he'd know to follow her. "Punkin, come with Mommy—it's time for your insulin."

She trotted off to the kitchen, breathing a sigh of relief that Kellen had agreed to stay. His beef with Marcella was valid on some levels. She *was* a demon. But she was a demon who'd made a very bad decision based on foolish emotion versus practicality.

Shit happened.

Marcella had spent a butt-assed long time trying to make it right on this plane. Not that it would ever do her any good. She'd turned her nose up at the Big Kahuna. Major bad juju. That wasn't something you could ever take back, but take it back she tried each time she helped Delaney convince someone that the demon who had showed up at a crossing—as some occasionally did—and was offering them riches beyond compare and a sea of tanned, toned, naked twenty-year-olds as far as the eye could see, was all just bullshit. You might see tanned, toned twenty-year-olds, but they'd have scales, or snakes writhing on their heads.

No one knew that better than Marcella, and Delaney was grateful for her—even if Kellen thought she was a turbo bitch with an agenda that still remained unapparent to Delaney after ten years of friendship.

She'd be bitchy, too, if what Marcella said about what her demon form really looked like was true. Scales and horns and the like were so far from Marcella's gorgeous human form. That alone was a good reason to be pissed off.

In Delaney's opinion, Marcella'd been ripped off, and now she had no hope of redemption. Choosing sides when you left this Earth, and having no guidance from someone like Delaney—especially if you waffled at the wrong moment—was a scary prop.

Yanking open her fridge once more, she dug out the insulin, reaching into the drawer beside it to find the packaged needles she kept there for dog number one. She filled the syringe as Kellen's chestnut-colored head peeked around the door frame of her kitchen and her pack tore around the corner, screeching to a halt at her feet. Positioning her diabetic pooch in her arms, Delaney injected his meds with a swift, practiced hand.

"Mind if I shower—or is the water still only hot from nine in the morning until ten forty-five?" he joked. His jaw was unshaven, his hazel eyes bleary. Probably from the long hours he put in at his after-school program for gifted children. He was a good teacher. He'd be an even better father, and that made her smile. She just might have offspring by proxy if Kellen ever settled down.

Delaney chuckled, then looked at her microwave clock. "You've got, like, eight minutes."

Her brood stared after Kellen's broad back, while he hurried off to catch the last of the hot water she'd see until tomorrow. And that reminded her . . . her hands went to her hips, her eyes zeroed in on her "pack." Hah! Pack, schmack. "Hey, philistines," she called to them. Five and a half pairs of eyes sought hers. Well, four and a half if you counted out her sightless angel.

Six bodies lined up dutifully as though a treat were in order. "Oh, no, no, no. You guys are in deep doody with me. Wanna tell me what all that cozying up to Clyde was all about? Haven't I taught you, Grasshoppers? Demons are bad, bad, bad, and there you all were, climbing all over him like he was a mountain of T-bones. You've got some splainin' to do. *All* of you. Now let's get some sleep. Off to bed." She gave them a stern look before flipping the lights off in the kitchen and heading to her bedroom.

The pitter-patter of paws followed closely behind, each of them jumping up on the bed and sniffing the place where Clyde had sat not an hour before with looks of longing on their wee puppy mugs.

Delaney's lips pursed. What the hell was going on? Her dogs were as sensitive as she was to a bad spirit. How could they mourn his loss?

She grabbed the muzzle on her anxiety-laden pooch, turning

the dog to face her. "Sweetums? What about horns and scales don't you get? He's a bad spirit. Now knock it off and all of you settle down." Dog number three turned her wet, brown nose up at Delaney, returning to the task at hand, which was apparently to dig to China through the blanket until they all found out where Clyde had gone.

That should be reason enough to give her pause as she climbed into bed, soothed by the sound of Kellen's presence in her bathroom.

But she just wasn't ready to go there.

For now he was gone.

Gone was good.

As her eyes drifted closed, from the end of her bed a shimmer of multicolored light interrupted her fall into oblivion.

Was it asking too much that a medium get some shut-eye? If this kept up, she wouldn't be able to help people cross the street, let alone cross over into their own eternal utopia.

Hunkering down under the covers, she muttered, "Not now, Charlie. Everything's fine. Promise. Go find some movie grip to toy with because this medium is ass fried."

His smile lifted his mustache—a smile that was less like a comfort and more like a lethal promise of mayhem to come. The craggy lines of his face revealed a much harder man than was the reality of the total softy he really was. In death, he was as raw biker sexy as he'd been in his prime in the seventies. "*Death Wish,*" he said, his lips moving out of sync with his voice. Sometimes, when a spirit like Charlie came along, it was like watching an old Japanese movie translated to English—their lips moved long before the words came out.

She knew this was his way of offering his supernatural, albeit sometimes destructive, help, and it left her touched. Delaney yawned and flashed him a sleepy smile. "Nuh-uh, Mr. Bronson. I know you'd like to whip out an AK-47 and trash all moving matter, but I don't need that kind of help. No *Death Wish* tactics tonight. It'll all be fine. The bad guy's gone now, and that means I don't need Rambo-like help." She was prepared for that smile to turn to disapproval at the mere mention of another infamous movie and an even more popular actor. "And don't frown at me. You didn't corner the market on vigilante-like revenge. Think of it as passing the movie star action-adventure torch to Sylvester, and get over yourself. But thanks for thinking of me. You're a real peach." Her smile was warm when she winked.

His nod was short, his hand rising in a succinct wave before he vanished, leaving her feeling all warm and smooshy.

How many people could say Charles Bronson had just dropped by to offer up his own brand of justice in her defense?

Sometimes, there was small compensation for the fact that she'd probably never have real live sex again unless it was via a battery-operated love tool.

Really small.

three

"Darlink?"

Delaney wiped the back of her hand over the corner of her mouth, searching for stray drool. Her hair clung to her eyelashes and her right arm was sore from being pressed beneath her chest. Waking up to her friend's light Spanish accent, and the scent of her sophisticated perfume, might have made her smile if the night before hadn't been so craptacular. "Marcella?"

A husky chuckle drifted to her ears. Husky and sensual and totally Marcella. "Not so in the flesh," she confirmed.

Delaney struggled to open her eyes, reaching for whatever dog was in her immediate vicinity so they could snuggle. She came up dogless. Kellen must have taken them out for her. "Where are the dogs and what time is it?"

"Your cranky brother has the creatures and it's time to get up."

She felt Marcella's weight shift on the end of the bed. She could picture her striking demon friend from behind her closed eyelids.

Darkly voluptuous, olive skinned, green eyed, probably dressed in a curve-hugging black dress with a pair of matching heels, draped casually at the foot of her bed. Yet she kept her eyes closed. "I had a spectacularly shitty night last night, and you'd know all about that if you'd answered my nine hundred voice-mail messages. But my forecast is much brighter this morning. I'm all out of immediate danger right now—so be a good girlfriend and go catch up on your reality TV or something. *Wife Swap* was on this week. You don't want to miss that. Hook up with me in a couple of hours, 'kay?"

"No can do, *chica*."

Delaney groaned with a pathetic whine, rolling to her side. "Why is it that you can't do? I'm not getting any younger here. You, on the other hand, are forever young. I don't want to cast stones, but I lost my directions to the Fountain of Youth. I need some sleep here."

Marcella snorted. Delaney could visualize the delicate flare of her nostrils. "Don't you all go waving my misfortune in my face there, girlie. It has very few perks—one of them being eternal youth—but if you could get a gander at my demon form, you'd grow a mustache. It's unsightly. Heinous even. Now, get up, my pretty ghost magnet. We have business to attend to." Marcella grabbed her by the forearm, pulling her to an unwilling, upright position and propping a pillow behind her back.

Delaney dragged the covers with her, her eyes still closed. "Is there green tea involved in this getting up? Because if there's no tea, I just know I won't play well with others."

Marcella tugged a lock of her hair. "I don't do domestic, and you know it. No tea. But there is something that might interest you. You can't see it unless you open your eyes."

"If you were really my BFF, you wouldn't make me do this."

"Because I'm your BFF, I'm making you do this. Open 'em, or I'll set your curtains on fire with my bad aim."

Delaney finally laughed, opening her eyes with a slow shift of her eyelids. She snapped them shut much more quickly. "Yippee and skippee. Is that what I think it is?"

Marcella flicked her arm with what Delaney guessed was a French-manicured fingertip. "It is, *mi amiga*. Now up with you so we can get this over with."

"Nice coup."

"Yeahhhh," she agreed with smug satisfaction. "Even if I do say so myself. Now up, my friend. We have business to attend to."

"Will it be messy? I can't afford to clean the carpets this month. The till is dry." Resentment for Clyde's séance crashing resettled in her craw.

Marcella's green eyes captured hers with a familiar gleam in them. "When isn't it ever messy with me, D? No one knows better than you do, my demon skills"—she leaned in to Delaney, whispering the words—"suck hairy balls, for lack of a better word."

"That's a phrase," Delaney corrected.

She sat back on the bed with a smile. "What-the-hell-ever. Anyway, seeing as I'm all ju got—um, *you* got, we'll just have to make lemons out of lemonade."

"Lemonade out of lemons," a deep voice over by the radiator in her room corrected.

Marcella slipped off the bed as though she floated on a cloud. Leaning down, she dragged a slim finger over the hard shoulder that was duct-taped to Delaney's radiator. "Whatever, darling. You Americans and your language are just something I don't think I'll ever get used to. Every time I think I get it—I don't. Now, correct me if I'm wrong, but I think explanations are in order here, don't you?"

Delaney was off the bed in a shot, stumbling on her sheets, almost falling into Clyde's duct-taped lap. When the full picture became clear, it made her gasp. Poor Clyde held hostage by a mountain of sticky silver tape. "You captured him with duct tape, Marcella? Duct tape? What about this says securing the bad demon to you? This shows shoddy workmanship, if you ask me, Ms. Demonlicious."

Marcella gave her long, black hair an indignant swish over her shoulder. "I was in a pinch, okay? He was lingering right here in your bedroom, hovering over your dead-to-the-world body—I had to act fast. Jesus, you'd think you'd at least notice the circle of salt I made around him so he'd be immobilized—just like you taught me. Can you even imagine what kind of freakin' facial peel I'd have been up against if I had gotten any of it on me?" She shuddered. "Oh, and I think you're clean out of Morton. We can shop once we rid ourselves of him. But not before we find out what he wants—or more specifically, what *Lucifer* wants." Her green eyes narrowed in on Clyde, her full lips tilted in a seductive smile. "Though, I have to admit, the human form he chose is pleasant on the eye, eh, *chica*?" She glanced at Delaney and mouthed the word *meow*.

Yeah, like big meow. The hell she'd admit that out loud, no matter how true. But Marcella, sexually charged demon that she was, had no filter from brain to mouth when it came to expressing her sexuality. A hottie was a hottie in her world. They never lasted longer than a night for Marcella, but Delaney had heard the stories. "Hey! Libido check. Forget what he looks like. He doesn't even really look like that. That's just some body he chose from a magazine cover or something, and you know it," Delaney chastised, moving in to examine the job Marcella'd done.

Despite the fact that Clyde looked as though he wasn't going anywhere, and with all that duct tape around him, he might never go anywhere again, she wasn't even a little ashamed to admit, she hated the prospect of violence during expulsion. And if screaming fireballs and iffy attempts at levitation were involved, especially where Marcella was concerned, Clyde was leaving this plane violently if not expertly. It just took Marcella time to warm up.

"Then he chose well, no?" she purred again from deep within her throat, the rasp of her words slow and sensual.

Delaney nudged her with an exaggerated sigh. "Focus, tart. He's gotta bounce. Where he goes or if he goes with you before he gets there isn't for me to judge." Looking down at Clyde, fastened to her radiator with more duct tape than a Home Depot shelf and a circle of thick salt around him to keep him from escaping, her heart began to speed up. What could Lucifer possibly gain by sending him? Unless Clyde was just letting her think he was a lesser demon . . . "Now, suggestions on how to do that?"

Marcella shook her head stubbornly, bracing a hand on the small of her back. "Not until we find out what's going on. Your message said he came here to bring you back to that scum Lucifer. I want to know why. Is the head badass all of a sudden upset that you've kept a few souls from his slimy clutches? Or is he doing this because I help you keep spirits from ending up just like me? That worries me, D. That worries me all the time. That maybe that weenie Beelzebub will exact revenge on me through you. I won't have it." She returned her smoldering gaze to Clyde. "So, handsome," Marcella looked down at him and purred, "spill."

Delaney reached for the robe she'd left in the corner of her room last night, never taking her eyes off Clyde. The Clyde who'd mastered a very convincingly baffled expression.

Bra-vo, ba-by.

He was crazy tight with the "I don't get it."

She didn't need to hear why he was here. She was almost certain why he was here. To make good on a threat the devil'd made almost fifteen years ago. A threat she'd never shared with anyone but Kellen. A threat that now made her wonder if she'd drawn unwanted attention to her friend who always dropped everything on a dime to help her.

Oh, hellz, no.

Involving Marcella might make an already hinky Lucifer take out his ire on her. There hadn't been a lot of thought about repercussions when she'd dialed Marcella last night. The last thing her bound-to-Hell pal needed was Lucifer's attention focused on her.

The last.

He wasn't one hundred percent in love with the fact that Marcella refused to spread his evil, but he let her be, in favor of bigger havoc to wreak. She was small potatoes compared to most demons, who willingly followed Lucifer. According to Marcella, each new demon, upon creation, came readily equipped with a fireball or two, maybe some levitating abilities, but if you didn't hone those skills, create chaos on a regular basis, you didn't get much further than that. Sort of a use it or lose it rule.

Marcella flat-out refused to play demon games, and so far, the horned one hadn't seemed terribly interested that she helped Delaney cross people over, or even that she'd stopped a bunch of possessions in her time. The theory they'd concocted about Lucifer's indifference to it was simple. No demon wanted to go back to his level-four Hell boss and tell them they'd screwed up something as simple as a possession or talking someone into their way of life. Don't ask, don't tell. What your level boss didn't know couldn't hurt him—or, in the end, you. And it couldn't be reported to Satan.

So Marcella'd become a mere blip on Hell's screen.

But Lucifer might not be so in the game if he knew Marcella was helping to thwart an effort that had obviously been a long time in the making. One he'd ordered by sending Clyde with a specific message.

If she'd been a trifle concerned last night, that all changed with the idea that Marcella could be hurt. Fear sliced through her—fear and indecision. Delaney put a hand on Marcella's shoulder, hoping she wouldn't pick up on the fact that she was about to tell her a major, honkin' lie. "Know what, Marcella? Forget why he's here. In fact, forget I called you. I think I can handle this all on my own." Her words were clearly unsteady, absolutely unsure, but she wouldn't risk Marcella's involvement.

"You mean forget it? Just like that?" Marcella snapped her slender fingers together. "Um, no. You were freaked out on the phone last night, *señorita*. You said Clyde had come to collect you and bring you back to Hell, something I don't get because he can't get you there without whacking you and he can't whack you, according to the rules of Hell—unless he wins your favor by deceit, which will never happen with someone like you. Though, he can definitely freak you the fuck out—make you see and do horrific things as a result if your will is even a little weak, but that ain't you, *guapa*. Regardless, that's not something I'll ever let happen if I can prevent it. But it's a statement I still don't understand because you're hardly presenting a problem to Lucifer. Most of the spirits you cross over know exactly where they want to go, and it ain't down below. So no go. Call me curious, but I'm in it for the long haul."

Delaney rolled her tongue in her cheek. Fuck. She *had* said she was a little freaked in her voice-mail message when Clyde claimed he was sent to take her to Hell. But wasn't that a demon's goal to begin with? To drag your ass back to Purgatory by hook or by contract? "Well, take your curious ass home. All demons make threats, and you know it. I'd never had a direct hit like that before that was so personal, so I got a little hinky. But I'm over it. Now, I appreciate the duct tape and the circle of death constructed in salt, but I think I know exactly what to do." Which was an utter and complete lie. She didn't know much more about expelling a demon than nuns knew about riding cowgirl, but if it meant keeping Marcella from hacking off Lucifer, so be it.

Marcella's dark head tilted to the left, the sleek strands of her hair almost brushing her elbow bent at her hip. "Ah, no. I went to a lot of trouble to anchor our compadre's ass to your radiator—a lot—and not without risk to my personal well-being. I deserve some answers. Besides, you do realize, if Lucifer sent him, and we manage to get rid of him, which isn't looking like a problem seeing as I wrestled him with only duct tape, that that chicken shit will just send someone else in his place. Maybe someone who's bigger and badder. I say we deal with the wussy demon just for fun, because he has to go no matter what, and while we're at it, we get the 411. Know what I mean, ghost lady?"

She knew exactly what Marcella meant. Delaney's thoughts raced, her hands becoming ice-cold. If Lucifer wanted her and this demon didn't nab her, there'd be more to follow. But that still didn't mean Marcella had to be involved. And she definitely didn't want Marcella to know *why* the devil had come calling via Clyde. The less she knew, the better off she was. "I know just what you mean, but I also know you don't need to be involved. It's like you said—he's clearly not a very powerful demon. I just got all whacked when he said he wanted to take me to Hell. But again: so over it now. So go on—get to gettin'. Isn't there a sale at Pier 1 today? I bet they have pillows on sale . . ." she enticed with a smile and a singing lilt to her voice, running a hand over her robin's egg blue nightgown. Which was just a little skimpy to be prancing around with in front of a demon.

"May I say something here, ladies?" The silent, studious Clyde suddenly drew the women's attention to him.

Marcella leaned down and put a finger to his lips. "No."

"But—"

She pressed more firmly. "Shhhh. Just be pretty."

Clyde shook her finger off with a rough jerk of his head. "Enough!" he shouted, seemingly surprising even himself with his commanding tone. He paused only for a moment before adding, "If you women would stop yammering like I'm not even in the room with you, I can explain."

Delaney's eyes narrowed while her heart raced. "No, no, no. Whatever you have to say, I'm not even a little interested. Demons are all liars."

Marcella gave her a hurt look, her exquisitely plucked brows furrowing, her lips forming a glossy red pout.

She shot her an apology with her eyes, then threw her gaze at Clyde. "Sorry. *Except* you, Marcella. You, Clyde, on the other hand, can forget it. I wouldn't believe a word you said even if you conjured up the Big Kahuna to back you up. Now, for the very last time, I want you—"

"If you two would just shut up, you'd see I could care less if you go back to Hell with me or not, damn it, because I'm not going back!" The muscles in his neck bulged, his tightly bound arms and legs strained against the restrictive silver duct tape, and his glasses wobbled on his nose with his explosive statement.

Ohhhh. He looked pissed. Which was hot on a guy who exuded the epitome of calm. Even if that calm façade was more than likely bullshit. But he'd managed to pique her curiosity. The women exchanged confused glances, but Marcella was the first to speak. "See? I told you we needed to hear what his story was."

Yet Delaney remained skeptical. "Demons are liars. Who knows that better than you?"

"Excuse me," Clyde intervened, his hard face clearly outraged, as the widening of his eyes and the granite set to his jaw showed. "You don't even know me and I don't mind saying, I'm a little hacked off myself now. I'm no liar. I *was* sent here to bring you back to Hell—"

Delaney pointed a finger under his nose. "You see? You admit it!"

His gruff sigh virtually shouted his agitation. The heave of the duct tape around his lightly haired chest made a slight ripping sound as it tore at patches of hair. "Yes, and if you'd given me the chance to explain before waving that thing under my nose and screeching like some banshee, I might have been able to finish what I was saying. I was sent here to bring you back to Hell, but I have absolutely no intention of doing anything of the sort."

Delaney didn't budge. Like she'd ever eat that baloney sandwich. "I call bullshit."

Clyde's stern expression grew harder as his jaw clamped down and a throbbing pulse in his temple picked up speed. "Call it whatever you like, but it can't be called bullshit. I'm telling the truth."

"Care to swear on a stack of Bibles?" Marcella's question was followed by her signature throaty laughter.

"I'd be insulted if I didn't almost get your skepticism. In the three months I've been in Hell, I've experienced my fair share of liars. But I'm not one of them, and if I had a free hand, I'd be all over your Bibles, lady." He gave Marcella a "so there, take that" look, letting his mouth turn to a thin line of furious.

Marcella plopped back down on the bed, taking Delaney with her. "Okay. Soooo, ah . . . what's your name again?"

"Clyde. Clyde Atwell, and I'd shake your hand, but again— there's this." He let his square chin drop to his chest, directing his eyes to the duct tape.

"Okay, Clyde, why don't you tell us why you're here?"

Delaney clamped a hand over Marcella's wrist "No! I told you—"

Now Marcella used her finger on Delaney's lips. "Hush, *mi amiga.* Let's just hear him out." She followed that with a conspiratorial wink of her thick lashes.

Clyde cleared his throat while Delaney watched his Adam's apple bob with far too much fascination for her comfort. "I *was* sent here to torment Delaney—probably, if what goes on down there is accurate—to bamboozle her into a contract with Hell. That much is true. I don't know why they want her. I'm new to this demon game, and I think Delaney can tell you, I'm definitely not particularly intimidating because I don't choose to be. I've only been in Hell for three months—most of which I've spent pondering the whys and wherefores on how exactly I ended up there. Especially because I didn't believe in it when I was alive."

Delaney leaned forward toward him, pushing her growing fear as far away as she could and staring him straight in his deep blue eyes. "Isn't that what everyone says? 'I just don't get how I ended up in Hell,'" she mocked, using a tauntingly innocent tone and batting her eyelashes. "You chose to go there, you moron. As has been my experience in crossing hundreds of souls to the other side, when reaching your afterlife, you have two choices. Obviously you were swayed by the promise of eternal pairs of epic ta-tas and cash or something equally as nefarious. So save the innocent, wide-eyed fuckwittery for someone who'll believe you. I've been around the supernatural block a time or two and I know you and your kind." End rant. She sat back on the bed, squishing closer to Marcella in case he had the power to shoot her with his laser beam eyes. She'd totally forgotten to don her protective force field.

Yet Clyde's posture became more rigid, the tension on his face most evident around his eyes and mouth. "No, I absolutely did not choose to go to Hell. I wasn't given a choice about anything. One minute I was in my lab, the next I was in Hell."

Well, well. That admission, as utterly stupid as it was for him to make, explained everything. "You weren't given a choice because you lived a life that was shitty. People who do shitty things all their lives don't get a choice about where they end up. You were obviously on the Big Kahuna's naughty list, my friend. That means you did some freaky-deaky crap while you were alive, thus marking your ass for Hell. Shit I don't want to know about because to not even be given the opportunity to choose means you broke some serious commandments. And now, I do believe, that ends our discussion."

She waved a hand at Marcella, using her other to pat her friend's thigh. "Okay, do your thang, friend." Delaney rose, making her way out of the bedroom and into the kitchen with Marcella right behind her.

"Um, consultation, please, O Ghost Transmitter."

"Consult."

Marcella wiggled her finger at Delaney, summoning her closer so she could bring her lips to Delaney's ear. "What *thing*?" she hissed in a whisper. "*Aye Chihuahua!* You know I don't have a thing, D. I suck at things. I'm just the talker in this relationship of ours. You know, the one who shows up when a spirit is waffling and convinces them that all that glitters isn't necessarily golden down under? I don't know how to get rid of him any more than you do. His skill level, if he's telling the truth about only being three months old, is probably on par with mine."

Delaney leaned into Marcella and snickered. "And you've been around forevah. Slacker."

Marcella's accent grew thicker as her temperature rose. "Aye, *mi amiga*. It means fair fight. Which means I could break a nail, or worse, ruin my dress. Which isn't from Target. So do not even start this with me, ju—ju—"

"Oh, look. The chick from Hell's still here." Kellen interrupted them with his dry remark from around the corner of her kitchen. Her dogs skittered over the linoleum floor, skipped giving Marcella the stink eye because she never let them jump on her cute dresses, ignored Delaney altogether, and headed straight to her bedroom to the corner Clyde was still in.

Marcella rested a hand on the countertop, sucking in her cheeks before facing Kellen. "Oh, look, it's the crankiest man in the world, and you're not even wearing plaid pants and scheduling colonoscopies yet. You're like an old man with hemorrhoids, Kellen Markham. Cranky, cranky, cranky. And pissy. Definitely pissy."

Delaney instantly stepped between them, placing a hand on the wall of Kellen's chest. They bickered from time to time, and on most days it was pretty frickin' funny. Very transparent, but still very funny. Today, it just added to the chaos. "Not now, you two. Don't give me more shit to deal with. We have bigger fish to fry. Like Clyde here." She thumbed a finger over her shoulder. "Save the witty potshots at one another for some other time, and help me figure this out."

Kellen planted a hand on her shoulder, gripping it with light pressure. "He's here?"

Delaney clucked her tongue. "Yep. Tied up in the bedroom. Courtesy of the chick from Hell. So knock it off or the next visit you pay me might be while flames lick your keister."

"And he claims he's here to torment Delaney," Marcella added, her gaze scanning Delaney's face. "I didn't say anything in front of him, but care to explain a statement like that? Lowly demon or not, he was sent here for you, missy. We've run into a demon or two in our time, but never one with the express intent of making you his target. Your thoughts, O Wise One?"

Kellen and Delaney exchanged glances before Delaney shrugged her shoulders. "Nope. Not a clue. Which is all the more reason he has to go."

Kellen's face grew stiff, his grip tightening on her shoulder. "I guess it does me no good to tell you I'll kick his ass if you want, seeing as he can flambé me with fireballs, huh?"

Marcella popped her glossed lips. "Better watch out. I just might help him."

Kellen didn't even give Marcella a glance over his shoulder. He always talked about her in third person, knowing full well it left Marcella feeling dismissed. "Does she really have to be here?"

Marcella came to stand behind Delaney, letting her chin rest on her shoulder and looking directly at Kellen. "She does."

Delaney could hear the chuckle in her friend's tone, the taunting clarity of the joy she took in sparring. She loved to bait Kellen. Lived for it. Might one day find herself with the unlife choked out of her for it.

Kellen hitched his clamped jaw at her. "I don't see why. I mean, what good are you to Delaney when all you do is set shit on fire and float into walls?"

The smile never left Marcella's face. But Delaney knew without even looking at her—the instant tension in her body told her—that Kellen was pushing all of her friend's touchy buttons. "If you keep it up, I'll set *your* shit on fire." Marcella wiggled a finger in the general direction of Kellen's groin.

The dogs began to bark, whining that high-pitched yap of distress, ending the threat of someone's junk going up in flames.

Delaney skirted around Kellen and made a beeline for the bedroom to find that Clyde was gone—in all his duct-taped fabulousness. Her sigh was ragged.

"Holy frijoles. He can disappear already?" Marcela skidded to a halt at the spot where Clyde had been attached to her radiator. "Very, very nice. I still have trouble with that—even when I squeeze really hard."

Delaney rustled the dogs up, scratching heads and hindquarters. "Well, he's gone for now."

Marcella gnawed the tip of her fingernail with a sheepish look at Delaney. "Maybe one roll of duct tape wasn't enough?"

Kellen barked a laugh, gruff and cynical. "You used *duct tape* to capture a demon?"

Delaney held a hand up, palm facing Kellen. "Shut it. Not another word, Kellen. It's not like you have a better solution, now, do you?"

Kellen was immediately silenced.

Marcella stuck her tongue out at him before asking, "So now what, D?"

Her teeth felt gritty, and she needed some tea and a shower. "I have no idea. He's gone for now and that's all that matters. How he got gone is a mystery. All I know is, it's Saturday, and if I hope to rope some customers in, I have to shower and get dressed. I lost eight hundred bucks because of that asshole last night. I can't afford to whittle away another day worrying about something that hasn't happened. I have rent to pay, and you know how slow the fall and winter are for me."

Marcella's face was sympathetic, her blue eyes warm. "You know it doesn't have to be like that. I can lend you the cash."

Delaney frowned, though her friend's concern never failed to touch her. She reached for the clip she held her hair up with, wrapping a fist around the thick width of it and securing it behind her head. "Oh, no, sistah. I'm not borrowing money I might have to pay back well into the afterlife. But thank you. Now go. Both of you." She waved her hands at them, shooing them from her room. "Go beat each other down with your snark."

Marcella blew her a kiss. "Oh, I'll go, but while I'm gone, I'm going to do some digging to see what I can find about this particular demon."

Fear assaulted Delaney again, fresh and pungent. She couldn't—wouldn't—allow Marcella to become tangled up in this. Yet she kept her tone nonchalant to keep Marcella's alarm bells from ringing. "Don't bother, Marcella. Just stay out of it and do what you do best—buy things." Delaney smiled, giving them each a quick hug, watching as they left, the silent tension between them as thick as it always was. But no matter how much Kellen claimed he couldn't stand Marcella, it didn't stop him from eyeballing her stupendous ass on his way out.

And if Delaney were a man, she would, too. 'Cause Marcella was ass-tastic.

And she'd hate her for it, but she didn't have time for one of the seven deadly sins today. She had a business to run.

A shower and two cups of green tea later, she was ready to do the day. Penning the dogs in her living room with their assorted toys, she drifted to the front of the store, grabbing her feather duster as she went so she could wipe down the shelves lined with herbs.

A rustle of paper made her ears prick with curiosity; a tingle along her spine alerted her to a supernatural presence.

For fuck's sake.

This was turning into some kind of supernatural Grand Central. No sooner did she ditch one, than another spirit cropped up. She glanced around the empty store, rolling up the sleeves of her oversized sweater. The warmth in her chest, the shiver along her arms meant she had someone's full attention. "Whoever you are, I'd really, really love you into the next lifetime if you popped back onto this plane, like, *later*. I promise, whatever the problem is, I'll help, just not now. I can't afford to shoot the shit and Sherlock Holmes my way into your mystery at the moment. So cut a medium some slack, and let me have just a couple hours of peace. There's squat on TV tonight, so come back then. We'll conversate. Promise." She held up her hand in the symbol of a Girl Scout's honor.

The air hummed with the slightest of vibrations, then stilled.

Thank. You.

But the flutter of paper caught the corner of her eye.

Green paper. On the old antique desk that held her cash register.

Green, cashlike paper.

Her fingers reached out and grabbed it, flicking through it, then she flipped through it again for good measure.

Well, if she was counting right, the pieces of green paper added up to a nice number. The number eight hundred.

Word.

four

Delaney held up the thick wad of one-hundred-dollar bills, waving it around her empty store with an angry fist. "I cannot be bought, demon! Take your money, ill-gotten, I'm sure, and hit the highway to Hell." She plunked it down with a flat hand, shaking the cash register, her breathing choppy with rage. The fuck she'd take money he'd probably stolen from some little old lady.

Clyde appeared with the blink of an eye. He sat casually—on the top of an old armoire that held books on herbal remedies located in the corner of the store.

Naked.

With a patch or ten of hair missing from his arms, legs, and chest.

The sticky residue of duct tape glue covered him from his ankles to his breathtaking chest. His hawklike gaze behind his square frames turned on her as he looked down to the spot where she stood. "I'm only trying to undo what you've obsessively declared over and over I've done. Robbed you. Blind."

Delaney looked upward, her eyes connecting with his, desperately trying to avoid the elephant in the room.

His junk, covered—just barely—by his lean hands.

Only a male demon would conjure up a love shank like that. Even in death, the male ego won out on the list of things they were shortchanged with in life. "I don't want money you most likely stole from someone else."

His look said offended. "I can assure you, I would never steal."

Her nose wrinkled. "I can assure you, you're full of horse puckey."

Clyde moved his head back and forth in an adamant gesture. "No. I absolutely did not steal it."

Hookay. "Then how'd you get your hands on eight hundred bucks?"

"The explanation is easy enough. It would seem my accounts aren't so otherworldly. At least one isn't. I had a safe deposit box. No one knew about it but me. While I hate to admit it, I used one of these demon skills I now have to get into it."

"How convenient. If bullshit was a corporate position, you'd be a CEO."

Clyde's face never changed. He never batted a single thick eyelash. "I'm not bullshitting you. If you'd like, I'll give you the name of the bank and you can see the account for yourself. It's in my name and has been for almost eighteen years."

Her eyes rolled at him. "Don't bother. Even if I did believe your half-baked baloney, it isn't like you couldn't conjure something like that up with your demon prowess."

"Hah!" he barked, making her jump with the sharpness of it. "I believe that particular skill is a level-six ability. I haven't made it past level one—as you clearly saw after that woman with the accent attacked me from behind, wrestled me to the ground, and duct-taped me to your radiator. I'm just now learning how to disappear. I don't like using anything that even remotely has to do with these demonic powers I've been given, but it gave me an advantage I needed today. I'd be a liar if I didn't say it helped in a pinch, but it was no cakewalk getting in and out of that bank—*naked*—even if it was closed."

Touché. Or not . . . she was having a hard time believing he wasn't just playing poor widdle weak demon to fool her.

"So now we're even," he concluded with a satisfied nod of his head.

"No. We're nothing. I don't want your money. I do want you to get out of my house—my store. I only aid spirits who need help crossing over. You've officially crossed, and there ain't no comin' back from where you landed. That means I can't help you and I'm not interested in why you showed up here." Though that might not totally be the truth. She was a little curious after his admission that he was sent here to torment her. But demons loved to play games, and that was probably the case with this one. To waste time playing with them, asking questions, was fruitless and would only heighten a demon's lust for the sheer joy of toying with a mortal.

Now his patience was running thin. She could see it in the hardening of his eyes, and the pulse at his right temple. "Then don't take the money. Give it to the poor. Buy dogs one through six a helluva steak. In my mind, my debt to you is paid, and honoring a debt is important to me—no matter how skewed and misinterpreted by a medium the debt is."

"Very civic, with just the right touch of Boy Scout. Now get out." She'd deal with the temptation of coveting thy demon's eight hundred smackers later.

He remained where he was with a posture that dared her to get her prism. "Nope. I'm not leaving until you listen, and if I have to,

I'll use one of my demon skills to make you. I won't like it, but I'll do it if the end result is we get this cleared up."

He. Did. Not. "Pop off, demon. I know you didn't just threaten me."

Clyde narrowed his gaze.

She sighed, when he didn't move a muscle, letting her irritation bleed through the long exhale of it. "Are you gonna make me get the prism again?"

His game face changed a hair. Not nearly as determined as it was a minute ago. "Please don't."

Delaney mentally took the metaphoric reins back. "It got rid of you the first time. Wasn't that you who got all girlie about a little piece of glass? You back for more, hero?"

"If your eyes burning holes in their sockets is girlie, then just call me girl. You had an unfair advantage—a weapon I knew absolutely nothing about. But I'm learning . . ." He let his words drift off, then gave her a smug grin.

Delaney's snort ripped through the silence between them. "Puulease. You know damned well what's damaging to a demon. Don't they give you classes on it in Hell? Isn't that, like, Demon 101?"

Clyde's lips thinned, his cheekbones becoming sharper, more defined, giving him a whole new appeal. "As I said, I've avoided as much participation in anything demonic as I could."

Her arms crossed over her chest; her stance grew defensive. "Really? That sounds like a very convenient answer. Like maybe something I want to hear to pacify me until you wail me when I'm not looking?" She cocked a suspicious eyebrow at him.

His wide chest heaved in a ragged sigh. Aw, look. The poor demon was fed up. Wah-wah. "That's why I was sent here, Delaney. I've been trying to tell you that since you accused me of bilking you out of eight hundred bucks. My *original* assignment was supposed to be some sort of punishment for my refusal to be a team player—if I don't do what I'm supposed to, my eternity will be spent in the pit."

The pit? What the frig was the pit? Marcella'd never mentioned a pit . . . "The pit?"

His nod was curt. "All your worst fears come true—for *eternity*."

God, that would totally suck. For her, that would mean they'd take *Ghost Whisperer* off the air or something . . . how heinous.

As she pondered the potential for a Friday night disaster, Clyde finally asked, "Aren't you even a little curious as to why Satan *himself* would send someone to terrorize you? That's a pretty strong message he's sending, if you ask me."

Yes, she was curious. No. Yes. No. Delaney shook her head as though that might clear up her misgivings. She refused to delve into this any further. If Satan wanted her, he'd just have to get his spineless ass in gear and come get her himself. She wasn't indulging, or for that matter divulging anything to, this Clyde.

Before she had the chance to voice her rather ballsy thoughts, Mrs. Ramirez appeared at the store door, pressing her round face to the glass and motioning for Delaney to open the door.

"Who's that?" Clyde asked from on high.

"Crap. Mrs. Ramirez. She comes to help me in the store sometimes and she loves to play with the dogs. She *cannot* see you or there'll be no keeping you under wraps. Disappear or something, would you?"

Clyde cringed, attempting to make his body smaller. "Do you have any idea what it took for me to do that the last time? I nearly burst a blood vessel."

Mrs. Ramirez pounded on the door, shaking the handle. "Ju open de door, Mees Delaney. Ees locked."

Delaney looked up at Clyde with a ragged sigh, hoping Mrs. Ramirez couldn't see with great distance into the depth of the store. "Can't you squeeze really hard or something? She can't find you here or the whole block will know about it."

Delaney went to the door, popping the top lock and sticking just her nose out. She faked a sneeze in the general direction of Mrs. Ramirez's cherubic face. "I'm sick, Mrs. Ramirez. I've got it covered today. You go home."

Her black eyes pierced Delaney's with sympathy. "Oh, ju seeck. I come een an' make ju soup, jes?"

"Jes, I mean, no. I don't want you to catch it. Go home and come back next week. I'm sure I'll be better then."

Her brow furrowed with deep lines. She planted chubby hands on her stout body while the wind whipped her salt-and-pepper hair from its tight bun at the back of her head. "No. I come een an' take care of de store an' de babies. Ju go to bed."

Delaney shot another fake sneeze at her and followed up with the best hacking cough she could summon. "I'm going to leave the store closed today, Mrs. Ramirez. Promise. Hurry up and go home before you catch something." She sniffled for good measure.

"Ju sure?"

She nodded at her friend who was more like a grandmother. "Jes . . . er, yes. Thanks, Mrs. R. Give Alonzo a big hug for me, okay?"

Mrs. Ramirez ran a finger along Delaney's nose, then turned to stroll away from the store, her luggage-sized purse swinging from her elbow.

Relief escaped her lungs in a whoosh of air.

"She gone?"

Now back to Clyde. "Yes, she's gone. Okay, so I have a question."

"Fire," he said, stretching his legs back out, defining every last sexy muscle in them.

"If your mission is to capture me and get me to Hell, why

would Lucifer send a noob who hasn't learned his demon ass from his fire-breathing elbow? Dude, that's just insane. Especially when you're dealing with someone who knows the spirit world like I do, not to mention the talent for bullshit you demons are so gifted with."

Now Clyde snorted, long and loud, making the notion of his ability to capture her seem even more preposterous. He shrugged his shoulders indifferently, but his eyes left her face and stared down at his toes. "If you know the spirit world, then you know sometimes it has no rhyme or reason. And Satan doesn't need a reason to do anything. He does as he pleases."

"So he sent you here with absolutely no backup? No heavy hitters to help you out?" This made no sense.

"None of that matters now. That's why I need you to listen. Satan sent me on a mission I have no intention of completing." He looked around as if someone—someone they couldn't see—might hear them.

Delaney looked around, too—because he'd passed the suspicion baton on to her and she was beginning to feel pairs of invisible eyes on her that probably didn't exist. "And why's that?"

Clyde's voice was low when he spoke again. "Okay, one more time for posterity: I don't belong in Hell." He held up a hand to stop her from interrupting him, thus revealing far more flesh than her almost reconstituted virginal eyeballs could take in all in one gander. "Before you say another word—no, I absolutely did not choose Hell as my eternal destination. I didn't have a choice. Like I said, one minute I was in my lab, the next in a place that's beyond Africa hot. And forget the idea that I led this shitty life you accused me of earlier. I've never raped, pillaged, plundered, cheated, or committed any of the deadly sins I'm sure you know by psalm and verse. I was a decent guy, if distracted by my work and sometimes forgetful that there were other people with feelings that occupied my space. I highly doubt being so absorbed in my work was how I ended up in Hell. Now I have a month back here on Earth to figure out how a decent guy ends up in Hell. That's how long Lucifer gave hi—er, me to bring you to him. Now, if I'm completely honest here, I'll admit I'm pretty bent out of shape. I have to tell you, it really doesn't pay to have any morals at all in life if you're only going to be screwed in death. If the life I led was what put me on the path to Hell, I expect the reigning pope to show up any minute in my 'Demons Do It Better' class."

Delaney looked down at her slip-on shoes, waving a hand in the general direction of his southerly locales, her cheeks hot and pink with embarrassment. "Put that thing away."

Clyde cleared his throat, slapping his hand back in place over his goodies. "Shit. My apologies."

She heard him shift on the armoire, his skin sticking to the wood when he did. And now everything was situation normal all fucked up—which gave her a thought. One she couldn't let go of. A little factoid that didn't connect all of Clyde's dots. His story was a good one, unusual and unique, but he could have made all of it up to string her along. Sort of a reverse psychology thing. Play nice, pretend you despise your horned leader, suck in the medium, then nail her balls to the wall for the coup of the century. Satan pats him on the back, and he earns another rung on Hell's ladder.

Perfect, right?

But this had been nagging at her since last night when he'd been on her bed in her bathrobe, jacking up her Friday night.

Her dogs loved him.

To some that might seem really odd, or even weak, that she was toying with the idea that her dogs could determine good from pure evil. But animals, and even some children, had a keen sixth sense, and her dogs had literally mourned his leaving her bedroom not just last night, but this morning, too. She knew her babies like a mother knew her human offspring, and her babies knew a malevolent force when they saw one.

She hoped.

Another thought occurred to her, too. Her dogs also loved Marcella. Totally dug her. She didn't love them back much because they were always tearing her nylons or chewing up her shoes, and even then, they still loved her. Had from their very first meeting when she'd called them some name, one that probably wasn't full of warm squisheys, in Spanish. Marcella was definitely a demon. Not a demon that would hurt a fly without cause, but a demon nonetheless. If Marcella could be a peace-loving unwilling resident of Hell, why couldn't Clyde?

Delaney grabbed an old throw she kept in the store due to the draftiness in the winter. She hurled it up to Clyde so he could cover his fun stuff just as she caught the glimpse of a woman standing in the corner by the rack of herbal oils. She froze in place, forgetting that she really should ask this errant demon what his supposed mission was about and how it involved her, because the familiar goose bumps rising on her arms while her chimes swayed with a shiver took precedence.

"Delaney?"

"Shhhhh," she whispered up to Clyde. "Do you see her?"

"Her?"

"In the corner. The lady with the poofy dress and the thing on her head that looks like a doily."

Clyde shifted to crane his neck. The moment he did, the woman began to fade, then her wavering form turned fuzzy like snow on a television set. Like when the picture faded in and out. Clyde stirred again, running a hand through his hair, and once more, the apparition crackled with static—almost in sync with his movements.

"Sit back up," she ordered.

Clyde grunted, leaning back to his left and centering himself atop the armoire again. "Is it Aunt Gwyneth again?"

"No, definitely not, and if you don't hold still I won't be able to help her. Quit squirming." Each time Clyde moved, the presence slipped in and out of vision, syncing with his every move. How utterly bizarre. "Stop moving!"

"Sorry, I had an itch."

Delaney moved closer to the woman, squinting her eyes to bring her into focus. "Clyde," she threatened, "if you breathe the wrong way, I'll hack your limbs off."

Moving with cautious steps, she approached the woman. Whoever she was, sucked to be her in that drab dress, wearing a doily on her head. Clearly she was from another century. Though the outfit didn't ring any history bells with Delaney. The woman's lips were moving, but the words rang with only the slightest whisper. Delaney leaned in as far as she could to try to catch what she seemed so desperate to say, watching her lips move as she did. *"DasKomadasKomadasKoma,"* she said, her face filled with a sense of urgency.

Was that German? Oh, fuck. What did she know in German? "Uh, Volkswagen. Oh! Sauerkraut and Wiener schnitzel—oh, oh! And knockwurst. And, uh . . . *Der Kommissar*!" she shouted as though they were playing charades.

"*Falco*, 1981, *After the Fire*, 1983."

She tilted an ear up at Clyde. "Who? Never mind, demon—shut it. I'm working here."

"DasKomadasKomadasKoma," the woman repeated with fierce insistence, extending a hand toward Delaney as though summoning her.

Pinching her temples, Delaney gave them a hard squeeze. "Aww, crap, lady. You *are* foreign. That so sucks. You know, as a medium,

I've given a lot of thought to taking some foreign language courses. I've had a visit or two from a group of Dutchmen, and once, even some gondola driver from Italy. But I just can't seem to find the time, ya know? Shit. If you tell me how to spell it, I can go look it up online." Which was probably ridiculous to ask because the woman wouldn't understand her any more than she understood the woman. But the image began to fade before Delaney could turn to retrieve her laptop.

Her shoulders slumped. "Damn. She's gone."

"And this would be my fault, too, I suppose," Clyde stated dryly.

Delaney rolled her eyes at him. "No, Clyde, though whatever mojo you have going on is screwing up mine. Did you catch a glimpse of her? Do you know if she was speaking German?"

"Foreign languages were one thing I didn't tap in my lifetime. And how do you get used to something like that? People just showing up out of nowhere?"

"You mean like you?"

His blue eyes colored with amusement, and he conceded. "Touche."

"Are you sure you didn't see her?"

"You did tell me not to move. I listened. And I definitely couldn't hear her because I was concentrating on not moving." His tone held a glint of accusation.

Delaney scratched her head, deciding she'd just have to hope the woman came back. "That's right, I did. Okay. Forget the lady with the sucky dress and doily hat for now. We have other business to attend to. So I have a thought."

Clyde pulled the throw around his shoulders, letting the ends fall to his lap. "Which is . . . ?"

She backed away, setting her butt on the edge of the stool she kept behind the counter. "Why the fuck do you suppose I'd believe anything—anything—you tell me about your story? You know firsthand that demons are liars. You said that yourself. How do I know you're not yanking my crank, making me think you're all jacked up by some mistake so you can hoodwink me and drag me back to Hell with you? Maybe you're just playing the 'I don't belong in Hell, poor me' story to court me into believing you. So I want an answer. And I warn you—your answer better be really, really solid, or I'm getting the prism and the salt."

"Maybe I am."

"Maybe you're lying?"

"Maybe."

Her face went slack with disbelief. "That's all you have to offer?"

Clyde's lightly bronzed shoulders hitched upward, allowing the blanket to fall to his biceps. "Yep. That's it. As you said, demons are all liars. I won't even bother to try and deny the truth of that statement. Yes, I could be lying to you. Yes, I could be trying to pull the wool over your eyes with a song and dance. I've tried to explain my situation to you under some abominable circumstances, like the potential loss of my eyesight and the peeling of my skin by way of pillars of salt, but you refused to listen. It's like beating my head against a brick wall with you. The more I say, the deeper I dig myself. So yeah, that's all I have to say. But there's just one more thing."

Delaney made an arc with her hand. "Please. Do share."

Clyde's glance was evasive at first, but then he appeared to gather some steam. His shoulders pulled back, and his eyes held a hard determination she hadn't seen before this. "I have no intention of leaving this plane without figuring out why I ended up in Hell, Delaney. I have limited time and limited resources. I don't want to do it, but I will if I have to."

Her head cocked to the left. "Will *what*?"

Clyde hopped down from the armoire, his feet slapping the

bare floor hard. He caught a toe on the rug, pitching forward for a moment before stumbling to right himself.

She fought the urge to mock and point at the bad-ass, mofo demon all frontin' like he was some gangsta on a killing spree.

If he was embarrassed, he was damned good at hiding it. Clyde threw his shoulders back, sauntering toward her.

Her eyes met his when he approached her, refusing to stray beyond the dark blue of them for fear she'd catch another glimpse of his man-tool. "Use my demonic powers."

Her chest puffed outward—defensive and at the ready. "Are you threatening me? *Me?*"

Gone was the confused man she'd met yesterday. Gone was that look of innocent displacement. In its stead was a jagged resolve of flashing blue eyes behind the glimmer of his square frames and teeth, clamped and on edge. "Yep."

Hoo boy.

It was, apparently, on.

"Do you have any idea the shit I could stir up? I know people from the other side—people who'll whip your satanic ass into a frenzy, noob."

Clyde rolled his tongue along the inside of his cheek. "I hate to be the one to burst your bubble, but if you're talking about that OD'd-on-too-much-nail-polish-remover Marcella, she's probably as much of a joke downstairs in Hell as I am. And I don't want to point out the obvious, but I will because I'm all about fair warning. If you had someone who could help you, you'd have called them by now."

In Clyde's favor, that would be game, set, *match*.

Because she really didn't know anyone with heavy-duty Hell powers, that was fo sho.

But her pride wouldn't allow him to threaten her—the frig he'd threaten her—and to hell with his reasons for being here. She didn't care anymore why he was here, just that he wouldn't be as soon as she could make that possible. "You picked the wrong medium to tango with, brotha." Delaney waved a finger under his nose when he drew closer, ignoring the pure maleness of him. And while she was at it, she'd ignore that waist that tapered to lean hips, and the scent of his aftershave.

His breath fanned her face when he let out a raspy sigh. "I didn't pick anything. But I'd suggest you listen to me before things get out of hand."

Okay, so maybe she was getting a little nervous now, but in the interest of never let 'em see you sweat, she threw her head back and laughed. "He with the duct tape glue residue all over his body said."

Clyde let the blanket drop to his chest, securing it by tucking the ends in. "You were warned."

Uh-huh. She'd been warned. Now she was going to take that warning and keep it ever so close to her heart as she swept the floor. Turning from Clyde, big, muscular, and okay, dweebishly hot, she went in search of her broom, ducking behind the counter to see if her dustpan was still on the shelf.

A sizzling crackle made her head snap up.

Stop.

He didn't.

Oh, but he had.

If the roar of flames was any indication.

five

"Omigod! You feeb! You set my grandmother's chair on fiiire!" Delaney ran for the broom, waving it in the air to slap at the flames before the smoke alarm went off.

Clyde appeared out of nowhere again with a soggy, wet towel. He handed it to her with a casual pass, then took a step back, crossing his arms over his chest. "I did," was the cool response. "But I was actually aiming for the bookcase behind it. So, oops."

Delaney swatted the chair with the towel, tamping out the flames shooting from the arm while large drops of water splattered over the fabric. He'd only managed to torch the one arm of it, but she was no less hacked off about it. "Oops? Like oops, my bad? This—was—an—antique—you—fucktard! Look at it!" she yelped. "You've ruined it. You can't just order fabric like this anymore. Arghhhh!"

He yanked the towel from her, pressing it into the cushiony material with firm hands. "I told you I would do what it took. I'm sorry it took this, but you have this way about you that demands proof by action."

Using the back of her hand, she pushed her hair from her forehead before nudging him out of the way, yanking the towel from his grip. Clyde's hand grazed hers while he held strong. "Give me that, firestarter," she huffed, pulling it from his grip. "This wasn't just my grandmother's chair, it was my *story time* chair."

Now he looked remorseful. Good. Very good. After the fact was hugely helpful. "She read you stories in it?"

Delaney grunted with the effort to blot the now sopping wet fabric. "No. I mean, yes—when I was little. But I also hold a story time for kids once a month here at the store with sugarless wheat cookies and soy milk. How do you feel about fucking up some poor kids' night out, you jackass?"

Clyde looked doubtful. "What kind of kid eats sugarless wheat cookies and soy milk and actually *likes* it?"

All right, so the sugarless cookies weren't always a score with the kids. Point. "The kind who have parents who're trying to keep toxic chemicals out of their offspring's bodies. Preservatives and additives and all the junk that clogs your pipes up. What difference does it make now? I have no chair to read to them from. That means you've not only ruined my cherished memory, but crapped on a bunch of kids who'll be very sad they can't sit by this very chair and hear the story of how Mr. Herb goes to Washington."

"Mr. Herb? Whatever happened to some good old-fashioned Dr. Seuss?"

"Well, we'll never know, now, will we? Even if I could have read Dr. Seuss to the little beasts, I can't do it now because you burned the goddamned chair!"

Clyde's he-man, take-no-prisoners posture slumped; his expression grew somber. "I had no idea. I think we should just have a running apology from here on out in our relationship. I'll always just be sorry and you can always be angry that I had to be sorry for whatever reason I'm sorry. Deal?"

Delaney threw the lumpy towel right at his not so lumpy abs, winking decadently at her from beneath the blanket. "No deal, Howie. We don't have a relationship, you inheritance wrecker."

Clyde caught it with a grunt and a sidelong glance. "We will. That's what I've been trying to tell you, but you keep ignoring me—brushing me off."

Duh. "In the hopes that you'll fade to black. Yes, I'm ignoring you—or at least I was trying to. Nobody threatens me, you Purgatory pimp. Especially not a pathetic demon like you."

Clyde planted a big hand on the back of the chair. "I had to find a way to make you listen and I'm not done yet. There's still more."

Delaney sucked her cheeks in, assessing the singed chair. "If you thought this was the way to get a woman to pay attention to you, a playa you ain't."

Nodding an agreement, he flexed his fingers. "Established—and not just by you. I'm not here to play you. I just want your cooperation. I just want you to relax and listen to me."

Her wide eyes and raised eyebrows said it all. "By setting fire to my stuff? I don't think I'm being too ballsy when I say you're not endearing yourself to me, *Clyde* the demon."

"I don't want to endear myself to you, Delaney the ghost lady. I want to find out why I'm in Hell and, if you'll let me, help you in the process."

Her hands went to her hips as she took in his tall form. She let her head tilt back on her shoulders to gaze up at him. Way up at him. Delaney was short by today's standards at five foot one, but right now she felt dwarfed, eaten up by his looming, darkly handsome bulk. "Oh, I'm all atwitter. Help me? How do you suppose you can help me?"

Mirroring her stance, he placed his hands on his own lean hips.

"Because I have information about you." He returned her shocked gaze with a cocky, all-knowing one.

"Reaaaallly?"

"Reaaaallly," he drawled, dropping his head to his chest to roll it on his shoulders.

The problem was, would that information be true? But she'd play, because she had some doubts she had to address about Clyde. Delaney sensed she was giving poor old Clyde a run for his money by the set of his tense shoulders and the way he twisted his neck back and forth. "Okay. Hit me with your best shot." Whiner.

"Pat Benatar, 1980, off the *Crimes of Passion* album." Clyde's lean fingers began to massage his temples in absent circles.

And now we had the crazy. Maybe he was more confused about how he'd landed here than he was letting on. "Uh, you just crossed the threshold from creepy and annoying to crazy. Repeat?"

His head popped up, and he gave a push with two fingers to settle his glasses back on the bridge of his nose. "Forget it. It's just a habit. I have a lot of useless trivia in my head. Sometimes words—songs trigger it. It just flies out of my mouth before I can stop it. Especially when I'm stressed, and getting you to give me your ear for more than the time it takes you to make my eyeballs feel like they're being grilled on hot coals is damned stressful, lady."

Delaney forced away the smile she almost let happen from hitting her face. "Okay, so how about we leave the era of leg warmers and Madonna, and you tell me what information you have about me from, of all places, Hell."

Clyde scowled. "Madonna didn't happen until more like '82."

"Right. Like a—a—"

"Virgin. From her *Like a Virgin* album, circa 1984, if I remember correctly."

"I'll be sure to make a mental note. Now spew, demon."

Now he frowned, the vein in his temple pulsing. "I hesitate to say this, but I'm guessing you won't believe me."

"And that's stopped you from yakking my ear off before? You set my chair on fire to get me to pay attention to you. Whatever it is, it must be serious—so tell me what the frig you want from me, and let me decide if I believe you." Which she probably wouldn't, but who didn't want to hear the gossip they'd evoked straight from Hell? If she was all the rage down there, she wanted every juicy detail.

"All right. So it's just like I told you. I don't know how I ended up in Hell. I'd swear that on the Bibles that crazy woman offered me. A stack of them. I've been there for three months—in the file room."

A snicker escaped her throat. "Hell has files?"

Clyde's face grew strained, almost as if what he claimed to have seen in these files really did trouble him. "A shitload of them," he said with a gruff note to his tone. "On *everyone*—the incoming, the due to be incoming, potential visitors, the easily corrupted, the want to corrupt but haven't decided what road to take to the land of corruption—plus, mission assignments for all the demons in Hell, et cetera."

Mayhem, madness, and chaos—all in one neat little filing system. Very clean. "So what does that have to do with me? I can't be corrupted, believe me. I know." And know she did. She'd been offered wealth and power once before by the very definition of evil. It'd been ugly, ugly. That warning shiver ran along her arms again with just the hint of the long-ago memory.

Clyde's jaw shifted. "You weren't in those files, Delaney. You were in the files for 'vengeance—long overdue.'"

Her bravado slipped from her hands like sand in an hourglass. Her breath wheezed out of her lungs, leaving a heavy pressure in its wake. "Meaning?"

The pained expression left his eyes and they took on a solemn, direct stare. "Meaning, someone was assigned to come here and taunt you, to torment you in whatever way they had to, to get you to give in and follow Satan. From what little I read, your file was flagged. It's the kind of file that's in the equivalent of the urgent basket, which means a demon given the assignment is supposed to do whatever it takes to bend you to his will—make a contract with you—because, as Marcella said, demons can't literally kill anyone. They can only coerce you into doing something that will land your soul in Hell upon your death—make you see your worst fears by creating illusions. I gather they were going to try and make you so crazy that you might end your . . . commit . . . suicide," he said with graveness so gravelly deep, she couldn't ignore it.

Huh. Surely the devil, after his run-in with her fifteen years ago, knew that just wasn't gonna happen. Hadn't he already tried, indirectly anyway, to corrupt her and found out he was SOL? But *suicide* . . . that was playing some serious hardball. Fighting to find her calm, Delaney popped her lips. "Well, if you were sent here to make me want to end it all, you're doing a phenomenally shitty job, my friend. Though, if you hang around much longer, temptation might not be as mighty an effort to resist."

For the first time, Clyde laughed, but it wasn't the kind that dripped with sarcasm. It was hearty, rich, deep. It left something warm in her belly, right in the deepest depth of it, stealing another gasp of air from her she had to hide. "But that's what I've been trying to tell you. I don't belong in Hell and I'm damned sure not going to participate in helping you take . . . well, you know. When I realized no one was doing anything but laughing at me behind my back, and sometimes boldly to my face when I told them I'd been gypped, I decided to figure out a way to get out of Dodge without doing anything too heinous to anyone. Especially after I found out what those beginners' demon classes were. When I refused to participate in learning how to create mayhem, or study 'Possession—Your Guide to Rebirth,' I was sent to the file room, and for someone like me, all that paperwork really is Hell—a punishment I can't quite describe, and my level boss knew it. I was eventually labeled difficult, but not untrainable. So I lay low, learned a thing or two. Learned newbie demons are granted day-, week-, even month-long passes all the time. But, some of the things I've learned—seen—I'd like to forget. So there it is."

Her lips pursed. "Still doesn't explain why Lucifer sent you to do this particular deed. You're a noob. Unless he thought you had some innate ability. Like driving mediums crazy with a demon's constant yapping."

His sigh expelled from his chest, making it expand and push at the throw she'd given him. "You're right, I am a noob, painfully so. But Lucifer doesn't do much more than leave the assignments up to his level bosses—most times. Though your file had his handwriting all over it. But here's the clincher on this whole mess. I wasn't really assigned to you."

Now that made her pause. "So who was?"

Clyde's eyes held guilt in the way they flitted from her face and focused on something behind her. "Some guy named *Clyve* Atwell. It was easy enough to change the letters in the name on the file from a *v* to a *d*. Like I said, I wasn't totally above using these demonic powers, mediocre as they might be, to get me the frig out of there. I can't think of much that would be worse than the punishment I was due for my refusal to attend classes. I'm also not proud of what I did—but this Clyve was a total waste of skin in life. He deserved what he got when I pulled that off."

"Well, now I'm really dying here, *Clyde*. What kind of assignment did poor Clyve get that you were supposed to get?"

His next sigh represented a man truly torn—or really good at faking it. "Keep in mind, my original assignment was meant to debase me, humiliate me for not joining the freak show down there," he hedged.

"And?"

"He's Paris Hilton's newest Chihuahua . . . well, he's possessing it, anyway—for a year. I have a feeling he'll be wearing diamond-encrusted collars and having his renal glands milked on a regular basis until the punishment is up."

Laughter bubbled in her throat and spilled out in a burst of snorting giggles. "I can see how that'd be a sentence worse than death. But this also begs the question: did this Clyve with a *v* deserve what he got? The word according to you, of course."

Disgust was written all over his sleekly chiseled face. "He was a pig, one of the worst humans to roam planet Earth," he spat with a flex of his big fist. "A bastard. A vile bastard. Clyve with a *v* deserved to rot in the pit for eternity. He had a laundry list of criminal activity. A rap sheet so long I'd still be reading it if I wasn't worried I'd get caught. But the worst of it is, he was responsible for a hit-and-run that killed a kid. A *seven-year-old* kid."

Clyde shook his dark head, clearly because of the senselessness of something so tragic. "Never even looked back, the drunk ass. He knew he did it, too, and to this day, no one knows who killed Katie Martin. Except Clyve. He knew he'd snuffed a kid. He made a comment about it that I can't repeat without the threat of losing my lunch." Clyde's last words were riddled with such repulsion even she paused.

A somber moment lingered between them. Delaney reached for her grandmother's chair behind her, sitting down and gripping the arm that wasn't charred beyond recognition. If Clyde wasn't telling the truth, he was damned good at spinning some smack, because a tale like that was . . . vile, unimaginable. "Jesus Christ Superstar," she muttered. A sharp pain clutched at her heart for little Katie Martin and a family that would never have justice.

"Tim Rice and Andrew Lloyd Webber, 1970, I believe."

She raised a bewildered stare at him.

"You said Jesus Christ Superstar," he offered reasonably, the sudden directional change in conversation appearing completely normal to him. "It was an album, then a musical—"

This demon . . . "Yeah, yeah. Broadway. I got it. Okay, how about we move on? Because if I linger over what you just told me, I'll never sleep again."

Clyde cupped his jaw, then ran his hand up and over the planes of his face to scratch his dark head. "Right. Anyway, I switched the files because I knew it meant coming back to this plane or whatever you call it if I did. I need to find out what happened the day I died, Delaney. I was a chemical consultant doing freelance research, for God's sake. I was about as tame as the Dalai Lama. I wouldn't hurt someone physically or otherwise. *Ever.*"

Said the wolf in sheep's clothing. Maybe. "And how did you die again?"

Everything about his demeanor changed with one sheepish grin. "I wasn't the most coordinated man . . . I had an accident . . ."

"Clearly. But there's more . . ." she coaxed. Because there always was with Clyde.

"Uh, I blew myself up." He held up a hand to stop her from what he must have known was coming next. "I know, I know. The particulars of what I was researching are probably far more detailed than you'd care to hear and about as evil as a newborn kitten. Just know I did something unbelievably stupid, and I should have known better. I was always careful, if not about my paperwork, that's what Tia was for, anyway, then definitely about my surroundings and my chemicals. But I sure didn't intend to end up dead—so forget the suicide theory I just know is milling around in that pretty head of yours, and nothing about what I was doing for research was diabolical or important to anyone of importance, if that's where you're headed next. So I took this mission because it put me back here on Earth, first and foremost, but I also took it because there's no way I'm living out an eternity down *there*. I don't know that in life I was much of a believer in Heaven and Hell and everything they teach you in catechism because it just isn't logical to me, but in death, I believe."

Yeah. Death had a way of conforming nonconformists.

And the demon had called her pretty. Christ, was she so hard up for male attention she'd preen over it when it was served up by a demon? "And again, who says you couldn't have made this all up? I hate to keep bringing up the treacherous deceit your kind are known for, but wellllll, I have to look out for my ass, too. Ya feel me? For all I know, this biz about me and Clyve and Chihuahuas is all just so much crap." No doubt she wished the bit about little Katie was just that. Crap.

"And again, I'd have to agree. But if that wasn't enough, there's more."

"Wow. How much better does it get than when a demon says he's here to convince you Hell is the new Paris?"

Clyde snickered a deep chuckle. "You know, sometimes, you're pretty damned funny."

Delaney slapped her hands on her thighs and nodded. "Yeaaaah. I'm a fucking riot. All the demons say so. I have to have a sense of humor or I'll go batshit in my line of work. Now get on with it before I lose my patience again."

Again, Clyde looked around with caution as if someone might hear what he was going to relay.

Delaney's reaction was to reassure, stemming from years of guiding spirits, a reaction she couldn't seem to help. "It's okay. I can feel an entity for the most part—good or bad. It's just you and the entity you are, for the moment. No worries we'll be overheard."

The intake of breath Clyde sucked in was long-winded, the stiff set of his shoulders relaxing but a hair. "They talk about you in Hell—that's how I recognized your name on the file, too. I've only heard short snippets of conversations, but what I heard is something you need to know. Something I couldn't live without telling you, or not live, or whatever it is that I'm doing."

Delaney rolled a hand in front of her. "So get jiggy wit it. And before you say anything else, I know. Will Smith—"

"Nineteen ninety-eight, from his *Big Willie Style* album. I'm a fan."

Jesus. He was a veritable font of useless crap. "Fab. Now out with it."

Clyde's face said he was uncomfortable, but he never let his eyes stray from hers. "I was at the water cooler one day—"

"Because Hell is Africa hot and naturally they're obligated to provide refreshment." She let the sarcasm drip from her words with a snicker.

The joke clearly escaped Clyde. He was all business now that he had free rein. "Right. Whatever. I was at the water cooler and your name came up. The other demons said you were a real ballbuster. That they were glad Satan was finally paying the kind of attention to you that you deserved—sending in the big guns like he was. A couple of them mentioned how they'd tried to interfere in that crossing thing you do and that you'd made one too many pairs of eyes bleed. So it served you right that your head was on the block."

Amusing shit, indeed. That she'd pissed ole Lucifer off was cause for celebration in her book. It meant breaking out her best party dress and high heels—maybe some confetti. It didn't upset her even a little that those fuckwads were kvetching over her past expulsions when they'd interfered with a perfectly good crossing. Though she didn't chase demons purposely. So they didn't worry her—much.

But that joy came at a price, and clearly, she'd just been put on Satan's clearance rack. That did worry her, and it made her worry for the few people in her life she loved. "I bet they hate my guts, and I gotta tell ya, I can live with that. So big deal. Some demons hate me. I'd slap on my sad face for you, but alas, that news makes me smile and smile. See?" She grinned wide.

But Clyde wasn't smiling. "And still there's more." His tone was grim.

Again with the serious. "So get on with it already. This little interlude's been like that song that goes on and on. Um, 'In-A-Ga—'"

"'In-A-Gadda-Da-Vida.' By *Iron Butterfly*, 19—"

"Enough with the useless trivia, music man. You get my drift. Now get to the 'there's more' point."

His eyes scanned her face in earnest, probing and deep. "There was another name involved when you were mentioned. Let me preface this by saying I don't know who this person is, and I have no idea what the name means in correlation to you."

Hackles rose along her neck, but she managed to push out, "What name?"

"I remember it distinctly because it's a nice name. It means . . . shit, I forget. I just know it's Irish—Gaelic."

The air evaporated around her, stilling to a thick pea soup. The blood drained from her face. "The—name," she prodded.

"Kellen. It was Kellen."

She knew what Kellen's name meant. At least in relation to it being bandied about a water cooler in Hell.

Mud.

Which meant they were toast.

six

Clyde stood in front of her in his impromptu throw blanket, his face a handsome mask of concern. "I should have known the name was important. Who is Kellen, and is another apology in my future?"

Delaney hadn't even realized she was holding her breath, but for the hiss of air that escaped her lungs when she finally spoke. "My brother."

"Can he see dead people, too?"

Her mouth was dry—words came at a heavy, substantial price. "No. No dead people."

Clyde put a hand on her shoulder, obviously hoping to lend comfort, reassurance, but it only served to make her uncomfortable, and it had nothing to do with the fact that he had a demon's hand. It warmed the cold front that had settled over her body, and that wasn't copasetic. "So they hate your brother, too? Just because he's *your* brother, I'm assuming."

Delaney shrugged his lean fingers off, hoping the warmth that seeped through her sweater would dissipate. Yeah, they hated her brother, but it didn't have as much to do with her and her gift as it did for her and that night.

That night.

That fucking night.

When all that had once made sense suddenly and inexplicably made about as much sense as a Rubik's Cube. The night Satan had promised to obliterate the people she loved—the people she might potentially love—during a bitter rage filled with all the unimaginable elements most only watch come to life on a movie screen.

"Yeah, I guess that's it," she lied with an ease she was left feeling dirty about. But she wasn't about to tell Clyde anything more than he needed to know. First, if he was telling her the truth, her issues with Satan would only compound his. Second, this was between her and the pitchfork lover. "Because he's my brother," she finished.

Clyde's eyes sought hers, darkening to a deeper blue behind his glasses. "I wish I had more to give you about why Kellen was mentioned in regard to you and Satan. The only thing I can think of is that Lucifer wants Kellen because hurting him would hurt you."

"So there was nothing else in this file about Lucifer's reasons for wanting me to damn myself for eternity? No specifics? Nothing about what he may or may not have planned for Kellen?" She had to know. In order to know, she had to pretend she didn't know anything at all. If Clyde was lying, and he brought back her apparent ignorance to Satan, then all the better. Not in a mill would she let the devil catch wind of the fear she'd harbored all these years or the terror that kept her sometimes rooted in isolation.

"Nothing. Just his orders to get your soul at all costs."

Closing her eyes, she fought to keep her rising panic at bay. She'd come across demons in her fifteen years with this gift of talking to the dead, but they'd never brought her this kind of specific information. Obviously, the time had come. Oh, but the hell she'd cower because Satan and his band of weenies had threatened her. The. Hell. She stuck her hand out at Clyde as she rose from the chair. "Thanks for the heads-up. You're crazy swell, Clyde. Really. Now go Matlock your way out of this supposed mix-up you're messed up in with my blessings."

He hesitated when she shook her hand at him so he'd take it in his grip. "But wait . . ."

With a nonchalant shrug of her shoulders, Delaney stuck the hand she'd offered in her pocket and shuffled to the door, unlocking it and flipping the Open sign over. She turned back to face him and his once again bewildered yumminess.

It would so help if he hadn't chosen such an unassuming, yet ultrafine human form. When he stood there, looking all like someone had just stolen his lunch money, but hot as the day was long doing it, making him nothing but a blip on her radar would be so much easier. "Wait what? You did what you needed to, and I'd bet, if you really did end up in Hell as some kind of cosmic mistake, this little random act of demonic chivalry will go on the pro side of your scorecard from upstairs. So thanks and all that jazz. Now go figure out what happened to you—you're absolved."

Clyde remained rooted to the center of her store on the big braided rug she'd bought at Rasheem's Rug Palace with a stance that said he wasn't going anywhere. "It's not that simple."

It would seem nothing with Clyde was. "What's not? You pulled a naughty by switching some file names, which, if what you're saying about your former life is true, was completely warranted— total validation is on your side. I'd be pissed if I'd been jacked like you have, my friend. So now you have however much time Satan gave this clown Clyve here on Earth to figure out what happened to you in your final moments. Use them wisely, Grasshopper." She waved a hand at the door, dismissing him. But her eyes couldn't watch him leave. Despite what he'd told her, if he was telling the truth, then as a medium, technically, she should be helping him.

Yeah, that was it. She just wanted to help. It had nothing to do with his dork appeal.

Nothing.

He strode to where she stood in two long steps, gazing down at her. "I can't just leave you here alone after telling you something like that, Delaney. You're in danger."

An odd twist in her chest made her that much more determined to get rid of him. Because if he wasn't telling the truth and she let him play her, she was fucked. "Aw, look. A demon with a Superman complex. I don't need your help, Clyde, for all the good it'd do me, anyway. Let's face it. You're not exactly all about the fear factor. Marcella did secure you with salt and duct tape."

He needed to go away. If he was as innocent as he claimed, Lucifer would spit fireballs and pitchforks if he found out what Clyde had done before Clyde could take care of his earthly business. Especially if he helped her. If the devil wanted her lock, stock, and crossings like Clyde said, he'd get all hinky over one of his minions stopping that. Clyde might not be telling the truth, but one thing was abundantly clear as of this moment: he wasn't much of a threat. She was as sure of that as she was the size of her panties.

Why she should care if he was hurt in the making of this Hellavision was something she had no time to dwell on. The idea that Kellen was even mentioned in passing in all of this had her terrified, and that had to be her focus.

Clyde's long arms, not too bulky, but with just the right amount of muscle, crossed over his wide chest. His lips formed a thin line of resolve. "I'm not leaving."

Whew, when he had that oh so focused look of determination

on his face, he was downright hawt, dweeb glasses and all. "Clyde, Clyde, Clyde. Do I have to get the prism?"

"Do I have to set something else on fire?"

Sweet mother. There was no denying his beefcake status when he was being pushed. Now she crossed her arms over her chest, rocking back on her heels. "You wouldn't dare."

He cocked an eyebrow, dark and condescending, at her. "We've traveled this road."

Rolling her tongue along the inside of her cheek, Delaney narrowed her eyes at him. "Time's wastin', Clyde. How much time did your level boss give you—er, sorry, *Clyve*—to drive me to the brink of insanity again?"

"A month."

"Hoo boy. You'd better make haste. According to my calendar, you have twenty-nine days left."

"I know how much time I have left, and I plan to use it wisely—while I'm here—with *you*."

Was this like an episode of *Geeks Gone Wild*? A sort of uprising—rage against the machine—like the meek shall inherit the Earth and all? "Uh, no. You're not staying here, if that's what that chest-beating, knuckle-dragging statement was about. There's no room at the inn."

He barked another laugh, only this one didn't make her belly experience the release of a thousand butterflies.

"That's funny, how?"

"No one's ever implied I was a Neanderthal. I find I don't so much mind the reference." He grinned again, changing the whole landscape of his face from just moments ago.

Just as she was about to go get the prism, the bell on her door jingled, signaling a customer. Then two things happened almost simultaneously.

Her first, albeit brief thought was, she had a man in the middle of her store in broad daylight who was wearing a throw around him like a bath towel while a customer strolled into her store. And the man was naked underneath.

Na-ked.

The second was Clyde's lips.

Attached.

To hers.

And of all the species of men, geeks being the least known for their prowess, Delaney decided they'd been sorely underrated.

Because bow-chick-a-wow-wowwww.

Clyde's arms were confident and hard as he scooped her up, dragging her to his chest, molding her hips to his as though they'd been made for just such molding. He slanted his mouth over hers, using a forceful but light pressure to coax her lips apart. The slither of his tongue into her mouth was silken and tasted minty fresh.

Warm heat gathered, and not just in her cheeks. Her arms had hung limp in surprise at first—until he slid his tongue into her mouth, drawing it with silken skill across hers in a smooth pass. His hard abdomen, flush with hers, was maddeningly covered by the throw blanket she'd given him, but the heat he emanated caressed her even through her sweater. The space between her legs rubbed against his hard shaft, leaving her deliciously aware of his maleness.

His big maleness.

A groan from one of them sounded low and husky, thrumming in her ears. Her arms, now with a will of their own, circled Clyde's neck. Her fingers found the crisp hairs at his nape, stroking them with a hand that surely didn't belong to her.

Her breath came in one single, short pant, then left her body entirely as their mouths fully entwined, meshing with one another's so completely the kiss became almost as familiar as it was new.

Surprise, shock, heat, among other things, assaulted her subconscious. But it sure wasn't enough of a shock to make her stop him from kissing the living shit out of her. Not even the dogs, shrieking like someone was peeling their skin from their wriggling bodies, made her want to stop. Their barking became muted, blending into the street noise from outside the store.

Clyde pulled away first, a mere inch to whisper, "Shut up. Trust me. Play along."

Oh. Okay. Like she was all about tearing herself away from him, anyway. "Why?" she whispered back against lips she wasn't quite ready to part with. Ashamed she wasn't ready to part with them, but there it was.

"Because I said so."

Delaney hung from his neck, tilting her head back just enough to watch his lips move. "And that should make me quiver with fear why?"

He didn't have time to answer, instead, he buried his face in her neck, dropping kisses along the column of it and making her groan with reluctant realization.

The customer chuckled, low and knowing. A chuckle that snapped the kissing slut right out of her. Those hackles were back—loud and proud, racing along her arms, but she couldn't quite pinpoint why. "I see you two are busy. I'll come back another time," a distinguished voice rumbled.

Clyde lifted his head from the warm spot on her neck, smiling lasciviously at the man, and gave him a nod of thanks. "Verrry busy," he muttered by way of acknowledgment, then replanted his mouth on hers.

When the tinkle of her door chimed again, Clyde dropped her like she was hot, backing up and smacking into the counter with his hip. He rubbed it while he yelled over his shoulder, "Dogs! Knock it off!"

And they did.

Knock it off.

The motherfuckers had shut right up as if Clyde was the King of Canines and they were all sent here to do nothing but his bidding.

Goddamn it. *She* was their pack leader.

Which again reminded her—her dogs dug Clyde.

And that reminded her, she'd just been diggin' on him, too.

Oy. And vey.

Her legs had wobbled when she'd hit the floor and they remained like room temperature butter. So much so, she had to grab for Clyde to steady her, but she snatched her hand back, wiping it on the leg of her jeans. When she found her voice again, it was a weak effort. "What. The. Fuck?"

His cheeks had two bright red spots, but other than that, Clyde the demon remained unruffled. "Demon."

Her eyes glazed over. "Huh?"

"He was a demon. I thought you knew when an entity arrived, Ms. Gateway to All Things Ghostly."

She did. Always. Almost. She was just off her game. Clyde was screwing with her mojo was all. But it explained her dogs' yipping reaction.

"Exactly. Your silence confirms what I thought. You had no idea he was a demon."

Nope. Not even an inkling. Not with her tongue down Clyde's throat she hadn't. Bad medium. Bad. Bad. Which called for some defensive action on her part. Like deny, deny, deny. "Well, it wasn't like I had time to assess the situation with you all up on me like that for reasons known only to you at the time." Again, weak, but it was all she had in the way of justification for turning into a total ho. Lawd. She'd clung to a demon—a *demon*—like he was the last bottle of Saint-John's-wort on the island. She was rattled—discombobulated—all shook up over a kiss. A demon's kiss. The bowels of Hell were on their feet and cheering.

Clyde's brow rose with a sardonic lift. "I'm sure that was it, and there was definitely a reason for that kiss. FYI, that demon was sent here to check up on me. I was just doing my job so he wouldn't rat me out."

What did his job have to do with kissing her? Her addled, hormone-driven brain was recovering in slow increments, though her lips still tingled and her heart still had an erratic moment or two. "I thought you were sent here to make me want to end it all."

His expression said annoyed. "Here we are again."

"Where are we again?"

"Doing that damned circle dance."

"I thought we'd moved on to our finale—sort of like the last waltz?"

"Engelbert Humperdinck, 1968. And no, we're not waltzing at all. We're still circling each other."

"How so?"

"Because there's still more. But you're always chasing me away with the threat of eyeball bleed before I can get you to listen. You never let me finish what I start."

"That's because you take light-years to get to the point, for Christ's sake."

He gave her a disapproving, sour look. "You take the Almighty's name in vain a lot. Doesn't that pose a problem for someone who's shipping people upstairs? Aren't you, like, a vessel of all things righteous?"

"I figure *He'll* forgive me that small sin if I don't do something way bigger. Like murder you. Besides, there's no law that says mediums have the market cornered on Mother Teresa–ish behavior. I *am* only human, and this gift can be akin to waxing your bikini line sometimes. I'm hoping *He'll* cut me some slack because of it."

"Presumptuous much?"

"We're getting off topic. We were circling another point at the airport. Land or I'm getting the prism. How is kissing me a part of this job you mentioned?" *Because job well done. Bra-freakin'-vo.*

The line of his mouth, so easily led to a smile, thinned again with a grim slant to it. "The assignment meant for Clyve was worse than you think, Delaney."

"Uh, how much worse does it get than trying to get me to off myself?"

"Much worse. Well, worse in that the plan was to get you to do something else before you ended your life."

"I can't even imagine what's left after suicide. Murder, maybe? Serial killing?"

"Okay, you're right, that probably tops suicide. Definitely commandment breakers."

Her hand slid to the back of her neck to massage it. The day was only a few hours old, but it felt like they'd been getting to this point for an eternity. Add in that kiss and she was ass fried. "Clyde? Heads up. I think my patience has worn thin. We've been around the block and back again and while I get your dilemma, we really need to wrap this up. Put it in the can, so to speak. Lay this shit to rest so I can get on with the business of living. So if you have any compassion at all for this weary medium, tell me what else there is and why it had to include macking on me." Because the macking was some of the best she'd ever experienced and while she'd like to chalk that up to her irresistibility, she knew she'd only be conning herself. There'd been a purpose for that kiss. Clyde's face had it written all over it in black and white.

He smiled, the grin spreading from one end of his face to the other. "Me."

"You?"

"Me. I'm what else there is."

Delaney's response was dry, her defeat evident. "I don't know if anyone ever told you this while you were alive, Clyde, but you're the most infuriating man I've ever known."

He smirked, though clearly from his tone he didn't harbor any resentments. "There was Tia. She said my lack of focus on anything else but my work was sometimes infuriating, if that makes you feel less alone."

Tia. There was a Tia. That's right—he'd mentioned a Tia. Who was Tia? Why should she care who Tia was? Did he kiss Tia like he'd kissed her? Kee-rist. "Good to know. Now quit with the unsolved mysteries and tell me 'what else there is' means and how that had to involve your lips on mine. Please, before the devil gets his way and I OD on green tea or something."

"I had to kiss you."

"Because?"

"Because that's what lovers do."

Just the thought made her shiver. Lovers. Oh, Gawd. If she didn't go to Hell with the help of some demon, she was going there for even thinking about them in a very nonbiblical sense—like the limbs-all-tangled sense—like the sweat gluing their naked bodies together from the motion of the ocean sense—like . . . "How'd we get all carnal in the space of a mere twenty-four hours?"

"We didn't. Not literally speaking—just figuratively."

Around and around they went. "We figuratively were lovers, and I missed it? Damn. You know what? I hate when that happens. I haven't figuratively boinked anyone in forevah and when I do, I, like, sleep through it. I. Suck."

Clyde gave her another smart-assed grin. "I mean, I wanted that demon to think we were lovers, but we're really just lovers on a figurative level."

"I'm lost. You play the guide role this time."

"That demon was sent to check up on me. I kissed you so he'd think we're involved."

"And the reason for that is ... ?"

"Because I'm your new boyfriend."

Tight.

Look at the medium all gettin' herself a main squeeze without even trying after all these dry, dry years.

Way. To. Score.

seven

"You know what talking to you is like, Clyde?"

"No, what?"

"It's like going through one of those corn mazes at Halloween. You know, the ones you go to to humor your stupid college friends, but you really just want to get the fuck out of because it's time wasted that you could have spent having bamboo stuck under your nails—yet you keep wandering in and out of rows of corn because you're lost and you have no choice but to keep wandering aimlessly 'cause if you don't, you'll never frickin' get to the end?"

"I've never been in a corn maze, so I can't say," he said with all seriousness.

Delaney fought back the scream she wanted to shout. Instead, she stuffed her fist in her mouth while she composed herself. "That's not the point! The point is, you take forever to get to it—the point, that is—and when you do, it makes no sense to me at all. How did you go from handing me some information about me directly from

Hell to being my boyfriend?" Because for real, if that was all it took . . .

Clyde's sigh was one of a man dealing with a small child—fighting to keep his patience, but coming close to taking her Fruit Roll-Up away. "The man who just came into your store was a demon—one you didn't recognize. He was checking up on me, and I guarantee it'll happen again. The worst part of this assignment was what Clyve had to do to get you to agree to sign a contract with the devil."

There was more. Foreboding skittered along her spine. "I thought the plan was to get me to hack a vein."

Clyde grimaced. "It was *how* he was going to do it that's the most fucked-up part in all of this, and excuse my foul language, but that's just what it is—fucked up. And it's also why I kissed you."

Her stomach turned, tying her intestines into knots. Dread called her name to stop, but she'd come this far, she may as well not stop now. "How was he going to do it?"

"By making you become romantically involved with him."

Ludicrous, that's what that notion was. "And he was going to do that how? Even if I'm a little off my game today, and I missed this demon, I know a malicious entity. I can *feel* them. So how did he plan to make me hot for him when I get the skeeves just breathing the same air?"

Clyde ran a hand over his short hair with an open hand. "I'm guessing there are much bigger fish to fry than the demons you've come across so far. Clyve was assigned to you because he's capable of some huge deceit, and his experience with those who possess a sixth sense, or are mediums as you call yourself, is renowned in Hell. I'm guessing there are some demons that can get past this antenna of yours—you've just been lucky till now. Clyve was, for lack of a better word, a sociopath. A real prick without a conscience. He was made for an assignment like this, Delaney. Satan said to step up the game where you were concerned—he was doing that by sending Clyve in to win your trust, your heart. I was pretending to be Clyve when our demon spy dropped in. To do that I had to behave as though we were becoming romantically involved. He'll go back to Hell and tell the level boss I'm right on track. That's what we want."

Sweet, fancy Moses. "So Clyve was supposed to be like some kind of love decoy?"

"Love. Or the promise of it."

That stopped her cold. It was the one thing she knew she might never achieve because of her ability to talk to people no one else could see. Love. Children. Cookies and milk. Crock-Pot dinners. Soccer games and tutus. And Satan wanted to mock her for it. Fuck-tard. "Okay. Give me the details and don't stop until you've told me *everything*."

Clyde's face darkened, and that told her she wasn't going to like hearing the details. He moved the chair, motioning her to sit. "Please, sit. I'm just going to get this all off my chest at once, okay? Do me a favor and don't stop me until I have. It's enough I've been carrying this shit around with me, feeling as crappy as I have about it, but I have to just say it—and then we'll attack, okay?"

Delaney nodded, mute and slow, backing up to the chair, grateful for the support it gave her. She just wanted this over with. "Okay, I'm ready. Just say it."

Clyde stood in front of her, ridiculously handsome in the throw still wrapped around his chest. "Clyve's assignment was to come here and make you fall in love with him, Delaney. Fall in love with him, and then he'd promise you all the things couples promise each other when they fall in love—children, white picket fences, whatever it is that couples want to share when they commit. Then Clyve was supposed to either drive you to hurt yourself or make you an offer to sign a contract with him to keep him from some kind of harm. If you know anything about Satan, you don't ever want to sign a contract with him because there's always some loophole that'll leave your neck on the block. I don't know the exact details of the assignment—I only skimmed the files. What I do know is he wanted you wrecked emotionally. In Satan's mind, a relationship, children, are the one thing you've always wanted, but can't seem to find due to your gift. You said as much yourself when you talked about your last date and your dogs. It's your Achilles' heel—a weakness in an otherwise strong resistance to Lucifer. A resistance he wants to come to an end. He wanted you so broken at the idea of losing something you were so close to but yet so far from, that you'd do anything to keep it. What you might do as a result of that kind of emotional turmoil was left open-ended."

The air in her lungs evaporated. She felt naked, exposed. If she had a moment alone, she'd break things. As many things as she could possibly touch. Things that would shatter into thousands of pieces with satisfyingly obliterating crashes to her floor. Her cheeks grew scarlet, first with humiliation that Lucifer had her deepest desires so rightly nailed, then with infuriated, flaming anger that he was preying on the one thing in the world she might never find with someone as long as she had this gift and his threat hanging over her head. Love, a family, and yes, children.

And no, she didn't need an episode of *Oprah* to tell her that beyond her love for animals, and her hatred of any kind of suffering, she adopted pets with no futures because by nature, she was a nurturer—she needed to be needed. So she filled up her longing for children with pets who wore BeDazzled diapers and had missing parts. That Satan was trying to make her feel pathetic because she wanted something that was so simple made him a sorry piece of shit.

If she had something breakable on hand, she'd hurl it.

But the luxury of ravaging a pantry full of dishes wasn't something she was going to be afforded right now. Not with Clyde here to witness it. Not with the possibility that he might still be full of crap and he'd skip on off to Lucifer with maniacal glee in his black heart.

Clyde spoke her name, deep and low. His tone held pity, and that was something she just wasn't into. "Delaney?"

She turned away from him, letting her hair fall around her face. "Don't say anything, Clyde, okay? Don't apologize anymore. Don't rationalize. Just go do what you have to, and let me figure this out."

The timbre of his voice was deep, his words sober. "I'm sorry, Delaney. There really wasn't any other way to tell you."

True that. "I know. So thanks for telling me all of it. That was all of it, wasn't it?"

"That's everything I know."

Her gut tightened. Wasn't that enough? "Hookay, then. Like I said before, we're golden; and obviously I have some stuff I'm going to have to deal with. So you go deal with your stuff and I'll deal with mine. Free and clear, okay? No more prisms and salt and whatever else I have in my bag of tricks. Promise."

He shook his head. "No. While I appreciate the fact that you won't be burning my eyeballs at the stake, I'm not going anywhere. And if you'll just skip the histrionics, I'll tell you why."

She had no histrionics left in her. What she did have—or at least needed—was a plan. Lucifer had sent in what he thought was a serious player to make good on his longtime threat to punish her.

Delaney closed her eyes to stave off the gruesome memory of a rainy night long ago—and Vincent. Simply thinking his name made her skin crawl. She'd stolen something from Vincent that Satan thought was rightfully his—and he wanted it back. Yet, to this day, she still didn't understand what she'd stolen. And why did he want revenge *now*? What had taken him so long to come calling?

Clyde's arrival meant one way or the other, she and Satan were bound to mix it up—soon. "But I can't help you. You're not stuck here. My job is to cross you over. I can't cross what isn't available for crossing."

"But I do want to cross," was his bullish reply.

"Tell me something, Clyde."

"Okay."

"Do you see a light—like, anywhere? And I'm not talking like football stadium lights, maybe just a dim light far off in the distance? Or maybe a lab filled with every desirable item for a brainiac like yourself, maybe?"

"Uh, no."

"Then my job here is done. If you don't see anything that even remotely looks like something you'd consider your eternal paradise, I really can't help. And I'm sorry, but that's just how it goes."

"But you can help me. Don't forget why I'm supposedly here. To win your heart, remember?"

Her stomach sank again. "Well, that's not happening." Not even to keep Hell's minions at bay. Not even. That was a game she just couldn't play.

"Again, maybe not literally, but we can shoot for the figurative. We'll just pretend."

Which was probably about as close to a committed relationship as she was getting. "So play house?"

"That's right. Look, Delaney, I'm being watched. I've been here a whole day and my level boss has already sent in someone to check up on me. I have to, for all outward appearances, make like we're—we're—you know . . ."

"Hooking up."

Clyde's brow furrowed again. "Yeah. That. Besides, I have nowhere else to go."

"And this benefits me how, Clyde? I'm not seeing what I'll be getting out of this but another body taking up my limited space."

"I'll look out for you."

Delaney barked a skeptical laugh then covered her mouth with her hand. She didn't want to openly debase his manhood, but hellloooo—he had been secured in duct tape by a woman who hated to even chip a nail. "Look out for me? How do you suppose you're going to do that? With your one fireball? You're a one-trick pony, my friend."

"Maybe. But might I point out, it was just me who spotted the demon, wasn't it? Before you, all knowing and all seeing, I might add," he volleyed back.

"Smug much? Yes, you spotted the demon, but like I said, my radar's all wonky. I was distracted. It'll get better if you go away."

"I just can't do that. I know my motives aren't totally altruistic. I do have an investment in this, like covering my own ass, but I don't want anyone hurt while I do it. You need someone to look out for you, and maybe I'm not exactly the best demon, but that should just prove to you that I shouldn't be a demon to begin with. Now that I've told you everything, I can't just leave you all alone to fend off demons who're much bigger than I'll ever be. So how about we strike up a deal? You let me stay here, and I'll keep whoever my level boss sends in to check up on me from getting to you until we can figure out what to do."

"Why can't you just go back to wherever it is you go when you disappear?"

Clyde gave her another grim glance. "Do you have any idea what that place is like? It's just a prettier version of Hell. Lots and lots of doomed souls wandering around, crying, bemoaning their fates, and wringing their hands. Best I can figure is it's some sort of holding room—or plane, as you call it—for those who've led questionable lives. Very depressing. You don't want me to be depressed, do you?" He flashed her a grin—one that made her pulse jump. "Aren't you all about spiritual wellness? My spirit would be sucking wind in that place. And besides, for some reason, I couldn't keep myself there—I kept ending up back here." He pointed to the ground by his bare feet.

Crazy that. But she'd had enough. Clyde couldn't help her, and while she understood his dilemma, she still wasn't sure he was righteous. So no go. Sticking her hand in her pocket, she whipped out the prism, swishing it in the air. "I know I promised, but . . . you do know you made me do this, don't you?"

"Christ!" he shouted, his hands going to his eyes, rubbing them. "Would you cut me some slack?"

Delaney popped up off the chair when his human form began to shimmer. "No slack. 'Bye, Clyde." She waved the prism once more, watching his broad chest become transparent, and then he faded completely.

She stooped to pick up the throw and had a moment's remorse. Now Clyde was off on some plane that was a prettier version of Hell—naked.

Way to cheer up the tortured souls.

A few hours later, after a long stint on the Internet, searching Google for anything she could find about Clyde, she decided another shower was in order for her achy muscles. If he really was who he said he was, she wasn't going to find that out on the World Wide Web. There'd been several Clyde Atwells and none had died within the last three months. The rest of the information was limited to some pretty general stuff from phone directories across the country. Every clue he'd given her about his life, she'd put into a search engine, only to come up empty-handed.

Stripping her clothes off, she ran a weary hand over her grainy eyes and flipped the shower handles on, then reached for her favorite oatmeal and seaweed scrub while the water warmed. If she was quick, she just might get enough hot water time in to wash her hair. Eyeing the dogs all sitting in a row on her bed, plumping her decorative pillows with their scruffy paws, she gave them the look. "You guys behave, got that? I have to say, I'm just a little disappointed that Clyde seems to have no trouble getting you knuckleheads to pay attention—and he ain't the one with the kibble. So you'd all better start listening to me. I find one pillow out of order, I'll know who was humping it, and the shit will fly. I'll call Cesar pronto, and then we'll just see who's your pack leader. Understood?" She scratched heads as she hurried to get in the shower before the hot water disappeared.

Sprays of water, blessedly hot, slid over her skin in cascades as she wet her hair, grabbing the shampoo and working it into a soapy lather. Her thoughts strayed to Clyde and how she'd shipped him off to planes unknown on a rather harsh note. Why she was having bouts of regret in the way of stomach clenches was something she couldn't pinpoint.

Or maybe she could. She was a sucker for anything or anyone hard up. If Clyde was telling the truth, he was undoubtedly hard up.

And hard.

Sweet mother and all twelve apostles. She was having naughty flashbacks to a kiss that he'd claimed was nothing more than some kind of covert operation. Yes, she was. Epic naughty thoughts.

Clenching her eyes shut, she gave her hair a good scrub. This was one of the few times in her life she decided she wasn't going to behave like she'd just fallen off the turnip truck—no matter how convincing Clyde had been.

He was a bad dude.

End of.

She was officially absolving herself. Clyde'd been right about one thing—she had bigger fish to fry, and that included figuring out what Lucifer's next move was. So she'd just have to go on believing that this story Clyde'd given her was just a way to get her to let his demonicness into her life and then he would do exactly what he claimed his mission was—trash her.

There it was again.

That infernal, nagging niggle in the pit of her belly that said she'd maybe possibly misjudged him. She'd never had so much one-on-one contact for such an extended period of time with a demon like she'd had with Clyde.

That had to be it.

Delaney went back to scrubbing her hair, eyes closed, enjoying the oddly blissfully hot water. She gave her scalp a good massage, but the rustle of plastic stilled her hands.

"So this could be labeled awkward, right?"

Get. Out. "What about me naked and you in my shower while I am isn't awkward, demon?"

"Before you go screeching at me, just hear me out."

Her hands immediately went in ten different directions at once to try to cover her girlie bits while shampoo dripped into her eyes, blinding her. "You know, I have something to say here, and I'll try not to screech, but I make no promises. You evoke screeching."

"By all means, say something."

Her words came out in a watery, garbled drip of shampoo when she spat, "What, in the ever-loving fuck, are you doing in my shower? I'm naked, for Christ's sake!"

"Yeah," he said on a gusty sigh. "Me, too."

"Still?"

"Yep."

"But you've been naked since I met you. Me? Not so much. For you it's a standard in our budding relationship. I personally like to get to at least share a granola bar before I consent to take my clothes off."

"Well, my eyes are closed, if that's any consolation," he offered with a dry sarcasm she could almost taste on her lips.

For some whacked reason, it left her deflated that he hadn't at least peeked. Gee, twisted much, Delaney? That ridiculous notion only made her angrier. "I don't believe you."

"Swear it."

"What is it about me that you can't seem to resist? I've all but made your eyeballs bleed. Yet here you are. This could be considered stalkerish behavior, Clyde Atwell," she drawled.

"I'm no stalker, Delaney Markham."

"Then explain, demon," she growled, finally gathering enough of her wits to begin rinsing her hair, but too afraid to open her eyes. She'd seen him in almost all of his glory. In fact, she'd just been strolling down the memory lane of nudity when he'd popped in. It'd been hard enough to resist the throw-blanketed Clyde. Wet and wild was definitely out.

"I swear to Christ, Delaney, I have no idea how I ended up here. I was off on that dismal, dreary plane you prismed me back to, and I admit, I was thinking about our predicament, and then wham, here I am." His voice rumbled with gravelly irritation, leaving a vibration in her chest that made it tickle.

She squinted one eye open while water battered her face, keeping her chin up so she could only see from the tops of his shoulders up. She was in treacherous waters if she didn't. What she found was a rather shamefaced demon, huddled in a corner, dwarfing her small shower space.

Wow. The demon was a gentleman. He really did have his eyes closed.

"Didn't I tell you pink wasn't a good color for you?" she chided, letting her hands slide to her breasts. Whether he was ogling them or not, modesty must prevail.

Clyde's hand went to his head, pushing her shower cap up on his forehead. "Noted, and I have no clue how I ended up in this—it was just here on my head—I was just here. It's like I said before, I keep ending up back *here*. With you. I'm convinced that has to mean something."

"It means you're ruining my shower. Wasn't it enough that you screwed up *Ghost Whisperer*? I don't get to indulge in a hot shower often because I hardly ever have hot water, and now you're sucking it all up. So, please, I'm begging you, get out, and keep your eyes closed while you do it." The last thing she needed was a critique from Body by Bowflex. Demon was definitely the new sexy.

"I can't do that without opening my eyes, but I'd be happy to open my eyes—with your permission, of course." His affable smile turned into another cocky smirk.

Her sigh filled the small shower with her exasperation. There was only one way out and that was by squeezing past her. The other half of her cheap shower doors didn't open enough for someone as large as Clyde to get past. "Give me your hand. I'll guide you out. You're going to have to step around me, so watch those klunky feet."

Clyde placed his hand in hers while she maneuvered him around her, biting the inside of her lip and sucking in her stomach to keep their bodies from touching—all while she kept her eyes affixed to his face. His grip was tight around her fingers, their wet flesh connecting and leaving a raw trail of jumpy nerves that sizzled along her arm.

When she tugged him around her body, their chests touched, the patches of hair he still had scraping deliciously across her nipples. Her gulp was thick, her head light. Delaney blew out a shaky breath before she spoke. "I'm going to open the shower door, so step up when I tell you to."

"Okay," he grunted, sticking his other hand out as a guide.

"Step up now." Sliding the creaky door open, she fought the impulse to look down at his ass, knowing full well it'd be as hard and sculpted as the rest of him.

Though, seriously, what would a peek—just a quickety-quick glance—hurt? It was, after all, just a butt. Everyone had one. And while she noted that she definitely didn't want to see everyone's and she was overly curious about his, seeing Clyde's wasn't against the law. Her eyes, with a will of their own, cast downward.

Jumpin' Jehoshaphat.

Everyone didn't have one like *that*.

Holy ba-donk-a-donk. Woo to the hoo, baby.

Her face grew hot, her cheeks flaming though the water had grown cool. She darted her guilty, prying eyes back to his broad back just as Clyde stepped up and out of the tub, forgetting to let go of her hand and pulling her out behind him.

The wet slap of flesh as she lost her balance and fell into him, knocking him forward to the floor, was sharp, Clyde's grunt when he hit the floor with her on his back, sharper still.

And then they were pressed together in a mass of crooked, bent limbs on her tiny bathroom floor.

Naked.

All this nekidity might have been redundant but for the fact that lying front side down on Clyde's big back was, for the tiniest of moments, hawt, hawt, hawt.

His skin was supple, firm, slick with droplets of water. Delaney's cheek fell to his shoulder, her nostrils flaring with the heady scent of man. She didn't care that his neck was at an awkward angle, jammed up against the vanity, and she cared even less that his foot had been left hooked on the edge of the tub. It wasn't every day she was able to indulge in the raw sexuality of a man. For as totally wrong as that thought probably was, she just wanted a moment . . . to linger . . . on top of Clyde . . .

"Delaney?"

"Hmmm?" Yes, she could fully acknowledge that was her voice doing a breathy Marilyn Monroe imitation.

"Please don't take this as an insult, but I can't breathe, and I think I might have broken my toe. So do you think you could get up? Please?"

Like now? When she was just getting the taste of her first real, live man in years? How selfish. But, an inner voice, scathing and derisive, reminded her, *He's not a live man, horn dog. Demon, remember?*

She popped off of Clyde's back, once more silently thanking Pilates for her core strength—for any strength that allowed her to unglue herself from him and his tasty bod.

Her hands fumbled for a towel, yanking it off the rack with hasty fingers and wrapping it around her. She turned her back to him, handing the other towel to him over her shoulder. "Put this on." *And make it snappy,* she thought, or all this pent-up sexual energy was going to become a long-ignored, libidinous shitstorm worthy of the apocalypse.

Clyde's groan signaled he'd untangled himself from her shower. The dogs began to whimper their love for Clyde's return with whining joy. He cleared his throat. "I'll wait in the bedroom."

With the sound of the bathroom door closing, she covered her face with both hands. She'd just plastered herself to a demon—and had liked it. There was nothing about this that was good. Nothing.

Squaring her shoulders, she wiped the condensation off her bathroom mirror so she could untangle the mess her hair would surely be in without having been conditioned. She frowned at the reflection peering over her shoulder, perfectly cool, perfectly blonde. "Ah, Miss I Vant to Be Let Alone, now isn't a good time. I'm taking a page from your book. I'm a sopping-wet, half-cleaned mess, and I'm sure you wouldn't have been caught dead looking like this—even at your worst." When a girl really wanted to experience low self-esteem, all she had to do was get a little visit from Ms. Garbo to set her straight. Whenever she appeared to Delaney, she was permanently the bodacious babe of her 1920s fame.

Her ruby red lips moved before the whisper of her voice flitted to Delaney's ears, the striking clarity of her cheekbones adding to the stunning entity, paling Delaney in comparison. "*Flesh and the Devil*," was her less than remarkable, but suggestive advice.

Delaney wrinkled her nose at Greta. It'd taken some time to understand exactly what her otherworldly celebrity clientele were trying to tell her, but once she'd figured out they all spoke in reference to their famed movies, it had made conversations much easier to participate in. What Greta was suggesting was—was—gasp-worthy. There'd be no getting a freak on with Clyde just for the pure pleasure of freaking. "You bet your silent movie bippy he's the flesh of the devil. And I know exactly what you're thinking when you suggest such a thing, you risqué broad. No. Absolutely not. I work for the other side. There'll be no hanky-panky with his flesh—especially because it's from the devil's."

Her thin, pencil-rounded eyebrow arched in mockery. "*The Kiss*."

Okay. So there was that. It had been a stellar kiss even though the reasons for it were hardly based on anything more than necessity. "Guilty. It was fantabulous—he's a consummate kisser, okay? Now quit making me feel worse than I already do, and while you're at it, take your perfect size zero butt outta here. I can't concentrate when you're all looming over my shoulder being so coolly blonde and breathtakingly gorgeous."

Greta smiled with warmth and sympathy, winking an eyeliner-rimmed eye at Delaney before she faded.

A grip she hadn't even realized she had on her sink tightened, then released, leaving the muscles in her hands jittery. She dried her hair, dragging a brush through it, fuming the entire way right up until she yanked her nightgown down from the hook on the back of the door.

Her behavior had been appalling, she acknowledged, reaching for the bathroom doorknob. But that was all going to change right now.

Clyde was on her bed, a pile of puppies surrounding him, wearing her pink bathrobe.

"If this keeps up, you're going to owe me a trip to the bathrobe store," she remarked before picking her discarded sweater off the floor and pulling it over her head.

"If this keeps up, I'm hoping we'll find something that's more suitable to my coloring," he joked.

Laughter burst from her lips while weariness implored her to just give in. "Look, Clyde. I'm ass fried from our shenanigans. I don't know that I believe your story, but if I'm honest, I will admit to having reservations about disbelieving you, too. I don't know why, I just do. Don't screw that up. We're precarious here, you and I. We're teetering on the brink."

His whole face relaxed, the small lines around his mouth easing. "Jesus. That took long enough. If you'll just look at this with some logic—"

Delaney scowled. "There is no logic to this. If I've learned nothing else since this ghost chat gig happened, I've learned there is no rhyme or reason to the spiritual world. If what you say is true and you can't keep yourself from ending up back here, I'd have to wonder if Lucifer didn't put some kind of binding magic to this assignment, so that you'd have no choice but to stay glued to my side. Or, if you're telling the truth, so that Clyve would stay glued to my side like a thorn in my ass. But I'm too tired to care right now, and

I'm too tired to explain binding. So you can sleep on the couch for tonight, and tomorrow I'll try to figure this out. But by no means is this, in any way, shape, or form, me conceding total belief in you or your cockamamie story. I reserve the right to take it back and nail you, balls to the wall, with my prism if I have even the remotest hint you're full of shit. Got that? You win the first round for wearing me to a frazzle—so take my bathrobe and just let me get some sleep. No arguments, no discussions. Deal?"

He clamped his delish lips closed for a moment, but no sooner had he done that than he opened them back up again. "Will I fit on the couch? It's pretty small."

"Will you find a couch, small or not, on that plane you keep ending up on?"

"Point."

"But remember, I'm keeping my prism under my pillow and a box of salt under the covers. Don't frig with the medium. Now, good night, Clyde."

He rose from the bed, moving with caution around the side of it to avoid stubbing another toe. His face held a thousand unanswered questions, but for the first time since she'd met him, he appeared to find his shutoff valve. "Good night, Delaney." Clyde turned on his heel, the width of his pink back disappearing out of her bedroom door when he pulled it closed behind him.

Dogs one through six sniffed the air, noting Clyde's departure, and then the pitiful whine began. A whirring sort of hum peppered with the occasional yip.

They defected off the end of the bed, jumping like lemmings at the edge of a cliff, and headed straight for the door Clyde had just exited.

Dog number three, not known for her social skills, scratched beneath the gap of the door. Dog number six, using the one good front paw he had, joined her. "Heeeyyyy!" she whispered on a hush, kneeling down alongside her faithless pack, all lumped on top of one another in a ball of fur and whimpers. "You're shitting me, you bunch of traitors. Is he the one who feeds you? Is he the one who cleans your puke up after you've snarfed down one of those damned rawhide bones like you're rabid? Most importantly, did he save your asses from the guillotine? You'd all be kaput if not for me. I can't even believe this is happening. What if he *is* a demon? Then where will ya be? Do you suppose old Clyde there is going to change your diaper?" she asked her BeDazzled canine. Her gaze turned to dog number three. "And if you think you have phobias now, miss, hah! Just you wait until Lucifer makes you his lapdog."

A low growl, menacing and distinct, sounded behind her. Her head whipped around in surprise as her dearly departed Rottweiler appeared from thin air. "Darwin. Finally, the voice of reason," she said with a welcoming smile. "How are ya, pal?"

But he growled up at her again, his large jaw quivering. In life, Darwin hadn't been very intimidating. In fact, the guard dog she'd hoped would defend her with a snarling, drooling intimidation factor to the *n*th degree was more likely to slather your face with his unbridled affection.

Confused, and knowing she couldn't touch him, instinct still made her hold out her hand to him anyway, but Darwin snapped his deadly jaws with a sharp chomp and eyeballed the bedroom door. He blatantly ignored her hand, pushing his transparent, sleek, black bulk to the forefront of the pack, joining the rest of the clan as if he was still of this plane.

Her gasp of surprise was hard to conceal. "Noooo, not you, too!" she groaned. "Are you out of your gourd, Darwin? What kind of loyal companion are you? Even dead you're still a candy-ass, huh? I'm not a little ashamed to tell you all, this—is—bullshit!"

The dogs' scratching grew to a fevered pace, paws digging madly, their cries of desperation rising to a desperate pitch.

So there was nothing left to do with the little bastards.

With a cluck of her tongue so they'd hear her disgust, though clearly they cared little, she popped open the door.

In a massive collection of fur and riotous barking, they fled like they'd just been released from a puppy mill. She heard the customary "Oomph" from Clyde as she supposed they'd hurled themselves up and onto his stomach with the excitement once reserved for only her.

"You all suck!" she yelled out the door, slamming it with a satisfying thunk.

Clyde's laughter trickled to her ears, amused and just a little neener, neener, neener thrown in to prove his "I'm not supposed to be in Hell" point.

Fine.

He'd find out what Hell was all about tomorrow in the morning when he had to keep all six dogs from eating each other's poop.

eight

"Delllllaaaney?" someone singsonged her name while trailing a finger over the shell of her ear.

She waved a hand in the air to ward off whomever was ruining the bliss she'd finally found once she'd gotten over the epic betrayal her dogs had doled out last night. "Go away."

"But I made tea. I'm not sure if all the stuff floating around in it is supposed to be floating because I don't remember floaties when you make it, but it smells like the stuff you make. And it's the effort that counts, right?"

Marcella. It was Marcella and she'd made tea.

Wait, she needed to run that past her demon-fried brain again. Marcella had made tea. Like, touched the stove. Omigod, that meant the world was coming to an end or her kitchen was torched. "It's the *thought* that counts and you made tea? For me?" To hide her surprise would be a feat likened to the second coming.

"Who else would I make this stuff for?"

"You touched the stove? Oh, shit. I'm afraid to open my eyes. So which is it? Is my kitchen blackened Cajun style or did the world as we know it end last night?"

She clucked her tongue. "You're such a pessimist. No, the world didn't end, and yes, I touched the stove. Why can't a BFF make tea for her BFF?"

Delaney pried her eyes open to find Marcella sitting beside her on the bed, her long legs crossed as she examined her fingernails, her glossy black hair sleeked back behind her ears. "Why would you?"

"Because I figured you needed it."

Yeah. Yesterday had been a butt licker. She could definitely use some tea to soothe her weary soul. But Marcella had no idea yesterday had sucked big, fat hooters after she'd gone home. None. Marcella had no idea that Clyde had worn her to a frazzle until she'd finally given in and agreed to try to help him. She had no idea that Satan wanted to ruin her, and she wouldn't if Delaney could keep her out of it. And as a final act of utter humiliation, Marcella had no idea her dogs had gone to the demon side, either. "Marcella?" She spoke her name with the greatest of hesitance.

"*Sí, mi amiga?*"

"*Why* do I need tea?"

"Well, after last night, I figure refreshment is in order. To replenish and all."

"Replenish what?"

"Your strength."

"For?"

She sighed, so obviously impatient from the roll of her eyes to the flick of her fingers on Delaney's arm. "For another round, I suppose, and I say good for you. It's about time you took charge of your life and your needs as a woman. Congratulations are in order. In fact, I think we should shop or something—maybe have a facial so you can maintain that healthy glow you have now."

Delaney grabbed her friend's wrist. "What in all of hell are you talking about?"

Marcella curled her hand around Delaney's and entwined their fingers, giving her a catlike smile. "Dunking the demon, sweetie."

Delaney rolled her head on the pillow. "Dunking the demon . . ."

"Slamming the succubus, hooking up with the hellhound, boffing the—"

Delaney put a hand to Marcella's mouth. Everything was instantly clear. Not only because of what Marcella was implying, but because her words dredged up those forbidden, naughty thoughts she'd had last night about the demon. But she figured protesting was a necessity because Marcella'd probably seen Clyde on the couch. "He's not a succubus, and if he were any bus at all, he'd be an incubus. You know, a man-demon. And I did not either dunk, slam, or boff. Not a single, solitary thrust of my anything. The demon slept on the couch."

Marcella's lips pursed in obvious doubt, taking Delaney's hand back in hers. "Then I have a question."

"Go."

"Why is he in your bed in your pink Friday night, eyeball-bleeding fashion faux pas?"

Delaney bolted to an upright position, pushing away the hair stuck in her mouth, her eyes widening when she found not only Clyde beside her, but her dogs, all crammed up against him, snoring peacefully. Her mouth fell open, yet no words came out. His chest rose and fell in slumber, revealing a bit of patchy hair through the fabric of her bathrobe while one hand curled possessively around dog number one's overly rounded belly.

Marcella smiled her sly, sensual brand of grin. "Oh, D. You don't have to be coy with me. I say hoorah to getting a freak on. The only thing I'm a teensy bit worried about is what your boss upstairs might have to say about this little meeting of the bump and grind. Oh, and I have another question—whenever you're ready to stop pretending you're all horrified and when you close your mouth, that is. I can smell your morning breath from here." She wrinkled her pert nose in distaste.

Delaney let her eyes stray back to Clyde. In her bed. Like he'd always been there.

In her bathrobe.

With her fucking dogs.

Blasphemers.

Marcella waited, and when she garnered no answer from Delaney, she plowed onward. "Seeing as you're all stupefied, gnaw on this. You said we couldn't keep the demon. You were adamant. I was okay with that. Actually, after thought, while I was having a pedi and a vanilla latte, I supported it one million percent. But what I wonder is this. Why is it that you get to keep him and I can't? You called me a tart for even suggesting it. And doesn't this mean you've broken a commandment? Isn't there one about sleeping with the enemy?"

Clyde's eyes had popped open, and so had his ever informative mouth. "I think that's your neighbor's wife."

Marcella crossed her arms over her tight red T-shirt, shooting Clyde an icy look. "Right. Neighbor's wife, Satan's spawn—technicalities. Whatever. I just want to clear this up so I know what we're in for. So again, Delaney, while I'm all for you finding your inner hootch and letting her run rampant, madre santa—could you have picked a worse candidate? Isn't he the bad guy? Or has something happened to change our minds about the dorky demon? Because while I applaud your freak being satisfied, I worry for your soul. So please—puh-lleease—tell me what gives here. Did you do some crazy herb last night and tie one on? Are there pharmaceuticals involved I'm unaware of? Wait . . . did he force you to do this? Now if that's the case, then Clyde"—she shot him a glacial stare—"I have to tell you—it ees on. See thees shoe?" Marcella pulled off her black shoe with the red, pointy heel and waved it at him. "I'll shove thees so far up jour ass, jou'll blow stiletto chunks for a week! *Comprende?*"

Hoo boy. When Marcella's accent slipped—it meant she was cranked.

Delaney propped a hand between the pair, the only thing she seemed capable of doing at this point. She looked from Marcella to Clyde, mute. It wasn't that she didn't want to offer an explanation, and she knew it better be a good one, she just couldn't remember any words.

Clyde pulled himself to an upright position, disturbing the dogs who'd nestled closer to his side. His eyes took them both in, as serious as any impending heart attack. "I think this demon thing is way out of control. Last night, Delaney agreed I could stay here to figure out what's going on. I was on that little couch last night when I went to bed. I swear to you, I have no idea how I ended up in your bed."

Marcella licked her full lips, her eyes hard pinpoints of glittering green light. Her laugh, deep and throaty, was totally tinged with her skepticism. "I know exactly how you ended up here, Clyde." She swept her hand along the bed like she was a *Price Is Right* girl showing off a brand-new refrigerator. "We're demons, we sometimes have *needs*," she drawled, throwing him a team spirit look. "But if you used some kind of demon magic to coerce my friend into—into whatever happened here—"

"No," Delaney finally managed.

Marcella puffed her cheeks out, her patience evaporating in a flash. "Yes, darling. Oh, I think, *yes*. And I'll say it again—booyah for you. And now that we've dispensed with the 'you go, girl' pats on the back, what—the—hell—were—you—thinking?" she screeched.

Clyde leaned in to her ear, making her heart race stupidly when his lips momentarily brushed her flesh. "Are all your friends this dramatic? You're all so loud and always threatening anything that moves. It's a little jarring this early in the morning."

Marcella's breathing hissed from her nostrils in angry puffs.

Delaney leaned back in to Clyde, working to ignore the warm wall his chest made, and finally found her voice. For his sake, and the sake of a pending fireball war her bedspread would never survive, it was a good thing she was able to pony up. "Clyde?"

"Yes?"

"If I were you, I'd put a sock in it, and let me do the talking."

Thankfully, he heeded her warning. "Shutting up," he replied, plumping a pillow behind him and latching his fingers together behind his head.

Turning back to Marcella, Delaney put a hand on her shoulder, giving her a firm shove away from Clyde. "Sit back down, Buffy—"

Clyde stuck his face between the two women. "Not Buffy. Technically, she was a vampire slayer. I'm not sure if she was ever involved with demons. In fact, I don't know if there's been a commercial demon slayer—"

"Did I tell you to put a sock in it?" Delaney asked.

"You did."

"Then heed my warning, especially where the feisty, scarier-than-she-looks demon is concerned. Think buttloads of duct tape."

Clyde leaned back once more against the pillows, letting his mouth turn into a thin line of silence.

"Now, Marcella, listen to me. No, we absolutely did not—not—"

"Have intercourse," Clyde finished for her, looking too pleased that he'd helped her out.

Intercourse? How interesting. How institutional. How rather trip-to-the-gynecologist's-like. Who said *intercourse* anymore? She gave Clyde another warning glance to clamp it. "What he said. Nothing happened. Nothing. Swear it on my poor, dead granny Glenda. As to why he's in my bed, you got me. Now relax, Marcella. Everything's fine."

Now Marcella's mouth fell open. "That's all you have to say?"

Delaney nodded, pushing back the covers and grabbing her discarded sweater from last night. Less was always way more around Clyde. "For now, yep," she said over her shoulder as she went to gather leashes to take the dogs out.

Both Clyde and Marcella were right behind her. "How about I do that?" Clyde offered. "You and your friend can talk." He took the leashes from her hand, stooping to hook them on various collars while Marcella simmered.

The moment he went out the back door, Marcella hooked her thumbs in the loops of her hip-hugging black jeans and moved in on her. Delaney acknowledged the fear in her friend's eyes, mingled with her outrage. "What have you done, Delaney? Do you have any idea what you've done? Jesus! You slept with a demon! If I sleep with a demon, it's all good because I *am* a demon. Horns, scales, ugly shit. You? Not—a—demon! Remember? You know, that whole crossing over into the infernal light I haven't even had a glimpse of? Remember that place? The one with wings and halos and puppy dogs' tails or something. Have you lost your faculties? You're a good guy, and good guys don't do demons! What in the bloody fuck is going on?"

Delaney winced. Marcella was roaring—seething. That meant explanations better happen or she'd levitate. She'd lose her focus about halfway and crash to the ground, maybe break a high heel or something. With Marcella, that meant war.

If she told Marcella anything about why Clyde was here, it meant Marcella would have information she could eventually be hurt for. Possibly tortured for, and that left Delaney's gut twisting and churning in absolute fear. What Clyde had told her last night left her afraid for everyone closely involved with her. So what to do, what do to? Stall. Think. Fast. "No, Marcella. I didn't sleep with a demon."

Marcella scoffed at her. "Okay, so you didn't *sleep*. I imagine if I were in the same bed with Clyde, I wouldn't be asleep either."

She had to be very careful here. "You know exactly what I mean, Marcella. There was absolutely no hanky-panky. None. I'll say it again. I don't know how he ended up in my bed. I swear it on my secret stash of valerian root."

Marcella's stance eased a little. "Then what's going on?"

Delaney blew out a breath, her stomach a tight ball of tension with what she was about to do. "Okay, I just need you to trust me here. We've been friends a long time, right?"

Her eyes narrowed in rightful suspicion. "Don't play the friend card with me, Delaney Markham. Yes, we've been friends for a long time and in that time you've never done anything this dangerous or this stupid. Something's up—I wanna know what."

Her friend knew her well. "Answer the question. Have we or haven't we?"

Marcella's agitation grew in her terse reply. "We have."

"Then I want you to remember that when I ask you to leave and not come back until I tell you to."

She hardened, not just in her posture but in the tight fists that clenched at her sides. "The. Hell."

Delaney kept her face unreadable, or at least she hoped that was the case. "Don't give me that infamously stubborn, mouthy bullshit you pull like I'm Kellen. *Go home.* Trust that I can look out for myself, and I know what I'm doing, and that I wouldn't ask you to leave unless I absolutely *had* to."

"Nope."

Damn her. "Do you remember when I once told you to keep

our friendship on the down low? Like don't go broadcasting our long lunches and flea market sprees? Remember, I made you swear to try and keep your mouth shut about it?"

"Yeah, and I didn't make you tell me why. I thought maybe it was because it'd look bad for you in the spirit world if the ghosts knew you were BFFs with a demon. Now I'm convinced that's not what it was."

And now for the big guns. The guns she never thought she'd use on someone who'd been one of the best friends she'd ever had. Dead or not. There wasn't much they hadn't shared in ten years, and within a matter of moments she'd create a gulf of distance between them that she might never be able to bridge once all was said and done. But if that long-ago threat from Satan still stood, if he'd taken the time and effort to send someone in to whip her like so much cream, it meant he was looking into her life. When he looked, he'd find Marcella. "Marcella. This is me not kidding with you. Go home or I *will* use the salt. I don't want to, but I will." May the forces that be forgive her for even thinking it.

Marcella's mouth fell back open, her beautiful face openly showing her hurt. "You wouldn't . . . You've never . . . Not even when we first met . . ." Her words stumbled, then failed her.

Delaney steeled herself for Marcella's verbal outburst—the one she'd have once she caught her breath. Braced herself for the look of angry, hurt outrage Marcella was so gifted at. "I would." Amazingly, the stutter in her voice she expected to hear didn't make an appearance.

Yet her longtime friend surprised her, making her final statement a twisting knife in an open wound to Delaney's gut. "I'm going to say one last thing to you, and then I'll go, and I promise to never darken your doorstep with my stubborn, mouthy bad-ass self again. You're the only friend I've had in almost seventy-five years as a demon. That's a long time to be friendless, and I know it's nothing less than I deserve for doing what I did when I bit the dust. I've always known that someday you'd go on to a much better place, and I'd still be here doomed for all eternity. But I made my peace with that because it's the price I'll always pay for shunning Satan, and it's my own goddamned fault. I would have savored our friendship long after you kicked the bucket—I guess I'll just be doing it much sooner than I'd planned."

Marcella turned her slender back on Delaney, disappearing into her stunned silence with a gentle fade to black.

She was left in her small kitchen with the wind sucked right out of her, and even knowing she'd done the right thing, the one thing that just might keep Marcella out of trouble, it didn't make it hurt less. In fact, it hurt far more because Marcella'd left without a screaming match. She'd left defeated, and that was far worse than the spar of some heated words. It smacked of finality and that was something Delaney couldn't bear.

All because of the demon.

The stupid, fucking, pain in the ass, nagging fishwifey, interfering, clingy demon.

"She's gone?" Her back door slammed with a gust of October wind and a rush of sniffling, excited puppies.

She looked up at Clyde, his big hand encompassing six leashes, each dog dutifully sitting at attention. His short hair was windblown; his sharp cheeks had a healthy tint of color from the brisk autumn breeze. The dogs' obedience only served to fuel the fire that lit her chapped ass. "Yeah. She's gone, and you know what?"

"I'm not sure I want to know what, but what?"

"I've decided something."

His eyes grew wary with caution. "Does this decision mean I should prepare myself for the dark and dreary promise of the planes again?"

"No. I've decided that today, you're officially a stupidhead, and you've moved to the top of my stupidest stupidhead list. So go somewhere I'm not for the moment and just give me two whole minutes to myself." She stomped off to her room to dress and simmer, leaving a surprised Clyde standing in her kitchen in her pink bathrobe.

Tears stung her eyes when she threw the bedroom door shut. Logically, it wasn't really Clyde's fault she'd had to send Marcella away, but the clench of her heart overruled common sense. If he'd just kept his supposed good intentions to himself . . .

You'd what, ghost lady? Be blindsided without ever knowing what hit you? That's pretty bright. By all means, crack on the demon for giving you a heads-up. That makes all kinds of sense. If what he says is true, you'd be chicken fried without his input. Don't shoot the messenger and all.

Okay, so she'd be stewed.

Knowing her enemy was definitely half the battle. Knowing there was an intended battle, better still. And that left Clyde all magnanimous and worthy of things she didn't want to attribute to a guy she'd for sure thought was evil—lame evil, but evil all the same.

Now something had to be done to figure this out and there wasn't time to diddle. The sooner she figured out what to do about Lucifer and his wish to see her in his palace of pain, the better off she'd be, and the quicker she'd be able to make amends with Marcella—who'd probably demand some begging and pleading and a shopping trip to Ferragamo.

If she hoped to make up what looked like a betrayal to Marcella, that meant dealing with Clyde.

Who needed to know where he stood with her.

She yanked an ankle-length, periwinkle blue skirt out of her dresser drawer and dug around for her favorite gold poet shirt with the long, flowing sleeves. When she caught a glimpse of herself in the mirror above her dresser, she gave herself a critical once-over. She was pale, and her lips had no color to them. Shoving on some of her gold bangle bracelets, she blew into the bathroom to find some blush and the peach lip gloss Marcella had bought her on one of her shopping sprees. It was all natural, with no harsh chemicals and no animal testing, she'd said proudly. Running her finger along the tube, Delaney smiled with the memory.

Her stomach clenched. Who would buy her stupid stuff she hardly ever used if not Marcella? Her fingers trembled as she applied the gloss to her lips, then swiped the blush across her cheekbones, adding mascara as a tribute to her friend.

Better. That was much better. Marcella was right about one thing, sprucing up made her feel more in control, if only on the outside. Dragging a brush through her hair, she grimaced. She had more than her fair share of curly locks, hanging to almost the middle of her back and a shade of auburn Marcella said you couldn't get out of a bottle. It was unruly and almost impossible to tame with just a brush. She pulled it into a loose knot on top of her head, wrinkling her nose at the stray strands that refused to stay put.

"Delaney?" Clyde's sharp knock at her bedroom door came with the realization that she had to deal with this, and deal with it now. Kamikaze style.

She strode to the door, peeking around the corner, but she said nothing.

"Is everything all right?"

Yeah. It was shiny. "No. But I have high hopes for the future."

His blue eyes were rimmed with an emotion she might have labeled concern. Whether real or phony, it made her pause. "Can I ask what happened with you and Marcella and how I got labeled a stupidhead in the process?"

She pushed her way out the door and turned to face him, forcing herself to remember that Clyde was potentially a lost soul. Her job was to help lost souls—not call them names. Yet the dogs clung to his bare calves like he'd been dunked in brown gravy, and she found she still had to fight resentment for the intrusion he'd made in her closely guarded world. Which wasn't fair to him. "I was pissed. I'm sorry I called you something so childish. It was rude. So now I'm apologizing—bet that's a nice change of pace."

"What happened with Marcella?"

She rolled her lower lip to keep it from trembling. "What do you think happened after she found you in my bed?"

He threw up both hands, palms forward. "I'll say it again, Delaney. I swear I have no idea how I ended up there. I was on the couch last night, with a pile of dogs and I think your ghost dog, Darwin. When I woke up, it was in your bed. I don't remember getting up. I don't even remember falling asleep."

Delaney rolled her head, deciding they had bigger issues to tackle. "I say we just forget that. Nothing's made much sense since you showed up. Regardless, Marcella seems to think I've been swayed to the dark side by your charms, and that freaked her out."

Clyde smiled.

Which made her bristle. "That's funny how?"

"If you knew me in life, you'd find the idea of me swaying anything—no less a woman—is about as likely as two right angles in a triangle."

"I sucked in math."

"I didn't."

"Go fig. Anyway, Marcella thinks we—"

"Dunked, slammed, hooked up, wonked."

"All of the above, yes, and I didn't confirm or deny."

"Because?"

"Because I can't let her get involved in this. If she knew Satan was out for my blood, she'd do something impetuous and stupid—

like hunt his ass and offer to throw down. She's got a temper to rival an erupting volcano, and when she's angry, there's no thinking about anything but taking care of shit and paying for it later."

Clyde's eyebrows rose. "I'd have never guessed."

"So I sent her away and told her not to come back until I said so. I had to. She's not on Lucifer's most popular list, if you know what I mean. I can't take the chance she'd be involved in this hard-on he has for me."

"So you argued because of my presence here."

"Basically, and it's not your fault, and I'm trying to get a grip on that as we speak. If what you say is true, you did me a favor by telling me about this Clyve. But she left without a fight, and that's not like Marcella. Not even a little. Which means I cut her deep. We've been friends a long time. In fact, she's probably one of my closest friends, because she gets my gift, ya know?"

His silence ticked by, the wheels in his head visibly turning. "I have a question."

Her remark was dry. "What a revelation."

"What is Satan's hard-on for you about? Is it because you talk people out of choosing Hell as their final destination? Because you cross people over and that pisses him off?"

Shit. Here came another big, fat lie. She'd been a real commandment breaker as of late. Hopefully, in the end, the theory of greater good would outweigh the falsehoods she'd been slinging like breakfast hash. "I don't know," she lied, her answer evasive. If she kept it simple, fed him as little information as possible, she just might be able to keep him from finding out too much on the off chance he was a lying sack of shit.

His eyes met hers from behind his square-framed glasses. There was definite doubt in them. Doubt and possibly suspicion. He cracked his knuckles before he spoke. "I've never been a great judge of character, Delaney, and maybe that's because I haven't spent a lot of time with many people because of my work, but I think you're full of shit."

She averted her eyes in case mind reading was on his list of rapidly growing demonic powers. "You can think whatever you like. Whatever Lucifer wants is between him and me, and clearly, he's not sharing his motivations. So here's the deal. Seeing as you can't seem to resist my unbelievable charisma, you can stay here for however long you have to figure out whatever you need to figure out. Go on about your business, keep up the pretense you're doing what you were sent here to do. If I can help, I'll give it my best medium's shot. So ride 'em, cowboy."

Clyde shook his head, the dark chestnut of it catching the light of her overhead fixture in gleaming chunks. "Well done. I still don't believe you. There's something going on here that you're not telling me, and I get it—believe me. You don't trust me yet and if I were you, I wouldn't trust me either. That's just playing smart, but I don't want to see you hurt any more than I want to end up back in Hell when this stint is over. This isn't just about me."

Damn him and his sense of honor—all noble and moral. It did things to her insides she didn't much fancy—especially if he was lying to her. "Well, seeing as we don't know what Satan's whacked about, let's just focus on you for now. First things first. You need clothes. You can't go running around in my pink bathrobe if we hope to find out what happened to you the day you died."

He leaned an elbow on her countertop. "I think I might like myself a whole lot better if I at least had something that wasn't so pink. You were right, it's really the wrong shade for me," he joked.

Her giggle popped from her lips like a cork from a champagne bottle. "I have to go to my brother's for lunch today, anyway. We always have lunch together on Sunday at his place. You're about the same size give or take a couple of inches in height. I'll see what I can dig up. While I do that, you can puppy-sit." Maybe her resentment would dull if dog number three spent an hour licking the air for no reason other than she was anxious about absolutely nothing or if dog number four had to have his BeDazzled ass changed a time or one hundred. She'd feel much better if they weren't so well behaved around him—the sting of their utter compliance with Clyde just might find some relief.

Delaney went in search of her purse, digging around for some singles for the bus. He held out her coat for her to slip her arms into, leaving her with a residual temptation to lean back into the strength of his solidness.

Before she headed out to the storefront, she gave him one last glance. "And Clyde?"

"Yeah?"

"If you're fucking with me—if I find out you're full of shit about this assignment business—I promise you, I'll fuck you up. And when I'm done, I'll sic Marcella on you. You do not want the Puerto Rican all fired up, heading in your general direction. It's heinous."

His stubbled jaw lifted, but without defiance. "I still have the duct tape scars to prove it. I get it. Completely."

"So long as we understand each other." She rubbed each dog's head with a quick token of her love. "You guys behave, though I'm sure the demon Clyde here'll have no trouble with you bunch of traitors. You seem to listen to him far better than you ever have me. I'll see you later." She waved over her shoulder, making her way to the store's front door.

A glance at her watch told her she'd better hurry if she was going to catch the twelve fifteen. The cool air helped to clear her head, the crunch of fallen leaves under her feet forcing her to focus on the rich colors of her favorite season.

The bus screamed to a halt just as she hit the corner. Today it was mostly empty, she noted, making her way to the back of the bus, and she was grateful. As much as she enjoyed chatting with the regulars like Mr. Epperstein, she just wasn't up to barium enema horror stories today. A sigh of relief escaped from deep within her chest when she settled in her seat, resting her forehead against the window. The tension of booting her best friend out and the harried pressure of the last two days eased just a little. Peace. Quiet. All good things. Important things. Rejuvenating your spirit things.

She could use some of that today.

What could the devil possibly plan for her demise when he found out Clyde wasn't Clyve? There was no winning her over to the dark side. She'd cut him off at the pass once, she'd fucking do it again. And again and for as many times as she had breath left in her lungs.

Delaney sucked in another cleansing gust of air through her nose and caught the faint scent of a now familiar aftershave.

"You forgot your scarf."

For the love of all things shiny. "You know, if I wasn't so tired, I'd give you the look."

"Roxette. As in, 'you've got the look.' From the album *Look Sharp*. Nineteen eighty-eight or eighty-nine."

She lifted her head, glancing to her left at Clyde in all his bathrobed fantasticness, sitting in the parallel seat as though riding the bus in a woman's bathrobe was an everyday occurrence. "Well, I don't think anyone could deny you've definitely got 'the look,'" she muttered under her breath, slumping down in the seat.

Clyde ran his burly hands over his jaw, slumping with her as though he could hide his brick shithouse–robed pinkness. There was no hiding his bulk. "Again. Awkward."

She snorted. "I'll say. So what happened and how did you end up glued to my ass again? What is it about you and the 'stay-put' theory that I keep missing the mark on?"

Clyde's expression was sharp. "If I had the answer to that, don't you suppose I'd stop doing it? This defies every law of physics I've ever studied. But then, so does Hell."

"And you've defied it in a pink bathrobe. Score."

"On public transportation, no less."

She pulled her purse tighter to her chest to fight a chuckle, then sobered. What was wrong with her? This wasn't funny. Him popping up in her shower unannounced—not funny. Him seeing her naked in her shower—not laughing. "Okay, how about you explain what happens when you leap from place to place like you're that guy from that show *Quantum* something."

"*Quantum Leap*. Scott Bakula, 1989. And he leaped from body to body. That's not what I'm doing. I'm just following you around like we're Siamese twins." His snort held disgust.

"Just tell me what happens and save the inane trivia."

"The moment you leave, it's almost like we're tied by a rope or something—tethered is the best way to explain it. You leave, and without so much as a blink of my eye, I'm right there with you. I don't feel anything. I don't have any warning—it just happens. Hey, didn't you mention something about a binding last night?"

She had, and that was the only thing she could think of that would make him keep popping up the way he did. "It's called a binding spell and I imagine explaining that to you is about as easy as you explaining trigonometry to me. If that's what this is, the simple answer is this: you're attached to me and before this thing with you is over, we're sure to have plenty of embarrassing encounters. Much like this one. You need clothes and shoes—fast."

The bus ground to a halt, the screech of its brakes reminding her she was just one stop away from Kellen's.

She slid farther down in the seat. If they could just make it through one more stop without causing a scene . . .

"Hey, duuude, nice pink swag."

Or not.

Delaney peered over the top of the seat to see a group of six or so kids plunk themselves into the seats.

Clyde ignored the group of kids, who'd decided to sit two seats away from him, leaning back in the seat and crossing his ankle over his knee while tucking the bathrobe's ends between his legs. He crossed his arms over his chest and stared at them dead-on. They nudged each other, laughing with a mocking cackle only snotty teenaged kids were capable of. The tight knit caps they wore in various colors covered their shoulder-length, stringy hair; their hoodies were oversized and bulky; their jeans clung to just above the tops of their butts. They mumbled something about an ass, but she didn't quite catch what they were referring to.

Clyde's jaw set hard, the grind of his teeth reaching her ears.

Ever nonconfrontational, she offered advice to Clyde. "Ignore them," she whispered. "They're just smart-ass kids."

"Who need an ass whoopin'."

Wow, look at the geek go all ghetto. "I'd have never guessed you were this easily riled, Clyde. Wasn't it you who said you were tame?"

He shrugged his wide pink shoulders. "Oh, I don't care what they say about me, it's all the wondering what your ass looks like that I object to."

Delaney's eyes instantly narrowed in the boys' direction as they whispered and laughed.

Thug motherfuckers.

When the bus stopped, Delaney rose with caution, but Clyde nudged her along, sliding behind her, placing one hand at the small of her back and the other on her shoulder. Passing the group, she grew tense, her steps stilted. Yet Clyde's strong, quiet presence urged her forward.

As they reached the stairs one kid leaned over the seat and muttered just loud enough for them to hear, "Man, I'd so tap that." His friends chuckled with conspiratorial snorts.

"Tap this, you rude little shit," Clyde growled under his breath, raising his index finger and pointing it at the boy's backpack, resting at his feet. A spark shot from his digit, lancing the pack and creating a puff of gray, sooty smoke, leaving each boy blissfully speechless.

"Wow, nice aim, huh?" He chuckled the words low in her ear when they took the last step onto the sidewalk. "I'm getting pretty good at that," he said with arrogance, then tripped into her back, knocking her forward with a lurch.

Whirling around, Delaney poked a finger at his shoulder. "Are you fucking nuts? You can't do stuff like that, Clyde—not in public. What if you get caught?"

Clyde pulled his foot up to knee level, rubbing the toe he'd apparently stubbed. "By a bunch of teenagers? Who'd believe them, anyway?"

"No, what if someone else saw that, like the bus driver? It's bad enough you're in a pink bathrobe, barefoot, wandering around New York like some homeless-shelter reject, but shooting fireballs from your fingers just might be the noose for your thick neck. You don't need to draw any more attention to yourself—so knock it the hell off and quit showing off your demonic prowess." She pivoted on her heel, marching toward the deli where she picked up her and Kellen's lunch every Sunday.

Clyde's footsteps slapped against the pavement as he followed behind with big, klunky feet. At the deli's door, she faced him, caring little that people milled about the sidewalk, casting confused glances their way. "Now, I'm going in to grab a fried tofu and watercress salad. You want one, too?"

He made a face at her, clearly not at all bothered by the fact that people were eyeing him like he was a sociopath loose on a day pass from the funny farm with his nurse. "A *fried tofu salad*? I can't think of anything less appealing. But if you wouldn't mind, I'd appreciate a pastrami on rye, extra brown mustard. I only like the brown mustard."

"All that fat and protein will clog up your arteries, Clyde Atwell."

His expression was deadpan. "I have no arteries, Delaney Markham."

Oh. Yeah. Dead. "Fine. Eat dead animal. Now, here's the score. Don't move from this spot," she ordered, pointing to the cracked, lumpy pavement. "In fact, stand over there by the side of the building and hold on tight so the next time I turn around you're not up my ass. Feel me? We don't need the Sunday lunch crowd mocking and pointing."

But Clyde wasn't looking at her, his eyes, sharp and clear behind his glasses, were focused on the interior of the deli.

"Yooo-hooo, demon light? Pay attention." When he didn't stop gawking, Delaney turned to see what he was so enraptured with. The fingerprint-smudged glass gave her a direct view to the deli counter, where a long line had formed. "Clyde? What's wrong?"

He pointed a finger at the glass, right between the *O* and the *L* in *O'Leary's*. "Tia."

"Who-a?"

"Tia."

"And Tia is . . . ?"

"My girlfriend."

nine

Enter Tia.

The ridiculously, sickly hawt Tia. Just what they freakin' needed to make this day perfection. "Where?" she asked dumbly, hoping against hope it wasn't the hot broad with the bod of steel.

"Right there." He pointed over her head.

Her stomach sank in defeat. "Who is she again?"

"She's my girlfriend, er, ex-girlfriend, er, whatever she is to me now that I'm dead."

Right. He'd mentioned a Tia in one of their conversations. Delaney turned fully, gazing into the packed deli. "Which one?"

"There. The one with the short, platinum blonde hair, the clingy, light blue dress, and white heels."

The one with the ass so pert and tight you could crack hard-shelled nuts on it by dropping them from above her prone body? Well, of course *she* was Tia.

Tia, Tia, Tia.

Neener, neener, neener.

Whooooah, sistah.

Where'd that come from?

Delaney looked up at him, setting aside her sudden stab of jealousy. "She's damned fine, Clyde. Überhot." *Good on you.* Clyde'd hit it big with Tia. She was Hawaiian Tropic model hot. Long lean legs, toned calves, a belly so flat it was almost concave, wide blue eyes, and pouty lips. Definitely fantastical. But then, so was Clyde, in his own college professor way. The only person who didn't seem to know that was Clyde. He'd made mention several times of his lack of finesse with the ladies—which made her wonder why someone like Tia had hooked up with him, and if he'd looked like he did now before his death. She definitely didn't look like she'd spent more time in a classroom than she had being spray tanned in some pricey salon.

Ooooh, Delaney—judgmental much? Looks were sometimes deceiving, and maybe Tia had an IQ to rival a Mensa member.

Maybe. Or maybe it was only her bowling scores that could rival a genius IQ.

Me-ow.

"Yeaaaah," Clyde agreed on a sigh that, to her ears, sounded wistful and faraway, thus jabbing the tip of the jealousy stick right in her left eyeball.

"Okay, so established. Tia's sickly hot," she acknowledged.

Good gravy. So Tia was spectacular on the eye. There were lots of women in the world who could hold that title. Marcella was one of them, and Delaney wasn't jealous of her at all. Well, okay, so she did feel some envy when Marcella wore all those tight jeans. But that was it. Really . . .

What Tia looked like shouldn't make a difference to her. What should was grilling the shit out of her bleached blondeness until she got some answers about Clyde and his life and now death. "Hey, stud muffin, want some advice? You'd better hit the bricks. I think she'd shit the aerobics instructor she got that rockin' ass from if she saw you. You're dead, remember? For three months now. If that won't freak her out, she's got bigger balls than most, but I get the feeling that's not the case."

Her words snapped him back to attention. "Damn. You're right." He instantly ducked down, hanging his dark head to his chest to push his way through the crowd, then latched onto the side of the brick building.

Delaney followed right behind. Tia might be the key to what had happened to Clyde the day he died. Maybe they shouldn't let this chance meeting pass them by. "Do you think Tia knows what happened the day you died, Clyde? Maybe I could talk to her."

His face went blank in thought. "Couldn't say for sure. I imagine she got the gory details from the coroners. I'm sure there had to have been at least an investigation into my death because the chemicals I was working with were my demise, but she wasn't there, if that's what you mean. I sent her home hours before it happened. I'm grateful for at least that much. And even if she did, what would you say to her anyway, Delaney? Hey, I talk to dead people—got a minute for your iced squeeze Clyde?"

Yeah, early on, when this thing had been thrust upon her, she'd innocently enough believed she could approach people and just tell them what their loved one wanted to share from the great beyond. But she kept running into roadblocks like, "You're nuttier than squirrel shit, hack," and her all-time favorite, "freak," no matter how much proof she had that she really could talk to ghosts.

She'd learned a few hard lessons that way. That no matter how dead-on you were, no matter how secretive the information was that you shared with a grieving relative, the skeptical, the fearful, just weren't going to buy it. She only shared with those who were open to the possibility of the other side, and those who weren't, she tread ever so lightly with.

So he had a point. Which brought up another point. "You know, I did a Google search on your name the other day and found next to nothing. I searched obituaries for the last three months all over the country for a dead Clyde Atwell and came up dry—why is that?" There was no keeping the suspicion out of her question. "It's like you said, wouldn't there be a coroner's report? Unless they haven't released your body because the circumstances surrounding your death were suspicious . . ."

"I have no answers for you. I've already told you what I know—what I remember. I screwed up. It was late, I was tired, and what I was working on exploded. I only remember seeing the flames and hearing the explosion for a split second—after that, I was in Hell."

She ran her tongue over her lips. "What chemicals did you mix and is it likely that whatever you mixed and blew yourself to smithereens with was so stupid the police might find it suspicious that a smart guy like you would do something like that?"

Clyde became clearly chagrined. "I cut myself on some metal, so I cleaned the wound with some H_2O_2, more commonly known as hydrogen peroxide. But it wasn't the kind you buy over the counter. It was highly concentrated—sort of like the kind hairdressers use to bleach hair. Like an ass, because I was, as usual, absorbed in my work, and me, me, me, as Tia used to say, I was trying to dilute it when I knocked the *entire* bottle over. It collided with some sulfuric acid I was using to clean metal, fell into the Bunsen burner I could have sworn I'd turned off, and exploded. And yes, I can see the police finding it pretty ironic that someone like me with a degree and a rather above-average IQ would do something so goddamned dumb. So sure, they could find it suspicious that I mixed those two chemicals together, because it was damned careless, but I don't think they'd get very far."

"Why's that?"

His impatience became crystal clear in not just his face, but the agitated tension in his stance. "I've said this a thousand times, Delaney. What I was researching was absolutely harmless. I wasn't on to the next cure for cancer, or even the common cold. I was researching a new hypoallergenic coating for jewelry—pretty innocuous. I don't have a lot of money—or didn't. I made a decent living, but not sizable enough to kill me over. I have some stocks and bonds, but nothing substantial. No valuable property or jewelry. No inheritance. So if the coroner is holding my body for investigation, there won't be much to find and certainly nothing suspicious."

If that was true, Clyde was a strange, strange bird, and she said as much. "You're a strange bird, Clyde. I don't get it. I don't get how you ended up in Hell, but the more you show up in your pink bathrobe in places like the bus and my shower, the more I want to figure out why you did. And don't think I'm going to take everything you say at face value. We're going to start picking apart your life like meat off a chicken carcass."

"Could I have clothes before we do? This whole half-naked and exposed thing has become a lot. Not to mention, my feet are freezing," he said on a grin, the serious, staid attitude replaced by a boyish smile.

"You wait here. I'll go get lunch, and then we'll get those clothes. Do. Not. Move."

"Roger that."

"No matter how tempting it might be to approach Miss Hawaiian Tropic," she warned before heading back to the front of the deli.

Just as Delaney reached for the door, Tia skipped out on her heeled feet, clinging to a man's arm.

A damned good-looking one. All sleek and wearing a designer suit she was sure was a big-name label.

Hoo boy. Poor Clyde.

As Delaney slid past the couple, she gave a quick peek over her shoulder, hoping Clyde wouldn't see the pair when they sauntered out of O'Leary's. The look on his face when he'd seen Tia had been a little too lovesick for Delaney. It had almost made her heart clench. She could only hope, when she had more time to examine it, that clench had everything to do with her sentimentality for love lost and nothing to do with the color green.

Twenty minutes later, lunch in hand, she breathed a sigh of relief. They'd managed to be apart for twenty whole minutes without him attaching his big self to her.

And that's when she began to panic.

Christ, if he'd disappeared without warning, she'd kick his ass for all the trouble he'd been. Her stride was quick, her heart hammering while she threaded her way through the Sunday lunch crowd, pushing her way to the door.

Flying out the deli door, Delaney made a direct left and went straight for the corner she'd left him in.

Lo and behold.

No Clyde.

The spot she'd left him in was empty. Her heart began to pump irregularly; her legs became the equivalent of lead poles. If the motherfucker'd jacked her up, and she found his brainiac ass, she'd dump a whole case of Morton on his head.

Goddamn it, goddamn it, goddamn it.

Shoving the bag from the deli under her arm, she stomped down the street toward her brother's, where a crowd had begun to form in front of the 7-Eleven.

And whose head stood out in that crowd?

Delaney gritted her teeth and made a beeline for Clyde, who stood front and center, staring at something inside the store. Had Tia'd gone into the 7-Eleven with Mr. Fine, and Clyde was preparing to throw down in a fit of jealous rage?

She discarded that thought. Clyde just didn't seem like he got het up over a whole lot—even if his girlfriend was prancing about with a good-looking guy. Delaney grabbed his upper arm and hissed, "What are you doing? Either I can't get rid of you or you're off attracting a crowd like you're the new orca whale at Sea World. Did I tell you to stay put?"

"I forgot the 7-Eleven was here."

It struck her at that moment—she had no idea where Clyde came from. She was so slacking when it came to her medium duties these days. "You've been here before?"

"Once or twice," he replied, the fog he was in refusing to lift.

Delaney tweaked his arm. "Hello in there. Just a reminder. You're a fully grown man in a pink bathrobe out in broad daylight. All you need is a shopping cart full of soda cans to complete your crazy portrait."

He looked down at her, the glazed-over look in his eyes clearing. "They have Slurpees . . . 7-Eleven has Slurpees. I love Slurpees."

"Do you think you might love the nuthouse?"

"What?"

"The nuthouse. Because if you keep wandering off in your bathrobe and bare feet, I can almost guarantee you, they're going to drag you off to the place called crazy. Now come on. I'm late as it is." She grabbed his hand, dragging him close to her side so he couldn't escape while everyone they passed stared at them. "Move, people! Crazy guy in a bathrobe here," she said to them by way of explanation. "Totally harmless unless he misses his meds. Then shit gets ugly. We only have about ten minutes before everything goes south. So excuse us, because when he realizes he has the color pink on, I make no promises he won't react. *Violently*," she added with a shiver of horror for the gawkers, giving them all a furtive glance.

The ten or twelve people who'd gathered around Clyde parted, allowing her to drag a reluctant, heavy-footed Clyde behind her. "Do you think on the way back to your place we could get a Slurpee? I haven't had one in a while. They used to be my mainstay. I hope they have banana. I love banana Slurpees. Helped me get through many a long night while I studied. But I'd settle for a Full Throttle Frozen Blue Demon."

"Throttle and demon. How ironic those words being in the same phrase," she commented.

"So would you mind?"

"Mind what?"

"If we stopped on the way back so I can get a banana Slurpee."

The mention of banana Slurpees made her stop almost cold. The memory of why something as ridiculous as a banana Slurpee was relevant slipped away like a cube of melting ice in her grasp. She shook off the faint recollection and plodded ahead. "I can't think of anything worse for your innards than a Slurpee. The sugar alone is enough to leave you snockered."

"I think I'm beyond worrying about my cholesterol levels and blood pressure and pretty much anything that has to do with my health. Again, I remind you, I'm dead. If I drank a hundred Slurpees consecutively, I wouldn't stop ticking because I no longer tick. And don't you ever live a little? Like have a cheeseburger or some greasy fries? Or do you always eat food fit only for gerbils and goats?"

"I try to maintain a nontoxic existence. I've gone green, I avoid preservatives, additives, dairy, and most bread, and I believe for every bottle of aspirin out there, there's a form of meditation or a root extract that'd be just as helpful."

His chuckle was deep. "Are you one of those people who hums while you're in downward dog position in search of your happy place?"

She made a face at him, giving him a jab in his ribs. "It's downward facing dog. Don't make it sound so crazy. I'm not the fruitcake in this deal, bathrobe man. Yoga's good for you. It not only increases your flexibility, but releases energy blocks, and with the lot of you bunch running around, always jumping into the middle of my life, I could use less in the way of energy blocks. Christ knows I need more energy to keep up with all these ghosts. You'd be surprised how calming yoga can be."

"Doesn't change the fact that I'd like a banana Slurpee on the way home."

"We'll see. Right now, I'm almost forty-five minutes late with lunch. Now step on the gas." She let go of his arm and hurried up the steps of her brother's apartment building, punching the buzzer for his apartment.

"Christ, D. Where you been?" Kellen barked out of the intercom. "I only called you five times. That's what the cell phone is for—so I can call you. Then you answer. It's called keeping in touch."

She cast a gaze of admonishment in Clyde's direction when Kellen hit the buzzer, opening the door. They climbed the stairs together in silence. It was just now occurring to her that she was going to have to explain Clyde to her brother. As they stood at Kellen's door, she looked up at him. "Just let me do the talking. Don't say a single word or I'll superglue your lips together."

Clyde leaned his bulk against the black enamel door frame, tightening the robe around his waist until it almost met. "So this is the Kellen whose name I heard in Hell. Your brother, right?"

"The one and only, and though he knows about the dead people thing, and he knows about you, too—he's not much of a demon lover."

"Really, Delaney, who is?"

"It's not something you'd understand. Believe me when I tell you, if you thought I was a hard sell, with Kellen it'll be like trying to sell rhythm to J-Lo. Now seeing as you're in the habit of jamming feet in your mouth on a regular basis, and you have all the sensitivity of an earthworm—just be quiet. Okay?"

The lone bulb hanging above his head highlighted the sharp planes of his face while the wheels of his fact-loving mind visibly turned. "Interesting fact, earthworms are hermaphrodites. They can have relations with either male or female worms and still reproduce. I'm unsure whether they have emotions, though."

Again with the intercourse. Delaney narrowed her eyes at him. "If only to be an earthworm. Just lay low and can the Discovery Channel regurgitations from out of nowhere." She rapped on the door, slapping a smile on her face for Kellen, remembering to step in front of Clyde to prevent her overprotective brother from right-hooking her demon's jaw.

Kellen threw open the door wide, stopping short when he saw Clyde standing behind her. Both men sized each other up. Kellen's narrowed gaze honed in on Clyde.

In a pink bathrobe.

And that had to be anything but a testosterone boost for Clyde.

Yet Clyde never left her back, though she sensed his nostrils were probably flaring much the way Kellen's were.

"So this is the demon, huh? Nice robe, man," Kellen drawled, jamming his hands under his armpits.

"Kellen," she warned, "just listen before you drag your knuckles on the floor. C'mon, Clyde," she prompted, placing his hand in hers and taking him to the kitchen. Delaney threw the bag on Kellen's small dinette table, handing Clyde his requested sandwich. "Here. Clog those arteries. You"—she pointed at Kellen—"sit down. We have some really serious stuff to discuss."

But her intentions were all but forgotten when the cabinets above Kellen's stove began to open and shut with crackling thwacks to the wood.

"Visitor?" Kellen asked—used to the interruptions Delaney's mad, mad world presented.

Her eyes scanned the room, searching for the entity. Goose bumps came and went, skittering along her arms and down her spine on spiderlike feet.

Clyde rose to his full height. "Where?"

The instant he did was the moment the cabinets stopped clattering and the chill disappeared. "Sit down. Don't move."

As though the man himself had arrived and given him an order, Clyde actually listened to her, his ass hitting the padded chair hard in obedience.

She placed a finger over her lips, glancing at both men. "Helllllloooo?" she called to the room. "Oh, c'mon, don't be shy. It's really okay. Come out and talk to me," she coaxed, hoping her light tone would extend her willingness to talk and inspire trust.

When the slither of a black shadow took form, Delaney cocked her head, gazing at the spot just above Clyde's head.

Weee doggie, that had to have been major suckage.

"Delaney?" Kellen's concerned voice broke her fixated stare at the image in front of her. "Who is it?"

"Well, could be a doctor—definitely someone in the medical profession because he has scrubs on."

"And that's unusual why?" Clyde questioned.

Delaney grimaced at Clyde. "First, *do not move*. He's coming in loud and clear, and every time you so much as blink an eye, he fades. Second, don't freak on me, okay?"

Clyde's face darkened. "Why would I freak?"

"Because he's resting his head on your shoulder."

"That's not so freaky."

"Well, here's the thing."

Now his gaze grew wary. "What's the thing?"

"It could be interpreted as such if it's in his hands."

ten

Clyde bolted upright, shoving away from the table and brushing at his shoulders, knocking over the soup she'd bought for Kellen with a wet splat of chicken and dumplings.

She flicked his arm with an angry finger. "I told you not to move! Jesus, Clyde—now he's gone again." Her eyes darted around the room, searching for the spirit.

Clyde whipped around, eyeing Delaney with a visible shudder. "Call me all kinds of sorry I scared the guy with the head in his *hands* away. Jesus." He gave a vigorous rub to his broad shoulder again for obvious good measure.

"I told you not to freak. It's not like it's *real* real. He was just a ghost. Transparent, ya know? No substance—honest. Don't be such a candy-ass."

"Says you. It wasn't *your* shoulder his head—not attached to his body, I might add—was resting on."

"Don't be such a total girl. You're a demon, for crap's sake. Some people would call *that* creepy."

"But I'm a demon with my head. Not as creepy."

"I hate to defend the demon, Delaney, but I have to side with the lackey here," Kellen offered in a dry response, pulling napkins from a holder on the table and wiping his pants.

Clyde's tongue rolled on the inside of his cheek, his fists balled by his sides. "I'd refrain from using words like *lackey* when referring to me. I'm no one's lackey. That's a polite request, but I'll back it up if I have to. You're Delaney's brother and for the most part, Delaney's been pretty decent to me if I don't grudge and hold the salt and the prism thing against her. I'm trying very hard to respect her relationship to you," Clyde said, directing his pointed gaze at Kellen. A tic in his jaw pumped furiously as the air between the two men filled with the pungent scent of a point being made.

Kellen scowled at Clyde, his shoulders slinging back when he rose from the table. "And you'll do *what* if I don't? Set me on fire?"

Delaney was between them in a shot, backing up against the table to glare at Clyde, reaching behind her to hold off her brother. "How about we go all Neanderthal another time? I have a spirit world that needs me. The one I can't seem to communicate with these days because everything's all fucked up. Adding more chaos by throwing down will just piss me off. You don't want to do that. I'm raw, boys. Fragile. Teetering even. All made worse by threats from Lucifer. Now sit—"

Kellen put a hand on her shoulder, the concern on his face clouding his eyes. "Threat? Lucifer made a direct threat?"

Delaney nodded. "Hoo, yeah. And we need to talk. So let's go do that. Clyde? If the headless dude shows back up again, call me."

She pulled Kellen through his living room and into the bedroom, sitting down on the edge of his bed. She held out her hand to him. "Sit next to me. We have trouble. Clyde brought me a message from Hell. He just doesn't know the depth of it."

Kellen's eyes grew stormy and dark with disbelief and anger. "And you know he's telling the truth how, D? He's a demon, for Christ's sake! According to you, they're all liars. Oh, except Marcella. She just got a *crappy* deal, right?" he said with a sarcastic grunt.

Her eyes began to water at the mention of Marcella's name. Fuck. "Leave her out of this. *Please*."

Kellen threw his hands up like white flags. "Okay, okay. Sorry. Did you two have a fight?"

"No, I sent her away."

"What?" The surprise on his face was evident, but there was more than just the shock of hearing she'd sent her friend packing. And that only confirmed her suspicions, which would leave her pleased under any other circumstances but the one Marcella was in—doomed for eternity. "What the hell happened?"

She toyed with the line of bracelets on her arm, the jingle of them soothing her. "Listen to what I have to tell you and you'll understand."

While she explained what Clyde had told her and her pseudo argument with Marcella, minus what she suspected was some kind of binding spell, she kept an eye on her demon, pacing up and down the wide expanse of Kellen's living room.

"This has to go back to Vincent," Kellen said with a sneer and clenched fists. "That son of a fucking bitch."

She leaned her head on Kellen's shoulder. Recalling that night brought nothing but heartache and pure terror. All because she'd defied Satan. Because she had, she'd dragged Kellen by proxy into something he shouldn't have ever been involved in. "I guess so. You heard what the pitchfork lover said that night as well as I did.

He said he'd see me in Hell and basically said he'd take anyone I loved with him, too, and if what Clyde says is true, I guess he meant it."

"But it's been almost fifteen years, Delaney. And how do we know this Clyde's telling the truth? If all demons are liars, why isn't he?"

"Look at him." Delaney pointed a finger out in the direction of the living room.

"He's kind of hard to take seriously. He's got on a fuzzy, beat-to-shit bathrobe. A pink one. So what am I looking at?"

"Look at your cats." Kellen's cats, Vern and Shirley, swirled their tails around Clyde's bare ankles while he stroked their backs. It wasn't easy to admit, but that he liked animals, and they liked him back, was a huge plus on Clyde's scorecard of pros.

"Yeah, and . . . ?"

"They don't hate him, do they? They don't hate Marcella either," she said pointedly. "As a matter of fact, they don't like a lot of strangers, but they sure are clinging to Clyde the demon."

The slap of his hands on his thighs made her jump. "Is this going to be the paranormal edition of Animal Planet again? You're trusting two cats who hack up hairballs just to give me a reason to buy paper towels and who play in the toilet for amusement, Delaney. Don't be ridiculous."

"Don't call me ridiculous, smart-ass. I know the supernatural and I know animals. My dogs love him, Kellen. They know an evil entity, and as crazy as this all sounds, I don't think Clyde is one, and neither do they. He's almost too much of a dork to be one, in my opinion. But that's neither here nor there. He's here and I'm dealing with him. Live with it."

A sigh of defeat, meaning she'd won this round, blew from between Kellen's lips. "Fine. Like I could talk you out of anything anyway. You can be so damned single-minded. Someday, it may be your ass you hand over. So what's the plan now? We wait until Lucifer sends in reinforcements? I'm supposed to wait around until something or someone hurts you? And what the fuck are you going to do with Clyde?"

She'd finally resigned herself to giving Clyde's problem her all. It wasn't like she could get away from him, anyway. There was a reason Clyde was here. Whatever it was, it was karmic, cosmic—something-ic—and she'd always been a firm believer in the universe's plan. "Help him. It's kinda what I do. I'm going to figure out how he ended up in Hell and try to cross him over—if he's been truthful, that is. If Clyde's the man he claims he was in life, then he should be in the biggest, baddest chem lab ever with endless resources and supplies—*upstairs*, not down.

"The rest"—she shrugged her shoulders—"what else can we do but wait it out? This is the devil we're talking about, Kell. It's not like we can anticipate what he's up to, or what he'll do when he finds out Clyde's one-upped him in the smarts department. He's got shit going for him we don't. Like flaming fingertips and those freaky snakes he's so fond of. I just want you to promise you'll be really careful. He'll do whatever he has to to hurt me, and if he hurt you, it would kill me. We only have each other now. Whatever's going to happen, I need to know you're safe. So watch your ass."

"And wait around," was Kellen's dull response.

Delaney rose from the bed and pinched his cheek with a fond tweak. "Yep. That's all we can do. We can't control what we don't know. When and if I figure out what's up with Clyde, I'll let you know. I doubt it's related to us, but having an in, in Hell can't hurt. And keep your mouth shut about Vincent. No one—not Marcella, not Clyde—can have that information, especially Clyde. If this turns out to be some big hoax on his part, I don't want him taking the kind of intermittent fear I've experienced since that night back to Hell. I won't give Lucifer the satisfaction. He'd definitely hurt Marcella to hurt me, and that's not something I think I could take. That's why I shipped her off—because if she tries to interfere, she won't be a nobody to him anymore."

Kellen leaned back on the bed on his elbows. His attempt was for clearly casual, but he only achieved it partially. "Is she okay?"

Her eyebrow rose and her lips blossomed into a knowing smile. "And you care why?"

His expression fought to remain impassive and nonchalant. "Because she's your friend. I know it would upset you if anything happened to her."

"Right. Which has absolutely nothing to do with her ass. Which you watch. Often. Every time she leaves a room, in fact. This is all just concern for me."

"I'm a man. Demon or not, she has a sweet ass. So what?"

Delaney chuckled at him. His attraction for Marcella was so blatantly obvious, but knowing her brother and his hatred of anything smacking of Hell, he'd never act on it. On a rational level, she knew Marcella would long outlive Kellen. To become involved would be mostly insane. Her heart said something much less rational. "So nothing. I have to go. I need to get moving on this thing if I hope to help Clyde cross."

Kellen snatched her hand in his once more, gripping it tight. "Do you really believe crossing is what he wants? Really?"

She glanced at Clyde once more. Now Vern and Shirley were in his lap, rubbing their faces against his arm and vying for his attention. "I think I do." Without warning, she definitely did think just that. Why, when, how, was a mystery. Yet she was convinced in that moment that Clyde was for real. Though she still wasn't ready to tell him the details of her run-in with Satan.

"Okay. I'll shut up. I won't like it, but I'll do it if you think it's the right thing to do. But call me. Call me often so I know you're okay."

She planted a kiss on his cheek and followed up with a quick squeeze of a hug around his wide shoulders. "Will do. Oh, and one more little favor?"

"What?"

"Can I borrow some clothes and a pair of shoes? I can't keep dragging him around in my bathrobe. People stare, ya know?"

Kellen went to his closet and pulled out a couple of shirts and a pair of old shoes, then got some jeans from his dresser drawer. He threw the bundle at her. "Keep 'em."

She blew him a kiss over her shoulder and went to get Clyde. Dumping the clothes on the couch next to him, she grabbed her coat from the back of the sofa. "Get dressed. Please. So people will stop staring at me like I'm the keeper of the loons."

The grin he flashed was lopsided. "Have I told you you're funny?"

"That makes two times now, and yeah, I'm a fucking riot. Go get dressed and we'll go back to my place and figure this out."

Clyde unfolded his big body, setting cats aside with careful hands and one last stroke of his palm. His eyes pinned hers, solemn and studious behind his glasses. They sent a thousand messages. Some she understood, some went without saying, and some she wasn't able to identify. "Thank you."

And hell if that didn't make her stomach flop like a fish out of water. "You-you're welcome."

Slipping past her, he headed for the bathroom to change, passing Kellen on his way. "You fucking hurt her, and I'll—"

He and Clyde were eye to eye when Clyde said, "You'll what? Kill me? Afraid you missed that boat, partner. But if it's any consolation, I promise to do whatever it takes to keep her out of harm's way." Clyde made the first move by offering Kellen his hand.

Kellen took it, but the tension in his bulk was apparent from the stiffness of his shoulders and the clench of his teeth. "You make sure you do that—or I'll chase your ass into the afterlife."

Clyde's nod was curt when he stepped around Kellen, closing the bathroom door behind him.

Okay, so maybe chivalry hadn't died a merciless death.

Hot.

To discover that about Clyde was unbelievably hot.

To have a man other than her brother stick up for her was just plain smokin'. And pathetically, desperately, sadly a statement that it had been far too long since she'd had a man's attention.

Weak.

Very weak.

Clyde sipped his banana Slurpee with a blissful grin on his face. The dogs, littered in a clump at his feet, slept in peaceful silence. He tilted the large cup at her in gratitude. "Thanks for this. I really missed them. You think if I get the frig out of Hell, they'll have these wherever I end up?"

Banana Slurpees.

Not so profound unless you connected the beverage back to someone she'd like to erase from her memory.

It had hit her when they'd stopped at the convenience store on the way home. Not only was it an out-of-the-ordinary, disgustingly sugary drink to crave, it was a weird coincidence to run into two people in a lifetime who loved them the way Clyde did.

And Vincent had.

Vincent had loved banana Slurpees, too. The memory had made her shudder in the store, and it made her shudder again now. Vincent holding court in her head the way he was as of late made her feel dirty, but he'd had a way of making even the most innocent of things seem dirty. The kind of dirty she just couldn't wash away. He'd lied, cheated, stolen, and eventually killed . . . even if she could soak in a vat of disinfectant, it would never wash away the stench of his filthy memory.

Delaney gritted her teeth and realigned the bottles of herbs she'd already straightened for the umpteenth time to keep her fingers busy, looking away from the beauty of Clyde. Since this afternoon at Kellen's, the impulse to tuck fistfuls of his hair between her fingers while he kissed the living shit out of her had been impossible to shake.

Dressed in her brother's old blue polo shirt and jeans, he was unquestionably one delish package. It'd been an effort to keep her distance. The soft glow of the storefront, where all of her beloved remedies and books were, didn't help either. It was too cozy and their silence too comfortable.

"I'm hoping for row after row of 7-Elevens with nothing but banana Slurpees," Clyde said on a watery chuckle, cutting into her haze of growing lust.

Her expression went into instant consolation mode. She knew this role—the role of spirit guide. It was like an old shoe. She slipped it on with ease, relishing the buttery soft, worn leather of it.

She was at her best when she was reassuring someone they were making the right choice by choosing the up button on the elevator of eternity. "I can't say for sure. I do know that some of the things I've heard uttered were said with big-time awe and wonder. I can safely say I haven't had a single customer shriek in horror when they cross. Wherever you end up, I hope it has endless banana Slurpees, if that's what trips your trigger." And she did—hope that for him.

Clyde's eyes sought hers, his glasses mirroring her reflection. "Did I mention I never believed in Heaven or Hell when I was alive?"

Her hand covered her mouth to hide her snort. "You did. I guess the logical team lost a player, huh?"

Pausing, Clyde took another long draw from his Slurpee straw. "It just didn't make any sense from a scientific point of view. The devil and angels were myths as far as I was concerned."

"Well, the devil's no myth. It's good you're clear on that now." She checked off a box on her inventory sheet, then said, "So tell me a little about what Clyde Atwell was like when he was alive."

Rocking back on the stool, he propped his feet on the counter by her register. Pensive was the best word she could think of to describe the set of his face. Pensive with splashes of some distant regret. "The truth is he was self-absorbed, sometimes to the point of driving people away. His mother and father were gone, and he had no siblings, but he hopes if there really is a better place, they're there when he gets there. Clyde Atwell spent a shitload of time in a lab, tinkering with his experiments and not nearly enough time doing life stuff. He read manuals and annals and prided himself on his research. But he never took a vacation. He never saw all the things, the places, he was so good at researching. He saw them from a computer screen and history books. He liked facts and figures and everything to make perfect, logical sense. He liked order in his world and in his theories about said world. Clyde's come a long way in just three hellish months."

Those facts were no surprise to Delaney. "And how old was Clyde when he died?"

"Almost thirty-seven."

"That's a long time to not do any of the things you wanted to do."

There was definitely a trace of sadness to his next words. "Yeah, yeah it is. But I was sick for the better part of my early years and in bed more than out—books, facts, figures, television, and eventually the Internet were my friends. I had trouble relating to people because of it."

"Sick?"

"Long story."

One he wasn't ready to share by the closed-off look his face took on. She got that. She could wait. If she were to treat him like any other crossing, she'd do it with a light, noninvasive hand. That's what the plan was for now. "Were you close to your parents?"

The smile on his lips was fond, his whole being lighting up with affection. "I had great parents."

"And they've passed?"

"Yeah. My mom just last year of pancreatic cancer and my dad about four years before in his sleep. I was a late-in-life baby for them. My mom found out she was pregnant when she was thirty-nine and my dad was forty-five. According to them, after almost twenty years of marriage, I was a miracle." He shifted positions, dropping his feet and pulling the stool closer to where she was checking her inventory. "So how about you? I know about Kellen. Any other sisters or brothers I need to watch my ass with?"

Her laughter filled the store, but her eyes strayed to the floor to avoid his. "Sorry about that. Kellen's very protective, and part of that has to do with the fact that we only have each other now. My mom died about thirteen years ago of Alzheimer's and my dad a couple of years before my eighteenth birthday of a heart attack. So Kellen and I look out for each other."

"It's good to have someone to lean on." His statement held hidden emotions she guessed had to do with not having any family left when his parents were gone.

"And you were a scientist or something smart, huh?"

"Freelance chemical research consultant. I was my own boss."

"So where did Clyde Atwell hang his hat?"

He cocked his head. "I never wore a hat."

Delaney sighed. "I didn't mean literally. I mean figuratively. Like where did you live?"

"North Dakota."

Well, there went the idea of making a visit to his swinging bachelor pad. Though, now that she had a definitive place he'd once resided, she could look more closely at the obits online in the North Dakota newspapers. But what the hell was Tia doing in New York if she was from North Dakota? And why had she shown up at that specific deli—one Delaney frequented every Sunday for lunch . . .

Suspicion reared its ugly head again. "If you're from North Dakota, what was Tia doing in New York?"

"That was her brother you saw her with. He lives here—works as a stockbroker. She came here often to see him—so I'm vaguely familiar with the area."

"You saw him?"

"Yeah, and thanks for trying to protect me from seeing what you thought was her boyfriend."

"Don't you find it suspicious that she was in a deli I go to every Sunday? That she was right in our immediate vicinity?"

"Not even a little. I think it was just a really big coincidence. Nothing more."

Maybe. Maybe not. Maybe Tia knew more than Clyde thought. Hmmmm.

While she was dipping her toes in the pool of Clyde, she decided to wade further in. "So how about Tia? I'm sorry about that. Bet seeing her cut deep." She was being a meddling, nosy bitch— even if she was sorry he'd lost someone he clearly still loved. But by God, she had the craziest urge to know how deep their relationship had run. It didn't make her a bad person—just a curious one.

And this information will help you cross him over, how, Delaney?
Curious isn't the only thing you are . . .

"Don't sweat it," he offered as though they'd seen his dry
cleaner or the bagger at his local grocery store in that deli rather
than the woman he'd loved.

Her heart clenched. Maybe he was trying to hide his pain over
seeing her by drowning his sorrow in his banana Slurpee and pride
laced with testosterone. "Do you need some time alone?"

"Why would I need time alone?"

She clucked her tongue at him. "Because you just saw the
woman you love and you couldn't even talk to her. That has to be
hard. At the very least, frustrating."

Clyde was so obviously confused, she thought the word "huh?"
might transcribe itself on his forehead like a stigmata on a grilled
cheese sandwich. "And that means I need to be alone?"

What. A. Simpleton. "Well, yeah. Like time alone to do un-
manly things like sulk, pout, maybe even cry."

Clyde's lightly tanned brow wrinkled. "Why would I do that?"

Alrighty then, her sympathy cup had just been bled dry. "Because you *loved* her. Because you *miss* her. Because now you're
going to spend the rest of your eternity with winged people, if all
goes as planned, and not the woman you love!" Nimrod.

"Oh," was his dull response.

"Oh? Ohhh?" she almost shrieked, throwing her clipboard
down on the counter between them.

The glance Clyde gave her said he was tired of explaining
things that were rational to the exceptionally irrational, slightly
overreacting ghost talker. "These are the cards I've been dealt. I
can't go back to Tia now. It isn't practical or logical. What's the use
of mourning something that won't ever happen? I think you have a
very romanticized view of love, Delaney. I think it's pretty clear,

'happily ever after' only lasts for so much 'after'—everything changes when one half of the equation kicks the bucket. I kicked the bucket. How fair would it be for me to show up and make her life a mess, only to have to leave again if you can cross me over?"

How very no-nonsense and unbelievably logical with a big side order of insensitive and about as romantic as a trip to the gynecologist. How totally Clyde. "Well, I dunno if my view's been romanticized, demon. I mean, if I'd had a girlfriend as wonkable as, say, Tia, and I blew my ass all over the joint, yet never had the chance to say good-bye, never was able to say a final 'I love you' to her, I'd be feelin' some regret. So, yeah—color me romantic. My view is idealistic. But you, on the other hand, can't even seem to remember what your last moments with her were like. And you call yourself decent? What kind of boyfriend are you?"

"Well, from your point of view, I'd say I was a pretty shitty boyfriend," was the sarcastic reply.

The snort she spat in his direction returned his sarcasm. "I'll say. How can you so callously dismiss what you shared with her? I thought, from the look on your face when you saw her, that you were a guy who'd been in complete love. Maybe your bad judge of character is rubbing off on me."

His one eyebrow rose above the frames of his glasses. "That look was for the pastrami on rye. It's been a long time since I had one, and I'm not callously dismissing anything. There wasn't much to dismiss. Do I regret not having the chance to say my good-byes? Yep. I do. But I don't just regret not being able to say good-bye to Tia, I regret not being able to say good-bye to several people. Mostly my cat, Hypotenuse."

She shoved all the bottles back on the shelf with disgust. "You know what, Clyde? You're a schnutz. Chivalry really is dead and that death unlives in you. That you miss your cat more than Tia says a lot about you."

"What does it say about me, crazy dog lady?" His remark was glib and, she was sure, meant to remind her that if not for Kellen, she'd have some dogs to say good-bye to and not much more. But that wasn't so much by choice as it was by circumstance. No one wanted to hang out with, date, or even do something as simple as take a walk with someone who talked to dead people—not to mention live with the threat of Satan walloping your ass if you got too close to the medium. *Thanks for the reminder.*

Her eyes narrowed and her fingers twitched. "Don't you dare compare us, Clyde Atwell. My life isn't anything like yours. Mine is all about connecting and even if it's just with dead people, it's for a good cause. My situation isn't by choice. Yours was, filled with cold, sterile labs and some law of averages. I think what yours says is that you think love is a useless emotion that takes up too much of your time—time that could be spent researching the Striped Marsh Frog or something. It says that you don't think love can be bigger than you are. That you can't be swept away by it. And now that you're deader than the extinct Wannanosaurus, you'll never be able to find out. That should make you very, very sad. Instead all I'm hearing in your voice is dismissal for the silly medium and her idiot notions."

"Ahhh, the Wannanosaurus. Probably one of the, or maybe even the, smallest bone-headed dinosaurs. Not one of the more infamous either. I'm impressed."

"Thanks. I'll tuck that away in my 'useless bullshit' files. I think I'm done for tonight." She threw her inventory sheet on the countertop, then yanked off the full-body apron she always wore in case she spilled a bottle of oil and threw it on the counter.

Rising from the stool he'd been sitting on, he clasped her arm in a light grip when she tried to pass him. "Why are you so angry?"

Yeah. Why was she? Maybe because he'd debased the idea of falling in love to a level that made her feel mocked for believing in it. He'd simplified it, analyzed it, deglorified it to something silly and wasteful. Like it was some chemistry problem to be solved on a chalkboard. And the really horrible thing about that was it was her deepest desire. It was like attacking her dream with an AK-47 and unloading the cartridge.

It was only an opinion, and not one she hadn't heard before from plenty of men. Why it rubbed her raw because it came from Clyde made no sense. "I'm not angry. I just find this conversation pointless. We have very different views on what love is or isn't. I'm all about diversity. Vive la 'behave like a stupidhead.' I'm good." And that didn't sound at all sullen or spiteful. She tried to shrug away from his grasp, but he wouldn't let her.

Realization spread from one corner of his face to the other. "Ah, wait. I get it. Because I'm not totally wasted, all curled up and fetal over never seeing Tia again, I'm a cold-hearted asshole, right?"

Right. "Whatever."

Clyde let her arm go, folding his arms over his chest, and loomed because, it would seem, he was gifted like that. "Here's a little something you don't know. Tia and I were once involved, yes, but was she the love of my life? No. Was I hers? I doubt that because if that were the case, and your version of love is real, I gotta think she wouldn't have been skipping off to New York to visit her brother just three months after I annihilated myself. We did date for *two* years. If your version of love was what she and I had, she'd still be home, sobbing in her pillow and wearing one of my old shirts while her hair got greasy and her hygiene became less of a priority as she grieved me. I liked Tia a lot, but at the point of my death, she was pretty fed up with me and my single-mindedness. She was halfway out the door of our relationship when I blew myself to smithereens. And I wasn't *in* love with her, though I did care a great deal about her. I guess if I had been, my work wouldn't have interfered the way it did. It isn't that I'm mocking your views on happily ever after, it's that I haven't experienced that kind of desire or need with anyone."

So, yeah. Shit, she'd gone all fist to the sky in protest on him. "Oh," she muttered with far more contrition than she liked hearing.

"Yeah. *Oh*." He stuck his face in hers, craning his neck down at her when he did.

A faint woo to the hoo that Clyde hadn't been wild about Tia, Hawaiian Tropic hot as she was, made her a little giddy. Dangerously so. She knew what her love-starved mind was toying with, and in her head, she knew that shit had to come to a screeching halt. Loneliness could make you do stupid things. It put your defenses at an all-time low. It was her loins that just didn't seem to want to play. They needed to be girded. She gave him a coy glance. "Okay. So I made an assumption about you that was unfair. That makes it my turn to apologize again. Sorry."

Clyde's gaze eased just a little, shifting from the arrogant cast it had to it to a more affable, albeit cocky smile. "For someone who's so open to life after death, and ghosts and demons and all the other crazy shit that really does exist, you can be just a bit judgmental, but apology accepted."

In guilt, she looked down at her toes. "You're right. I was being judgmental and biased because of your fascination with facts and figures, and obscure shit like music trivia. You yourself said you were wrapped up in manuals and your research. Those can be cold things. They don't allow for gray areas. Possibilities that involve emotions."

Clyde's fingers tilted her chin up so she was forced to look at him. "So you immediately came to the conclusion that I'm incapable of believing in things like soul mates and true love. Which also meant I'd be attacking what you hope someday you can have. A husband. Children. Someone to love you until death do you part.

So here's something else you don't know—my parents had that. I've seen it firsthand. I lived it with them. Their marriage was a testament to true love. A deep, unconditional match made in soul mate history. I wanted the same thing—I just didn't find it with Tia. Conclusions without all the facts can be a tricky thing, Ghost Lady."

Delaney gulped, but the truth was the truth, painfully naked as it was. "I did jump to conclusions."

His eyes compelled her to hold his gaze, his grip on her chin almost forcing her head back and her neck to arch. "I'm not done. A few months ago I might have agreed with your assessment of me. I'm the first to admit, I didn't believe in a lot of things. Then Satan called my bluff. My perspective on things has changed since then. I had three months in Hell to give a great deal of thought to a lot of things in my life—things I missed out on, even some regrets. And while the logical side of me reminds me I can't go back and undo the time I didn't spend with people or the Christmas dinners I missed because I was wrapped up in my work, the other half of me, the half that's become maybe just a little sentimental, bordering on maudlin, wishes he could." His nostrils flared, his eyes flashed her "take that information and shove it up your ass" signals.

So shut up, you presumptuous, nosy, discriminatory, conclusion-jumping, ghost-channeling bitch.

Dude.

He was hard-core when he got riled up. So much so that she couldn't tear her eyes from him—or back away from the heat of his body, now so close they just missed touching one another.

The air in the room was suddenly gone—whether from his unexpected rant or from the breathlessness he created by standing this near, she wasn't sure. The lack of sound, the slowing of her heartbeat, the narrow pinpoint of vision that only included Clyde captivated her.

He leaned in even closer to make another point, but his voice had a low husky tone to it that was unmistakably sexy-serious. "I'm not mocking your secret desires, Delaney. I know how much you want those things. I didn't just read it in your file in Hell, I see it in the way you treat your dogs, in how much you seem to love Kellen, in your dedication to helping spirits cross over. In how you sacrificed your friend for her own good—and mine. I. Get. It. Don't ever mistake my love of science and logic for lacking a heart. I had one—I just didn't spend a lot of time listening to it when I had the chance."

Somewhere between the words "secret desires" and "dogs," her hands had somehow landed on his biceps, rounded, hard beneath hot skin. Her breathing had stopped entirely. Her libido had decided now was the perfect time to fire it up.

The choice was made before Delaney even considered not only the consequences, but that there would be an act that required consequences.

That choice being her lips all in attack mode, latching onto Clyde's like they were on lockdown. The force of their contact made Clyde rock backward, but he took her with him, crushing her against the length of his sculpted frame until her chest ached and her toes curled.

His tongue, silken, hot, drove into her mouth, pulling a gasp from somewhere deep in her throat. Her back was hard up against a wall, all at once, and without any memory of movement. Clyde's hands kneaded her spine, hoisting her legs up around his waist, dragging them lower and lower until she lifted her hips upward in soundless approval.

Reason flew out the window and hot on its heels was her sanity when Clyde pulled her skirt up, grazing fiery fingers over her thighs, caressing the sensitive flesh at the tops of them.

Her muscles clenched in aching response.

So did her ears when dogs number one and five began to howl.

Dogs two, three, four, and six joined the mix, their toenails clattering against the hardwood floor, bringing the clinch they were in to an abrupt halt.

Delaney tore her mouth from Clyde's with reluctance, leaning her head back against the wall to find air for her tortured lungs.

Clyde let his head rest against her jaw, his breath coming in jagged huffs. "Do they have to go to the bathroom?"

She pushed her head from the wall, directing her gaze at her puppies, scratching at Clyde's ankles, their tongues lolling from their mouths.

You had to love the timing of the departed.

This—this was the very reason she was never, ever going to get laid again.

Maybe not even in the next lifetime.

Delaney sighed the sigh of the defeated. "No. I don't think they have to make potties."

"I fed them. They can't be hungry," he said against her neck, tickling her flesh with a fan of his hot breath.

He'd fed them? Her gut fluttered in time with her heart because he'd done it without her ever mentioning a word. But no, they weren't hungry. "No. They're not hungry."

"So what are they?"

"Excited."

"About?"

"Remember back at Kellen's when I told you not to freak out?"

"Delaney?"

"Uh-huh?"

"If there's a guy without a head and he's anywhere near me, you're going to be a casualty I can't avoid—'cause I'm out."

"Understandable."

"Verdict?"

"Nah. His head's not on your shoulder this time."

A clear, relieved sigh escaped his chest, pushing against hers. "Location?"

Delaney said nothing. If she did, he'd get the squicks and flip again. How could she possibly help a lost spirit if Clyde, and whatever craziness he'd brought with him from Hell, kept chasing them away?

"Delaney?"

"Yes, Clyde?"

"Where's his head?"

"Do you mean the exact, exact location?"

"Yep. I mean the most exact location you're capable of giving me."

"Can you try not to freak out again if I tell you? Whenever you move, whatever kind of vibe you give off makes the spirits fade in and out. I can't do my job and help them if I can't see them for more than a couple of seconds. So if you promise not to move, I'll tell you."

"Uh, no. I'm trying to be a gentleman here and stay calm, but it wasn't your shoulder his head was on today. That's too much for even me. Now answer the question or it's your ass and the floor. You'll make the perfect couple. The head. Coordinates. Now."

It was so crazy hot when he made demands she had to force back a breathy sigh from escaping her lips. "Your foot."

"His head is on my foot?"

"Yeaaah. His expression, from here anyway, screams exhaustion. Maybe he was tired from carrying around his head. So he put it down. I can't blame him. Carrying your head around has to be a lot."

"A human head can weigh up to ten pounds, or so I think I've read. I could see him being tired." And then, as though he'd caught himself being practical when he really wanted to display his disgust and fear by brushing the head off his foot, a violent shudder ran the length of his body.

"Again, another useless fact I'll keep near and dear."

"Delaney?"

"Yes, Clyde?"

"Remember my standing apology between us?"

Uh-huh. She did. "I do."

"Good. Don't forget I meant it. Oh, and don't forget to bend your knees," he warned.

With those words, he dropped her.

eleven

Delaney hit the floor with a sharp, breath-stealing bounce, her ass scraping the wall on its way down. Thankfully, she did remember to bend her knees, the jolt to them no less jarring, but manageable.

Clyde shook his left foot with vigorous jabs at the room while he hopped on one foot. "Jesus Christ! What is it with these damned ghosts?" he yelled. "And before you say anything, I'm sorry for dropping you, but for shit's sake, his head was on my foot. His *head*." He shuddered once more, his large body visibly convulsing.

The dogs ran to the back of the store, stopping between the exit of the storefront and the entrance to her living room. Delaney ignored Clyde and ran behind them, hoping they'd sniffed out the entity's location.

Delaney found her spirit on the couch, his head neatly sitting in his lap as though he held nothing more significant than a plate of

Christmas cookies. The dogs hopped up on the couch, sniffing the air and stumbling over each other.

If you put the spirit's two pieces together, he'd probably been a decent-looking guy when he was alive. His hair was the color of straw, with white-blond highlights that poked out beneath his scrub cap. His skin was the ruddy color of someone who liked the outdoors and clean living. Eyes, a milk chocolate shade of brown deeply set beneath thick brows much darker than his hair, moved with animation. From his shoulders down, he appeared to be in pretty fine shape. The scrubs he wore clung to wide, lean shoulders. His fingers toyed with the scrub cap on top of his head, readjusting while it rested in his lap.

Delaney honed in on his lips, kneeling down in front of him to watch them with hawklike eyes. They moved, but no sound came out. Most likely because whatever had happened to him when he died had severed his vocal cords. Major suckage, in her opinion.

Clyde lumbered behind her with raucous clomps of his feet, stopping just behind the couch, making the entity's transparent form flutter.

She threw her hands up to keep him from going any farther. "Stop!"

Clyde froze in place like they were playing a game of freeze tag. One foot, mere inches from the floor, stopped midair. His eyes and nothing more moved from side to side, attempting to scan the room. "Where is he?"

She approached Clyde with care. "Right on the couch. Look down."

Clyde averted his eyes, staring straight ahead. "Uh, no. No headless guys for me, thanks."

"Just hold still. Not a muscle," she warned with a finger.

"Call me statue."

"Your mouth is a muscle."

"Actually, it's your tongue that's the muscle and it has—"

"Clyde!" she admonished low. "You're gonna be in the market for a new one after I yank it from your head if you don't can it. Be quiet!"

He clamped his delicious lips, lips that moments ago she'd accosted, shut. But then he lost his balance and his foot, almost to the floor, dropped like a rock.

Again, the entity crackled like snow on a television set. Shit, shit, shit.

Clyde instantly froze again, the glance he sent Delaney's way was one of apology, but the spirit kept fluttering.

Out of the blue, an idea came to her. "Clyde, move your head."

"My head . . ."

"Just do it."

"Which way?"

Her eyes darted from Clyde to the ghost. "To the left."

"Like this?"

The silvery transparency of the doctor began to fill in like a small child with crayons had begun to color in his outline. "Just a little more to the left. Like an inch. Oh! And hold your right arm up, too. Do it until I say stop."

Clyde did as she asked, tilting his head to the left and raising his right arm in an arc to just above his head.

Better. The doctor was coming in much better. "Stop. Now lift your left leg, bend it at the knee."

"A contortionist I'm not."

Her look was pleading. "Help a sistah out, okay?"

Clyde mumbled under his breath, but obligingly moved his leg up.

"Stop!" she whisper-yelled. "That's perfect." A sidelong glance at Clyde's awkward position almost made her burst out laughing. "Very *Crouching Tiger, Hidden Dragon*."

"Released in the year 2000—directed by Ang Lee—"

"Clyyyyde," she warned.

He scowled at her. "Hurry up. My arm hurts and my nose suddenly itches."

Delaney knelt back down and watched soundless lips move in the repeated pattern over and over. Fuck, if she could just hear him . . . "Oh, wait! There's an *o* in the word. Yeah, an *o* . . ." She paused, wracking her brain. "Wait, maybe it's not an *o*. Maybe it's a *u* . . . *uma*! I think he's saying *uma* . . ." But that made no frickin' sense. "I know it makes no sense, but that's what it looks like." She watched his lips once more, squinting to get a different perspective. "Uma? What the hell is an uma?" She directed her question to the dead guy. The corpse rolled his eyes upward with decided impatience.

"Thurman? Uma Thurman?" Clyde blurted out. "Born April 29, 1970, in—"

"Don't be ridiculous, Clyde—" The entity stopped her midsentence, shaking his detached head left then right on his lap. "See? He says that's not right," Delaney said over her shoulder.

The tension in Clyde's voice mounted. "Well, there is no such word as *uma*, Delaney, and could you hurry up? The Mr. Miyagi in me is about to crumble, Grasshopper."

"Omigod—*The Karate Kid*! I was ten, so, like, 1984 or so. Just starting to like boys. Ohhhh, I had such a crush on Ralph Macchio." She smiled fondly at the memory. "Remember wax on, wax off?" Delaney flipped her hands up and made swirling movements in the air. "Take that, trivia man."

"Delaney," Clyde said through teeth that were clamped, "now isn't the time to best me in movie trivia. I'm sweating bullets here, and my muscles are this close to spasm and becoming so bunched, I'll permanently be three inches shorter. *Hurry up*."

Delaney clucked her tongue at him. "If you'd taken yoga and

found your happy place, you'd be there right now and your muscles would be all yippy-skippy."

"*Delaney . . .*"

Okay, he was growling, and sweating, if the glisten on his forehead wasn't the lights in her living room playing tricks.

Her attention returned fully to the spirit, but she continued to remain as baffled as she'd been when he'd first moved his mouth. His insistence that she was wrong was compounded by the continual shake he gave his poor head in the very distinct manner of the word *no*. Desperation became helplessness. "Dude," she muttered to him, "I don't get it. Let's try something different. Are you a doctor?"

His fingers, nestled just above his head's ears, tilted it forward.

"Yes!" she shouted triumphantly. "Okay. A doctor. What kind of doctor? Pediatrician? General practitioner? Chiropractor? Ooooh, what about brain surgeon?"

The head moved to the left and the right again while his lips kept moving in the same pattern.

She bit a fingernail in concentration. "Damn. Okay, forget what kind of doctor you were. Is the reason you found me because of your profession? Like you want me to pass on a message to a patient, or their family?"

The spirit's outline began to fade again, frustrating her.

Clyde let out a grunt, his arms and legs giving out.

The moment Clyde slumped was the moment the spirit slipped away, evaporating into the air like a sliver of smoke. "Damn."

His look was apologetic. "I'm sorry. I'll get right on those yoga classes the moment I'm free of a little thing like Hell."

She pressed a finger to her temple. "Did you see him? Maybe if you'd watched his lips move, you might have caught something I didn't."

Clyde's body did that shudder thing again. "Delaney, I'll say this one more time. No. I didn't see him because I didn't want to see him. He has no head. I repeat. No head. I can't stress that enough. That's just too weird for me. Besides, I was too busy clenching every muscle in my body to focus on much else. I'm also not ashamed to admit I'm just a little squeamish about blood and detached body parts anywhere on my person. So what more do we know about him tonight than we did this afternoon? He's a doctor?"

"Yep, I think so. At least he made his head nod yes when I asked him if he was. Or he did something in the medical profession. He definitely lost his head in some kind of accident that had to suck big fat weenies. He was decapitated, I'm guessing. Can't think of another explanation for why he'd be carrying around his head."

Clyde jammed his hands in his pockets. "And we have the word *uma*. Which isn't really a word."

"Yep. Maybe he's foreign like the lady with the doily on her head." Damn, she should have asked him that, but with Clyde being her conduit for all things spiritual, it was distracting.

"Well, shit. I have to give you patience. This would drive me out of my mind."

Her shoulders lifted, then released. "It's what I do and sometimes, that's how the spirits roll. They aren't always sure why they're here either, or the message they're trying to send. It's all a part of my medium package. Sometimes I have to figure it out on my own with most of the pieces of the puzzle missing."

"Decapitated . . . you know, ironically, I once knew a guy who was decapitated."

"Ugh. Really?"

"And as a matter of fact, he was a doctor, too. Brutal car accident."

Maybe the spirit wanted to talk to Clyde? He'd said he was sick as a child . . . "Was he a young guy? Really blond with brown eyes? Very fit?"

"He did have brown eyes, but he was balding and had a paunch. It was a shame, too. He was a nice guy."

"And he was a doctor?"

"Yeah. Geriatric. My mother's."

Damn. "Well, your doc doesn't match my ghost's MO, anyway. So back to square one for the headless scalpel wielder. That's two ghosts in the matter of days who've shown up and I couldn't help them."

"Does that happen often?"

"Nope. So far, the only ghost I don't get is Darwin. I don't know why he won't hit the field of endless tennis balls and rawhide bones. But it's early in the game. Some spirits require more investigation than others and longer periods of interaction. But it's bothering me that they don't come in as clearly."

Clyde put a hand of sympathy on her shoulder, creating mayhem in her stomach. "And I realize that's my fault. However, I know what'd make you feel better."

Your rock-hard body up against mine? On mine? Under mine? In a boat, on a float? Or even in a moat . . . She mentally gasped. *Enough.* Delaney cleared her throat, moving away from Clyde. "What'd make me feel better?"

"My Slurpee. Bet if you had some of my banana Slurpee, you'd feel better."

She grinned. "Bet I'd rather just hand over my left lung and a kidney."

Clyde laughed. It rumbled from deep in his chest, making it strain against his borrowed polo shirt. "Don't knock it till you've tried it."

His laugh was sexy when it was unbidden. The word *unbidden* sounded a lot like *forbidden*—which Clyde was. As had been that kiss she'd thrown at him like she was whoring for dollars. She needed space to recover. Like big. "It's on my list of things to do. And now, I have to finish my inventory. Go amuse yourself. In fact, why not teach the dogs how to eat with the proper fork and polish my toenails for me. You're good at making them listen."

"You sure you don't need help?" His stance said, *I'm just trying to be polite by offering*, but his eyes said something different.

Something she couldn't quite read and was better off remaining illiterate to.

Flapping a hand at him, Delaney turned and backed out of the living room. "Nah. Go watch TV or something. It's just boring paperwork," she offered dismissively, turning toward the storefront. "I'll try to be quiet if you crash on the couch. But be warned," she called over her shoulder, "tomorrow—we go digging around your life and death." *Because you have to go—soon—if not sooner*. He was too appealing on too many levels to be ignored, and that just couldn't be.

End of.

"Clyyyyyyve . . . How's it goin', brother?"

The voice from behind Clyde, gravelly and harsh, crackled in his right ear as he sat on the couch, watching some inane program about a chef attacking unsuspecting women in a grocery store and taking them home to teach them how to cook. He didn't turn around, keeping his face impassive and his tone cool. Whoever it was, it was someone who'd come to check up on him, and they expected to find that psycho Clyve, not the tame, unassuming, nonconfrontational Clyde. So this would be where he could rely on all those movies he'd watched when he was so sick. "What the hell are *you* doing here?" he said, dry and disinterested, cracking his knuckles.

"My job, asshole, which is checking up on your sorry behind."

Clyde's jaw clenched while he ground his teeth together. It was crucial he remember he was pretending to be a sociopath. "Fuck you. I don't need a goddamned babysitter." *Niice,* he commended himself. Nice snarly quality to his tone with just enough affront in it to make it sound like he was really that freak Clyve.

The voice hopped over the couch, slouching down next to Clyde, his greasy stench, like dead, rotting flesh, putrefying in his nostrils. "Don't you think I fucking know that? I'm just doin' what I'm supposed to do to get by. That psychopath Pauley sent me to check up on you because I was in the area. So here I am. Nice cover, by the way. You never woulda gotten within a hundred yards of this chick looking the way you did before you left Hell. What made you pick a guy who looks like a reject in a Calvin Klein underwear ad?"

He grunted, jamming his fingers under his armpits. He hadn't picked anything. This really was what he looked like. But he remembered what Delaney'd said when he'd been duct-taped to the radiator and how some demons chose other forms to appear in. Clyde shrugged indifferently. "Saw it on the subway, and it wasn't Klein, it was Kors somebody. You know, like the beer?"

The demon beside him cackled, revealing missing teeth and breath that smelled like a Dumpster. "Good thing, too. You were one ugly son of a bitch."

Yeahhh. "Okay, so you've checked on me. Now get the fuck out."

The demon screwed up his ugly, bony face, his skin mottled with pockmarks. "Christ. Don't be such a fuckhead. You know what Pauley's like. Since he made level boss, he's up in our shit all the time. If he says check up on you—I'm doin' it, motherfucker."

He craned his neck around, eyeballing the living room, the stretched skin of his face shiny under the lamp. "Where is she, anyway? Shouldn't you be banging the shit out of her by now? It's almost eleven o'clock."

It was all he could do to keep from ramming his fist up this dick's ass and leave it tangled somewhere in his esophagus. "Walking those stupid mutts," he muttered. "But she'll be back." He gave the demon a sly grin, punching his fist into his hand. "You better get the hell out of here before she gets back. Her damned dogs can sniff out demons."

"And they didn't sniff out you?"

Clyde shot him another smug smile, adding a touch of lascivious and sneaky. "I'm that good. Don't forget it."

The demon slapped Clyde on the back. "She's pretty fuckin' hot. But I gotta tell ya, for the time she made my damned eyes feel like they were on fire, I can't wait to see her dead. But just before she bites it, I wanna give it to her good." He bent his arms at the elbows and made a lewd gesture with his hips.

Dead. The idea that Delaney'd miss out on all those things she wanted so much because she was dead made him want to heave. Clyde rolled his head on his neck, fighting the sudden burst of total rage at even just the hint this prick would come anywhere near Delaney—let alone touch her. It made his stomach roil, but he had to play along or he'd be fucked. He held his tongue instead. He'd never been one to rush into anything; keeping his head was more crucial than it'd ever been before.

"So we're cool, man?" he held out the top of his fist to Clyde.

With a sneer, Clyde ignored the dirt embedded under his fingernails and dropped his fist down on the demon's—hard.

He snapped his hand back, shaking it out. "Ow! What's your hard-on?"

"Pussy," Clyde spat, letting his own cackle erupt from his throat.

"Now get the fuck out of here before she comes back in and catches you here. I'm workin' her like a snitch works the feds."

He snorted. "You oughta know." The demon grinned wide, the rot of his teeth making Clyde want to turn away in disgust. But he couldn't do that. Apparently, whoever this asshole was, he'd known Clyve. That meant Clyde couldn't take a chance the man'd figure out he wasn't Clyve at all—and rat him out. The shit would get ugly if that happened and then he wouldn't be here to watch Delaney's butt. So he played along like they were long-lost buddies.

He slapped Clyde on the back again. "Yeah, yeah. Just remember, man, you're being watched. The big boss wants this chick— bad. Don't fuck it up or you'll never make level four. I'll tell Pauley you said hello."

"Do that."

The demon disappeared, leaving behind nothing but the foul stink of his rotting soul.

Dropping his head to his hands, Clyde inhaled a deep breath, shaking off the fear that rose in his throat like sour bile. How in the frig was he going to keep Hell from getting to Delaney? He was only one demon, and a sorry-assed one at that. Even if he could accumulate a power or two to help her, the shit he had to do to acquire them went so far against his nature, he couldn't even think it.

He'd never forget the kinds of things those demons had laughed over around that water cooler. He'd never forget how their black gurgles of laughter had erupted when they'd talked about Delaney's demise.

Now more than ever, he wanted to know what she'd done to have this much heat from Lucifer. The problem didn't just lie with her crossing over souls. She'd said herself that most of the people she'd crossed weren't the bottom-of-the-barrel souls. They were just indecisive, or needed to pass on one last message. She was their conduit for safe passage.

Something was out of whack with her claim of innocence. Something he had to make sure he found out before he had to leave her, or he'd risk leaving her to fuck knows what.

What would Satan do to her when he found out Clyde had fucked with his plans? How could he even consider crossing over knowing he'd leave her behind to face that alone? What would happen when his month was up and they came looking for Delaney's soul?

While he'd like to believe his fears for Delaney were nothing more than humane, he knew better. He hadn't experienced many women in his life, but he'd never experienced one like Delaney.

Right out of the gate, when he'd been looking down at her from that plane he'd been stuck on during the séance, he'd found her compelling. He'd been drawn to how utterly unaware she was that she had this fresh innocence about her. She had a sharp tongue, no doubt, and every time she used it to lambaste him for something new, he wanted to make it stop wagging by clamping his mouth over hers. And each time he was close to her he discovered something else he found attractive about her. All that red hair with darker strands of golden brown in it, for one. When was the last time he'd noticed fucking highlights in a woman's hair? Yet the compulsion to run his fingers through it tonight and take a deep whiff of the apple shampoo she used was driving him out of his mind.

As was the soft, supple melding of her body to his and the curve where waist met hip.

To make this attraction to Delaney even less likely, she had fluky ideas, crazy notions, and a healthy sense of humor, considering her lot in life as a medium. She ate things he couldn't pronounce that smelled like a Jersey dump, and believed in things he'd never heard of and couldn't be swayed to change her mind about.

Yet, he found he respected that—much more than he would have if he'd known her when he was alive.

Alive . . . now that was a problem. If he'd known her in life, he might have missed her due to the fact that he'd once thought clairvoyants like her were quacks. Now that he knew her in this unlife, there was no chance this could go any further because his time would be up in a few weeks.

But then there was that kiss. Two of them, to be precise. One just as hot as the next. Her lips had done things to him. Things that had never been done before her. Her body, clapped up against his like plaster on a wall, had left him with a raging hard-on and a lust that tore at every nerve ending he possessed. It'd been a while since he'd been intimate with anyone, and he realized that could play a part in how much she turned him on, but not all of what he'd felt with Delaney attached to him had to do with sex.

He liked her.

He didn't want her to be hurt.

He found he wanted her to have all the things she seemed to want so much.

He also found himself wondering if he were alive, with the kind of view he had on how precious life was now, if he wouldn't want to explore her desires *with* her.

Clyde halted those thoughts with a mental screech of metaphoric brakes.

That just couldn't happen. He'd come here, taken this bloodsucking assignment so he could get out of Hell with no idea he'd find himself attracted to this free spirit. Whether he succeeded or not, he had an egg timer attached to his time on this plane.

When it dinged—he'd never see Delaney again.

And that made his gut clench into a tight, unwelcome fist.

Fuck.

twelve

"Oh, Clyde. Is it my perfume? No, wait, I know. It's my animal magnetism. My va-va-voom. Yeah. 'Cause I have so much of that. It just oozes from my every pore." Her laughter tinkled, but her body was on fire. Clyde's arm around her waist, the crisp hairs on it brushing against her arm, made her nipples turn to tight beads—which was totally and utterly *pathetic*. Given how little it seemed to take to turn her on these days, she might as well start humping lampposts.

No disrespect meant to Clyde, who was far and away much more attractive than a lamppost.

Clyde stiffened behind her, stirring to the sound of her voice.

In fact, every part of his body was stiff.

Every. Part.

"I'm in your bed again? How do you suppose this keeps happening?" His voice rumbled, groggy with sleep in the deep velvet of the night.

"Uh-huh, and I'm taking a stab in the dark, but I think it must have to do with the binding."

"Right. The binding. Am I naked?"

Oh, sweet Jesus. Was he? "Were you nak—uh—nu—ah . . . when you went to bed on the couch earlier?"

"Affirmative."

Perfect. "Then I imagine not much's changed. And you're sucking up more than your fair share of the bed. Not to mention, you have all the covers. So you know what that means, don't you?"

"I'm apologizing?"

She giggled despite his sinfully tempting nudity. "No, you're taking the dogs out—as penance, bed hog."

His groan tickled her ear before he lifted his head to look at her alarm clock. "They're still asleep. It's three in the morning. So I say we go back to sleep, too. We deserve to sleep in, don't you think? It's been a rough few days." He burrowed closer to her; the impulse to lie back into his strength was pushing overwhelming, bordering desperate. Clyde curled his fingers into her waist when she tried to get up.

Delaney fought the hitch of her breath. "You're right. We have stuff to do, demon. So hit the bricks so we can get some sleep and call Tia in the morning. I'm still not convinced her being here at exactly the same time as you is a coincidence. I find it very strange rather than coincidental. I know you don't want—" Clyde rolled her over with swift hands, pulling her flush to him, making her forget why they had to call Tia.

But it was important.

Really important.

His blue eyes gazed into hers, glittering despite the late hour, and his hands spanned the width of her back, creating an arch in her spine that made her hips lift toward his. "We definitely have stuff to do." His nose pressed to hers, his breath caressed the corner of her mouth.

Wow—way to put some distance between you and the demon, Delaney. Get up, tard. Get up from this bed right now and don't look back. But . . . this was soooo nice. *And so wrong. Very wrong, Delaney Markham.* "This presents a problem, doesn't it?"

"I think it might."

The breath she took shuddered with nervous hitches, but if she was about anything, she was about honesty, and that was required here. "Let's just lay this on the line. If we do this, Clyde Atwell, you know it can't go anywhere, and I'm not just saying that like some standard 'no strings attached' line. I'm saying that because it really, really can't. *Ever.* We won't have to wonder if it'll end because it *will* end. No ifs, ands, or buts. Which might be completely fine with you. For all I know, you were a real playa in life and all this 'I was a lab rat always wrapped up in my work' is just crap." And even then, she didn't know if she'd still turn him down because if that really had been the case in Clyde's life, what diff did it make if in the end he'd be gone anyway?

Well, the difference is, you'd be shimming his shank just to shim.

Yes, indeedy.

Okay, so that was different, but not by a lot. Him and his shank would be on the highway to Heaven either way if all went according to what she hoped would happen to Clyde's soul. Yet, there was a safety in knowing he couldn't dump her because her gift interfered in their lives. There was also a safety in knowing he understood her gift and wouldn't be troubled by it the way anyone who didn't believe was. Plus, he didn't think she was a nutjob for talking to dead people. It was hard to deny the overall hotness of that.

"So in closing, this won't ever be anything but two people fulfilling their baser needs. As a demon, and if you're anything like Marcella, those needs can be demanding. If you're the nice guy you say you are, I don't want you all whiny with regrets after the fact because we just did it to do it."

The nod of his head against hers was in agreement. "First, even if that were true, and when you dig into my life, you'll see it's so far from the truth it borders ridiculous, that I have to leave when my time is up is also true. Second, I can't remember the last time I whined. So the question then becomes, do you want to take that risk, knowing what you know? Or maybe even what you don't know?"

"Do you?"

"I'm pretty sure I do."

Her cheeks warmed and her stomach fluttered. "Then I'm just going to be straight with you because I have absolutely nothing to lose. It's not like I'll ever run into you—there'll be no awkward encounters where I have to hide at the grocery store in the feminine protection aisle behind the pads with wings because you're there with your new hottie. I can't make an ass of myself with all that senseless begging and pleading with you not to break up with me, because you have no choice in the matter."

Clyde's eyes flashed an emotion she was unsure of before he said, "That much is true. So be straight."

"Alright, but here's the deal. Don't let me embarrass myself."

His laughter was deep, his hands warm and firm. "Deal."

It was do or die. "Okay, so straight up. I'm all about owning my needs. I haven't met a man yet, aside from you, who doesn't think I'm some fruitcake, making things up. I'm good with this being something temporary, knowing an opportunity like this might never happen again in my lifetime. Which is pathetic, and very, very sad, but whatever—my life is what it is. Not that you're just an opportunity . . . I mean, well, I'm just going to have to hope you know what I mean. But I want to be clear about me and who I am—this isn't something I . . . well, I've never had a one-night stand or anything even remotely like it. I'm no man-eater."

"Hall and Oats—"

She sighed.

"Sorry—it just happens." She could faintly see his grin was sheepish, the lines by his eyes crinkling with laughter.

"Could I just get this off my chest so I know we're not going to have any ugly misunderstandings?"

"Shoot."

"Okay, so I've had one serious relationship my entire life. And one sort-of relationship when my ghosts were off on sabbatical on some tropical island or something. I had a blissfully quiet period for about a month. They showed back up—he caught me in the bathroom talking to his shower curtain because my ghost was an old navy sea captain and the bathtub was his ship, labeled me batshit, and it was over. I don't have those hurdles with you, and that's fine by me. And on that note, I'm also going to be honest about something else, too. I find you okay looking. Seriously, like really okay looking . . . I don't know what you looked like before, but the human form you chose deserves a standing O." Delaney paused, shifting her eyes down to his chest, a mere silhouette in her darkened bedroom. "And I'm okay with this just being what it is." Though the regions of her heart were clearly less okay with it, judging from the size of the compression she'd just had in it.

Clyde tipped her chin up, catching her gaze with his. "Are you done?"

"I think my pop-up timer just popped." Delaney took a deep breath, the inhalation forcing their chests to once more press together. The rigid line of his body pressing against hers became maddening; the rigid line of his everything else wasn't helping either.

"I'd like to clear something up."

"Go on with yer bad self," she encouraged.

"This *is* what I look like. I didn't steal my image from anywhere. When I look at myself in the mirror, it's exactly what I looked like before I died."

Tight. "Consider that cleared up, then. Anything else you want to add?"

"Is this where I confess my past relationships, too?"

Delaney's laugh was hoarse and gritty. "You suck at small talk."

"Guilty again. But I just want to interject one thing."

"Interject."

"I find you really okay looking, too." He pushed the strands of hair clinging to her cheek away with gentle fingers.

Fire shot from her toes to her cheeks. So okay. Golden.

It was on.

Let the sexcapades begin.

Hell to the yeah.

But Clyde didn't make the first move. She wasn't sure if he was waiting for her. It'd been so long, she wasn't clear on what meant all systems go.

So she went for both of them.

Clenching her eyes shut, Delaney threw her arms around his neck and smashed her lips to his with fierce intent, but Clyde set her away from him with a flash of his white teeth and a rumbling chuckle. "Breathe. I need to do that in order to do this properly."

Delaney reared her head back, mortified. Oh, the shame of in-experience. "Sorry. All of a sudden, I'm just nervous . . . it's been a long time . . ."

Clyde hauled her closer, spanning his big hands over her lower back. "Understood. You can relax," he coaxed, nipping at her jaw with his teeth and lips.

A wave of shivers clung to her skin as he worked his way

toward her lips, grazing the shell of her ear, tracing a slow methodical pattern over it. Heat built in her chest, a simmer of blood sparking in her veins and nerve endings sizzling to life. Her heart began to thump so loud, she heard it in her ears, crashing erratically. The thickness in her throat created a lump of anxious energy.

Yet Clyde soothed her with confident, strong hands, allowing her time to not just anticipate, but acclimate.

His fingers slipped beneath the straps of her nightgown, dragging them over her shoulders. She let her arms slide free, the thin material falling to her waist, exposing her breasts. The cool air stung them pleasantly, making her nipples harden to tight peaks, rubbing against Clyde's chest with delightful friction.

Lips, molten hot and silken, trailed along the curve of her neck, teasing the sensitive hollow with flitting strokes. Delaney gasped when he finally took her mouth, gripping her shoulders, kneading her flesh. Clyde devoured her lips, skimming the crease between them, slipping his tongue inside the hot cavern, stroking the inside of her mouth.

Her arms wound around his neck, her fingers drove into the raw silk of his hair, clinging to the strands in pleasure. Clyde shoved the blankets that separated them away, pushing at them with impatience. Dragging her nightgown over her head, he tossed it to the side, then yanked her panties to her ankles. Even her feet trembled when she kicked them off the bed.

His groan was a husky moan when their bare skin collided, filling her with hot lust. Clyde pulled her thigh over his hip, caressing it with confident hands, leaving her quivering when he dipped his fingers between them.

Wet warmth flooded her, dizzying flashes of light behind her closed eyelids came and went as Clyde explored deeper, lower. An almost violent shudder ran the course of her body when he parted the curls of her sex, and stroked her with a light digit. Slipping down her length, he whispered kisses across her collarbone and along the indentation of her shoulders, stopping only when he reached a painfully tight nipple.

The first thrust of his hot tongue against her long neglected breast was lost to savoring when it created such an electric current. Delaney gasped, sharp, clear, leaving a ringing in her ears as she bucked up against his hand still between her legs.

His tongue rasped at her nipple, licking it to a fine point, blowing on it with a soft caress of air. The muscles of her stomach clenched so tight they coiled with pleasure/pain.

Slow, soft sips at her breast became hot, forceful tugs, creating decadent swirls of building excitement. Pressure between her legs mounted when Clyde drew the nub of her clit between two fingers, rolling it, stroking it until it swelled.

Her fingers drove into his hair, clenching fistfuls when he left her breasts and shimmied down along her body. Clyde knelt before her while his strong, urgent hands parted her thighs. His head dipped, his breath whispering over the most intimate part of her before his tongue took the first sensual stroke.

Delaney's hips bucked upward, reaching for the silken rasp of his tongue. Hot, sharp stings of pleasure taunted her, teased, building, pushing, driving her to find relief. Clyde's tongue grew more insistent, he drove a finger into her, reaching a place she didn't know existed, drawing a soft cry from her lips.

Tension mounted between her thighs, hot, wet, spiraling out of control until the last slick thrust Clyde took with his mouth and finger sent her head spinning. She clutched the sheets, driving her flesh against his mouth, gyrating against it, riding the sweet crest of orgasm.

Muscles flexed, clenching and unclenching with rigid jabs to her every nerve ending. Her chest rose and fell in heavy thrusts while she gulped for air.

And then Clyde was over her, demanding and hard, straddling her body with his. His cock jutted from between his strong thighs, her curious fingers grasped him, sliding her hands along the flaming silk of his length. Delaney couldn't see him very well in the velvety dark of the night, but she memorized every sharp angle of his body, caressing the rippled dips in his stomach, tracing a finger along the indentations at his hip bones.

Smooth skin fluttered under her fingertips when she kneaded the muscles of his thighs. Clyde groaned when she reached for his shaft once more, taking long passes, smoothing her fingers over the silken tip of it.

"*No more,*" he said with a gruff, husky demand, drawing her hand to him, bringing it to his lips and pressing an urgent kiss against it.

Her legs opened on instinct when Clyde sank against her, lying on top of her, skin against skin.

Delaney's sigh was from deep within her throat at the contact, her arms reaching upward to wrap around Clyde's neck. He pulled her legs high over his hips, teasing her swollen entrance with the tip of his cock. Their skin connected, searing her, lighting her flesh on fire.

The first thrust was slow, deep, exploratory, measuring her reaction. Her hips lifted upward to encourage him to go deeper as a flush of heat began to once more rise in the pit of her belly. Clyde lifted up on his hands, his face a shadow in the darkness, and his moan when he sank balls deep into her was one of satisfaction.

They found a rhythm, hips driving against hips, increasing in tempo until they crashed against one another's. Sweat glued their lower bodies together as Clyde stroked her, long and deep. The heels of her hands dug into his back when the torturous friction of the hair nestled between his legs rubbed against her clit, and her teeth clamped down on her lower lip to keep from screaming out.

He ground into her, rocking against her in a circular motion, changing her need for relief from intense to almost unbearable. When his head bent so he could capture a nipple between his lips, Delaney lost all sense of time and space.

There was only Clyde, driving more wildly into her with each thrust, stroking her nipple with his tongue, wringing her dry of all sanity. Her orgasm exploded, digging so far within her it made her stomach muscles clench, her nipples tighten unbearably, pinpointing every erogenous zone in her body.

When Clyde stiffened, his head fell back on his shoulders, his last thrust gliding effortlessly within her. He came with a low, soft moan, clenching his jaw so tight, she could see it even in the black of the night.

Delaney's breathing came at choppy intervals, wheezing from her lungs as though she'd smoked a thousand cigarettes.

Woo to the hoo.

Demon could wonk.

For all of Clyde's reason, for all of his logic and calm rationality, for all of his dweebiness, he ruled the bedsport like a mighty warrior. She'd have never suspected he'd be so amazing. Amazing at chess. Yeah. For sure. That just made sense. Solving trigonometry problems and doing some calculus for a chuckle. Yeppers. Book smart—no doubt.

But for the love of voracious, all-consuming sex, who knew he'd be such a wonderland of skill and vigor?

Dayum.

Clyde had obviously caught his breath. "So here's what I'm thinking, and I suspect as a woman, you want to know what I'm thinking, right?"

Oh, the brilliance. "If you want to tell me, sure." She gave a vague note to her tone so he wouldn't suspect she wondered if maybe all the time he'd spent reading books they hadn't been chemistry books at all, but more along the lines of stuff like *How to Make a Chick's Eyes Wobble with Your Tool of Love.*

"I think you didn't expect me to be very good at this."

Bagged and tagged, baby. She struggled to keep from squirming under his microscopic gaze. "I think you shouldn't think so much."

Clyde winked a sumptuous blue eye. "I think I'm okay with you thinking that. I'm not upset at all that you're surprised. It comes with the territory. I'm used to it."

"The territory?" she said, playing dumb.

"Let's not kid one another, Delaney. The nerd factor for me is high. I know a lot of useless stuff like '80s trivia, percentages, chemical mixtures—boring shit to most. No one expects me to have any prowess in bed. I don't mind saying, I like your look of sheer astonishment."

"And the geeks shall inherit the Earth," she teased.

"That's meek, and you just never can tell, huh?"

The dogs began to stir. When dog number two stuck his one eye in Clyde's face, the urgency in his vacant stare meant some serious potty. Clyde rolled off her, planting a light kiss on her nose. "You recover. I'll take the dogs out." He gave her a very pleased-with-himself, arrogant smile before rising from the bed and pulling on his shirt and jeans. He scooped puppies up with an ease that made her heart ooze warmth, dropping them to the floor, and whistling on his way out into the kitchen to gather leashes.

Delaney sat up, easing her feet to the floor and making her way to the bathroom on feet that wobbled and thighs that ached with each leaden step.

Recover. How rude—how presumptuous.

How true . . .

Landing at the sink in her bathroom, she gripped the edges while the cool, white porcelain of it seeped into her hot skin. She grabbed for her pink bathrobe from the hook on the back of the door and shrugged into it, inhaling the scent of Clyde the manly man when she did.

A splash of cool water to her face did nothing to cool the fiery mess her stomach was in.

Her reflection said it all. Clyde was right. She was astonished. She'd expected he'd be okay, maybe awkward because he wasn't exactly grace incarnate walking. She figured they might need to find a happy sexual medium, overcome a hurdle or two, but she'd never in a mill suspected he'd be so completely fantabulous her eyes would wobble.

There was nothing awkward or self-conscious about Clyde between a set of sheets. Dude had mad skills.

Or maybe she just thought they were mad because it'd been nigh on a friggin' millennium since she'd been so blissfully stomped.

But if she remembered her old life correctly, the one before ghosts and Lucifer and his demons had shown up, the sex hadn't been that fucktacular. Not on the level Clyde had taken it to. Of course, she'd been very young when her sex life had been in full swing. Maybe age and maturity, and okay, a dash of desperation changed your perspective.

Or did Clyde's demonicness play a role in his mastery?

Suck it up, princess, maybe it was just one helluva mating.

How depressing and exhilarating all at once.

Depressing because she might need to get as many rounds in as she could before Clyde blew this Popsicle plane and left her with nothing but erotic memories—her probability for any kind of relationship beyond a chance supernatural one was slimmer and slimmer by the year. Especially one as fulfilling as that encounter had been with Clyde. Yet she couldn't deny this slinky, I'm-a-total-woman, sex-kitten vibe she had going on—the shine of her eyes and the blush in her cheeks—was exhilarating.

She'd irrevocably changed the dynamic of their relationship, and that Clyde would leave had begun to fray her nerves, gnaw at the edges of her heart. Though, the risk she'd just taken by letting her instincts take over was one that had proven worthy on an intimate level she hadn't experienced with a man in many years.

And might not ever again if the only man on the planet willing to become even just a little involved who understood what she did, who believed, was Clyde.

What if she never had sex like that again? Was there anyone, dead or alive, who did what Clyde did?

Of course there was. It was silly to believe he was the only man ever to possess such incredible aptitude.

But what if there wasn't . . . if she ever became involved again, and the poor slob didn't live up to Clyde, what was she going to do? Ask him to do it like Clyde did it?

Deaf, dumb, and blind had a whole new meaning. She'd been better off in the dark about that particular brand of banging. The can of worms was officially open—Pandora's box blown wide-open.

The torrent of emotions involved in what she'd thought was just two people relieving some pent-up sexual energy was turning too deep, and that couldn't be allowed.

She inhaled, closing her eyes and searching for some inner calm.

But a familiar shiver called to her, forcing her to open her eyes. "Now is a bad time, Michael," she whispered, pushing her fingers through her tangled locks, trying to tame them.

The ghostly form nodded in agreement, but she wasn't sure if he was agreeing this was a bad time to catch her in the bathroom, or a bad time because she'd created a situation that might cause a great deal of pain—for her. Typically, he was playful and as well known for his pranks in the afterlife as he was in his life on his ghostly plane. Tonight? Not so much. "So what's up? What's on your mind tonight? Wanna hit Walnut Grove and play Name That *Little House on the Prairie* Episode? I think I've proven I know 'em all. You just can't stump me when it comes to the Ingalls clan, bud. And I'm really tired. So make it snappy or better yet, maybe we could hook up tomorrow?"

His dark, curly hair shook when he moved his head to the left, then the right.

No. He definitely didn't want to piddle tonight. She held her hands up in defeat. "Okay. I'm all out. Tell me what's on your mind."

Michael pointed a finger at her in an almost accusatory way. "*Highway to Heaven*," he said, but it was minus the fond smile that normally accompanied what Delaney considered reminiscence on Mr. Landon's part about his heyday as Charles Ingalls.

Delaney rolled her eyes—okay, message sent. Yes, yes, yes. Clyde should be upstairs. God, the pressure to perform. "Dude, I'm doing my best here. I'm pretty sure he shouldn't be in Hell, and yeah, yeah, what I just did in there was probably a bad idea. I don't need you to tell me that. And knock off the voyeurism—it's creepy. I'm going to help Clyde—swear it, okay? Is that what you want to hear?"

Michael frowned, the beauty of his smile fading, replaced with concern.

Her head cocked to the left. Her brain was addled by the wonk of a lifetime and her patience was all but shot. Yet, Michael without a smile on his face troubled her. He was her good-time Charlie ghost. Nary a trouble. "I don't get it? Is there something else you're trying to tell me that I'm failing miserably at understanding?"

Now he graced her with a warm, gleaming smile of acknowledgment. The laughter he'd been known for in his life whispered all around her in a swirl of delighted echoes. "*Bonanza*!"

She slapped a hand to her forehead, letting it slide over her weary eyes. "Oh, good. I hit the jackpot. Thank God I got something right, because Christ knows I've done nothing right so far. Wanna tell me what I hit?" Her hand fell from her face only to find him gone.

"Hey," she shouted at the ceiling. "Come back here. Was this one of your jokes? 'Cause I'm eggshell fragile right now, friend. This is me telling you, not flippin' funny."

The knock on the door startled her. "Delaney?"

She flung it open with a grunt. "Yeah?"

"You okay?"

"Dope."

"Am not."

"Not you, Clyde. Dope means I'm fine. I'm so fine, I couldn't be finer."

"Then why were you yelling?"

"Because Michael Landon makes me crazy sometimes."

He looked at her like she'd just gotten her crazy on. "Like *Bonanza* from 1959 to 1973 Michael Landon? Like *Little House on the Prairie* 1974 to 1983 Michael Landon? Little Joe? Charles Ingalls?"

Oy. "The one and only. I take it you were a fan?"

"My mother was. Loved him. So you don't just talk to dead people, you talk to dead famous people, too?"

"I talk to anybody who wants to talk to me, including dead celebrities. They pop in from time to time. I'm a captive audience, what can I say?" Her eyes cast downward, refusing to get lost in the depths of his. Lord only knew what her now awakened libido would do if she lingered.

"Someone's here to see you."

She poked her head around the door to scan her alarm clock.

"It's five in the morning. Is it Kellen? Is he okay?" Her heart began to thrash against her ribs.

"No. It's not Kellen. It's Marcella."

Oh, that meant hard-core.

Let the Spanish Inquisition begin.

thirteen

Clyde dragged a finger over her cheek, holding out his hand to her. She let him tug her to the kitchen, where Marcella sat at her small Formica table, drumming her pink nails on the surface.

"You girls talk. I'll take the puppies to bed." He planted a kiss on Delaney's forehead, corralled the dogs, and left her in awkward silence with her friend.

Marcella swung around in the seat, straddling the back of it with her long, bare legs. The olive of her skin gleamed under the kitchen light; her eyes, dark like the blackest coffee, were hard. She pinned Delaney with her gaze and held it like she was holding on to a sale item at Ann Taylor.

"You're in for a world of hurt, Delaney Markham. When this is over, you'll need someone to listen to you whine and snivel while I pass tissues to you and talk you out of eating the whole bucket of Kentucky Fried Chicken that'll only end up on your ass. You're short—all that extra weight's going to be very unattractive on someone of your stature, and I refuse to pacify you with bullshit like you're just big-boned. That someone should be me. You don't have any other friends. So the responsibility of keeping you from going emo with a blunt object and leaving this cruel world when that Clyde goes falls on me. I'm all about burdens." Her gaze dared Delaney to defy her assessment.

Her throat tightened. She so wanted to share everything with Marcella. Yet she knew she couldn't—shouldn't. "It's none of your business," she said with an offhanded tone.

Marcella shrugged her shoulders with feigned indifference. "Of course not, darling. It isn't my business until he runs over your heart like a Sherman tank. Then what will happen? You'll be calling me on the phone crying, apologizing, telling me how right I was and how wrong you were. Why not just let me save you the trouble by crucifying him now so we don't have to shop for wrinkle reducers? They're so overpriced."

"You're not right." Shit.

Marcella's eyebrow rose, condescending and sure. "How do you figure? Is he or is he not a demon?"

Vague. Be vague and noncommittal, Delaney. "Sort of . . ."

Marcella leaned forward with a hand on her full hip, pressing for an answer. "Is he or is he not here on some kind of day pass that has no choice but to be revoked?"

Her gut shuddered hard. Her throat clogged. "Maybe."

Marcella went for the jugular with her brand of steely determination. "Will he or will he not leave you when whatever he's here to do is *terminado*—er, finished?"

Delaney averted her eyes. "Yes." And if she could only express how rank that was. If she could only put her head on Marcella's shoulder and just have a good cry. If she could only figure out why Clyde's leaving was turning into a big deal . . .

"So how am I not right, *chica*? Please, commence with the explanations." Her face was smug. Smug and really, really pissed.

She had no defense against the stark truth. The coyote ugly truth, so she went for a different tact. "Didn't I tell you to go away and not come back until I told you to?"

"*Sí,*" Marcella said with a jut of her chin. "But this is me not listening to you. So go on, ghost whisperer gone over the edge, tell me how not right I am."

Tears, from frustration, from the reality of this situation, from anger because her friend was spot-on, from fear for her friend's safety, began to threaten. "Marcella, you have to go. *Please.*"

"Nope. I don't have to do anything I don't want to and I'm absolutely not leaving here until I have an answer."

"I'll get the salt." Her lower lip trembled as her resolve weakened.

And Marcella pounced all over her resolve, rising up over the back of the chair and thrusting her neck out. "Oh, the fuck you will. Ju arrre *mariquita*—a big-ass sissy. Ju—*you* hate demon expulsion and the mess it leaves, so save the threats. Now tell me what's going on and tell me now before my fiery temper makes me do something hasty. I want to know why you're sleeping with Clyde, and the reason better be good or I'll put a spell on him that makes his winkie shrivel up and fall off!"

"I can't." She looked down at the floor at her purple-painted toes.

"Oookay, then maybe you can tell me why you're all the rage in Hell these days? Your name's been tossed around more than a whore in a frat house."

Fuck. Now she was angry that Marcella just didn't know when to stop. "Marcella, I can't tell you anything. I can't. I won't. Go home. Go shop. Go do something far away from me."

"Aha! That's fear I hear in your voice. Fear for *me*—which

explains everything. It's not like I can't find out if I want to, Delaney—so you might as well knock the bottom out of it. Now. Because I'm not going away until I have some inkling as to why you're boffing the big boy. That bad big boy. The *very* bad big boy. I want to believe there's some logical explanation for it—but I'm having a really hard time putting it all together. So you do it for me."

Guilt infiltrated her morality, spreading like Ebola. "I wasn't. Boffing him, I mean. Not until tonight, and that's all you need to know."

"You're going to make me use plan B, aren't you?"

"What's plan B?"

Her smile became suddenly playful. "That's where I duct-tape *you* to a chair and dangle red meat in your face while I mainline icky preservatives into your veins to make you talk. I may not be a very good demon, but I can totally take you."

Delaney burst out laughing, quivering with partial relief. "If I could tell you and know it wouldn't put you right in Lucifer's line of fire, I would."

"So threatening me with monstrous acts of salt hurling was to protect me?"

"Yes."

"And fuck Lucifer. Like that asshole's stopped me so far."

Delaney waved a warning finger under Marcella's nose. "That's only because he's chosen not to stop you, Marcella. You might be one kick-ass broad, but you're no match for Satan. You know it and I know it. Let's not pretend anything different. Don't go talking shit because you're angry. If you weren't already dead, I'd say your temper would be the death of you."

Understanding spread over her beautiful face. "So you're worried about trouble with the pitchfork lover. You never have been before—what's the deal now?"

"Yes, I'm worried, and stop asking me questions."

"No. Then what's the sleeping with the enemy about?"

"He's not the enemy."

That stopped Marcella cold. She shook her glossy black head. "Come again?"

"He's not the enemy, Marcella. That's all I can tell you. The less you know the better off you'll be."

"And you're sure he's not the enemy, how? Divine intervention?"

Her fist tightened at her abdomen. "Gut instinct."

"Oh. Good. Your gut tells you he's not a bad guy, but he comes from Hell and he's a demon. Good instincts, D. Remember when your gut instincts told you Jennifer Aniston and Brad Pitt were soul mates?"

"He's not supposed to be a demon, Marcella." That she was jumping to Clyde's defense was so transparent. She felt like she was telling her mother he'd only been convicted of one little felony—it wasn't like he'd committed homicide.

Her look screamed scathing. "Yeah, me neither, but whaddya know—I am."

"His story's much different than yours, Marcella. I just need you to believe that and knock the interrogation off. *Please.*"

"Well, his story must have some similarities to mine or he wouldn't be in Hell. Did he fuck up going into the light, too?"

"No," she gritted out. "And I'm not saying another word."

Marcella flipped up her palm. "That works. I'll say all the words. First, I've been hearing your name from some of the other demons I sometimes run into when I'm trying to well, you know . . ."

"Hook up?"

Marcella's expression soured, but her eyes glittered. "Don't hate. I'm a demon. We have needs that can't be denied—they're bigger than we are. It's more of a curse than anything—so save the Bible thumping. I am what I am. I'm always careful, and I never see my prey again. That's all beside the point I'm making here. What's going down with you and Hell? Why are you all of a sudden prom queen there?"

Delaney tugged at her lip with her fingers. "I'm not budging."

"Wanna know what they're saying?"

Damn. And then it happened. She cracked—big—wide-open. "Yes," Delaney sputtered.

"They're saying you're due some serious throwdown from the boss and they all seem to be getting a real kick out of it. Oh, they were having a fine time talking smack about you at this club I was in. I almost ruined a perfectly good purse, beating the snot out of one slug for it. That makes me really angry. It was a nice purse—red with gold piping. So what did you do to piss the fucker off?"

If she were truthful by omission here, she truly didn't know what Lucifer was so het up about other than she'd beaten him to the punch. The punch that still made no sense to her. He'd still won in the end, though in a roundabout way. So she was going to lie—again. It was becoming a habit. "I don't know."

Marcella's huff was harsh. "I get the feeling I'm being bamboozled here, *amiga*, and I don't like it. You might not know the exact origins of Satan's issue with you, but you have an idea what his freak is about and it has to do with Clyde . . ."

Among other things. "In a very roundabout way. Look, Marcella, I'm begging you here—stop asking me questions. When the time comes, I'll tell you whatever you want to know, but I can't right now. Not now."

The chair scraped the floor as Marcella rose, smoothing her short, floral dress over her legs and straightening her cropped blue denim jacket. "You do know what you're doing is *loco*, right? Toying with Clyde, even if only on a sexual level, that just isn't you, D. You're going to get hurt. I can feel it, and I don't want that to happen. You're vulnerable to a man's attention. *Any man*. You haven't been even a little involved with anyone for a very long time. The last man's name I heard you utter was the fuck who cheated on you back in college—Harry—Larry—whoever."

"Gary," she provided helpfully, then cringed at the mention of his name. Gary was a large part of the reason she'd had the run-in with Satan to begin with. Gary and Vincent.

"Yeah, him. So stop this now before it goes any further. You'll only end up with red eyes and a runny nose, but worse, a broken heart."

"Then remember the bucket of chicken. Extra crispy, no wings, please."

Marcella tweaked her cheek, but her eyes were on fire. "If Lucifer plans to harm one hair on your head—"

"You'll go all gangsta on him."

She nodded her head in the affirmative. "With every pathetic fireball I've got. I'll go, D, because I get now that you're looking out for me, and as much as I appreciate that, as much as I love you to itty-bitty bits for it, I can take care of myself. I've been doing it for a long time now. My friendship with you has never been a problem for Satan before. I'd have to wonder if he even knows about it. But the talk I've been hearing says you're going to get yours in a big way, and it scares the living shit out of me. And for what? You cross over souls who are nothing more than disoriented. You don't steal potential clients bound for Purgatory. Sometimes you cause a good eyeball bleed with a demon or two. Big deal.

"If that's what Lucifer's so pissed about, why is he taking action now? You've been doing it all your life. So whatever's going on has to do with something that happened recently. Why you can't tell me is very suspicious—especially seeing as I'm probably the best connection to Hell you have and more than likely could help you. So okay, because you keep giving me those pleading eyes and vibing some fucked-up body language, I'll go, but I can't promise I'll stay gone."

Delaney bit her tongue to keep from refuting her friend's statements. On impulse, she grabbed Marcella's hand, squeezing it. "Just stay out of it. *Please.* Don't ask questions. Don't go fishing for information from demons in bars. Satan barely knows you exist, but if he finds out we hang, you're toast, seeing as I'm in his sights these days. Please, just trust me."

Marcella squeezed back, letting Delaney know everything between them was okay. "Right. Oh, and I'll expect apologies and shopping when all's said and done for the trauma you've caused me this past week. You'd better line up some séances soon or you won't have the kind of cash I'll need to cover my trauma. Later, *chica.*" She waved a finger before disappearing into the dark of Delaney's living room.

On a shaky release of breath, Delaney sat in the chair Marcella'd vacated. Christ on a cracker—this clearly wasn't going to go away. First Clyde and his water cooler confessions, now Marcella and rumblings of demonic glee at her downfall.

Waiting for the blow—wondering what she was in store for—was like watching toxic ketchup drip.

Marcella was wrong on so many counts, she'd lost count. Her assumption that Delaney'd been connected to the supernatural all her life was wrong. She hadn't been born with the gift—she'd acquired it.

After Vincent.

Hands, big and all encompassing, lay with flat palms on her shoulders. "So how'd it go?"

"Well, I still have curtains and I don't think I learned any new cusswords in Spanish—so not too shabby, I guess," she joked, though she didn't lift her head. She let Clyde's soothing hands melt into her, reveling in the calm they attempted to bring.

"So here's my question. What is it that you're not telling me about this beef Lucifer has with you? There's more. I want to know what."

"Just because you got into my knickers doesn't mean you're entitled to know everything, demon." The effort to keep her voice even and light was monumental. Clyde had to leave and do it before he found anything else out about her torrid past with Satan. If she could get him gone before Lucifer found out Clyde had switched assignments, she'd breathe so much easier. If he got wind of the fact that Clyde wasn't doing as ordered, and he came calling, Christ only knew what would happen to not just her, but Clyde's soul.

"Remember when I told you, you were funny?"

"Yep."

"It would seem that's not always the case. Stop making light and tell me what's going on."

The more concern he showed, the more Delaney believed Clyde was totally capable of sticking around in his noble efforts to help her, and she refused to jeopardize his crossing. "I don't know, and right now, I'm too tired to care."

"You do know, and before you ship me off, I'll find out."

If the gods were kind, he'd ship off long before he had the chance to find anything out. If the gods were kinder still, they'd make his exit as painless as possible for her. "I got nuthin', Clyde Atwell. What we do have to do is investigate your death. Today. It's almost five thirty and I'll never get back to sleep now. So go find your brainiac tools and meet me back here in the kitchen so we can call Tia."

Clyde's hands gave her shoulders a gentle squeeze before he left her alone in the kitchen.

Alone to ponder Lucifer's next move and batten down the hatches.

Now, to find something to batten with.

fourteen

By late afternoon, they were no closer to finding out what had happened to Clyde than they were to finding the exact location of the Bermuda Triangle. Tia's cell phone number had apparently been disconnected, Clyde couldn't remember exactly where her brother lived, and he was unlisted. The North Dakota newspapers had not a single obituary listed for a Clyde Atwell in the last three months, and absolutely no mention of a police investigation involving his accident.

They sat together at her kitchen table with her laptop popped open, heads pressed together deep in thought. The dogs scattered at their feet sighed contentedly on occasion, stirring if Clyde made like he might move out of their direct line of vision.

Rubbing her eyes with the heels of her hand, Delaney asked, "How about a neighbor? Did you have a neighbor you were friendly with who might be able to tell us what the frig's going on? Because this makes no sense, Clyde. It's like you never existed."

Clyde rolled his head from side to side, massaging the muscles of his neck with the palm of his hand. "I didn't talk to my neighbors much."

Delaney slapped her palm against her thigh. "How silly of me to think you might have actually been sociable. So backyard barbecues and block parties weren't your thing?"

"Nope."

"A friend? Got any? Even just one? Maybe someone you worked out with? You didn't get that Body by Jake from sitting on your ass all day."

He smiled, clearly pleased by her assessment. "Actually, it was Body by Chuck Norris and I jogged. No workout buddies."

Te-rrific. He had to be the most isolated person she'd ever met. Aside from maybe her and she at least had a friend. Maybe it was only one, but one was more than none. "Oh, wait, I know! What about the freelance work you did? Couldn't we call one of the companies you did work for and see if they know what happened?"

"Now there's an idea . . ." Clyde's posture changed from slumped in defeat to upright and ready to attack.

She reached for her cell phone. "Number?"

He slumped again. "Shit. I can't remember it."

"Name of the company?"

His face was completely blank.

"Clyde?"

Shock was an absolute in Clyde's expression. "I can't remember. Holy shit. I can't remember."

Convenient? Maybe. "You do realize how suspicious this looks, don't you? You have no friends back home. There's no obituary for you—no police reports. Tia's number is disconnected and you can't remember the company you were freelancing for. Crazy that." Her response to his sudden blank spot was dry with sarcasm.

His fingers flitted across his temple as though he were searching for his memory. "I swear to you, Delaney, I don't know why I can't remember—I just can't."

"But you had no trouble remembering tons of other stuff about what your life was like, where all this work that blew you up took place, where your lab was . . ."

"I hear the suspicious tone in your voice, Delaney, and I'm not liking it. I can't remember, and I'm not lying. *Don't* go there."

God, even if he was lying—it was hot when he did. Extra hot because Clyde didn't strike her as the kind of guy who liked to throw down unless he had to. Conviction suited him—but he'd remembered plenty about his life before today, and that bothered her. "Well, where the fuck am I supposed to go, Clyde? You knew plenty of details a few days ago, and now you expect me to believe you can't remember who you were doing work for?"

His blue eyes narrowed to slits. "Yeah, I do."

"Why's that? Because you got in my drawers?" *Oh. Low, Delaney. Way.* Even as the words slipped from her fresh mouth, she knew it was low. And so uncalled for. Weariness and frustration were always an ugly combo for her.

Clearly Clyde was preparing his windup, but they were interrupted by the tinkle of the chimes on the door of the store.

"Meees Delaney! I am here. Ju are better, jes?"

Crap on a stick.

Clyde looked at her with a question.

"Mrs. Ramirez—short, chubby Puerto Rican lady, remember?" she whispered, jumping up from the chair. "She helps me in the store. I've got to get rid of her before—"

"There ju are! Oh, Mees Delaney—" Mrs. Ramirez's words stopped short when she came around the corner. The dogs jumped at her ankles, but she paid no mind. Her mouth fell open in the shape of a perfect *O*.

Clyde rose from his chair, sticking his hand out to her. "Clyde Atwell. Pleasure." He grinned all pearly white and gentlemanly.

Wherein, the romantic in Mrs. Ramirez appropriately melted. That perfect O her lips had created turned into a grin that spanned her entire face. Her head bobbed with understanding, her heavy floral perfume wafting to Delaney's nose. She nudged Delaney with a secretive glance. "Now I know why ju are seeck. Ju are loveseeck. Ees soooo nice." She nodded her approval while her eyes roamed the length of Clyde.

Hoo boy. She had some splainin' to do. "No, Mrs. Ramirez—this isn't what you think—"

"Ju no be chy, Delaney. Ees won'erful!" She clapped her hands together with a girlish giggle of pure delight.

"Chy?" Clyde asked.

"Shy," Delaney translated. "Just hush," she said out of the corner of her mouth.

Mrs. Ramirez made a circle around Clyde's body, lingering momentarily on his backend. "Ees about ti', too, jung ladee. Ju is always talkeeng to de dead persons dat nobody see but ju. Thass no good for de soul. Ju is alone too much. Now ju ees not alone. Ees soooo good!"

Delaney bit her tongue before saying, "No, Mrs. Ramirez, this isn't what you think. Clyde's just a friend and someone has to talk to the dead persons. That's my job."

Mrs. Ramirez clucked her tongue. "Ju make de persons up because ju are lonleey. Ees okay. I un'erstan'. An' I don' know no frien' who looks at his other frien' like dat. Ees okay. I no tell nobody."

Right. An hour from now the entire East Village would be doing the wave in her honor because Delaney Markham's dry spell was over. "I don't make them up. And I'm telling the truth, Mrs. Ramirez, this isn't—"

She flapped a pudgy hand in Delaney's face. "Now, ju two go. Ees almost ti' for deener. I watch de babies—ju go eat or someting. Ju take my Delaney so'where nice, hookay?" She patted Clyde on the back before rooting at her feet to scoop up dog number four to check his diaper. "Ju are wet, Meester Fancy Pants. We feex." She gave Clyde and Delaney the stink eye. "Whe' I co'e back, ju be gone." She turned her back on them, making a beeline for Delaney's bathroom and leaving no room for discussion.

Clyde held out his arm to her, his smile cocky and condescending. "So whaddya say we go and eat and you can attack my character, say, somewhere much more public? You know, so you can tell me how you really feel with a live audience."

She pursed her lips, grabbing her coat and scarf. "You know, it's not impossible that you've been lying to me, Clyde Atwell," she said in hushed tones, letting him help her with her jacket. "This sudden blank you've drawn would be stupid of me to ignore."

"Yep." He sauntered to the storefront, opening the door for her.

"That's it? That's all the denial I get?"

"Yep. What good does it do me to defend myself when those wheels in your head are turning at a pace faster than the speed of light? It's wasted energy."

"Which is very practical," she said, fighting the grin she wanted to let loose when he laced his fingers with hers. "However, not terribly passionate."

"Passionate?"

"Yeah. Passionate. To defend yourself would show some passion."

"To defend myself would be useless. You'll think what you want whether I tell you differently or not. Until you have solid proof to the contrary, you want to find something to harp on me for, some imperfection, big or small, to make me a bad guy. That means when I go, which you were all about reminding me I have to do last night—you can console yourself with the fact that I was just a jerk. A liar. The other possibility is, if you can catch me in a lie, you don't have to let your guard down. You don't have to let me in. I get it."

Delaney stopped dead in the middle of the sidewalk, ignoring the people who passed by. Right in front of Anthony's ("All You Can Eat Kielbasa and Pasta"), she decided to let him have it. "Let you in? Where am I not letting you in to?" Besides her drawers. Done. She'd done that. In fact, she hadn't just let him in, she'd thrown the door open for him.

The cool night air settled between them before he spoke. "Your life. Don't kid yourself into thinking I don't get you, Delaney. You're as isolated as I ever was. My situation was work related, yours is just situational, but it's the same damned thing. You haven't had a relationship in a long time, and now you're afraid. You're ready to condemn me because it's as good an excuse as any to stop any more intimacy between us. That means you can't be hurt when I have to go. That's because you like me. If this is your way of subconsciously telling me you're freaking out because last night was that good, let 'er rip, but don't hide."

She didn't even lower her voice when a young couple strolled past them hand in hand. "Wow, Freud, thanks. My life in a paragraph. And quit patting yourself on the back about last night, Dr. Love. You'll pull a muscle." She cast him a scathing glance, tucking her purse back over her shoulder.

"I'm only speaking the truth, and, I might add, I did it with passion." He chucked her under the chin, then kissed the tip of her nose.

But she shook him off. "I'm not accusing you of lying because I don't want to sleep with you again, Clyde." Or was she? Was she just looking out for herself and the possibility that if she let Clyde have too much of her, she'd end up hurt because there was absolutely no doubt he was hitting another plane and soon? It dawned on her that she was afraid she'd become too attached. This fear she carried around didn't solely have to do with the terror of retribution from Satan if he found out Clyde wasn't breaking her.

His gaze held hers for an uncomfortable period of time before he responded with an easy smile. "Yeah, you are. You don't want to get too attached. Each time you've gotten attached to someone or something, it ended. And that hurt. I make it worse because I understand your gift. I believe in it, and it doesn't freak me out. It's not something I couldn't learn to live with. That makes me one step ahead of everyone else you've been involved with. The others found out about it by circumstance and freaked out and the relationship ended—with a navy sea captain, as I recall. If you can keep me from you by pretending I've been lying to you, not only will you not end up being what you call played, you'll protect yourself from the end result of this fiasco. Me leaving. What I wonder is this. What's going to happen when you find out I'm telling the truth, Delaney?"

Her stomach rose and fell like the swell of the ocean; her heart pounded in loud, harsh beats. The neon light of Anthony's blared with its annoying redness, exposing her. Horns blared, people meandered along the sidewalk, yet all she could feel was the night swallowing her whole.

Okay, so she didn't want to get too attached and for all her "I'm an informed, mature woman of the new millennium" talk last night, for all the "this has to end" rhetoric, Clyde had hit the nail on the head. It must not be in her to live for the moment. She wasn't the kind of chick to tap it and skip back off to her life with a satisfied smile. Her desire to have children, to create a family, was stronger than even some mind-blowing sex. She wanted more, and even if she wasn't sure something like that could ever develop with Clyde at this early stage in their relationship, he had so many of the right qualities that it sent her into a full-on freak.

But there were facts she couldn't ignore.

He liked her dogs. They loved him to the point of ignoring her as of late. He was wicked-ass hot, but had no clue how brick shit-house he was. He was smart. Most of all, he understood the life she'd been living—the ghosts she communicated with. That was half the battle in finding someone to share her whacky life with, and that he'd have no choice but to go before she could get to know him better just plain sucked wankers. That she wanted to know him beyond this fairly superficial level troubled her more.

"Ms. Markham? Care to elaborate? Maybe fight back with some of that *passion*?" he taunted.

"No."

"Sulking much?" He grinned, obviously to show her he was teasing, but she wasn't laughing.

Her arms crossed in protective mode over her chest. "What's all this about anyway, Clyde? You don't strike me as the kind of guy who likes to get deep unless it's knee deep in H_2O_2, or whatever it was that you creamed yourself with."

The hand that had held hers tucked deep into the pocket of his jeans; his lips were grim. "I think I'm turning over a new leaf. Maybe it's a little late, maybe it's well past the time it was due, but there it is. I spent ridiculous amounts of time buried in books about life, but I didn't gorge on life itself. Looking back, I would have done it differently. So I'm paying closer attention, and paying closer attention means that I see you, Delaney. I know you and how you tick. I want you to see that interacting only with the dead has left you with blind spots to everything else. I want you to see what I see now that I'm dead. And I don't want you to miss out on what you want because you won't at least try or realize that you're not really trying at all."

Her mouth might have fallen open in astonishment if not for the fact that she had so much to say. "Have I mentioned what my life's like, seeing dead people? Were you not present for the overall synopsis?"

Clyde's head dipped. "I was there. I'm here now, and from my vantage point, I'm seeing someone who's been rejected because of something she can't control, and then decided it was much safer to stay at home with her dogs and Melinda Gordon than it was to take a risk."

If only that was the entirety of her self-imposed isolation. It would be a much simpler explanation than the real reason. Sure, the medium thing was a difficult pill to try to make someone swallow, and that she'd given up on a relationship was just as well, because Satan's threat to hurt anyone she came in contact with brought her more fear than telling someone she talked to the dead.

Delaney threw her hands up in the air in disbelief. "A risk? Risk? Did you smoke a bong when I wasn't looking? Maybe hit my herbs and some paper towels for rolling? That's not all this is, Clyde. This is about something much bigger than a risk." A risk. Risk this, asshole. He had no idea what it was like to have to explain why and how lamps and dishes and a host of other objects had managed to become airborne without her moving a muscle. Or why she was in the coat closet, talking to fucking nothing. Risk *that*.

But Clyde wasn't letting go. Yet he appeared neither angry nor even a little frustrated. His quiet urgency set the hairs on the back of her neck standing on end. "No, that's exactly what it is. If you live the rest of your Friday nights at home on your bed with your dogs, watching *Ghost Whisperer* in that ratty bathrobe, it's a much safer bet you won't meet someone who thinks you're a kook. It's easier. But I'm here to tell you, *Ghost Whisperer* will be canceled someday. I know that offends your sensibilities, but even J-Love won't be around forever. You can either replace it with some other show, or you can go out and get a life. Getting a life is a lot harder than finding something new to watch on TV. It's work."

She was aghast, but it didn't keep her from defending her position. "When prospective dates think you're crazy, when even the average female you meet at the gym finds out you think you see ghosts, shit changes. Save the speech."

"Know what I did when you went to help that customer today while we were surfing the Net?" The smug look he gave her, right there in the middle of the sidewalk, said he'd found some fact about something he could throw at her like a fastball to back up his new life plan for her.

Delaney stuck her neck out while she shook her head. "No, Clyde, what did you do? Absorb a class in psychiatry at the speed of light so you could tell me what's wrong with me?" She chose not to hide the sarcasm in her tone this time. In fact, she let it drip right off her words and into the space between them like puddles of melting hot chocolate on ice cream.

But he smiled wider. "Nope. I searched mediums, and forums for mediums. I'm laying bets there's plenty of them out there. Mediums, that is. People who feel just like you do. People who have the same sorts of social problems you experience because ghosts show up at inopportune times. Don't think you're all that special, Delaney. You're not the only woman with a burden to bear. Maybe you should get over yourself."

Get over herself? Get. Over. Herself. Easy for him to say. Red flooded her cheeks and fire raced along her neck in a flush of color. "I never said I was special, demon. I said it was hard to meet people. And hey, Mr. Supernatural—why don't you saunter up to someone and tell them you're a real, live demon? See how well that goes down. And P.S., over ninety percent of those people you found online are all full of shit. I've seen some fruit loops in my time, and they don't even see their own shadows, let alone the spirits." She'd been to some of those forums and discovered the real shysters. She was accused of being one all the time, and yeah, it had put her off most of the human race. So the fuck what.

Clamping his hands on her shoulders, Clyde forced her to look him in the eye, and he wasn't smiling anymore—he was intent. "Then that leaves ten percent who aren't full of shit. Go figure. But you wouldn't know that because you won't even give it a chance. Why couldn't one of those people be someone you spend some time with? Get to know. Have some goat cheese with? Get off your ass and try."

"I hate goat cheese." Which was a lovely defense and totally not true.

Clyde shook his head with a firm not-buying-it. "No, you hate *rejection* and the smallest hint of it. You don't do it because it's the looking for what you want that you don't want to do. So let's say you hook up with someone—or a hundred someones and they all call you a kook. You didn't lose a limb—it won't kill you. It's just words, Delaney. You're not afraid of words, are you? You call me enough of them. But what if there's just one someone in that bunch who doesn't think you're a nut? Imagine that . . .

"This isn't about me lying to you. This is about me giving you some hard truths from a perspective you have to admit is pretty damned accurate. It's about indulging in the possibility you'll end up alone, and not only letting it happen but wallowing in it. It's so much safer, but look where alone got me. I can't even find my cold, dead body, and I have no one who's alive to do it for me. Some would say that's pretty pathetic. Is that what you want?"

Her eyes rolled, and her mouth opened. "I want you to get off my ass and stop projecting your postmortem introspections about how insulated your life was on me. My life isn't anything like yours." She bit the inside of her cheek to keep from gearing up for a good smackdown. He was rubbing her raw, and it was pissing her the fuck off.

"Because my introspection's too close to home?"

"Because it's a retarded comparison."

"Because it's a comparison that's relevant."

She finally shrugged his hands off her shoulders with a shake. "Why do you care how I end up, Clyde? What goddamned difference does it make to you if I end up in a rocking chair at a state-run nursing home and die with the title Crazy Dog Lady?"

"Because I like you. When you like someone, you want good things for them. See? That was easy to say. Now you say it, too. I—like—you—Clyde."

Poof, her anger was gone. Just like that, and the bubble of a giggle formed in her throat. "No."

"Then at least admit it was hasty to call me a liar, and answer the question. Am I right when I say you're afraid to be shot down?"

She giggled without thinking, her anger ebbing. "Look, this blank you've drawn—or *claim* you've drawn—is pretty suspicious. If you were me, what would you think?"

"That wasn't the question. Don't avoid the answer."

The sigh she expelled was exaggerated and ragged. Cool air blew from her lips in a puff of irritation. "Fiiiine. I'm afraid I'll get too attached to you because you understand me and my life and my stupid, traitorous dogs. But I'm also afraid to mistake those qualities for something more than what they are and what this is. It would be stupid of me to think that, just because you acknowledge I can see ghosts, you're the missing half of me. So get the proverbial grip. We're about as different as two people can be thus far. You shovel the most offensive crap into your body—dead or not. I'd rather die than drink a banana Slurpee. You're passionate about percentages and the square root of five, and I'm passionate about herbal remedies and ghosts and dogs who have no homes and no one to love them.

"Okay? Yes, it's damned hard to be rejected and called crazy. Yes, it's hard to put yourself out there when you know most people think you're a cracker. My shot at all the things Satan wants to see me trashed over lessens all the time. But my shot for those things isn't any greater with you because you're outta here in a couple of weeks. Yes, you get it—you get what goes on in the madness of my communication with the dead—but you don't know me and I don't really know you. Letting you in won't make a difference one way or the other because a few weeks is hardly enough time to know someone." Right?

"And you like me. Given the chance to spend some time with me, if you weren't such a chicken, and we had more time, you'd do it."

And? "But we don't have more time."

"Now who's the logical one?"

When your heart's at stake, logic can be your BFF. She'd had enough. Hurling the obvious in her face had become tired. "Aren't we supposed to be eating?" She pushed off on her heel, turning to head down the sidewalk. Her fears were hers—kook that she was. Talking about them with Clyde would only mean she was allowing herself to be exposed. You didn't do that with someone you'd never see again. There'd be no bonding over her supposed isolation.

He caught up to her, grabbing her hand once more. Against her will, her fingers curled into his. Clyde leaned down and chuckled in her ear. "Avoid, avoid, avoid. And if you're taking me to one of those places that specialize in goat's milk and seaweed, you're dining alone. I'm up for a greasy cheeseburger or some pasta. How about you?"

There went the Souper Salad buffet. "Oh, definitely—color me all in. With a banana Slurpee on the side," she scoffed, then mentally slapped herself. Clyde should be able to enjoy whatever the hell he wanted. She didn't know if they had banana Slurpees where she hoped he was headed, or cheeseburgers or whatever, but if they didn't, she had no right to deny him simple pleasures. "That was catty. Sorry. You should have whatever you want to have, as much of it as you want, before you . . ."

"Go."

Jesus, he was all about the making his point tonight, wasn't he? "Right. Go."

"Something you don't want me to do. Even if you did call me a liar."

"I didn't call you a liar." Not out loud.

"Well, technically, no. You didn't. But it's what you were thinking. I'm still working on not being offended."

"You do that. And while you're at it, let's go stuff your mouth and clog your arteries so you'll have something to do besides psychoanalyze me and air my dirty laundry in a public forum—"

"Don Henley, 1982—"

She flicked a finger to his biceps. "If you don't quit that, I'll take you to my favorite organic restaurant and stuff some marinated burdock root down your throat, followed by some tofu hummus."

His eyebrow raised in disdain. "Perish the thought."

Delaney stopped outside of Ishmael's all-night burger joint, the only one she knew of that was close by. "Aw, look. By-products and animal fat, Clyde. This must be the place." She went to reach for the door, but Clyde's big hand stopped her, swinging her around to face him. Her look of question turned to a hitch in her breath. His face was all hard planes, his eyes epitomized somber, and his vibe was once more urgent.

"Don't grudge, Delaney. Don't be angry because I've opened wounds you'd much rather slap Band-Aids on. Don't. I get it now that I'm dead. I want you to get it before you are, too. I'm being very serious when I say that I like you. You have a razor-sharp tongue, and you're too damned cute for your own good, but you're also *alone*. Because I like you, and I can't be here to do a proper job of it myself, I want you to have those things you want. I don't want you to sit at home and hope it'll find you."

They had to lighten up or she'd be crying buckets of wasted tears. And what did "do a proper job of it himself" mean? "So are ya giving me permission to date other guys? Does this mean it's over between us, Clyde? Are we"—she made quotation marks of her fingers—"seeing other people?"

Without warning, he pulled her into his embrace, jolting her senses. "Don't make light. Just promise me you'll give it a try when I'm gone."

When he was gone.

That the words still stung after he'd said them for the hundredth time, that she was feeling even the slightest bit of dread for a lost soul who was by far going somewhere better than this, meant heartache would follow. Clyde belonged up yonder. Any suspicion she'd had earlier was gone. Ghosts had blank spots in their memories all the time. Demons probably could, too. Whatever was keeping Clyde from remembering who he'd done work for, she was ready to admit it had nothing to do with dishonesty.

That made him even more wildly appealing, and nothing scared her more. Clyde was right in his assessment of her life and the potential to become attached to something she just couldn't have.

Scarier still.

"Sure, Clyde. I'll give www.mediumsaren'tbatshit.com a shot just for you." She turned to pull out of the arms that were feeling far too insistent, and way more secure than she was comfortable with.

Yet Clyde held fast. "Light."

"Huh?"

"You're making light. Stop. Just do it."

Yeah, she'd do it, and while she was at it, she'd avoid any more sexual healing in the process.

Marvin Gaye, 1982 . . .

Oh, Hell's bells.

She'd caught the disease known as Clyde.

The only cure was to get him out of here and off to higher ground.

Pronto.

fifteen

Mistake number one—putting something as undeniably romantic on her CD player as Michael Bublé while she packed.

Mistake number two—being anywhere in the same small space as Clyde.

So here they were.

In a clinch, swaying to the strains of "Lost."

Delaney wasn't even sure how it'd happened—how his arms, like granite, had encompassed her, or how his chin had come to rest on the top of her head while their feet found a slow, rhythmic pattern.

Her eyes closed without her realizing, her head lying nestled in the crook of his shoulder. Dogs one through six lay splayed out across the bed after they'd thoroughly sniffed her half-packed suitcase.

Clyde's hands moved across her spine, trashing her resolve to keep her hands off and get to the business at hand—getting Clyde to where he belonged.

And she'd been doing a fantabulous job of it until now. First, she'd called Kellen and alerted him to what was going on, offering to send Marcella to look out for him while she was gone. In light of the fact that Kellen's name had been brought up in the conversation Clyde had heard before he left Hell, Delaney couldn't take any chances he'd be caught off guard. But Kellen had refused Marcella's help—which didn't surprise her. He'd even offered to come along and help them, and she'd refused. She needed someone to check on Mrs. Ramirez for her.

Second, she'd made reservations to go to North Dakota and Clyde's house. He'd assured her that he had money for plane tickets in this account no one had come across since his death to pay for them. So she'd used her credit card to secure two seats to North Dakota.

The only way to end this was to go back to the beginning.

And to the scene of Clyde's death.

There had to be a clue, a body, a cemetery that had a tombstone with his name on it. Something.

They were on a fast train to nowhere if they kept looking for clues on the Internet. Time was running out for Clyde. If he didn't decimate her all right and proper like he was assigned to do, Hell and all its minions would come looking for him—for her. She had to find out what was keeping him in Hell and cross him over.

So you'd think that'd light a fire under their respective asses.

However, Bublé's "Lost" turned into "Home" and "Home" turned into something she couldn't recognize for the plunking of her heart and the peaceful utopia of being held by Clyde while they shuffled their feet.

"I was never a Bublé fan in life," Clyde mumbled.

She sighed. "Yet another stark difference between the two of us.

I'm not only a Bublé fan, but a Feinstein fan, and I'd probably hurt little old ladies to sit front row at an Andrea Bocelli concert. Not to mention the damage I might be inclined to do if someone were to rival me for five minutes alone with David Cassidy. It would so be on."

His chuckle vibrated against her ear. "I'd have figured you for a Shaun fan, not David."

She tilted her head back to gaze up at him, wrinkling her nose. "Again, might I point out, different, we're very different. No way was Shaun cuter than David. I lived—*lived*—for *Partridge Family* reruns."

"I stand corrected," he said with a chuckle.

She let her head fall back to his chest, allowing the moment to just be.

"Mind if I borrow your Stephen King book for the plane ride?"

"I'd have never pegged you for a King fan. I thought you'd be more of a *Calculus in Your Everyday Life* kind of guy," she joked.

"Then you were wrong, and maybe that makes us not so different."

"Well, then, *I* stand corrected."

"You reading Stephen King makes some kind of weird sense to me."

She giggled. "It should. His imagination is far creepier than almost anything that happens to me in real life." *Almost.* "I always end up feeling two things when I close one of his books: lucky and superior."

"So you're an action-adventure, supernatural kind of girl—movies, I mean."

"I haven't been to a movie in ages, but if I had my druthers, it'd be a thriller or a horror flick like they used to make them—*Halloween*, Michael Myers style."

"Again, not so different. Though, for me, it was *Friday the 13th*."

"So tell me something?"

"You bet," he hummed against her ear.

Why was he making it a point to mention their commonalities? Her head fell away from his chest to tilt upward. "Are you trying to rub in the things we have in common for a reason—or do you just have to be right?"

"Do you have to be a sore sport or are you just sensitive? I was just making conversation. Ease up there, ghost lady." He smiled, all bright and cocky, before he tucked her head back against his chest. "If neutral's your thing, we could always talk about the theory of relativity or the evolution of man."

"Again, *very* different. I'd rather have my eyeballs gouged out with one of Marcella's high-heeled shoes."

Clyde laughed. "What do you like to do besides read and watch *Ghost Whisperer*? Got any hobbies? Like decoupage or sculpting?"

She paused for a moment, then frowned. Okay, enough with how small her life was. "Nope, as of late my only hobby is crossing souls for sport."

"I didn't have any either, but I always wanted to try parasailing."

"I'm afraid of heights." So, yeah. Not so much in common. *See me stick my tongue out at you.*

"That's not all you're afraid of."

"You made your point, Atwell. Back the hell up."

Clyde laughed against her ear, but without warning, his voice took on a serious note. "I think we might need to stop now."

"Is it time to leave for the airport already? I thought we had another two hours."

"That's not why we need to stop."

"So why are we stopping?" she mumbled, forgetting her promise to herself that she wouldn't succumb to his charms. She didn't want to stop. She wanted to stay like this for as long as her legs would hold her up, and long after.

Clyde pressed her hips to his in answer.

Oooooh. Yeah. If there were a reason to stop, *that'd* be a solid one. Reealllly solid. Because she wasn't getting too attached, and what lay between them might be hard to detach her from if this kept up.

Yet neither of them pulled away.

The music had stopped, but the sway of their bodies hadn't.

"Your call," he murmured against her ear, sending a sinful cluster of tingles across her neck.

Yeah, like she should be responsible for calling a halt to anything at this weak moment. That was like leaving Bozo the Clown in charge of world peace.

Delaney knew this shouldn't happen again. Compiling the already fantasticalness of the other night with more of the same was asking too much of herself. She needed some willpower here—some nads—some something to stop this madness that would leave her doing exactly what Marcella had said she'd do.

Cry.

A lot.

Her body disagreed wholeheartedly and so did her fingers. Fingers that trailed up over Clyde's arms and wound around his neck, threading through the hair at his nape.

She stood on tiptoe, pressing her lips to his, coaxing, tasting, savoring the taste of his mouth. Clyde's tongue rasped against hers, dueling with it, demanding she submit to him while his arms dragged her closer. Their moan was shared, as though neither of them could survive a moment longer without each other's lips.

Clothes were peeled without hesitation from hot, achy bodies, falling to the floor without so much as a thought. Delaney moaned with husky need when Clyde lifted her, wrapping her legs around his waist, then sitting at the edge of her bed.

His cock slipped between her thighs, skimming the wet, swollen bud of her clit. Her head fell back, luxuriating in the press of Clyde's thighs against her ass, the stiff shaft of his cock seeking entry. All brain activity ceased, all common sense about the state of her heart followed.

A tilt of her hips allowed her to sink down on his rigid shaft; it filled her, stretched her with deliciously slow increments. Wrapping the length of her hair around his hand, he tugged her head back, making her spine arch upward. Clyde used his other hand to cup her breast, muttering his approval when she offered it to him in total abandon.

She rode him as he thumbed her nipple, tingles of ecstasy pricking her skin. Leaning back, she placed her hands on his hardened thighs, enjoying the feel of the springy hair that covered them.

His hips lifted upward, driving into her, surging, pushing her to yet another height. Lust drove her to reach between them and drag her fingers through the hair at the base of his cock. Clyde bucked, jerking inside of her, filling her so full it took her breath away.

Her climax was swift as she drove downward one last needy time, rolling her hips with a whimper. A trail of sweat trickled between her breasts, and Clyde licked it away, pressing his hot lips to her skin as he came, too. His grunt of satisfaction was thick, muffled by her exposed flesh. Delaney tugged her head back upward, loosening his grip on her hair, and laid her cheek atop his head, inhaling the shampoo he'd used when he'd showered earlier.

They sat for a while, Clyde still in her, drawing her close and pulling the throw blanket from the end of the bed to cover them when she shivered.

Delaney squeezed her eyes shut at the rightness of this. How easy it had been to make love to this man she knew so little about, but longed to spend every waking moment with discovering.

So this would be a primo moment to bust a move.

Yet she just wanted to rock back and forth like this forever.

At the edge of her bed.

With Clyde.

"Heeeeey, you two—stop, you're burning my eyes," Marcella said with scorn, parting the desire-induced haze Delaney was in with her cold words spat with rapid fire.

"Coitus interruptus," Clyde said with sigh and a frown, blinking his eyes at the light Marcella'd so rudely turned on.

Delaney fought for breath, struggling to right herself and shimmy off the end of the bed, but she dragged Clyde with her, his right ankle still wrapped around her left. "Did you forget how to use your phone, Marcella? You know, that cute pink thing with all the shiny buttons?"

She waved her hands in a flurry of agitated motion. "Get off of each other and skip being all offended that I've interrupted the festivities. You and me, D? We gotta talk and we gotta do it now. I'm not looking—get dressed."

Delaney pushed her disheveled hair from her face, untangling herself from Clyde and scooping up her clothes, throwing them over her head. "Wow, sounds urgent. Oh, no. Did you miss the buy one shower gel get one free sale at Bath and Body Works?"

"Yeah, yeah I did. So I'm cranky. And guess what? I missed it because of *you*. Now—get out here now." She stabbed a slender finger in the direction of the darkened kitchen.

Marcella's voice bordered on seething and hysterical, and while she might get upset over missing a sale at one of her favorite stores, she'd never get this hinky about it.

Which meant she needed to unstick herself from Clyde.

Delaney gave Clyde a sympathetic look before fully dressing and hurrying off to the kitchen. "What the hell is so important you couldn't wait until . . ."

"You were done? Sorry, *chica*. Next time I promise to put my social skills to better use, but this can't wait. Now sit. We've got to talk." Marcella yanked down the edge of Delaney's skirt and buttoned a button on her blouse with a look of disgust.

Delaney didn't want to sit. "So talk."

"Who's Vincent?"

Her stomach plummeted. "Why?"

Marcella rounded her, lingering with a menacingly close stance. "D? Now wouldn't be the time to play stupid. Don't fuck with me. Cut the bullshit, and answer me. Who—is—Vincent?"

Her mouth went arid with fear. "Someone I knew a long time ago." Which was totally the truth. Totally.

Marcella's lips popped in skepticism. "*How* did you know him, Delaney? Was he a friend, a lover you conveniently forgot to mention to me? What did he mean to you?"

"I don't get what this has to do with anything."

"If I didn't just have my nails done, I'd haul off and clock that fake question mark right off your pretty face. It has to do with your life, dipshit! Tell me what this Vincent means to you, and maybe I can piece this together."

"Piece what together?"

"The shit I heard tonight."

"How about you tell me what you heard."

"I heard that Vincent's time was up, and so is yours!" she hissed in Delaney's face. Fear, crystalline and bright, shone in her green eyes; it was visible in every line on Marcella's smooth skin.

But that was impossible. Vincent's time couldn't be up.

He was dead.

That meant no more time to be up.

"Delaney, I swear on every last throw pillow I have, if you don't tell me who the fuck Vincent is, I'll beat you until the words fall out of your toothless mouth! Who is Vincent, Delaney?"

"He was just someone I knew a long time ago—when I was in college."

"Was he your lover?"

Her face must have belied the bile that rose in her throat at the very thought. "No. Christ, no."

Marcella paced, her white wedge sandals clacking on the tile. "Okay, look. Now's not the time to hide shit from me, *mi amiga*. If you won't tell me how he's connected to you, then I don't get it—but here's the gist of what I overheard. Vincent's contract is up, and according to the evil, douchebag fuck I caught talking about this—so is yours. How in the bloody fuck can you have a contract with Hell, Delaney?"

Now that was curious. "But I don't have a contract with anything. Swear it on my echinacea."

Marcella latched on to Delaney's shoulders, digging her nails into her flesh. "I swear, you're going to make me kick your ass, aren't you? What are you protecting? *Who* are you protecting and why won't you just tell me so I can help?"

"There's nothing to help me with, Marcella. Vincent's dead." Dead, dead, dead. The whoring, boozing, fuckfest of a freak pig was cold and dead.

Marcella froze, the wild look in her eyes tearing at Delaney's gut. "That doesn't explain a goddamned thing and you know it, and admittedly, I only heard pieces of this conversation. But riddle me this, if this Vincent's contract's up, how does that have anything to do with you? I literally had to clamp my jaw shut to keep my mouth from unhinging when I heard the words *contract* and *Hell* with your name in the mix. The world's gone mad, and if you don't give me some answers, I'll hunt them down myself. Whatever you're doing this for—whomever you're protecting—they've got you by the short hairs and I promise you, I'll kill them before I'll let them touch one strand of hair on your head."

Marcella's cell phone chirped "A Rose in Spanish Harlem," breaking the intensity of their confrontation.

"Argh!" Marcella shouted, digging into her trendy, red leather jacket and yanking out her cell phone. Her brow furrowed as she flipped it open. "What?" she yelped into the mouthpiece, but then she grew silent. "Yeah, you prick—you can bet your slimy ass I'll be there." Her eyes narrowed in Delaney's direction before clamping the phone shut again with a snap. "I gotta go, but I'll be back, and when I come back, you'd better be ready to bring your toys to the sandbox." She snapped her fingers, turning first to a crackling white light, indicating her extreme displeasure with Delaney, then disappearing.

Delaney took long swallows of air, the thrash of her heart against her ribs almost debilitating. How in all of bloody hell was she connected to Vincent by a contract?

Yes, Vincent must've signed a contract with Lucifer for all the power and connections he'd had. For all the trouble he'd escaped in the short time she'd known him, he'd had something working in his favor. But Jesus Christ in a miniskirt, no—she'd had nothing to do with it. What did Vincent's time running out have to do with her? None of this made any fucking sense.

Her chimes tinkled in the store, then her flesh pimpled with familiar goose bumps. "Now's not the time, people! Can't you see I'm in crisis?" she called to the ceiling, hoping whoever was here now could just hang on. She couldn't piece other people's lives together if she couldn't even keep her own together.

But Robert Young, one of the most famous fathers ever portrayed on television, not to mention a cutting-edge doctor on a hit medical show in the late sixties and long into the seventies, wasn't about to be denied. What he appeared in always fascinated Delaney. Sometimes he was dressed in a crisp suit and tie, other times in his medical coat complete with stethoscope.

"Bob? Busy here, okay? Can you come back another time? And do me a skinny, tell everyone else I'm busy, too. I'm on hiatus or something. Sort of like those breaks you rich actors who star in a series take in the summer to sail off to exclusive islands or get massages and find Jesus in sweathouses, ya know? The breaks that piss the rest of us off because there's nothing to watch on TV but crap. It isn't like the viewing audience doesn't want you to have a vacation, but does it have to last for three damned months? And who the hell said you could have a midseason break on top of it, too? I don't want to be pissy here, Bob, but that's Easy Street. If they paid me the kind of money they pay some of these schmoes on TV these days, dude, I'd do a whole show with just me as the cast and I'd work even if I lost a limb—three hundred and sixty-five."

He stared her down, his expression grim.

She took a deep breath when she saw his look of concern. "Sorry, I'm grudging, and I'm tired—makes for a crabby Delaney, but when I come back I'll be all better, okay?"

His sweet, gentle face floated in front of hers while he shook his head no. When he spoke, she found herself confused by his words. *Lang Memorial.* The words drifted from his lips long after they'd moved.

"I don't remember that. Was it a movie you were in?" Delaney shook her head. "Never mind, I don't have time tonight. I've got a plane to catch and I'd really appreciate it if you guys didn't make an appearance on said bird of flight. The flight attendants frighten easily. Plane crashes and doling out half a shitty can of soda they can handle. Ghosts? Not so much. So shoo—go haunt Jane Wyatt.

She'd probably love to catch up, don't you think?" she muttered with distraction, trying to dig out all the dog food bowls for Mrs. Ramirez, lining them up on the counter.

Robert next appeared on top of the counter. He'd folded his hands over his knees, crossing his legs. His white medical jacket was crisp and clean as though it'd been freshly pressed. He said once more, *"Lang Memorial,"* enunciating each word with long drawn-out syllables that lingered long after his mouth had moved.

Delaney put her face in his. "Again, I'm on the fly—totally don't get your drift and probably can't hang around to try and figure it out. I have no idea what movie that was so I can't tell you how awesome you were in it—if that's what you're looking for. But I loved you in reruns on TV Land, how's that? I especially loved *Marcus Welby, M.D.,* and I always sided with you against that whippersnapper doctor James Brolin. He was a cocky sonofabitch, huh? Now skedaddle." She flapped a hand at him.

Robert reached out a hand to her, cocking his slick, dark head and giving her a beseeching look. He knew she couldn't take his hand, but she indulged him anyway, her fingers slipping directly through his milky, transparent flesh. *"Father Knows Best,"* he tittered, his intent gaze asking for something she just didn't get.

What the hell had gotten into this bunch of dead actors lately? Everybody was so serious when they showed up these days. Used to be they hung out, had a giggle, and then they were gone. Now they were all downers. Charlie, and then Greta, Michael, and now Bob. She clenched her eyes shut to ward off the headache she was feeling the beginnings of. "Yep, I liked that show, too. And now I really, really have to hit it." She opened her eyes only to find him gone.

"What is with you knuckleheads lately? Lighten up, already, huh?" she told the ceiling.

Christ on a cracker. She could use a little levity.

A little would go a long way.

"Uh, Boss?" He entered the room with soft footsteps—with reverence—with terror.

"Clyve?"

He cleared his throat, shuffling from foot to foot. "Problem."

"Continue."

"Well, it went like this—"

"Cut to the chase, Clyve. Now. Or I'll singe your sorry ass," was the muffled response.

"I'm not where I'm supposed to be."

"And where is it you're supposed to be, Clyve?"

"With that Delaney woman."

"Delaney Markham?"

Whatever. "Yes, Boss."

"*Interesting.* Explanation?"

"There was a screwup somewhere."

The laughter from the burgundy leather table was deep, rumbling—insidious. "Why don't you tell me where, Clyve, and I'll see what I can do to make everything rocking horses and rainbows for you. Wouldn't that be all sunshine and roses?"

Clyve gulped. He was in the shit. When he'd been alive, nobody talked to him with that condescending, bullshit tone. Nobody. He'd run the show. Things were just a little fucking different down here. "I'm not sure, Boss."

Satan clucked his tongue. "Not sure? That's a pity."

No lie. "Yes, Boss."

"So why don't you sit with me, Clyve, and tell me all about your woes," Satan invited with a sweep of his hand to the chair beside the massage table he lay facedown on while a nubile young woman kneaded his flesh. "Go on, Clyve, make yourself comfortable. Your comfort is my reason for being." He lifted his head briefly and flashed Clyve a smile, a brilliant, maniacal smile, before settling back into the hole carved out of the table made especially for his face.

Clyve eyed the chair suspiciously—when Satan was being so accommodating, something wasn't kosher. With his luck, the chair'd sprout teeth and gnaw his balls off.

"Do you doubt that I only want your comfort, Clyve?"

Fuck, yeah. "No, Boss." He sat with a hard thunk, figuring he'd better front fast and slap on his suck-ass minion face. If he had no balls by conversation's end, he'd have no balls with a fine display of bravery to keep his pride warm at night in the pit.

"Then, please, sit and clarify."

"The file with my mission assignment—someone screwed with it."

"Who, pray tell? Who would do such a dastardly deed, Clyve? I thought all the dastardly deeds were only done by you, being so skilled at dastardly as you are."

Right. Like he'd have ever purposely handed himself over to some rich broad who liked to dress him up in berets and have his hair clipped by some fag named Gustav. That had been its own special hell. Pomeranians had a shitassload of hair. It was hot. "No, sir. It wasn't me. I don't know who did it or how it happened."

"Then I say we launch an all-out investigation—bring in the troops—batten down the hatches until someone fesses!" he shouted with mock, almost giddy, exuberance.

Whew. The sweat that had begun to trickle down his spine slowed to a crawl. "I'd be happy to do that, sir."

"Oh, Clyve," Satan whispered so low he almost couldn't detect what he'd said—until he roared, that is. "You, goddamned moron!" Bottles of oil rumbled then tipped over in a crash of gooey, thick puddles. The walls shook like bolts of thunder had shot through them.

Clearly. Moron worked in this case. "Boss?" he offered in the form of a weak question.

Satan snaked a long-fingered, clawed hand out without looking up, snaring Clyve by the front of his T-shirt. A pink T-shirt that read *Cat . . . the Other White Meat* and was cut off at his hairy, protruding belly. He dragged Clyve to his knees beside the massage table, raising his head to assess his minion. "You idiot!" he screeched, opening his mouth wide to reveal Hell's very own breath, hot, rancid, flesh-eating.

Clyve knew to struggle would be his end, so he squinted his eyes instead.

"Do you have any idea the kind of stress I suffer when you half-wits can't get it right? If I weren't already dead, I'd have had a triple bypass by now—maybe two. What have you done, Clyve, and why are you wearing a shirt that looks as though you've been frolicking with pink poodles?"

Because he had. Lots and lots of poodles, to name just one yippy, snippy, snarling, diamond-studded-collar-wearing toy breed. Poodles, Pomeranians, those uglier than coyote ugly Pugs, Chihuahuas—you name it, he'd been in a cage with the fuckers, fighting for his right to a stupid rubber hot dog coated in beef broth while he waited for Gustav to milk his renal glands.

Yet, to deny he'd had anything to do with the fuckup in the Markham assignment would only enrage Satan to the point that he'd be in the pit for a year, his ass sizzling, his worst fear, snakes, slithering over him while he was chained to something, pissing in his pants. To offer a solution was the only way out. Thank God— okay, maybe not Him directly, but thank the universe—he had one.

And Clyve had one, all right.

The fight now was to keep his voice free of any hint of tremble; deliver the information; redeem. In that order. "I have a solution, sir."

Satan dropped Clyve with a jolt that might have broken bones, had his bones retained the ability to break anymore, sending him skittering sideways to crash against the far wall. Satan gave him an affable smile from his place on the table. "Oh, please share, Clyve. I so love resolution. It's very Oprah-ish."

Clyve bit back a whimper of agony. Even if he was dead, and his bones couldn't be broken, it still wasn't a warm fuzzy to end up with your face smashed against a wall. He couldn't wait to fucking hit level seven—you couldn't feel pain there. "I have information about Delaney, sir. Information I think will make you happy. Very happy."

"Suh-weet! Now get on with it, Clyve, before I pop out your eyeballs and play a rousing game of marbles with them right here on the floor."

When Clyve spoke next, he kept his words confident, and quiver free.

As Satan listened, his smile of malicious pleasure grew.

So, for the moment at least, he'd pleased the freaky fuck.

Meant he could keep his balls.

He had the world on a string now.

sixteen

"Holy explosion, Batman."

"I did say I screwed up, didn't I?"

"Yeah, you did. I just don't know that I understood fully how big you screwed up."

Clyde picked through the charred rubble of what had once been his basement, looking for even the smallest of clues regarding his accident. "Could we maybe not be quite so direct?" He pointed to his chest. "Sensitive here, okay? This is the scene of my *death*. Have some respect."

"You wanna hold hands and sing 'Kumbaya'?"

"Not funny."

Her tendency to crack wise, even in times of discomfort, sometimes went beyond couth. This was one of them. "Sorry. No fireside songs. Okay, so here's the thing—we've been here for two hours and nothing. I'm all about moving forward, and that's what we need to do here. You torched this place, there's not a lot left but a shell. I doubt we're going to find anything that helps us in this blackened Cajun-style mess. So let's go, okay?" She held out her hand to him, hoping to offer some comfort. His eyes held a million emotions behind his glasses, and he made no effort to hide them. "I say we go talk to the one lone neighbor you have over there in the north forty and see what he knows. He has to know something. An explosion this big had to have caught his attention. Now, c'mon," she coaxed when Clyde made no move to step over the heap he was almost knee-deep in.

"Hypotenuse."

"What?" She gave him a bewildered stare, twisting a strand of her hair in her fingers.

"My cat. He was in the house with me, probably upstairs in his cat condo sound asleep. I know it's ridiculous three and a half months later, but I hoped to . . ."

Her heart clenched into a tight fist even in the bone-numbing cold of North Dakota. "Find him."

"Yep."

"Maybe he was outside when it happened and he wandered off." One could hope. Delaney knew it was futile, but she offered the words of comfort anyway. She was all about realism for the most part, and facing the truth—well, except when it came to Clyde's theory that she wasn't living her life to the fullest because she was afraid of rejection—but now just wasn't the time for harsh realisms.

His lips thinned in apparent disagreement, the rustle of his hair against the collar of his thrift store down coat clear. "Hypotenuse was an indoor cat. He wouldn't know how to survive if he got out of this anyway—especially when it's this cold out. If I even opened the door to suggest that he indulge in outdoor sport, he gave me the look and headed straight for the comfort of my bed."

Shit. She blew warmth into her cupped hands. "I'm sorry, Clyde.

Believe me, I understand how you feel." And she did. She loved her furbabies, probably more than what some would term normal. But she loved them, and when they shipped off to the other side, it still hurt.

"I know you do."

She tugged at his sleeve with a gentle yank. "C'mon. Let's go see the neighbor and then go back to the hotel. I bet there's a 7-Eleven on the way. I'll buy you a banana Slurpee. My treat. Whaddya say?"

Clyde's smile was vague when he finally focused on her again. "Now I know you feel bad if you're willing to spend your hard-earned money for all that sugar just for me. You wear sympathetic and sensitive well, ghost lady." He took her hand and led her out of what used to be his basement.

Once outside, the cold air filled her lungs, almost stealing her breath away. It was buttfuck cold in North Dakota, yet the sweet, unsullied air cleansed her mind, leaving behind the scene of Clyde's death added to that calm. She slid behind the wheel of their rented car while a distracted Clyde handed her the keys and took the passenger side.

After checking in with Kellen to ensure he was still safe, Delaney drove the half mile or so to Clyde's neighbor's in thoughtful silence. Not having found anything in that mess he'd once called home left her desolate for him. If they didn't figure this out soon, his pass from Hell would expire. They'd come for him when he didn't show up with her death on his hands.

Bad shit would go down.

She refused to let any more bad shit happen to him.

Pulling to a stop in his neighbor's long driveway, she was grateful for some scattered landscaping lights. It wasn't just buttfuck cold here—it was buttfuck dark, too. Turning to Clyde, still broodingly silent, she said, "You stay here. Don't move. Don't even think about getting out of this car. If someone saw you, they'd shit a whole chicken coop. Got that?"

His laughter caught her off guard. It was filled with bitter regret. "They probably wouldn't know me if they saw me. Like I said, I didn't make an effort much."

The hand that reached out to comfort him had a will of its own, curling around his shoulder with sympathy. "I know, but we can't take a chance. You stay here—I'll be right back."

"What're you going to say to them?"

Delaney shoved open the door of the rental car, looking over her shoulder at him. "It'll go like this. Heeeey, I'm Delaney Markham—Clyde Atwell's spirit guide. You know, the guy who splattered himself all over parts near and far here in your fine state of North Dakota? I need your help . . ."

Clyde didn't crack the smile she'd hoped to elicit from him.

Delaney popped her lips. "Okay, totally inappropriate. Sorry—again. I don't know what I'll say, but don't sweat it. I'll figure it out as I go along." Hopping out of the car, she made her way with cautious steps to the double white doors of an updated farmhouse. There was only one light on inside, and peeking through the sidelight, she saw it came from the kitchen.

What was she going to say? "I'm Clyde's medium. Got any thoughts on his ghost showing up at my store in New York?"

Clearly, that'd never work. She was almost beginning to feel a simpatico with Melinda Gordon and all those stupid tears she shed week after week. Right now, she wanted to cry, too—and it was in helplessness and frustration.

Flexing her fingers, she jabbed the doorbell and waited.

The door cracked, revealing one light brown eyeball with long eyelashes. It looked like it belonged to a woman. "Yes?"

Delaney heard the fear in that one accented word. Who could blame the poor woman? Not only was it buttfuck cold and dark here in North Dakota—it was damned lonely. When someone rang your doorbell out here, it had to be, like, an epic event. "Hi, um . . . I'm Delaney Markham—from New York, and I was wondering if I could ask you a couple of questions?"

"The mister and missus, they not home. I am the housekeeper. Ju come back next week." Her accent was thick and slurred, thicker than Mrs. Ramirez's, and a far cry from Marcella's occasional slips.

Damn, damn, damn it all to Hell and back. Next week was too late. They were here now. "Do you work here?"

Her next reply was hesitant. "Yes, but I no alone!"

Delaney's eyes pled with the one eyeball in the crack of the doorway. "No, it's okay. I understand you're afraid to talk to me, all showing up at this late hour. Look, I really need your help, and I'm only here for a short time. I'm a friend of Clyde Atwell's. You know the guy who lives—er, lived down the road?"

Her one eye filled with sympathy. "Ack! Yes. Is bad what happen to him."

"Yes. It was bad, but we've been out of touch for a while, and when I dropped by, you know, unexpectedly, well . . . his house—it's gone." Tears weren't hard to summon; they formed in the corners of her eyes for Clyde's loss.

Instantly the eye went cloudy with concern. "Oh, I sorrrry. His house—it explode. Was very, very bad."

"Do you know what happened?"

Her tongue clucked, a sound almost deafening in the still of the night. "Boom! Big boom. I was cleaning the bathrooms and I hear. Was so bad."

Bad. Yeah. She got that. Delaney sniffed, hoping she could contain this sudden need to bawl buckets of tears. Whether it was lack of sleep or the fact that she was more than likely going to be staring at some cold, gray headstone with Clyde's name on it sooner than she expected, she didn't know. With a gulp, she asked, "Was there a funeral? Somewhere I can pay my respects?"

The door popped open a bit wider, revealing a petite woman dressed in a patchwork robe and blue, fuzzy slippers. She made the sign of the cross over her chest. "Oh, no. No funeral. He's no dead. Is a miracle. Thank Jesus."

Delaney's breathing stopped. "Wha-what?"

Her light brown eyes blinked. "He's no dead. He's in hospital."

Delaney had to grip the door frame to keep herself upright. Clyde wasn't dead. He'd survived that mess back there? It would be nothing short of a miracle if he'd lived through that. That couldn't be right. How could he have been wandering around in Hell for all that time, able to do all the things demons are supposed to do, if he was still alive? If he wasn't dead, what the fuck was he?

But hope, desperate, yearning hope, made her force her tongue to perform and ask, "Wait, he's not dead? Clyde Atwell isn't dead? Are you sure?"

The woman's head, securely wrapped in a white towel, nodded. "I sure. Very sure. I'm sorry for you to come to see him like this."

"Where is he? I mean, if he's in the hospital, what hospital? I— I'd like to . . . visit. Yes, I'd like to visit him."

"I don't know nothing. I jus' know he's not dead. The mister and missus, they have his cat. *Madre de dios,* what a mess he was. His hair burned, but he's okay. He was so hungry. The mister, he say to take the cat and feed him."

Sweet mother. Relief so sharp it was like a knife cutting through her soul made her gasp. "Are you sure?"

"Yes. I told you, I sure."

Delaney's head spun with a thousand questions, all of which she had to ask with care because this woman didn't speak English very well. "Have you heard anything about Clyde's condition?"

Because it damned sure couldn't be good after an explosion like that.

"I don' know nothing, I told you. Now I go." She waved a hand in the direction of the rental car with a shiver. "Is cold. I tell the mister you come, okay?"

"Okay," she barely muttered, hardly noticing the closing of the door.

Her mouth was hanging open. She knew it because gusts of chilling air swirled around in it, but she almost couldn't move. Her feet were icicles—unwilling to take the signal from her brain that movement to the car, where heat was wafting from a vent, was critical to warming them up.

Delaney's hands held fast to the front of her coat.

Clyde was alive.

She couldn't think that word enough.

Alive.

Living.

So not dead.

Yippee and skippee.

In a millisecond, the feet that had been unwilling to uproot themselves became all motion. She practically stumbled to the car, latching on to the door handle and flinging it open with a grin.

The car light over Clyde's head beamed. With life.

Life.

Like alive life.

"I take it from the grin on your face my neighbor's an upstanding guy?"

"I think you have to drive. Because I can't."

"Reason being?"

She threw the keys at him. "I can't. I'm shaking. When I tell you what I just found out, I don't know if you'll be able to drive either.

We may have to call the paramedics. Maybe we should just stay put while I tell you."

"I'll drive, and you're not making sense, Delaney."

"None of this makes any sense, Clyde." Slamming the door, she went around to the passenger side of the car. "Drive. Hurry, before I have apoplexy. We need to get back to the hotel."

Clyde slipped past her, the look of concern on his face clear under the starry night. He got in the driver-side door, turning the key in the ignition. "Speak, Delaney. You're freaking me out now."

She shook her head in astonished disbelief. "Well, it's good news, if that helps."

"What would help is if you'd stop looking like you just saw a ghost because on you, that just doesn't look right. You see them all the time. What happened?"

"Hypotenuse is alive. He's at your neighbor's farmhouse with the people who own it."

Finally, Clyde smiled in a sad sort of fond way. "I'm glad. I don't know if I could've forgiven myself for offing H. He was a good cat. So that's what's freaking you?"

"That's not all."

His nod was all-knowing. "I should've known. So what happened? Please tell me no one else was hurt . . ."

There was just no other way to say it. "You're alive."

Clyde didn't miss a beat. Not a single swerve of the wheel. Rock steady as always. The only hint he might be as shocked as she was came in the way of the roll of his tongue in his cheek. "Repeat?"

"You're alive, Clyde. You're alive. Omigod! You're alive!" she shouted, her voice rising with each word she managed to sputter, not caring that her joy about this news had come out of its closet in all its festive, revealing glory. Laughter spilled from her throat, tears wet her eyes. It didn't make any sense at all that he was here in the car with her, yet his body was in some hospital. But Clyde was still breathing. Somewhere. She was fully aware she was teetering on the brink of emotional overload, but she didn't care. Clyde, according to the neighbor's maid, was *alive*. What a fucking spectacular word.

"So a thought?" he offered in quiet tones.

Delaney slapped a hand over her mouth, searching for calm reason. "What?" she managed.

"If I'm now only sort of dead, does this mean I can really do myself in if I run us off the road and straight into a tree?"

Glancing his way, Delaney saw he fought to retain the control he was so practiced at. After a long shudder of breath, she replied, "I'm sorry. I should have driven, but you're always so rational, I figured it was better if you did. Just stay calm and listen to what I just found out. Keep your eyes on the road, because even if you're only semidead, I think, anyway, I'm not, and I don't want to be. We have shit to do." She filled him in with as much composure as she could muster about what the maid had told her, giving as many of the details as she'd garnered from their language-hindered conversation while Clyde kept the car at a steady pace, his facial expression never once even flinching.

"Say something to me, demon."

"You no longer have the right to call me demon, ghost lady."

True that. He'd have to be dead to be a demon. And Clyde wasn't dead. He wasn't deceased or dearly departed either. No sirree, Bob. "You're right. So say something to me, not so dead Clyde." Excitement that was hard to tamp down rose once more.

"This would be one of the times when I'm supposed to display passion, right?"

Her fingers gripped the sleeve of his jacket when he pulled into the hotel's driveway. "Yes, Clyde. Passion would be good. Better if it didn't have to be on command, but still good. You're alive,

Clyde. I don't know where. I don't know how in the fuck you survived that, but there it is, and if you don't at least give me a hell to the yeah, I'm going to explode."

"Hell to the yeah," he said, dry as a bone.

"Oh, come *on*, half-dead guy! This is *huge*. Monumental—ginormous—tremendous. Work with me, would ya?"

His hands tightened on the steering wheel, his face unreadable under the glow of the hotel's sign. "I'm still absorbing."

Delaney couldn't contain herself anymore. She grinned, giddy with excitement. "Okay, you process, I'll get a happy on. Don't you see? It explains everything! Jesus. That's why we can't find an obituary for you, Clyde—because you're not dead! You're alive—in a hospital somewhere. What I want to know is why there was no police report—arson, something. This had to be big news out here in Nowhereville. Why it wasn't reported in at least the local papers is beyond me. But that's neither here nor there right now." Delaney paused, taking another stilted breath as realization washed over her again. "Omigod—this is—is—amazing, and crazy, and amazing." How in the fuck did this happen? How had Clyde been able to pull off being out of his body for this long? But it also gave her hope. If Clyde was in a hospital somewhere, he was alive.

And she was überpsyched about that.

Because it meant he could stay.

With her.

She looked around as though she'd spoken the words out loud. Disentangling herself from the grip she had on Clyde's arm, she sat back in her seat.

"What hospital am I in?"

"Crap, I have no idea. I could just barely understand what she was saying, but I understood the alive part. That's all that matters. You're alive. *Alive*, Clyde Atwell. The rest shouldn't be too hard to find out. What I'm having trouble with is how your soul got out of your body and landed you in Hell . . ."

"Not nearly as much trouble as I'm having with it," he commented in wry observation—still showing no signs of even a glimmer of happiness.

However, Delaney was now lost in finding a theory about what had gone wrong. "It makes no sense. I just don't understand this. Your soul's all wandering around like you actually exist on this plane—you manifested, you can touch things—but your physical body's in some hospital?"

Clyde shrugged his wide shoulders in what almost looked like indifference. "Don't look at me. You're the ghost expert—got some ghost friends you might consult about it?"

"No . . ."

"Well, you might if you—"

"Got that life you keep trying to talk me into. Yeah, yeah. Whatever. Stop knocking my self-imposed seclusion and let's get to the business at hand—which is figuring out where you are. And getting you out of there."

"I suppose my chances are grim if I've been in the hospital all this time—I'm probably in a coma, and I bet I'm pretty crispy. My chances of surviving were . . ."

Clyde's voice became all slo-mo, warbling in and out, leaving her only a word or two about percentages to pick from the gobble-dygook of slurred sentences.

Because out of the blue—epiphany—stark realization—total understanding—had just wailed her like a punch to the gut.

Holy. Shit. A *coma* . . . she grabbed at Clyde's arm again, almost unable to string her thoughts into a coherent sentence. She bounced up and down on the seat. "Remember that lady that showed up— the ghost lady who spoke German or some foreign language?"

"I do. The typical blame on your part was involved. Then my usual apology for throwing a monkey wrench in your ghost communications. What about her?"

"Right! That's her. She said *Das Koma*, remember? She kept saying it over and over. I don't know who she was, but when we get inside, we're looking her and those words up online." Delaney's thoughts blurred together, stringing triggers of memory. Discovery, much the way it always does, claimed her thoughts in one fell swoop. The missing piece of the puzzle fell into her lap like manna from Heaven. All she had to do was put it into the puzzle to complete the picture. "And the doctor with the decapitated head, remember him?"

Clyde blanched with a shudder. "Unfortunately."

"We thought he was saying *uma*—but I'd bet my left ovary he was saying *coma*!"

Clyde's frown deepened, but Delaney pressed onward—her quest for an answer was right at her fingertips. "Don't you see, demon? The spirits were trying to give us clues all along. Whoever the German chick was, she was trying to help us—help you. She knew you were in a coma."

"Then who's the doctor?"

She rolled her eyes. "Does it really matter? Sometimes spirits, if they can help, even if the information they bring you is disjointed and often confusing, will try to help if they're invested in some way in seeing you cross over."

"So how's the doctor or the German lady invested in me?"

"Didn't you say your mother had a doctor whose head was decapitated in a brutal accident?"

"I did. But he didn't sound at all like the description you gave me. He was older. Not some young guy."

"I'd bet my right ovary he manifested in the way he most liked his physical appearance when he was alive, which was young and blond. And he wants to help because I'm guessing, during your mother's illness, you were pretty good to her."

"You'd better stop handing over ovaries if you hope to have those children someday. You know, with the guy you'll find once you get that life?"

Delaney knew he was teasing her, forcing her to continually face her boxed-in life the way he did, but his words had a tinge of regret she wanted to cling to. Savor. If Clyde was still alive, and could recuperate, would he choose her when his spirit no longer needed guidance? Thinking about that right now was selfish. There was no time for self-indulgence and pansy-ass behavior. Not now.

"Okay, so if he was an older doctor when he died, he was probably vain enough to miss his youthful form. So in death he chose to manifest in the body that pleased him most. I'd bet my uterus he's got pics online somewhere. If you can remember his name, that is. Maybe from the hospital he worked at—something. There has to be *something*."

"Stop handing out your birthing bits so casually. And Dr. Watson. Gordon Watson was his name. But I can't remember the hospital my mother was in. In fact, now that I try, I can't remember any of the area hospitals. One of those blank spots again. And don't feed me that shit that it's convenient for me to forget. Why would I want to forget I'm still alive and not tell you where the hell I am?"

Talk about clinging to one stupid remark. Okay, okay, okay. She'd been caught with her pants down. But they had bigger issues to address than her calling him a liar. "How about we don't argue about your integrity now? Let's just get inside and get online. We'll order a pizza and start digging. You can't be far."

The elevator ride to their room was spent in silence, Clyde brooding and Delaney lost in the possibility that his body still ticked somewhere—that somewhere in North Dakota, no matter the shape he was in, Clyde lived.

His heart beat.
His pulse throbbed.
He breathed.
His body had life.
She couldn't think any further than that.
She wouldn't.

seventeen

Delaney typed in the words *das* and *Koma* only to come up dry. Maybe she was spelling them wrong. She took a trip to Babel Fish, punching in the URL on her laptop while Clyde sat on the chair, facing the bed she sat cross-legged on. She'd been so absorbed in figuring out who the woman with the doily on her head was, she'd forgotten that Clyde had just found something out that changed the landscape of his life in an enormous way.

She'd just have to be overjoyed for the both of them because Clyde wasn't feelin' it.

Looking up, she took in his face, so somber and serious. "You still absorbing?"

"Yep."

"Okay, sponge. Well when you're done, you let me know. I could use some help deciphering this *das Koma* thing and figuring out who that ghost was. It sounded just like the word *coma*, but I need to double-check. With the way our luck's run lately, I'm probably wrong and it's another clue to whatever's going on that we'll miss if I don't get it right. Thinking back, she had big heavy skirts on and that doily on her head. I've seen that somewhere . . ." Delaney drifted back off, typing in the word *Koma* on Babel Fish, an online foreign language translator. "Aha! It does mean 'coma,' only it's spelled with a *K* in German . . ." Okay, so the woman had been trying to relay Clyde's condition to them. But why and who was she that she'd stepped up to the plate on Clyde's behalf, and if they figured out who she was, what difference would it make? She hadn't reappeared. Maybe all she'd wanted to tell them was that Clyde was in a coma. Mission accomplished.

"Describe her dress again," Clyde ordered.

Delaney eked out as much of the memory as she could. She'd been fuzzy and distorted due to Clyde's presence.

"That doily on her head sounds familiar. Here, gimme the laptop."

Delaney let him have it, pleased he was finally taking an active role in getting them closer to finding his body.

"Did she look like this?" He tilted the laptop to show her a grainy portrait of a woman.

"Holy shit—yeah, that's her. Who is she?"

"Well, it makes sense if we keep following the pattern that half of the dead medical profession is trying to give us clues. The picture is Florence Nightingale, probably the most common, well-known name associated with nursing, and she did speak German among other things."

He was right—it did make sense. Perfect sense. "Florence Nightingale showed up, even in death, to help you. That's monumental. And how do you figure shit like this out? You're way too smart for your own good, ya know that? I never would have made the association."

"It's just what I do—did—I don't know." He handed her the

laptop and sat back against the headboard, putting his glasses on the nightstand and sliding his eyes shut. She'd hoped a shower and some time to himself to think would improve his attitude, but he was still all dark thunderclouds.

"Clyde?"

"Delaney?"

She leaned her head back to cast him a sidelong glance. His profile was tense and rock hard. "What the hell is wrong with you? We just had the best news we've had since we hooked up. Could you at least crack a smile? I understand needing to absorb this, but we need to be looking up hospitals and locating you, er, your body, I mean."

"Locating me," he said with a flat note.

"Yeah! If we can find out where you are then we can . . ."

"Can what?"

Yeah. What? How were they going to get him back into his body? Shit, she should have watched *Paranormal State* more often—maybe she'd have learned something. "Okay, so we have a stumbling block or two, but that doesn't mean we can't figure it out, Clyde. C'mon, you're really smart—help me find some answers. I promise it'll be okay. We'll figure this out."

Clyde pounced on her like a cat pounces on a stuffed toy mouse, his legs straddling her hips, his arms bracketing her shoulders. His eyes lanced hers, intense and cutting. "Don't say anything else. I don't want to talk about my body or where it's at, or how in the hell we plan to get me the fuck back into it."

Whoa. "But we have to talk about it, Clyde. If we don't talk about it, we'll never figure this out, and then—"

Clyde's mouth was on hers, stopping her words, her thoughts, stopping everything but the pound of her heart and the heat gathering at all points on her body. His lips became aggressive—insistent—demanding. His rock-hard shaft pushed at her hip from beneath his jeans; he shoved her T-shirt up with hands that were impatient and held urgency.

His hands roamed her body. His lips followed close behind, licking, teasing, sucking her skin, taking her nipples in his mouth and laving them with fierce, hot strokes.

Deft fingers slipped under her panties and spread the lips of her sex, stroking them until they swelled with need, ached to be satisfied. Her clit throbbed, pulsing with wanton lust as she buried her face in the pillow, jamming it over her face when Clyde's skilled hands and mouth brought her to orgasm. The climax made her stomach muscles clench so tight, she had to fight for air. Delaney stifled a scream with a clenched fist to her mouth, rising up and driving against his hand.

Clyde pushed his hands beneath her, latching on to her waist and dragging her down along the bed to look him directly in the eye. Shocked eyes met blazing blue ones just before he captured her lips again and pushed the heel of his hand to her shoulder, driving her back against the bed to her back.

Commanding, *demanding*, *driven* were the words that flitted through her addled, lust-filled brain when he pulled her underwear off and chucked them on the floor. But Delaney wanted more this time; she wanted to taste Clyde, discover what else made him writhe with desire.

Slipping from beneath him, she rolled him to his back, slinking along his body until she laid her head against his pelvic bone. Clyde's cock strained against his abdomen, reaching upward, the smooth skin hot to the touch and lightly veined.

She snaked her tongue out, flicking it with a light lick. Clyde reached down between his legs, thrusting his hands into her hair with a feral groan. Wasting no time, she took him in her mouth in one downward stroke, letting her tongue follow with a leisurely pass. She grew bold with each plunge of her mouth, wrapping her fingers around his rigid length and pumping him until she felt him shudder beneath her.

Each groan she elicited from Clyde, each deep rumble of satisfaction spurred her on until Clyde's hands tightened in her hair. "Stop!" he growled, pulling her up to meet his eyes. "I want to be inside you when I come. *Deep* inside you."

Her chest shifted at his words, her heart pounding so hard and sharp it would surprise her to find only she could hear it.

Wordlessly, he rolled her to her back, spreading her legs and kneeling between them. His eyes held so many emotions in the light of the room, his teeth clenched with a clear struggle she didn't understand. Clyde's large hands clamped onto her thighs when the tip of his cock pressed against her entry, preparing to delve into the wet cavern.

She lifted her hips, welcoming the hard, silken length of him when he plunged into her. He moved within her with fevered strokes, as though each one would be the last, each slick glide melting into the next.

Her eyes clenched shut, her jaw locking at the sweet heat he stirred in her. Hot flames licked between her thighs, signaling the beginning of the end. Delaney couldn't fight the tendrils of climax, couldn't slow the impending tidal wave of sensation as it lifted her high, pounding into her, then dropped her with a sudden sharp jolt.

Clyde's thrusts peaked with a frenzied tempo, sinking deeper into her until he roared his satisfaction. He stilled for a moment, then collapsed against her.

Her breathing was irregular, hurting her throat on the way out of her mouth. Holy Clyde gone wild. Every inch of her body was sated, and unable to move a muscle.

Clyde rolled off her, pushing strands of hair from her face and mouth. "Are you okay?" His question was smattered with sweet concern she could clearly hear.

There were levels of okay. This okay was like a level nine point five on a scale of one to ten. Totally okay with the intensity of their lovemaking, but concerned about what had brought on the sudden need Clyde had displayed.

But as she came down, caught her breath, had a moment to reproduce a brain cell or two, she suddenly understood without him having to say a word. Clyde needed affirmation. He needed to feel—to connect—because he didn't know when he'd do that again after they located his body. He was on overload. That he'd turned to her, even if it was just for comfort of a physical nature, made her heart tighten.

When she finally answered, she looked him directly in his eyes. "I'm more than okay. The question is, are you okay? I was getting pushy in my excitement."

"I'm okay. It's a lot to wrap my brain around. All this time I thought I was outta here when my assignment was done, and now I find that that might not be the case. I'm just wondering what the hell we're going to find when we find me and if I want to get back into a body that's supposedly comatose. At least in Hell I'm not bedridden." The emphasis he placed on the word *bedridden* was hard to miss.

He'd mentioned being sick as a kid—it must be a sore spot for him. She rolled to her side. Seeing him fully naked in the light for the first time took her breath away. He was the most beautiful, magnificent man she'd ever seen, and she couldn't help but be thankful that wherever his body was, it was alive. Whatever that entailed, she didn't care. Just the thought that the possibility existed that he could recuperate made her want to do a happy dance. She just wanted to keep looking at him, soak in every last minute of time with him before they had to deal with what was next. "What is this from?" There was a scar on Clyde's chest, long but clean, extending from his clavicle to his breastbone.

"Heart surgery."

"Yeah. You said you were sick when you were a kid."

"I was."

"I can't believe I didn't see this when we . . . you know . . ."

He grinned and winked. "You mean when we wonked, slammed, hooked up?"

She playfully punched him on the arm. "You know what I mean." Unfortunately, it didn't mean the same thing for her anymore. There was no one to blame but herself and her Richter scale estrogen levels for the kind of deep she was now in.

Clyde wiggled his eyebrows, making them rise above the top of his glasses, which he'd put back on. "That's because we've done the wild thing mostly in the dark."

"So you were sick."

"Very. I was born with a congenital heart defect that worsened as I aged. I went through a bunch of corrective surgeries as a kid. I was in and out of hospitals most of my life."

"Well, that explains your over-the-top knowledge of useless facts like album names and song titles."

"Yeah. I spent a lot of time reading, watching TV. I'm a sponge, what can I say?"

"Which also explains your love affair with isolation."

"Thank you, Jenny Jones. What explains yours? Oh, wait—I know the answer to that. Fear." He smiled to soften the blow of his harsh words.

She ignored his jab. "That must've sucked."

"Not as much as you'd think. I had supportive parents. They tried to make up for my lack of friends in their own way."

"And your obvious distaste for the word *bedridden*. Is that what's upsetting you? Knowing we're going to find your body in a hospital bed?"

"That's part of it. I'm not loving the idea that my body's useless, because I worked so hard to keep it in tip-top physical condition, but what troubles me more is, if I can get back into my body, or whatever you're hatching in your pretty little head, who'll help you when Satan makes his next move? In all of this, we've sort of forgotten about you and your predicament with the devil, and I just can't let that happen."

Delaney's heart became erratic, wildly so, skipping beats over words she so wanted to believe meant more than just Clyde being noble. "Let's worry about problem number one. You have a time limit. I don't, that we know of, anyway."

Clyde kissed the tips of her fingers. "For the moment, but I'm not getting back into anything, bodies or otherwise, until I know you'll be okay. So where were we?"

"Sick, you were sick as a kid."

"Yes. I was pretty sick."

"But you obviously got better—this"—she waved her hand over his abs—"being your true human form."

"I did. I worked out, got a degree, and never had a single problem after that."

"After what?"

"My heart transplant."

"You had a heart transplant?"

"When I was twenty-two."

"Wait, you said you were almost thirty-seven. So in 1994?"

"Yep. November 21, 1994. It's a day I'll never forget."

Delaney bolted upright. No. Oh, fuck. No. Any date but that date. Delaney paled, her blood running through her veins like ice. "Where?"

"Lang Memorial Hospital in North Dakota. Where I had all of my surgeries." He said it with such clarity, it startled them both.

"You remembered . . ."

He smiled. "Yeah. Look at that . . ."

The room became a narrow pinpoint of nothing but the scar on Clyde's chest. It all added up. The doctor, Florence Nightingale, and finally, Robert Young. Fear threaded its way through her veins. Cold and throbbing. "Oh, Jesus, Jesus, Jesus." The words spilled from her mouth. She'd seen those papers. She knew where Vincent's heart had gone. *Lang Memorial Hospital.* Duh! That's what Robert Young had been doing when he'd popped up, handing her the last piece of this crazy jigsaw puzzle. *Marcus Welby* must have worked at Lang Memorial Hospital. She yanked the laptop from the edge of the nightstand and typed in the URL for Wikipedia. Her fingers trembled, waiting for it to pop up. Her throat tightened as she hit the backspace three times before she was able to type in correctly *Marcus Welby, M.D.*

Oh, God. OhGodohGodohGod.

"Delaney? What's wrong?"

"You got Vincent's heart . . ."

"Who?"

She gripped his hands. "Oh, my God, Clyde. Don't you see? This explains everything. There must have been some kind of mix-up . . . it explains how you ended up in Hell. It explains your ridiculous love of banana Slurpees . . ."

"Okay, slow down. Who the hell is Vincent and what does this explain?"

Her breath quickened, and a cold, clammy sweat formed in her palms. "Have you always loved banana Slurpees or did that happen *after* your heart transplant?"

He rubbed his jaw in thought. "I guess after. Wait. Definitely after. I remember going into a 7-Eleven and heading straight for the Slurpee machine without really knowing why I absolutely had to have one. I'd never had one before."

"And isn't it true that sometimes a heart transplant recipient takes on characteristics of the donor? Or in this case, the cravings of a donor?"

Clyde's brow wrinkled, his next words hesitant and measured. "I've read it's not uncommon."

Words were impossible. She had none. She'd done this. She was responsible. What she'd once thought was an act of redemption had turned into—into—Clyde being doomed to Hell.

How could that be? Vincent's heart had nothing to do with Clyde's soul. If Clyde's soul was clean, how could having Vincent's heart have destined him for this?

"This is my fault," she choked out, covering her mouth with her hand.

"What's your fault, Delaney?"

"Why you're in Hell. It's my fault. Oh, God, Clyde. If I had known I never would have . . ."

"Would have what? You're not making any sense."

"I never would have donated Vincent's heart. Never. I swear it." She'd condemned an innocent soul to Hell. Shit. She was officially a soul fucker-upper.

"Delaney, who is Vincent and what does this have to do with me?"

Her hands reached for the edge of the bed, seeking support while the world reeled.

Clyde pulled her back to him. "Talk to me. Who—is—Vincent?"

"My brother. My *half* brother."

"What does that have to do with me?"

"That has to be it. You got his heart. It explains all the road-blocks we've run into. You got Vincent's black, black, cold heart."

eighteen

Clyde's gaze never wavered. "So you owe me an explanation."

"Yeah, yeah, I do."

"So hit me."

"With my best shot?"

Clyde almost grinned, then sobered. "Now."

"I kinda like you when you get all alpha on me. It's super-duper hot—especially on a tame guy like you."

"Wanna see me not so tame?"

"No. I'm sorry. I was making light again, wasn't I?"

"No more light and no more secrets."

"Okay. So it went like this. Kellen and I had a half brother. His name was Vincent. We had no idea he existed. None. My mother never, ever mentioned him. She never breathed a word about another marriage other than the one to my father. As far as we knew, Dad had been her only husband, for reasons we found out much later. I was in college, studying veterinary medicine, and Kellen was bumming his way through life, delivering pizzas while he figured out what he wanted to do with himself. Mom was in a nursing home with Alzheimer's." She choked on the word—still so hard to say out loud, even now. Her mother's deterioration had been one of the longest, hardest, most draining periods in her move to adulthood. Draining and sometimes unbearable.

"And your father was already gone."

"Right."

"And?"

Delaney scoffed with a snorting huff. "This Vincent shows up, and he has proof he's our half brother. Real proof, Clyde. He had a bunch of pictures of my mom and him. All sorts of pictures. But it wasn't just that—he had other proof, too. Birth certificates and a marriage license—stuff we followed up on and found county records, divorce papers for." Even now, she still couldn't believe how Vincent's father had managed to cover it all up.

"And what was his explanation for why he lived with his father all those years and not your mother and you?"

Vincent had had an answer for everything. "His claim was that all of his life his father, Richard, had told him his mother—my mother—was dead. Vincent said Richard could barely talk about it without becoming enraged, but when his father died, he'd left a will with a confession about my mother in it. He'd told Vincent from a very young age that my mother left *them* before her eventual death. Richard knew all about my mother and us—he'd kept tabs on us over the years. In this letter, he made it look like she'd gone off and gotten herself some new family and that telling Vincent she was dead was easier on a little boy than telling him his mother ditched his ass, but just before his death, he had some private detective find us so he'd be able to leave Vincent the information."

"A coward even in death," Clyde said with distaste.

"Anyway, once we got past the shock and disbelief, the endless questions about why Mom had never breathed a word about Vincent and a former marriage—questions he knew damned well we couldn't ask her because of her debilitation—both Kellen and I decided he was family. Where we come from—how we were raised—you don't turn away family. Anyway, we were young. I was almost twenty at the time, Kellen was eighteen, and Vincent was pushing thirty-five when we met him. Thirty-five and rich. He had buttloads of money, and between college and Mom's care, well, we were drained. The life insurance policy after my father's death was slowly running out—which meant I'd have to leave college to keep her where she was."

"But Vincent had an answer, and I'm betting cash and a savior complex were involved." Clyde's words were snide, angry.

Delaney pinched her eyes with her thumb and forefinger to keep tears from flowing. "He said she was his mother, too. He was some rich defense attorney by then, and Kellen and I were stupid and hopeful—so hopeful we were willing to do whatever we had to, to give every comfort to our mother until she passed."

"And Vincent helped."

"Hoo boy—did he ever. But there were things about Vincent we could never quite pinpoint that made both of us really uncomfortable."

"Like?"

Simply remembering, dredging up all those times with Vincent, was like a shitstorm of painful memories. "Like he walked life on the edge. He drank too much. He was a pig when it came to women. He objectified them, leered at them, made remarks about my college girlfriends all the time, but he never lacked for one wrapped around him like some big bow. He was essentially a total scumbag. He defended the lowest scum of the earth, too—murderers, rapists, a pedophile or two. Yeah, I realize someone has to represent filth like that, but these defendants were prominent members of the community, most of them so guilty they may as well have had it written on their foreheads with a black Magic Marker, and all with buttloads of cash. Yet, Vincent didn't see it as such a big deal—not when he boldly told us about one guy he'd gotten off for murdering his wife even though he knew he was guilty. He prided himself on the strings he could pull with the cops. Then once, after we'd all been out to dinner together, we were pulled over. Vincent had definitely had too much to drink, and Kellen and I knew it. I know I should have taken the keys from him, but I don't know that I got just how trashed he was until the officer made him get out and walk in a straight line. I figured we're screwed. But nope. He hands the cop something, mentions a name or two, and it's over as fast as it started."

Clyde's lips thinned in distaste. "A bribe, no doubt."

"Exactly. Stuff like that happened all the time with Vincent. He greased palms and his were equally as greased. He had connections out the wazoo, and he wasn't afraid to use them or flaunt them to the point of uncomfortable. From having someone removed from his preferred table at his favorite restaurant to once demanding a poor woman's station wagon be towed because she'd taken his spot in his cushy law firm parking lot. Vincent loved showing off. His father was well known in the community and some kind of Supreme Court judge or something. Vincent told us how important his father had been all the fucking time, and when it became clear he was gunning for the same spot his father once held, I wanted to warn everyone I could get my hands on. I was sick at the thought that he might have the power to do something crazy."

"So you were between the proverbial rock and a hard place."

Delaney hung her head to fight the shame that even remotely knowing Vincent still brought her. "Yeah. We both were. He held the strings to Mom's care—and he knew it. If we cut all ties with him, he'd cut my mother's care off and he didn't mind telling us he would in his oh so subtle way. We were in deep and getting in deeper. It came to the point where I'd decided to leave college and get a job, and screw Vincent and his money."

But then came the day when it all exploded.

That day. She'd never, ever forget that day.

"I was at my breaking point. I had a boyfriend at the time. Gary. Gary hated Vincent, and Vincent hated him, but things had begun to unravel between us, compounded further by Vincent's appearance. Gary and I had been fighting a lot at about the time things started coming to a head with Vincent. We really needed to talk, so I showed up unannounced at his apartment one day and caught him with my roommate—in what I thought was our 'special' spot. The roof of his apartment building. We hung out there all the time because you could see the lights of the city. It was romantic. We'd sit up there for hours with a six-pack of beer and whatever our meager allowances afforded us to eat. So color me surprised when I found out our spot was anything but special.

"Now you'd think it would end there—poor Delaney gets cheated on, boo-hoo. But Vincent found me later that night in my dorm room; I was crying and doing all the stuff you do when you've been dumped in such an ugly way. You know, cursing his very existence, hoping his love shank dried up and fell off, making plans to sew a voodoo doll out of his underwear with the dental floss he used—"

"You can do that?"

"*No*, Clyde. It's just an exaggerated example. Anyway, I was a wreck and when Vincent showed up, I was at the height of a good freak and he was infuriated when he found out why. I ranted and raved, but Vincent said all those horrible things I was wishing on Gary really *could* happen if I wanted it badly enough. That stopped me cold. I didn't get it at first, and then he told me something that to this day, I might never have believed if I didn't see it with my own eyes."

"A contract. He had a contract with Satan," Clyde said with the certainty of his own name.

She pressed the heel of her hand to her head. "Jesus, did he. One that had been handed down to him from his father, Richard, was what he said. At the time, I thought he was nuts, completely nuts, and I threw him out, but not before he told me that he wanted Kellen and me to *join* him. He told us we could have whatever we wanted, money to take care of our mother, power—*anything*. When I told him to fuck off that's when he spewed some pretty crazy shit I wasn't sure I believed until . . . until I saw . . . He said little by little, whether do-gooders like us wanted it or not, believers like him would be in all places of power, sort of as a payment for doing Satan's bidding. He said he'd prove it. And that's when I got worried. Really worried about what he might do to Gary. Damn it, Clyde, if I'd just been a couple of minutes earlier. If I'd called Gary first, done something to warn him, he'd still be alive."

Clyde held up a hand, rugged and tan in the dim light of her room. "Whoa. Hold it right there. As demons we can't kill anyone, Delaney. That goes for any human who has a contract with Satan, too. I know that for a fact. We can freak them out, create illusions of their worst fears, and aid in driving them to the brink of madness so taking their own life appears almost utopian, but we can't physically harm them. I may not have liked attending the 'New-Millennium Demon and Your Role in Demonic Deviltry' classes, but I heard a thing or two."

If she didn't keep going, she'd never get it all out. "And that's just what Vincent did. Created an illusion. Gary was terrified of dogs. I know, me with a guy who's afraid of dogs, right? Either way, he was petrified of them. Some bad experience when he was growing up or something. Gary was on the roof of his apartment building. He and his roommates had been having some kind of party, and he was cleaning up while everyone else was puking down in the apartment."

Clyde's hand jerked through his hair in a rough motion. "Jesus. He didn't."

"Oh, but he did. I know he did because when all was said and done, some of Gary's roommates remembered hearing dogs growling. A lot of them, but the police chalked that up to their drinking because they found no evidence to support it. Gary must've seen those dogs, and in the kind of panic I just know they created for him, he took off running . . ."

"Right off the edge of the building."

Delaney closed her eyes. "An eight-story building."

"Holy Christ." He lifted his glasses to rub the bridge of his nose. "Okay, so what happened to Vincent? Where the hell is he?"

"It gets worse."

"As only it can."

"When Kellen and I got there, Gary was already dead. A crowd was gathering while someone else was dialing 911. In the middle of this already fucked-up mess, it began to pour. Kellen dragged me away from Gary's mangled body. God, it was so awful . . ." Her voice hitched, her chest a tight ball of knots. Her mind's eye had never allowed her the luxury of erasing that vivid visual.

Clyde drew her to his side, running small circles over her back, massaging the base of her neck, but he remained quiet, allowing her the time she needed to find her breath.

"So Kellen dragged me away from Gary—his body. I knew there was nothing I could do for him, and so did Kellen. In the middle of this, it began to pour. Thunder, lightning, the whole nine. Violent shit, and Vincent was still on the roof . . ."

Clyde's head cocked to the left in question. "I'm going to assume there is justice?"

Her shoulders sagged as Clyde continued to knead them. "In some weird way, yeah, I guess it was just. Vincent got nailed. We heard his scream, and the cries from everyone around us. Kellen and I both ran to the roof, and we found Vincent, but he was still alive."

"Alive?"

"He was when we found him—but just barely. I helped to keep him alive until the ambulance came. We spent hours in the hospital, and I hope the universe forgives me, but there were some moments when I hoped he wouldn't live—came close to actually praying for it. I was sick with myself for it—but at this point, even though I didn't know the whole story surrounding Gary's death, I knew how evil Vincent was. I knew what he was capable of, and I knew in my gut he'd killed Gary to prove to me what he could do—to show the fuck off."

The confusion on Clyde's face was blatant.

"Kellen and I were his only living relatives—me being the oldest of the two of us. When the doctors told us Vincent was virtually brain-dead, I felt so little remorse it disgusts me to remember it. But they also told us a decision had to be made about whether to resuscitate him if his heart began to fail. There was all this medical talk of DNRs and he was hooked up to all these machines, and then the words 'no chance of recovery' came up, and finally, organ donation . . . It's still kind of a blur, but I did know one thing—Gary was dead. Vincent wouldn't ever pay for that by doing time or whatever. He might not have paid for it had he lived because of who he knew, but I knew he was responsible—so I did the next best thing . . ."

Clyde's hands stopped moving. "I'm lost. Vincent's execution wasn't enough?"

"Vincent was healthy and strong. Vital, for all his faults. He took the 'body is your temple' to a whole new level. Despite his drinking, he didn't smoke, he worked out, jogged . . . so I kept him alive long enough to donate his organs. *All* of them."

Clyde's hands on her back froze, his body stiffening with a rigid clench.

Oh, God. What had she done in the name of revenge? "I kept him alive just long enough to offer up his organs for transplant. One of those organs was a heart. I know what I did was something Vincent would've hated, but he had to, in some way, redeem himself for the shit he'd thrown down. He killed another human being, Clyde. Gary may have been a cheat, but he didn't deserve to die for it. He was just a kid. *I* was just a kid. There was no way to make that right, so I did the next best thing—I gave every viable organ to someone who'd hopefully use them for good. And that's when Satan showed up. Right there in Vincent's ICU room when we were saying our last good-byes."

"If I wasn't lost before, I really am now. Why would Satan show up for something as inconsequential as some organs and a soul collection? He could've sent any one of his freaks in Hell to do that for him. In fact, he rarely if ever shows up. It's not like he cared about Vincent, Delaney. Satan doesn't have friends, he has pawns. Vincent was a pawn, and his time was done. Satan essentially won because I'm betting my own soul, Vincent went to Hell. So Satan got what he wanted—a soul."

That one fact had troubled her for as long as she could remember. "I'm as lost as you are on that. I only know this—whatever Vincent had was important enough for Satan to threaten me if I signed those papers. Vincent was already dead—if he had a soul, it was long gone from his body and probably well on its way to Hell. If that's what the devil wanted all along, if Vincent had really sold his soul to him, he'd won hands down. Vincent committed *murder*—he had no place to go but down. Why his eyes or his kidneys or his heart meant something to Lucifer, I still don't know."

"How did he prove to you he was who he said he was?"

Delaney snorted. "The usual. Horns, fire breathing, snakes, blah-blah-blah. At the time, I think I almost lost my bladder. Nowadays, it's like watching reruns of *Happy Days*. Not nearly as exciting or dramatic as it is the first time around, ya know?"

"I don't think I want to know. So next I'm assuming he threatened you?"

"Yup, and Kellen, too. He said he'd see me in Hell for signing that organ transplant document and having Vincent's body shipped off before he could get to it. What was worse was his threat to Kellen or anyone who came into my life from there on out . . ."

Clyde blew out a breath of pent-up air. "Which explains a shitload about how little you interact with the living."

Her shoulders lifted. "I was always afraid someone would end up hurt like Gary did. I was terrified Lucifer would send one of his lackeys in to hurt Kellen, but at least my brother knew what to be careful of—how aware he had to be that true evil exists. How do you explain the grim reality of the supernatural to a new girlfriend who isn't a demon—or to a possible date? I mean, I did try to get out and date. I told you that. But after a couple of failed attempts despite Satan's warning, the ghost talking only added weight to what was already a sinking ship. So I stopped trying. But I was successful in donating Vincent's organs—I decided that was enough compensation."

Clyde's eyebrows rose. "And let me guess—when you donated them, you did something completely Delaney-ish, like you stuck your tongue out at Lucifer and said, 'See this, asshole? Nyah, nyah, nyah.'"

Her smile was grim, but her nod was one of affirmation. "Nuh-uh. Though you did get the asshole part right. I said, 'The fuck I won't, asshole.' Oh, and neener, neener, neener. Not nyah, nyah, nyah."

He smirked. "Just as endearing as ever."

"Something good had to come out of that night, Clyde, and I was going to be fucked and feathered if I'd let all those good organs go to waste if they could give someone else life. A worthy life. A good life."

His finger traced the slope of her nose. "Hey, I'm with you one hundred percent. I don't know if I would have had the balls to do what you did, but I hear what you're preaching. So as his only living relatives, please tell me you got his money."

Her laugh was filled with bitterness for what that money could have done had they been in Vincent's will. He'd been smart enough to name Delaney on his DNR, yet keep them from having the help they'd needed for her mother. "No. No money. I would have had my hands severed before I took it even if we had. The only thing I would have definitely done was had my mother properly taken care of until she died. He owed her. The rest I would have given to some humane society or something. But Vincent left it to a political party."

Clyde's nod was of understanding, his eyes sympathetic. "And that's why you quit school? To work to pay for your mother's care?"

"That and the crazy shit that began to happen."

"The ghost thing?"

That first time had been killa. "Yeah. They were, like, everywhere. In my sociology classes, when I was in the dorm shower, in a lecture. Before I understood it, and what these spirits wanted from me, I really, really struggled. I went through the whole posttraumatic deal. Then I thought I was just nuttier than squirrel shit. At first it scared the bejesus out of me, then it drove me batshit for a time, and with that, my grades suffered—friendships were lost. I spent all my time at the library researching ghosts and mediums and Hell."

"So you weren't born with the ability to see ghosts? All this time I just assumed that was the case."

"No, it happened after Vincent's death. About two or three weeks or so after."

"And you don't see the connection here, Delaney?"

"Oh, I see it. I think the horned pitchfork-lover thought he could make me a loon by sending ghosts my way. When I finally realized I could communicate with them, I shoved it up his ass further by helping them cross. I did the lemonade thing."

When Clyde smiled at her, despite how dire their situation was, despite how the terror of that night still had the ability to affect her, it made her insides turn to utter goo. "You're a tough broad, Delaney Markham, but I think the connection goes deeper. I just don't know how."

His silence left her silent, too.

"And your mother? Did you ever find out why she'd never told you about Richard and Vincent?"

It still sounded crazy to her, and voicing it sounded like she really should be locked forever in a padded room with an "I love me" jacket. "You know demon magic exists—you made some when you went to your bank. Her memory, and the memory of anyone else even a little involved in their lives, was wiped clean. Richard stole Vincent and raised him for his own sick devices. He just didn't plan on Vincent being such a fuck-up."

"And I'm supposing Satan was happier than a cat eyeball deep in catnip to tell you that."

When Satan had shown up and began revealing what they'd done to her mother—that they'd taken her child—Delaney had wanted to scratch his eyes out. "About as happy as I imagine the fucker gets."

The breath Clyde exhaled was long. "So what exactly did you donate again?"

"His eyes, kidneys, heart, and other remaining parts to science."

"His heart . . ."

"A heart I'm almost certain you have. The dates match. November 21, 1994, is the day Vincent died. We need to get a look at your files, Clyde."

"It isn't just that, Delaney. Vincent's heart's somehow connected to you and your seeing ghosts. I don't know how, I don't understand why, but Satan can't send spirits who are seeking guidance—especially those who're stuck in limbo—to freak you out. He has no control over waffling entities. That much I know. He can definitely throw a monkey wrench in your plans to cross them, and send in a minion to try and talk them into coming to the dark side. However, he only has control over those who've landed in Hell. Period. Not those who're doing nothing more than questioning whether there really is an 'other' side."

She was at a loss then. "Then what's the connection? I didn't have the ability to see ghosts until Vincent was dead for at least a few weeks."

"I don't know, but we need to find out. And I'm not going anywhere—in my body—out of my body—nowhere until we figure this out."

Delaney leaned into him with a shaky sigh, their heads bent together. "This is what I wanted to avoid. At first, I didn't trust you enough to tell you about Vincent. I figured you'd go back to Satan so you could have a good chuckle over how freaked out poor Delaney's been all these years, and the hell I'd let that happen. I refused to give in to the fear. I decided to piss in his Wheaties by living my life—or semi-living it, if what you've labeled what I do is accurate. I was just really careful about *who* I let into my life. Because even if I wanted nothing more than to spite Satan, I didn't want to do it at someone else's expense. But then, I just wanted to keep you out of this thing Lucifer's got with me because I don't quite know if we've seen the extent of his wrath, but we might if he finds out you helped me and deceived him while you did it."

Clyde kissed the top of her head. "Now it all makes a bit more sense. That's why you sent Marcella away. If she heard no evil, she couldn't speak it."

"Exactly. She has no idea about Vincent. Well, not entirely. She did come to tell me she'd heard something about him the other night. I figured if I could keep my mouth shut long enough for her to grill me and leave, this would be over before she finds anything else out. If Satan knew she was my one and only friend, he'd try to hurt her—because he does have the power to do that. I don't want anyone hurt when he makes his next move. We'll have enough trouble if he ever gets wind of the fact that you duped him."

"Trouble has a shitload of different meanings, don'tcha think, *Clyde*?" a surly voice asked from the dark interior of the bathroom.

Both their heads popped up in surprise.

"Uh, bad guy?" she asked, so not wanting to hear the answer.

"Yep."

"How bad?"

"Scale of one to ten?"

"Sure."

"Twelve."

Hoo, shit.

nineteen

Delaney was powerless to move at the sight of the body attached to the voice. Clyde, however, stood up, taking the blanket with him and motioning to Delaney to put on the T-shirt he handed her. He tucked the blanket around his lean waist.

The demon hopped on the edge of the bed with a wink, walking his dirty fingers along the bed toward Delaney's leg with a cackle. "So what're ya doin' with my woman? You been stickin' it to her?"

Clyde was quicker than she'd ever have given him credit for. His hand snaked out, grabbing the demon's fingers and wrenching them with a rough jerk. "Get—the—fuck—away—from—her—or I'll *kill* you," he growled low and deep.

The demon's hand exploded out of Clyde's, roughly yanking his arm away, but his voice was sweeter than melted chocolate. "Aw, Clyde. Clyde, Clyde, *Clyde*. Play nice now, man. You had your shot at her, and I promise ya, I won't tell that whack Lucifer what you did, switching our assignments like that, if you let me give it to her.

Just once. You can watch if you want." His pockmarked face stretched into a leering grin, revealing blackened teeth.

Clyde dragged him to his feet, the muscles in his upper arms bulging when he shoved the demon up against the nearest wall, eliciting a harsh huff from him. "I said, get the fuck away from her, *Clyve.*"

Delaney scrambled to the floor, her eyes never leaving Clyde's back, strained from his grip on the key to this whole mess falling apart.

They'd been made.

The infamous Clyve Atwell had apparently found them—which meant Lucifer wouldn't be far behind.

The demon threw his head back and laughed until she could almost see he had no tonsils. "Or what, Clyde? You sorry piece of shit. You can't take me with your level one skills. Shoulda paid better attention in class, man," he taunted up into Clyde's face, breaking the hold he had on him with a swift shove to Clyde's chest. His dirty white T-shirt tore when Clyde lost his grip on him.

"Oh, you two—what is it about trouble and it always finding you when you're half naked?" yet another voice cooed.

And it had a slight accent to it.

It sang in Delaney's ears like a symphony of sweet violins.

Marcella.

Delaney's knees felt weak with relief, then weaker with terror. Marcella didn't stand a chance against this scum. Her protective nature kicked into high gear. "Marcella," she hissed, sending her a message with her eyes, begging her to stop. "Go shop, would you? Go home! Go do something other than get mixed up in this," she ordered.

Marcella sighed with obvious exasperation and it was directed at Delaney. "Have you no faith, *mi amiga*? Ju—" She paused, clenching her jaw to ward off the accent that she couldn't always hide in times of stress. "*You're* always so negative."

Inching closer to Marcella, and keeping an eye on an immobilized-by-surprise Clyve, Delaney pointed to her chest. "Me? Hell-loooooo," she whispered near her friend's ear, "who's the one who uses duct tape—*duct tape*, I remind you—to capture demons? Are you fucking crazy showing up here? He'll obliterate you! That means no more *Pier 1*. No more throw pillows. Get it?"

Crossing her arms over her chest, Marcella stuck her tongue out at Delaney. "Negative, negative, negative," she whisper-taunted back.

Her finger flew up under Marcella's nose. "You do that one more time and I'll snatch it out of your head—got that, demona-tor?"

"And I'll roast animal fat with your happy sticks, ghost trans-mitter."

"They're not happy sticks—they're smudge sticks, smart-ass."

"They look like rolled weed, and if you don't back off and let me do my thing, D, I'm going to singe your eyebrows." She clamped a warning hand on Delaney's shoulder, squeezing it hard, implor-ing her with her eyes to clamp it. There was a message in those green orbs—Delaney just couldn't figure out what the fuck it was. Marcella rolled her shoulders, letting go of Delaney and sashaying over to the demon, swishing her perfect ass in her friend's direc-tion.

Marcella cocked her head at him playfully, her smile cool, her green eyes, now glittering, almost black. "So you must be Clyve." She pushed herself between the two men, who'd both remained silent—one stunned, one unsure what was next. She flicked an ab-sent finger at Clyde, dismissing him as she stared the demon directly in the eye.

"Who the fuck are *you*?" he spat, though his roaming, beady eyes appraised Marcella's body with jeering approval.

Her fingers traced the soiled collar of his T-shirt with flirtatiousness. "Ohhhh, such harsh words, so big and mean. Grrrrrrrrrrrr. I *like* it." She squirmed, wiggling her hips with a saucy shift.

Clyve's chin lifted, a hard knot pulsing there, yet he couldn't take his eyes off Marcella. "I said, who the fuck are you?"

Smiling wide, flashing her perfect white teeth, Marcella closed in on him with a wink. She cornered him, eyeing him like he was what was for lunch. Her lips moved dangerously close to the demon's, so close Delaney cringed for her. Then she dragged a nail seductively over the stubble on his cheek, stopping at his lips, letting that digit tug at his lower lip with a playful tweak. "I'm the crazy Puerto Rican bitch that's gonna make you squeal for your mama, pig," she purred into his face, snapping her fingers together.

When the pads of her fingers released, she let her hands drop to her shoulders, stroking the sleek skin of a very long, black snake that had appeared out of thin air. Its head reared up in Clyve's face. "This is my friend. Pretty, *sí*?" Marcella wrapped her hand around the snake's head and held it next to Clyve's cheek, rubbing it with a sensuous glide over the surface of his skin. "He wants to be your friend, too, Clyve. Loooook," she said with a malicious smile and a coy, schoolgirl tone, "I think he likes you—wanna play with him?"

Clyve's face went white. His lips moved, but no sound came out.

With a jerk so quick Delaney almost couldn't believe Marcella'd pulled it off her shoulders, she hurled the snake at Clyve, who skittered backward, beads of sweat glistening on his forehead, his Adam's apple bobbing in rapid glides while he tried to swallow.

Marcella widened her stance, planting her hands on her jean-clad hips, watching with satisfaction as the snake gyrated at Clyve's feet.

Delaney's amazement at this new feat Marcella had apparently acquired was mingled with a mondo shudder. Bleh on snakes. Fuck, where had she packed her prism and salt? There must be salt in this hotel room—maybe she could help Marcella. There wasn't time to find out as the snake began to inch its way toward the demon, his tongue striking aimlessly in forked fury. She hated snakes—almost as much as it would seem Clyve did.

The demon hopped from foot to foot, a look of angry terror streaking his bony features. His greasy ponytail flopped up and down from behind his head while his face turned a lovely shade of crimson. "I'll fucking kill you, you bitch!" he hollered with a high-pitched wail.

Marcella pouted at him, her full, glossy lower lip distended while she toed the snake with a gentle nudge toward him. "You're hurting my feelings, Clyve, calling me names. Though *bitch* is rather all-encompassing, don't you think? Wise choice. And really, if you don't like this snake, all you had to do was say so. I bet I can find one you will like. I aim to please." She snapped her fingers again, this time letting them ball into a fist and plunging her hand toward the floor. A slithering swarm of coiled snakes, the color of garden hoses, appeared, hissing toward Clyve at a rapid pace.

Infuriated, Clyve screamed a shriek of whistling fury, hurling a fireball from his fingertips in Marcella's direction while he threw himself upward onto the small table in the room. Flames bounced off the wall behind Marcella and headed directly for her glossy, black head.

"Duck!" Clyde roared, throwing his body on top of Delaney's as they crashed to the floor.

Delaney peeked out from under Clyde's body to see Marcella roll her eyes at the demon's effort like he'd just lobbed a beach ball at her.

Dayum, who'd gotten her demon on all of a sudden? Since when did Marcella go all 666?

Marcella flicked her wrist, letting her fingers splay apart; from their tips came a crackling bolt of light aimed directly at Clyve.

The demon dove for the far side of the bed, the zigzagging current nailing the picture above the headboard and splitting it in half. Clyve recovered quickly, bellowing a "this is war" cry. He rose on his knees, his rotted teeth clenched together, and raised his fists skyward. Grimy palms fell open and out of them came flecks of color, becoming a metamorphosis of rats, twitching and scurrying across the floor in a million directions.

Oh, no. Nuh-uh. No can do. She loved animals, but rats should always, in her humble opinion, be loved from afar—like, big afar. Delaney heaved upward as the ball of rats raced along the floor, forcing Clyde's heavy weight off her. They jumped up together while Delaney made a beeline for his chest, throwing herself on him and wrapping her legs around his waist. Her ankles hooked behind his back and she wasn't letting go.

The first gust of wind made even Clyde and his thickly muscled thighs wobble. He gripped her to him with protective hands while swirls of bone-chilling air picked up speed. The room grew instantly arctic, small particles of ice forming on Clyde's eyebrows.

Marcella braced herself against the wind, turning her shoulder into it while she snapped her fingers once more. The velocity of sheer gale force pulled at the skin on her face, ripping through the room at warp speed.

From somewhere distant, over Clyde's shoulders Delaney heard someone call to the demon in a persecuted, nasally whine. "Clyyyyyyve! Clyve, what have you done, sweet baby boy? Oh, Clyve, you're so naughty!"

That this fuckwit had ever been anyone's baby had never even been a consideration for Delaney. Yet, the wind instantly ceased, the rats and their squeaking screams disappearing with merely an echo left in place.

Silence fell on the room—deafening in its suddenness.

Marcella whirled her hair out of her face, eyeballing the confused Clyve with disdain. "Tsk, tsk, Clyve. You've been a bad *muchacho*. But I brought someone with me who can teach you a lesson."

A sturdy, dark silhouette shaped into a rotund woman with several chins. Long hair, the color of a silvery moon, draped down her back, swishing across her wide, thick shoulders when she shook her head. The housecoat she wore had large red and blue flowers on it, and in her chubby hand, she held a rolling pin.

A big, wooden rolling pin.

Her eyes held pity when she gazed upon her baby boy, sorrow and pity. "Oh, Clyve . . ." she murmured with a cluck of her tongue, wrinkling her nose.

Clyve blanched from his place on the bed, sagging into it and cowering with fear. "Ma?" he said, weak and watery with a tremble he couldn't conceal.

"You've been so naughty, Clyve. Why are you so naughty? You promised you'd be good when I was gone, and look at you. Running rackets for the devil himself." She crooked her pudgy finger at him in her direction. "Come here, Clyve."

Clyve skittered back on the bed, fear and awe interchangeable in his beady eyes.

His mother moved closer, pity and sorrow turning to disappointment and anger. "I said, come here, Clyve. *Now*."

When it didn't appear as though Clyve was going to bend to his mother's will, she leaned forward, snatching his ear and dragging him to her.

Clyve's howl lingered long after their disappearance.

Delaney dropped from Clyde's embrace, speechless, her eyes wide when she caught Marcella's gaze.

"You know, sometimes, D, you just need to trust me," she remarked with dry sarcasm.

"I thought you were a level one demon," Clyde pondered more to himself than anyone else.

Marcella flapped a hand at them. "I am, but I've been practicing because whatever the frig's going on with you and Delaney here made me think I might need to. It also helps to have a connection or two and to know a demon's weakness. Clyve's being snakes and his mother—not necessarily in that order. So I learned a thing or two—and don't ask how, D. Just know there are ways around doing those things to poor innocents. So don't go all moral and righteous on me. And now, you can thank me for saving your asses. Oh, and P.S., do you have any idea how freakin' hard that snake thing was? Christ, Delaney—it took me four days just to conjure something that wasn't cold and lifeless. If you only knew how many goldfish lives I'm responsible for. I'm exhausted here, *guapa*."

Delaney lunged at Marcella, hugging her hard and giving her a sloppy kiss on the cheek. "Thank you, thank you, thank you. I love you. You're the most awesome friend I've ever had. You're like a demon queen. I'd be a puddle of shit without you. Now go home."

Marcella disentangled herself from Delaney, then smoothed her clothing. "Stop already. And I'm not going home. If I kept doing what you keep telling me to do, you'd be french-fried right now, and we couldn't take care of the biz at hand."

"The business at hand?" Clyde asked, coming to put an arm around Delaney's waist, rubbing her still frozen hands.

Marcella eyed him, her green eyes glittering with bits of suspicion. "Yes, lover. I admit, I didn't believe you, Clyde Atwell. I'm sure Delaney told you I thought you were full of shit. All that innocence and light was a little hard to believe, but we're good now after what I heard."

Delaney crossed her arms over her chest. "Spill."

"It ain't good."

"I don't imagine it could be any worse than it already is." Clyde's comment was wry.

"You"—Marcella pointed a finger at him—"are having a really bad week. Crazy bad. And Vincent's only part of the problem here."

Clyde looked down at Delaney. "She knows about Vincent?"

"She knows *of* him."

"Now I know *all* of him," Marcella interrupted, "and believe me when I tell you, this info about him and Clyde was some seriously guarded shit. Three demon bar hot spots and a carefully placed threat to a green, just-fell-off-the-turnip-truck noob or so later, here I am."

"So you know he was my half brother . . ." Delaney choked on those words. That label, in connection with her, disgusted her on so many levels she could yark over it.

Marcella squeezed Delaney's forearm. "I do—they always say you can pick your nose, but you can't pick your family. Vincent lived up to that. I also know that he had a contract with Satan, originating with his father—this contract his father, Richard, signed was handed down to him—sort of an all-in-the-family deal. It had details, stipulations of which I'm still not entirely clear. The only thing I do know for sure is this—the heart that beats in Clyde's body, wherever the frig his body is, was Vincent's."

Confirmation her suspicions had been correct. Delaney's nod was curt. "It's what we figured. What *I* figured, anyway. I'm betting it's at Lang Memorial Hospital. We haven't checked yet, and it's too much to go into now, but that's where Clyde had the heart transplant to begin with. I bet his body's there."

Marcella cupped Delaney's chin with cool fingers. "Wherever it is, D, we have to find it in order to set Clyde free. His soul's in limbo. How he got to Hell leaves me beyond mind-fucked now that I know the kind of person he was. I only know he has to be cut from the ties that bind him here on Earth in order for him to find any peace and free himself of Satan. Maybe the paperwork got screwed up or maybe it's because Clyde had *Vincent's* heart, and a person's heart, according to some tales of old, is the essence of your being. If that's the case, essentially, because Vincent's heart is still beating, his soul hasn't been collected. If that's the case, then you beat Satan by donating that prick's heart—big—and I'm pretty damned sure he didn't much like that. Basically, you stole from him. I still don't get what went wrong with Clyde's soul, but something did, and we have to make it right. That means we have to find Clyde's body."

Terror, real and like a living entity, gripped Delaney's insides, finally having confirmation of the suspicion she'd shared with Clyde earlier. "I knew it." She glanced up at Clyde, whose lips were compressed into a thin line. "I'm sorry. Jesus, I'm so sorry. I thought I was doing the right thing by donating Vincent's organs and now . . ."

"You didn't know, D. How could you possibly know the extent of that kind of evil or that it would ever harm an innocent soul like Clyde? Now, no time for regrets, *chica*," Marcella said, grazing Delaney's cheek with her thumb.

However, Delaney couldn't hear Marcella—she couldn't hear anything about freeing anyone. Free Willy, for fuck's sake, but leave Clyde alone. Clyde was alive, God damn it. *Alive*. He didn't need to be freed. She looked up at Clyde. "But wait, your neighbor's maid said you were alive. In a hospital. Why do we have to free anything if Clyde's still alive?"

Marcella's face expressed a million different things in one glance. "That's true, D. He is technically still alive." She grabbed at Delaney's hand, crushing it in her cooler one. "But it's only his body, honey. He's not really there, and that's because his soul is here, with us."

Delaney couldn't connect the dots. She gave both Clyde and Marcella a blank stare.

"I'm probably on life support," Clyde said, making the statement with such cold indifference, Delaney shivered, clinging to Marcella's hand. "And I had no will—no one to sign a DNR. It explains why there was no obituary for me. I'm lingering and probably pretty hacked up while I do it after what we saw at my house today."

No. No. That couldn't be true. *No.* "But the spirits said *coma*—they said you were in a coma—not on life fucking support!"

Clyde knelt in front of her, placing his big hands on her knees. "Listen to me, Delaney. You said yourself they get confused. Maybe they were confused, but if it's like Marcella said, that has to be what's keeping my heart, Vincent's, whoever's heart, beating."

Delaney's head shot up, her eyes pinning Clyde and his oh so logical, all about the rational self. Souls didn't just up and leave bodies before their bodies were good and dead. And Clyde wasn't dead. "Then how are you here—with me?" she yelled, in anger—in outrage—that yet again, the fucking devil would win. He'd win Clyde. He'd managed to steal her from him as indirectly as he'd killed Gary, and that made her so infuriated she wanted to break things—hurt something so she wouldn't hurt.

Marcella cleared her throat, brushing wispy strands of Delaney's hair from her face. "I told you. I don't know how Clyde's soul broke free from his body, sweetie. I don't know how in breaking free, that landed him in Hell. I do know he shouldn't be there, and I've spread the word far and wide that he's been unjustly placed.

I'm hoping someone will come and fix that. I don't even know where his body is, but we have to find it so he can be free, and we have to do it before Satan gets wind of what he's done. If Clyde doesn't cross, and no one's there to stop it, his soul's fair game." Marcella averted her gaze to meet Clyde's. "You did a good thing by switching those assignments, Clyde. I know it didn't start out the way it's ended up—you needed to figure out how you ended up in Hell, and the only way to do that was a pass here to this plane, but you were also looking out for Delaney, indirectly at first, I know . . ." Marcella shook her head. "Anyway, that's admirable, considering the shit you'd get if you got caught."

Clyde's expression turned to concrete. "I don't care about the shit, and I'm not leaving until I know Delaney's safe. Lucifer wanted her trashed, belittled, humiliated. That won't happen while I'm still here, even if it's only in spirit."

Marcella was quick to shoot him down. "Your gig's up, Clyde. Think of Clyve finding you two. You don't suppose a suck-ass like that didn't tell Satan what you two were up to for brownie points, do you? You'd be foolish to believe that. Lucifer knows about what you did, and you can bet your fine, sculpted bippy, he'll come collect you. You have to go, and you have to do it before Satan comes calling."

"Let him call," Clyde dared, his shoulders squaring off.

"It'll be okay. I promise. I have friends, some who sympathize with my plight," Marcella replied. "They'll help Delaney. She'll be okay. You have my word. Nothing will hurt her—*no one* will hurt her. Swear it, but you can't go on free-falling, Clyde. If anyone knows that, Delaney does. Your soul needs to find peace, and we need to do that before Satan decides he wants to play. You have to cross."

Clyde nodded his head with resolution—unbearable acceptance written all over his face. "So we have to pull my plug."

Marcella's nod of agreement was silent—foreboding—but definitely a confirmation.

And if his heart—Vincent's former heart—stopped beating, that meant so did Clyde.

twenty

"So you like the demon?"

Delaney wasn't sure when she'd begun to breathe again, but she must have been capable of it if she could spit out, "He's not a *demon*, Marcella. Or he's not supposed to be, anyway," and be able to pull it off with such defensive venom in her voice.

Marcella held her palms up like two white flags in a gesture of acquiescence. "Easy there, honey. Don't shoot the messenger."

But Delaney teetered between hysteria and fear, with a healthy dose of fury to keep her warm. She was at a loss for words, but at the same time, full of a jumble of angry, hateful thoughts she wanted to scream while she threw around the toiletries the hotel offered. Instead, she fought for clarity. In that clarity, one thing was sure—Marcella couldn't get in any deeper. "I'm sorry. I'm sorry for all of this. I swear to God, I never thought doing what I did all those years ago would come to this. But you can't be involved, Marcella. You need to go. You're already in deep with all of your poking around, any further and you're in way over your head, and the devil'll want payback. You don't want him coming after you with revenge on his mind. You do see where that got me, don't you?"

But Marcella was staunch, shaking her dark head. "Nope—not going, and forget the apologies. What I really want to know is this—and I'm only asking because it has to be asked. When the time comes, will you be able to cross Clyde over? Can you say good-bye?"

No.

No.

No.

No.

But alas . . . "I don't have a choice. It's what I do."

"No, you don't have a choice. I wish I could change that, Delaney. I don't have the power to do it, but if I did, I would." Marcella had always been about getting to the point, and Delaney admired that in their relationship—in Marcella. Yet tonight, she didn't want harsh realisms. She didn't need to hear what would happen next out loud. She wanted "Poor baby," and forbidden food filled with artificial dyes, or ice cream like Ben and Jerry's Chunky Monkey, a Butterfinger—hell, a whole pound of sugar she could suck on and wash down with a six-pack of Pepsi. She wanted something that would ease this inconsolable ache.

And then it hit her.

In the gut.

She swallowed hard when more of the information Marcella'd relayed sank further into her murky brain. "I'll never see Clyde in this life again. Ever." The whisper of that word swirled in ominous echoes.

Marcella's angular, perfectly structured face was the most somber Delaney'd ever seen it. "No, honey. No, you won't."

"Will you hang around . . . after we . . ." Delaney heard the desperation in her voice, she tasted it on her tongue, but she had no desire to hide it or the weakness it revealed.

"Of course I will, silly. Not even that arrogant, pigheaded brother of yours could keep me away from you. And he's fine, by the way. I peeked in on him when he wasn't looking because I figured you'd worry about him and he'd only freak if he knew I was watching his cranky ass." She held out a hand to Delaney, taking her trembling, cold fingers between hers and rubbing them with a brisk motion.

"As long as I still have you . . ."

"Oh, D. You'll always have me. Maybe even longer than you planned if I'm stuck like this for eternity. Demons are forever, right?" she teased, chucking Delaney under the chin. "So Clyde . . ."

"What about him?"

"You like him," she said again, as if reminding her wasn't like rubbing salt in a million open wounds.

Delaney's throat grew tight once more. "It'll be okay. He'll hit the great beyond and find some hot chick with big, honkin' wings who knows all about how to make a bomb from dental floss and nail polish remover or something."

Yet Marcella's face didn't crack the smile Delaney'd hoped for. "Don't make jokes. This hurts you. I hate that. In all the years I've known you, nothing would've pleased me more than for you to find your Prince Charming. Have kids so I could be Auntie Marcella to human beings instead of dogs. If this could be any other way, if I had the power . . . but just so you know, I'm here. When this is over, I'm here."

Delaney let her head fall to her chest. There was no way to hide the tears that fell in fat droplets to the bathroom floor she and Marcella stood on. She needed to gather herself together so she could give Clyde the send-off he deserved. With a smile—with the kind of joy one should have for finding peace on the other side.

For eternity.

But it hurt far worse than any other pain she'd ever experienced. It was different from the pain of losing her parents—different from the pain she'd suffered losing Gary.

Yet it was as raw, as real, as undeniably agonizing as any kind of torture could be. Counting the minutes until they had to take Clyde off life support in the hope that it would free his soul and she could cross him over was like playing Russian roulette—just waiting for the bullet to explode from the barrel of the gun.

Marcella put her arms around Delaney, pulling her into them to offer her ever-strong support. She surprised Delaney often, but her offer of physical comfort shocked her even more. Marcella hated crying; she said it was messy and did horrible things to your complexion.

The stream of tears she shed flooded Marcella's leather jacket, but she managed to choke out an admission that out loud cut far deeper than keeping it inside. "Jesus Christ. *Yes.* Yes, I like him. Damn it. I like him. The dogs like him. And I don't want him to go. I want to—"

Marcella squeezed harder. "Get to know him better. I know. But maybe—and I'm just throwing this out there—maybe this attraction is based solely on the fact that he's the first man who's been in your life in almost fifteen years."

That assumption, though she'd made it herself, made her angry again. "Would you say that about someone else? Say I met some guy online and he got the whole medium thing—totally accepted it—was wonking me until my eyeballs wobbled—wanted to marry me—give me a houseful of babies—would you say the same thing? No. You'd be thrilled Delaney was finally spending a Saturday night with something other than her battery-operated boyfriend and a bag of trail mix, wouldn't you? Just because I met Clyde under extreme circumstances, that doesn't mean I like him less. I like Clyde. I like him beyond the fact that he gets my ghost friends. I like his smile. I like the fact that he wears those glasses when he surely must know that he now has twenty-twenty vision. I like the dumb-ass crap he knows about the stupidest things like earthworms and '80s music. I like that he eats cheeseburgers like he's dining at some fancy restaurant. I like that he has no clue how fucking hot he is. I even like that we have almost nothing in common because you know what? I learn things from him because of it. The differences between us makes him that much hotter. I just like Clyde. The way I feel now, I figure given a couple of more months the *l* word I'm feeling now might have had a different spelling—but I'll never get the chance to fucking find out." She sobbed the words out, stuffing a knuckle in her eye to plug the wet tears that refused to stop falling.

Marcella held her away from her, gripping her shoulders. Her eyes held compassion. "And you're fucking angry about it! Good on you—you should be, *muchacha*. Wanna throw shit together? I'm all in for some glass breaking."

"I like you, too, Delaney," Clyde said from the bathroom door, his forearms braced on the frame, his face contorted in flashes of emotion. "And if things were different, I'd hunt your ass down, throw you over my shoulder, and *make* you eat cheeseburgers with me. I'd do all the things a man who wants to get to know a woman better does. I'd text-message stupid notes to you just because. I'd buy you flowers, even though they end up dead. I'd even put them in water with a smile on my damned face. I'd take you to the movies. I'd call you just to say hello. I'd even listen to Michael Bublé with you. I'd wear your ass down until you decided to consider a future with me and as many stray, helpless dogs as you could adopt and as many babies as we could make to fill a household. If this were different, if I had a choice in any of this fucked-up mess, I'd stay with you—and this time, I'd *pay attention*. I'd pay much closer attention to what was going on with the people in my life." Clyde's eyes clung to Delaney's face when he finished, blazing with conviction and all that passion she'd taunted him about not having.

And it left her breathless.

Wordless.

And so filled with anguish, it made it impossible to express it.

No one spoke—the tight confines of the bathroom suddenly became almost too much to bear.

Marcella grabbed a handful of tissues from the box on the long vanity, handing them to Clyde. "You two let me know when you're ready." She slipped under Clyde's arms and out of the bathroom.

Clyde cupped Delaney's cheeks with both hands. "I'd choose to stay with you if I could. I'd choose to *stay* . . ."

Her arms went around his waist, inhaling the clean scent that was Clyde, memorizing each ripple in his abdomen, each hard plane of his arms.

She had nothing left. For fifteen years she'd used words to help others, cajole, soothe, comfort. Tonight, she had nothing.

There really was nothing left to say.

They didn't have a choice.

Satan had made the choice for them.

Clyde's body was indeed at Lang Memorial Hospital—a trauma center for burn victims, the brain injured, and those with a host of other life-threatening issues. It hadn't been easy to get past the brigade of nurses, but Marcella and her charm should never be underestimated. In a matter of moments, Delaney'd slipped passed the trauma nurses' station unnoticed, with Clyde right behind her.

Marcella slipped back out of the room after squeezing Clyde's hand, then hugging her friend. "Safe journey, Clyde," she offered with a gentle smile. "I'll be right outside, D. Right there." She pointed to the long, sterile hallway. "Waiting."

So here they were.

Her, Clyde's soul, and Clyde . . . er, Clyde's body.

One big, fat, supernatural hoedown.

They stood by his bed. Parts of his body were wrapped in gauze, and he was hooked up to a ventilator and a heart monitor and some feeding tubes. According to the file Marcella had stolen, he had burns on only twenty percent of his body, yet another Clyde miracle, but that was only part of the problem.

He'd suffered severe head trauma in the explosion. The file was filled with complicated medical terms Delaney was only half sure of—the only thing she was sure of was that Clyde really was terminal. Essentially, this vital, smart, overly logical, fantastic man was brain-dead, and had been for almost three months now. Clyde had been right—there were no wills, and no living relatives to sign a DNR.

Every fiber of her being had hoped against hope that Clyde would have even a small chance of survival, despite what Marcella'd told them. She'd prayed Marcella was wrong. Seeing him this way, his strong frame helpless and pale with tubes and monitors, left Delaney barren of any optimism.

Clyde took in his lifeless form with grave silence. He neither moved toward the bed, nor away from it.

Hopefully, when they pulled the plug Clyde's soul would go where it'd always belonged, and this would all be over.

So. Over.

"So you have to go."

"It looks like it."

Puffing her cheeks out, Delaney fought to keep her focus on the task at hand. "Hookay, I say we don't linger because that'll just be bad for my already burning eyeballs." And her heart. Her aching, clenching, pounding, anguish-riddled heart. "So here's where we say good-bye. I ship you off to the big, white light and you walk into it, okay? No looking back—no waffling. Absolutely none or you'll be in some big pile of stank. So . . . okay?" Delaney finally looked up at him, clenching her jaw to keep tears from seeping out of her eyes.

"Not so much." He hauled her to him, pulling her close.

Delaney nestled her head against his chest and gripped the edges of his shirt with fingers that she feared might not let go. "It has to be okay, Clyde. It has to. We have no choice. You have no choice. For all intents and purposes, when I pull the plug—it's over. Really, really over," she whispered against his shirt.

"Understood. Doesn't mean it's okay." Clyde's hands kneaded her spine, gentle and reassuring.

Delaney rolled her head against his chest at the irony of this. "Crap. Only I could fall for a demon that isn't a demon but should really be upstairs, who's half dead on life support and *I* have to shut him down. Only me. Some might say that was pretty jacked up. Almost all my adult life I spent without so much as a god-damned date, and then you show up. Ya think maybe I could've gotten a break here?"

Clyde chuckled. "So you fell for me, is what you're saying?"

She clenched her eyes tight, knowing this was her last chance. "Oh, for fuck's sake. You're going to make me, aren't you? Fine. Cue weepy Lifetime-movie moment. I like you, Clyde. I like you a whole lot more than I ever thought I'd like a guy who thinks the way you do, lives the way you lived. Eats the crap you eat. All those things you said back in the bathroom—the flowers, the text messages—would have had my thong all up in a wad. Given a little longer, I might have considered stalking you if you didn't man up and beat me into submission. Okay? Are we good?" Her eyes ached, grainy and she was sure red from fighting off spending their last moments with her crying like a big, stupid girl.

But her big-girl panties just kept slipping and she couldn't seem to hike them up.

Clyde's fingers lifted her chin. In the dim light of his hospital room, he smiled—it held myriad emotions. "And all my life I was so self-absorbed . . . I would have had no one to help me figure this mess out because of it—until you. I want you to always remember how grateful I am for that, and that all the things I said back in the hotel bathroom were true."

Delaney snorted, thumbing tears from her cheeks. "Yeah, suuure. You can hand me a line like that now because you're hitting greener pastures and you won't be here to break up with me when I've driven you crazy with my herbs and self-help books—"

"And tofu . . ."

"And tofu," she agreed, giving in to the tears that wouldn't be thwarted. "So . . . if this—this," she stuttered, "is it—"

"Huey Lewis and the News, 19—"

Delaney planted a firm finger over his luscious lips to quiet him before she replaced it with her mouth. The salt of her tears landing on her tongue when she crushed her mouth to his, savoring, lingering . . .

Forcing herself to pull away, she took one last squeeze to remember him by, and gulped a breath of air before saying. "So here's the plan—when I pull the plug, I'm crossing my fingers that'll free you up. If you see the light—go into it. Hell, run into it, and don't look back, okay? Most of all, be happy, find your parents. I know they're waiting. I feel it. And do us all a favor—don't blow anything up, okay?" she squeaked, fighting for light and easy when dread was about to swallow her whole.

"Nope." Clyde looked down at her with an expression that had her worried.

Her head cocked to the left. "Come again?"

"I've decided I'm not leaving until I can assure myself you're safe. We can shut me down anytime, Delaney. I realize I have to go. I'm fully prepared to do that. I'm just not doing it until I make sure Lucifer's no longer interested in you. I don't care what Marcella said, I won't be doing any of this resting you all talk about when I cross if you're still Lucifer's target. So no can do." He crossed his arms over his chest and backed even further away from his hospital bed.

Whether by trick of the dim light or her tired eyes, she wasn't sure, but Clyde's form began to fade. Much the way the spirits had when he was around.

Yet her mouth fell open, her tears drying up with her disbelief. "Did you just fucking lose your mind? What about that statement is rational or logical? You have to go, Clyde. It won't be long before Lucifer comes calling because of what you did to Clyve. Marcella was spot-on. He'll go whining back to Satan and then we're fucked. *You're* fucked. There's nothing he can do to me that you didn't already tell me about. But you're a free-falling soul, pal. Up for grabs. You have to cross before he finds you—this is nonnegotiable." Delaney tried to keep her voice to a whisper, but it rose and fell with the fear that the devil would show up and make mincemeat of Clyde. If the devil snatched Clyde's soul back up, she'd never sleep a wink for the rest of her friggin' life.

"I don't have to do anything." His reply was unyielding and stiff as his big body began to shimmer, pieces of him falling away only to reappear.

What. The. Fuck? She fought her surprise and confusion and focused. "You do, too. Now quit playing Sir Lancelot and hit it."

"Nope."

Delaney waved a finger up at him. "Damn it, Clyde Atwell—I'll yank that cord so fast you won't have time to say banana Slurpee. Then I'll drag your ass kicking and screaming into the light. Don't you even think for a minute I won't."

His look dared her. "Try it."

Oh, no, he di'n't. "Argh! I'll be fine, Clyde. You wouldn't be in this mess if it weren't for me. This goes back fifteen years—this is my fault. Please, just let me make it right by getting you where you should be."

He began to move closer to her again, completely unaware that he was literally disappearing before her eyes. "I wouldn't have lived without Vincent's heart. I'd like to think that the fact that I lived was a good thing—not bad. And I wouldn't have known there was a mess to begin with or found out where I was—where my body was—if it wasn't for you, Delaney. And if I weren't in this mess, I'd be in another one. I was determined to get out of Hell. Clyve's assignment provided me the opportunity. That you were a part of that is coincidence. Plain and simple."

"Technicalities, Atwell, and enough with them. Now quit with the Neanderthal crap and prepare for the light." Delaney made a move toward his prone body on the hospital bed, preparing to do what needed to be done.

To make what she'd done all those years ago right.

Yet Clyde was right behind her, whirling her around to face him. His nostrils flared, his eyes shot flames of determination.

As for his right arm, well, that was so close to missing from his body it could have been on the back of a milk carton. "I said no, Delaney, and I meant no. If you touch that cord I'll haunt you into your afterlife. *Clear?*"

Her chest tightened and convulsed. Crap, he was so damned

hot when he was demanding, it made her stomach flutter. But she was just as determined. "Let me go or I'll—"

"What? Wrestle me? Did you remember the prism?"

Her eyes narrowed. "You cocky pain in my ass. You have some set of nads threatening me, demon. I'll—"

"Clyde! Get the fuck away from there!" Marcella yelled, skidding into the room on her high heels, slipping and sliding to a halt in front of Clyde.

Both Clyde and Delaney whipped around in unison to find Marcella, her beautiful features slathered in fear. "Don't touch that!"

Delaney instantly backed away. "What's going on?"

Marcella's chest heaved up and down as though she'd been running. "Two words. Lucifer's coming!" she gasped out.

Clyde glanced in Delaney's direction, his eyes wary, his left ear missing. "At my signal, unleash Hell," he muttered.

Delaney gulped and nodded, struck by how crazy it was to actually remember the line Clyde had just quoted in the midst of this madness. "*Gladiator*—Russell Crowe . . ."

Because certainly, Hell was going to be unleashed.

twenty-one

"I need you two to open up your ears and pay very close attention," Marcella ordered. "First, Clyde—get away from your body. *Now!*" she roared in command.

Clyde backed away from the bed, confusion clearly a close companion with his uncertainty.

Marcella gripped Delaney's arm. "Listen to me—we got big trouble, *chica*. No matter what, we cannot let Clyde's soul get back into his body before we're sure his body's dead. Understood?"

Delaney gaped at her. In, out. In, out. For the love of—pick one. "I thought we had to ship Clyde off—you know, free Willy, blah, blah, blah. The only way to do that is to unplug him, Marcella. What the fuck is going on?"

Her mouth set in a thin line of determination. "Don't say another word—just listen. We got beeg . . . er, big trouble. That fucking contract—the one with Vincent and his father? It's connected to you, D, because you're Vincent's half sister. When Lucifer struck the deal with Vincent's father, Richard, this Richard was one smart cookie. He had a clause in the contract: if anything should happen to either him or Vincent, the power he had, that you now have, would be passed on to any living relative—*forever*. How he got that past Lucifer is more mysterious than Area 51. But that's why you began to see ghosts—it had shit to do with the horned one and being good and pissed off. You see ghosts because of that freak Vinny. When he died, this ability to talk to the dead was passed on to you."

Delaney decided she might as well leave her mouth open— because each new revelation took too much energy for her to shut it only to have it slide back to the floor again. "What? Vincent didn't talk to the dearly departed—not by a long shot. He did shitty things and represented shitty people as a defense attorney." No, Vincent wouldn't have cared if he helped some lost spirit cross unless there was something in it for him.

"Here's the deal in a nutshell. The power given to Vincent was by proxy. When Richard died, it was passed to Vincent. When Vincent died, it was passed on to you, Delaney, because you were the next *living* relative in line. It's why you can see ghosts. Jesus, I thought you could always see ghosts. I had no idea this thing you call a gift happened just after Vincent died. How could we fucking know each other for ten years and you not tell me this?"

"Don't go all put out on me now, Marcella. I'll explain everything later—get to the point!"

"Either way, you began to see ghosts because of this power that freak Vincent passed on to you. The power you now possess is what's termed neutral, meaning it can be used either way. If you'd been, say, a serial killer or a murderer? The FBI, CIA, and Interpol would've been working some mucho overtime these past fifteen years. Because of the person you are, because you're undeniably a good human being, you used it to cross over people who were in turmoil. Helped spirits who needed guidance. Vincent used it to be a filthy pig and get away with murder. But it's also why Clyde couldn't stay away from you. You're connected by this thing—this contract and that transplanted heart—like some big cluster fuck."

"And you know this for sure, how, Marcella?" Clyde asked.

"Oh, brotha—if you had any idea the feelers I've had out since Delaney shipped my ass off. I knew something was up—who would want to get rid of *moi*?" She flapped an impatient hand at Clyde. "I don't have time to explain now. Just know I know people—have some contacts—and they paid off."

Delaney struggled for clarity, an answer to this tangled mess. "Okay, so what does that have to do with crossing Clyde over?"

Marcella rolled her eyes, but her grip had become more urgent. "Here's our problem, and this has to be done precisely right. Vincent's soul still lives because of that freakin' heart. He's still in there in some fucked-up way." She pointed to Clyde's body on the bed with a glossy, pink nail.

Delaney tried to grasp what she was saying, but her confusion only mounted.

"Don't you see?" Marcella shook her with a bone-rattling shake. "The devil never collected Vincent's soul the night he died. What does the devil love more than a fresh soul—especially a *contracted* soul? That's why he showed up the night of Vincent's death, D! He didn't get it when you donated Vincent's heart, and now Satan wants that shit back. But here's our fucking snafu.

"If we don't get Vincent's soul *out* of Clyde's body, which means pulling the plug, Clyde can't get back in because if he does before Vincent's kaput, his soul will once more be tied to Vincent and the devil will take him, too. He won't be able to cross. Lucifer'd eat up *Clyde's* soul like an ice cream sundae because Clyde deceived him by switching those damned assignments. We need to stop that heart from beating—get Vincent's soul out of that body—

and then we have to get Clyde back into his body, and cross him so he's out of harm's way.

"Look at Clyde, Delaney—look!" she demanded. "That's why Clyde's beginning to fade—because his soul needs to be freed. His soul, no matter what his brain's saying, belongs in his body, and before long, we won't be able to keep him from trying to get back in."

Delaney's stomach began to roll like waves in the sea as realization sank in. It was true. Clyde had been harboring Vincent's soul in his body for all these years . . . your heart, according to some, was the *essence* of your soul, Marcella had said. Not only had Delaney screwed up Vincent's soul when she'd donated his heart, but she'd screwed up Clyde's shot at going where he needed to be because he was all twisted up in Vincent. "So all this time Clyde's been keeping Vincent's soul from Satan because he had his heart? Their souls have been all tangled up?"

"Yes!" Marcella bounced from foot to foot. "And he ended up in Hell because somebody didn't keep track of his soul. It sprang free from his body before it should have. I swear, I don't know who's in charge up there, but bloody hell, they screwed this one up royally."

Clyde's nod of understanding was vague, his teeth clamping together as though he was fighting off something neither she nor Marcella could see. "So my body has to die to free both Vincent and myself up," Clyde assessed with his usual succinct logic, cutting into Delaney's own heart as surely as if he'd used a Ginsu. Yet his legs, filmy and becoming transparent, moved toward the hospital bed.

Marcella nodded with vigor, jumping in front of Clyde to keep him from his lifeless form. "Exactly, and we need to get on that shit now. *Now!*" She whirled to face Clyde, putting a hand on his chest. "Clyde, you have listen to me!" She snapped her fingers in his face, but only a flicker of awareness crossed his eyes, now intent on getting into his body. "Clyde!" Marcella roared up at him, her eyes blazing with urgency. "Stop—you have to stop! D," she shouted, "pull that fucking plug! Hurry up before he gets any closer!" Marcella butted up against Clyde's chest, expelling a harsh gasp of air in her effort to keep him from getting to his body.

It was as if he'd become transfixed, and stopping him was like trying to stop a steamroller.

Delaney couldn't take her eyes from Clyde's face, hard, intent, determined, all while Marcella butted up against him, the heels of her shoes leaving dark marks on the white floor. Her fingers clamped onto his arms, digging into his biceps to keep him from getting to the bed.

"*Madre santa*—Delaney, pull the fucking plug!"

In an instant, she knew there was no time for words, no time for good-byes—she had to end this so Clyde could find peace.

Delaney lunged for the back of the bed, fighting for focus to find the plug that connected to the ventilator. Fuck! There were so many friggin' cords!

"Delaneyyyyyy! Pull the fucking plug!" Marcella screamed so harsh and frantic it made her jump.

She dove through the tangled mess, landing on her knees, yanking at anything she could get her hands on. With trembling fingers she found the thick cord that led to Clyde's ventilator and yanked.

With everything she had in her.

Sending up a desperate prayer that Clyde's journey would be successful.

"Jesus!" Marcella huffed, the scuffle of her feet stopping as she expelled another breath.

Delaney's breath shuddered in and out, too, when she saw Marcella's feet stop moving.

It was done.

Let the weeping and wailing commence.

Her hands reached for the edge of the bed, hauling herself up off the floor to come only a hairsbreadth from Clyde's handsome face.

But the sob of agony she'd been about to wail turned to a gasp of surprise.

"Delaney, Delaney, Delaney. How goes it, sunshine? We really have to make it a point to get together more often than every fifteen years, don'tcha think?"

Satan strolled to the ventilator and flipped a switch with long, milky white fingers.

"Battery pack—every ventilator has one," he remarked with casual nonchalance.

And then he grinned.

twenty-two

Delaney looked to Marcella, whose chest heaved from keeping Clyde away from the bed. She clung to his big hand, positioning herself in front of him, clearly taking no chances he might make a sudden break for his body.

Delaney's hands went possessively to the shell of Clyde's form, prepared to shield him if need be. She clamped on to his forearm while beads of terror-induced sweat popped out on her forehead.

Satan clucked his tongue, leaning over the bed and chucking Delaney under the chin. "So here we are, Goody Two-Shoes. You, me, and the souls I'd better have when this conversation ends." He flapped his pale hands at her. The black T-shirt he wore, which said *Don't Say No until You've Seen My Dungeon*, stretched over his thin chest when he spread his arms wide. "Back up, do-gooder, or you'll force me to singe that pretty hair of yours. Vincent's soul is mine, and I think I'll take the rocket scientist's, too." He pointed at Clyde. "He did a bad, bad thing—punishment is my only option."

Delaney's eyes narrowed, her lips thinning. Not a fucking chance on earth she was leaving Clyde before he crossed. He'd have to tear her away from him. That meant stalling him. "The fuck I will," she spat, curling her fingers into Clyde's shoulder.

Satan heaved a playfully tortured sigh, his sculpted face taking on a put-upon expression. "Oh, Delaney. So righteous—so indignant—so old. Do you have any idea the shit you stir up? You're like this big metaphoric spoon in a pot full of perfectly good waffling souls. Not that I minded all that much. Most of the time your interference was pretty harmless. *Most* of the time. If you'd just stayed out of things, Delaney Markham, if you'd just kept your Susie Sunshine crap to yourself, none of this would be happening. But no—here you are, spreading your fucking rays of sunshine everywhere. Not to mention, you made me leave a perfectly lovely vacation in the Falklands because you just couldn't let this joker alone, and it appears my staff is incapable of collecting a simple soul. Do you have any idea the burdens I bear?"

Delaney narrowed her gaze, her eyes slits in her head. "Take Vincent, leave Clyde the hell alone," she growled.

"Yeahhhh, I'll get right on that," he taunted with glee.

Marcella's eyes captured hers for the smallest second—her lips moved soundlessly, repetitively, compelling her to read the message she was trying to send. The only thing Delaney was clear about was that she had to stall until she could figure it out. What better way than to poke at him? "Clyde's soul isn't yours to take, you freeloading asshole!"

Satan chuckled, thick and resonant. "Says you, princess. Besides, who'd stop me?"

Yeah. That presented a pickle. Truly, it was too bad these powers she'd been given didn't include the gift of screaming fireballs and the ability to produce, like, locusts.

He turned his attention to the soul in question. "And you"—he pointed at Clyde, who appeared incapable of anything more than remaining frozen in place—"are in for some really deep shit. Though I will say, I admire your craftiness, Clyde Atwell. Job well done; deceiving the entire filing department was brilliance. The only trouble is, you just didn't do it for the right reasons. If you'd just paid attention in class and taken to heart the whole 'evil is your ruler' message, I'd have personally planned your interdepartment celebration for induction to level two. We'd have had cake and ice cream and all the frills." Satan let go of a mockingly forlorn breath of air. "Sadly, now I have to drag your sorry ass back and throw you in the pit. I hate doing that. There's always screaming and loads of whining. A real yawn." He made an expression of supreme distaste.

Out of nowhere, Marcella hissed, "Delaney—get away from there. Get out of here *now*!" Clyde had begun to stir, pushing her forward again. Her face grew red from the effort it took to keep him at bay.

"You!" Lucifer roared, stabbing a finger in Marcella's general direction. "Shut the bloody fuck up, hot pants. You're next," he threatened, letting his fingers take the shape of long, thorny claws.

Delaney couldn't think, she only knew she had to stall the motherfucker while she tried to read the message Marcella was sending with her eyes, now nearly coal black, burning for Delaney to read the meaning in them. "Uh, question, O Horned One?"

He grinned again, innocent and boyish. "What's that, Gandhi?"

"Do you always wear that color? It's so wrong for you. It says nothing about who you really are. I mean, you being the supremeness of evil, well, I guess I just thought you'd have a better grasp on the best color to convey that. Black is so trite and overdone, don't you think? I'd so go red if I were you."

Satan threw his head back and laughed. When he tilted it upward once more, he popped his lips. "Clyde's right, Delaney. You're a fucking riot. Now move. As in *now*."

Delaney winced. "Wait! Just one more question, I mean, it isn't every day you meet the devil, right? If I passed up the chance to ask you a couple of questions, I'd never forgive myself . . . I have a million, but I promise to limit them to just a couple if it's not too much trou—"

"Ask!"

Ohhhhhh, if the twist of his mousy face was any indication, patience was wearing thin, and she still didn't understand Marcella's signals. "Um, who does your hair?"

He didn't answer. Instead, he narrowed his gaze, focusing on a prone Clyde.

"Wait!" she yelped, pulling the hospital bed toward her. "I swear, just one more thing, and I just know you're going to want to give me an answer because it's all about your maniacal genius. Honest. Why did you assign someone to—to—" Shit, she'd fumbled.

His eyebrow rose to a pointy arch. "To make you go all emo?" He drew a finger over his wrist with a lascivious wink of his red eye.

Delaney waged a battle with her flaring temper and the bile rising in her throat. "Yeah. That."

"Because you took something from me. On the off chance you didn't notice, I'm a horrible team player."

"Vincent?"

"Don't be silly, Suzy Q. Aw, sure, at first I was a wee bit angry that you'd kept Vincent's soul from me longer than necessary—I was sad because I made an extra effort to come and collect him personally. I don't do it often—delegation is a must when overseeing my den of iniquity—but I happened to be in the area, and it'd been far too long since I'd collected a soul. Being a hands-on kind of guy, I figured I'd roll out the red carpet for Vincent. Imagine my dismay when I found you'd ruined my grand gesture. Naturally, because you did steal from me, I was obligated to do the whole dramatic display of typical deviltry that night. You know, the one where I roared threats about your loved ones while I lobbed fireballs and screeched in my scary, outdoor voice? What kind of evil ruler would I be if I didn't? And look at what my crazy rant that night ended up doing to you—you have no human friends. No special someone to cuddle with while you eat grass and wheat germ. I took far greater pleasure knowing you'd turned into the Crazy Dog Lady all on your own than I ever could if I'd managed to expunge you that night personally. In fact, I was almost thankful it played out like it did, because it lightened my evil workload. You have no idea the pressure living up to a label like the Prince of Darkness has, honeybuns. But as for Vincent? You silly. I knew I'd have him back one day. It was just a matter of patience."

All these years she'd lived with that ominous threat hanging over her head had been wasted energy. Quite frankly, that burned her butt. But Marcella was still pleading with her eyes, so she kept poking him with her imaginary stick. "Ah, then it was the souls. I stole souls from you and crossed them before you could get to them. Methinks you're just a jealous weenie. Unattractive in a Hell lover, don't you think?" she taunted, followed by a giggle that would surely turn hysterical if she didn't figure out what in fuck Marcella was doing.

"I like you, Delaney. Nay—I'm enraptured by you. You're saucccyyy," he hissed the letter *c*. "I meant exactly what I said, cookie. I could give a rich man's dick *who* you cross. Most of the souls you cross belong to weak, pathetic losers who'd spend all of their time crying and cowering on my turf—droll, very droll. Not one of them had a contract with me either. Except this one particular soul . . ."

He was toying with her, the fucktard. It was all about the game, and she'd just have to let him poke her back because she just didn't get what Marcella wanted of her, and she needed time to figure it out. If she reached for that switch, Satan would fry her like so much chicken. Sweat trickled between her breasts and her mouth became so dry she almost couldn't pry her tongue from the roof of it, but she persevered. "Really? Huh. And that was whose soul?" She forced herself to sound interested while her bladder squealed its protest.

Rocking back on his heels, he shoved his hands in his loose-fitting jeans and winked at her. "Remember how delighted you were to see *Grease* on Broadway two months ago? Spectacular show, by the way. You know, all those gushes and sighs because you finally got your cute backside out of the house and spent time with real live people instead of those slobbering creatures, with any number of ailments, you've befriended?"

"I do."

"And do you remember what happened afterward when you used those backstage passes Miss Puerto Rico here so graciously gave you in honor of your friendship?"

Wee doggie—did she ever. There was nothing like crossing a diva actress who just didn't want to exit stage left. What a god-damned hassle that'd been.

Talking.

It took a whole lot of talking, coaxing, begging, and pleading to get that lovely, albeit vacant of any reason, twit to see that you couldn't just *fix* a broken neck, and really, you have to be more careful when you step on the slippery bathroom floor of your dressing room. The only place for her to go was up—and up she'd gone as Delaney beat feet out of that dressing room before anyone could see her. Harrowing indeed. "Yep. I crossed over the actress who played the lead role." Just as that thought flitted through her memory, Delaney knew exactly what this was all about. She'd fucked up his plans again without even trying. Suh-weet.

"Yeahhhhhh," he rasped. "Ya did. Tsk, tsk. Fool me once, shame on me; fool me twice, well, Hell ensues."

Buy time, buy time, buy time was all she could think. "So? Big fucking deal. It's just like you said. I do it all the time."

"Welllll, this time that particular soul wasn't so harmless. Don't play stupid—you don't wear it well. That soul got where she was on Broadway because she signed a contract with me. If you'd just left well enough alone, and the dim-witted demon I assigned the case to had shown up when he should have, she'd be greasing lighting downstairs—not up. You gave her a *choice* to go into the light—a choice she shouldn't have been allowed to make, but at that point she hadn't done anything so despicable she couldn't be forgiven for it or been kept from crossing because of it. See where I'm going here? You stole from me once and it was painful"—he thumped dramatically at the place on his chest where his heart would be if he had one—"but I healed. I even therapied—I faced my fears. Like I said, Vincent never stood a chance of going anywhere but to Hell 'cause he was a bad, bad boy, and I'm a patient man. I was willing to wait it out until Clyde here bought it, freeing Vinny's soul up. But surely you see, when you did it again, there was just no recovering. What would it say about me if I didn't lead by example? And that brings us to Vincent here." He cast a glowing, red glance at Clyde's body. "You donated his heart, and that was a lovely humanitarian gesture. Bravo. But his debt is long overdue," he remarked with offhanded dryness.

"Overdue . . ." Delaney knew exactly what was overdue, but the longer she could allow him center stage, the greater the chance she'd understand what the fuck Marcella was trying to convey to her. Jesus, Joseph, and Mary—what were her eyes burning holes in Delaney's about? If she rolled them in the direction of Clyde's lifeless form once more, they'd fall out of her fucking head.

"Indeed—his debt is handing over his soul. I so love souls. They're like potato chips—you can never have just one. I never thought I'd say it, and if you repeat this in polite company, I'll deny it, but the world is a better place without him in it. Vincent was an idiot who had no control. None. I'd have applauded the pig he was when he was alive if his living had done me any good. Was he off corrupting the government like he was supposed to—signing deals like all good demonic contractors do while he was dipping his wick in anything that moved? No, he was drinking himself into a stupor and chasing women. He was abusing *my* power, and I don't dig that much. In fact, it makes me pretty damned angry.

"But all's well that ends well because here I am. Just rarin' to collect. Your Clyde here was verrry sly. He's just not sly enough, and now I'll have two souls for the price of one. Isn't that a hoot? Oh, and there's one other thing."

Thing. There was a thing. "Thing?"

"Uh-huh. You might not have done something as dastardly as take your own life, but you do like my Clyde, don't you? C'mon, you can tell me. It'll be our little secret. He's cuuute, huh? In fact, you like him so much that you'll cry and cry when he's gone. I imagine you'll scurry back off into hiding in that pathetic store of yours and refuse to become involved with anyone again. If you don't become involved, those children and that house you so want with every precious breath you take will become nothing more than what they are now. A dream. An unfulfilled one, at that."

Satan leaned in close to her, laying a deathly cold hand on hers. "So maybe all that planning to torture you wasn't for naught after all, eh? You've been powned, sweetheart. Wait, hang on while I pat myself on the back in honor of my genius." A chuckle slithered from between his thin lips while he reached over his shoulder and patted his back.

She snatched her hand back, but just as she was about to call him the weak, spineless, fucktard motherfucker he was, she understood what Marcella was telling her without saying a word.

Pown this.

"Just one more question?" Delaney chirped, blinking her eyes, praying Marcella knew what had to come next. What she hoped Marcella had been signaling her to do.

"Just one more, sunshine, then it's lights out for Clyde."

"Why do you suppose you forgot?"

"Forgot what?"

"One really *important* detail."

Lucifer cocked his head in thought. "Damn, ya think? I've been doing that a lot lately. Do tell, cookie." He waved a slender, lightly veined hand for her to proceed.

God, please let her be right. *I don't ask a lot often, and I do send tons of biz your way. So help a team player out, would ya?* "Thisssss!" Delaney screamed, tearing the breathing tube from Clyde's throat with a roar—effectively cutting off his air supply.

In that precise, shared moment, Marcella yanked Clyde by the arm, swinging him forward and pushing him at his prone form, shoving him so hard, he fell face forward into his body, swallowed up like he'd been poured into a cup.

A black tendril wafted upward where Clyde lay on the bed, slinking, shrugging off the body it'd had been attached to.

With wild eyes, Delaney pinpointed Vincent's soul erupting from Clyde in an explosion of vile, rippling ebony streams.

Her half brother had arrived.

The suck-up.

So now it was two against two.

Without thought, without a qualm, Marcella launched herself at Lucifer, tackling him with a bone-crunching slam to the floor. The hospital bed swerved sideways, yanking at the machines and cords Clyde had been attached to with a precarious jerk. Lights blinked, alarms blared with ear-splitting quality. Yet no one came.

And then it got butt ugly.

Shrieks of thunder crashed, booming off the walls of the ICU room until she was certain she'd be learning some Helen Keller moves if she survived this. Rain, like wet little pelting needles, pummeled her exposed skin, drenching her in seconds.

As if in a dream, she watched Marcella scramble to her feet, slipping on the rain-slick floor, Satan but a mere infuriated step behind her and far more confident on his sneakered feet. "Get out!" she screamed to Delaney, her head snapping backward when Satan grabbed a long, dark handful of hair, wrenching it viciously. Marcella bit out angry words in her native language. *"Descarado sin espina, hijo de puta! Si tocas un pelo en su cabello, sea a verte en el hoyo!"*

Hissing infiltrated her ears, clawing at her eardrums, the screeching *sssss* pounding painfully against them. A shiver she had no control over skittered from her sodden head to her toes. What was it with the flippin' reptilian family, already? For the love of squirmy, slithering things—snakes, what seemed like thousands, shimmied across the floor, up her legs, wrapping around her ankles and edging their way to her waist. She screamed, shaking them off and shuddering, her chest heaving, her brain racing for a solution.

And then there were locusts, emerging from the dim light of the room in swarms, clacking to the ground and bashing themselves against her face.

Marcella clawed at the hands that dragged her, twisting and turn-ing her lithe body like some captured wild animal. "Get ooooout, Deeee!" Her hoarse cry mingled with the deep, crazed laughter of her captor.

Fury clamped down on Delaney like a vise, forcing her to take action. The hell she'd leave Marcella.

Her eyes scanned the room with wild desperation, pushing her to think. Delaney hurled herself at a lone chair in the corner of the room just as fire exploded in a starburst of blue and orange flames. They writhed at her feet, dancing their demonic rhythm to block her path. Terror made her legs pump like she'd run the minute and a half all her life.

She latched on to the chair's back, lifting it high over her head, bellowing in a wet warble, "Duuuuck!" before she sent it sailing across the room at Satan, only to have it fruitlessly slam against the far wall and splinter to the ground.

And that was when she heard it—the incessant rapid-fire bong of Clyde's heart monitor.

Oh, and then there was her friend's lithe figure, beautiful, fiery, hot-tempered, and the closest thing she'd had to a BFF, dead or otherwise, in all of her life, hurtling toward her. Marcella's glossy black hair billowing in soaking wet streams was the last thing Delaney saw before she was body-slammed with such force she crumpled, her head hitting the sink with a crack so sharp and ominous she knew it meant bad shit.

Slinking to the floor, helpless to save herself or her friend, Delaney had one last moment of consciousness.

In that moment, she heard the sweet, sweet sound of Clyde's heart monitor.

Flatlining.

Two thumbs up.

twenty-three

Victory just wasn't what it was cracked up to be.

For sure she didn't feel like going to Disney World.

Warm heat bathed her back, calling for her to turn around and lift her face to it.

But that was damned hard to do when you couldn't tear your eyes away from a train wreck.

Her jacked-up body being the train wreck and all.

Really, there was nothing like identifying with your work, Delaney thought while peering down at her broken, soaking wet, just a little too bloody for her taste, body.

Lucifer toed her using the tip of his foot, nudging her ribs with a look of disgust when Delaney's body gave him no reaction while he clung to Vincent's soul. He held up the struggling black wisp of light in his hand and examined it. "Oh, Vinny. Come to Papa. Did you miss me? And look at this mess, would you? Now I'll have to send in the cleanup crew. They need far more direction than I have time for tonight," he cackled.

Realization was slow and thick like pea soup.

When it finally came—it was much like that defining moment she'd heard so much about. She totally got it. Just like that.

Holy fucksticks, Batman.

She was dead.

Epically so.

She looked down again at her battered, broken body.

Yep, there was no recovering from that. Not even bionics and Oscar Goldman could save her.

Bummer.

Her eyes scanned the room for her friend. Oh, God, where was Marcella? Had she disappeared? She could only pray she'd escaped Lucifer . . .

Okay, okay, so she was dead. Delaney fought to compartmentalize. Pros and cons, pros and cons . . .

There were pros and cons to this whole dead thing.

Con—who'd take care of her babies? Kellen. He'd do it. *He'd better*.

Pro—up in here, no one would call her crazy for talking to ghosts. Nice.

Con—she'd never see Kellen again. Major suckage.

Pro—no more bills to pay. Her deflated bank account cheered.

Con—no more Friday nights and *Ghost Whisperer*. Boo, hiss.

Pro—dead meant Clyde was somewhere 'round here. So who'd powned who?

That brought a smile to her face and the desire to find the man she planned to make hers.

Delaney looked down at the bed where Clyde lay. Her warm fuzzies were quick to turn to dismay. Christ on a cracker, didn't he have his listening ears on when she'd told him to cross? Hadn't she said *go—into—the—light*? Clear as day. Not even a hint of an accent when she'd told him either.

But did he listen?

No. Because God forbid she should be right.

Frustration made her jump up and down.

For the love of valiant nobility, what the hell did Clyde think he was doing? Didn't he get dead?

After all that, he had the audacity to *live*?

Irony—she was all about making it.

How could he be anything but dead after she'd torn his breathing tube out? He was brain-dead, for Christ's sake. No one who was brain-dead got up out of bed.

No one but Clyde.

In the midst of the scattered equipment, torn curtains, locust carcasses, and machine parts scattered to infinity and beyond, a tortured grunt came from the bed.

Where Clyde better keep his ass if he knew what was good for him.

Leave it to a man to ruin a perfectly good plan.

Clyde's once battered form stirred, his chest blowing life in rapid, choppy breaths. With agonizing determination she could almost feel, he gripped the rails on either side of the bed in his hands, dragging his upper body to a sitting position. Each movement he made, each small victory his body was granted made Delaney scream, "No!" A no clearly only she could hear.

Raw grit was what led Clyde to the end of the bed, his determined eyes never leaving Satan's reed-thin back. Soundlessly, he slid to the floor, wobbling, then righting himself. The bandages on his right arm and foot were soaked and trailing in shredded chunks from his body. Every vein in his strained body stood out against skin that was pale and breaking out into a sweat.

The big picture she was getting blew chunks.

Clyde launched himself at her body. Kneeling beside Delaney, he pinched her nose shut, prying her mouth open with two fingers.

Wow. He was just determined to ruin everything, now wasn't he?

The Neanderthal knew CPR. That meant he was going to revive her and make a fantastic mess of a perfectly good budding afterlife romance for them.

Jesus!

"Clyde!" she yelled to deaf ears. "Nooo! What is it with you and the Superman deal? I'm dead, dipshit! You're supposed to be, too. Stop screwing everything up already, or I swear, the next time we meet, I'm going to force tofu down your throat and make you listen to Michael Bublé for an eternity!"

He slapped his stiff hands on her chest with clumsiness and began compressions. His eyes were filled with a look that could only be labeled hell-bent.

Lucifer squealed his fury, bellowing his outrage that Clyde lived. He threw himself at Clyde, landing on his back with the slap of Clyde's flesh against the tile leaving an echo in the room.

Clyde reared up, trying to shrug him off, but he was weak, his body slow and clunky from being sedentary for three months. The muscles in Clyde's chest strained when he lunged for her body again. He howled a cry of pure determination, dragging her to him and pinching her nose to begin the process once more.

Her eyes widened in horror, her throat became raw from screaming at Clyde to stop. Invisible hands dragged her, lurching her forward in unsteady, stilted tugs. Crap! Clyde's effort to save her must be working. In increments, her limbs melted, dragging, yanking, pulling her back away from the light.

Yet she could still see Satan and Clyde's struggle. They'd become one blurred ball, a slow-motion horror flick come to life.

When Clyde reared up for the last time, he managed to thrust Lucifer from his back.

But the devil didn't crash to the ground. Instead, he hovered helplessly in midair, his thin legs dangling, his white-blond ponytail streaming down his back.

Delaney felt the light pressure of a hand, strong and sure, stroke the top of her head, erasing the agonizing throb of her head. Then her chest heaved, filling with air. Without warning, she was no longer looking down at Clyde and Lucifer, but up toward the disembodied voice of a being who apparently held Lucifer effortlessly in his grip.

"Dude," its voice chastised, the tone rock steady and melodiously calm. "Chillax, horn dog." When the voice took shape, it was in the form of a young man who didn't look much older than eighteen. His hair, almost shoulder length, clearly kissed by the sun, swept over his forehead in a snaky wave of golden brown. The white puka shell beads around his neck enhanced his Hawaiian flowered trunks and golden berry tan.

He looked down at Clyde, who, shallow of breath, had wrapped protective arms around Delaney and he smiled—angelic and boyish. "Oh, dude! I'm so glad I found you. Do you have any idea how long I've been looking for you? Like, totally what seems like forevs. I've been all over New York, trying to fix this. Man, when you go for cover, you go deep—niiiice work, sensei." He bowed with a wink.

Satan, with blazing crimson eyes, struggled against the force this boy had created. He peered back at Lucifer with wide, childish innocence, giving him a stern shake. "Man, you need to chill. You are up-*tight*, my friend."

Delaney lay speechless on the floor, every nerve ending wracked with pain, but she grabbed for Clyde's hand and gave it a weak squeeze. His big body shook from the effort it'd taken to get out of that bed. "Who are you?" Clyde asked.

The young man cocked his head to the left and held up a finger to quiet Clyde. His soft eyes then captured Satan's. "Ya know, man, you're always all het up. Can't be good. So I have some advice—hear me out, Your Evilness. While I was looking for your *hostage*, I saw some pretty cool shows—even a coupla musicals—which mostly ain't my thing. Bet if you caught, like, *The Lion King* you'd totally give up this evil gig and quit stressin'. Must suck to be you, all angry and ragin' all the time, huh? So can't be good for your cholesterol. Bet those levels are off the charts. Oh, and dude, you should totally check out Coney Island hot dogs. This close to heaven with sauerkraut on them." He smiled a smile of benevolence, rubbing his stomach with childlike glee.

Satan writhed in his grip, yet he held on to him like he was holding up nothing more taxing than a helium balloon.

Now revived, Delaney struggled to sit upright, but it made her dizzy. She opted for vertical, slapping Clyde on the forearm with a weak hand and a shallow breath of her own. She ignored the strange man-boy, deciding to take the opportunity to give Clyde the hell he deserved before it was snatched from her again. Frustration welled in the pit of her belly. She was going to lose Clyde again, of that she was sure. Whoever this guy was, he had some serious power, and he was no friend of Satan's.

"Do you have any idea what you've done? I was dead. Dead was good, Clyde. It meant you'd have to forfeit all those flowers and text messages, you geek. If you'd have just left well enough alone . . . and now look. You're right back where you started. Why didn't you just go into the light, for God's sake? The plan was for you to cross. How the frig did you manage to summon the kind of will it must've taken to get out of that bed? And do we have to do this all over again?" she almost sobbed. "'Cause I gotta tell ya, I don't think I have it in me to yank that plug again. Which, by the way, smart guy, you weren't a whole lot of help with. I was supposed to turn off the ventilator *switch*."

Clyde gave her a weak, sheepish smile, kissing the hand that had swatted him, closing his eyes, and inhaling. "I know . . ."

The young man leaned down, holding Satan at arm's length, and eyeballed Delaney, interrupting the rest of the rant she wanted to stick to Clyde. "My man, that was some rockin' heroics on your part, gettin' up out of that bed like you did—suh-weet. Totally impressed me with your dedication, and how you've been looking out for the wahine here."

He stuck out his brown hand to Clyde to shake. "Okay, so here's the deal. First, I'm Uriel, ya know, archangel? I'm the dude the big guy's gonna be amped with when he finds out about this mess. I so owe you a mondo apology, boss. I should have been here to pick up your soul when you popped free of your body. But, my friend, the surf was rad in Big Sur that day, ya know? I mean, outrageous. Because you were a surprise, I didn't get the word about you until too late. My supreme bad. But seriously, who knew? Souls don't just pop free every day of the week. That happens almost never. But it made ya free game for Mr. Evil here, and that makes me total slacker material—sooo sorry."

Uriel . . . the Big Kahuna's eyes and ears. So he *was* here to collect Clyde. And that meant she had to say good-bye to him all over again. Tee-rific. Son of a bitch. If there was ever an example of a time when a man didn't listen to a woman, this was one of them.

Uriel held out a hand to her with a compassionate smile, pulling her to stand, then righting her when she faltered with a strong grip. "I'm stupid sorry you got all wicked tangled up in this, Delaney. But I'll take care of him." He nodded his head in the direction of a helpless Satan.

Delaney reached out to steady herself, only to find Clyde right beside her, placing a hand on her waist.

Clyde lifted his chin, straightening his hospital gown with his free hand, and looked Uriel square in the eye. "Appreciate the help, but here's where I'm at. If your job is to collect me, I'm not leaving Delaney until I know she's safe. I want someone's word—someone in charge—that she'll be looked after or you'll have to do far worse than he did to get me to leave."

Delaney stood on tippy-toe and whispered in Clyde's ear, "I know you don't know much about Heaven and Hell, but here's a tip. Shut up before you make this worse. Do you have any idea *who* he is? He's an *archangel*. Think wings and halos and omnipotence. Biblical lesson number one—do not, and I repeat, do not ever tell him no."

Uriel chuckled, slapping Clyde on the back with a good-natured thump. "No need to get hinky, boss. It's all good."

Good? No. This was anything but good. Instead of following her own advice in the presence of überangel, her frustration finally got the better of her.

She looked up at Clyde with blazing eyes. "And now, because of you, we have to do this all over again. Now my eyes'll be all red and my nose, which gets ugly and splotchy, is going to run because I'll be crying. How many ways can I define dead to you, buddy? What were you thinking getting out of that bed? I was going to meet you at the light. But no. You have to go all super Clyde on me and administer CPR. Is there anything you don't know how to do? You've got nerve saving my life. I think you were just trying to get out of listening to Michael Bublé because now you have to go and I have to stay. Good job."

Clyde kissed the tip of her nose, his eyes grim. "I promise to never save your life again."

"Swear?"

"Swear it on a banana Slurpee."

The panic, terror, complete helplessness she'd felt when Lucifer had hurled himself at Clyde battered at her again. The notion that he'd taken the chance to have his soul snatched back up and returned to the place he'd started, that he'd sacrificed himself for her, made her chest ache and warm simultaneously. "Why, why, *why* would you do that?"

Uriel leaned in between the two of them, his shiny eyes amused. "'Cause I'm thinkin' he's crushin' on ya, and that's crazy cool. So stop beating him down and listen to where we're at. First up, Clyde, dude, get back in the bed—Vincent's soul is outta here and you're clear for takeoff. Then I want you to go to sleep. Tomorrow's a big day. You're gonna have a miraculous recovery, all unexplainable and medical mystery-ish. You got some bogus deal because I didn't show up when I was supposed to, man. So I figure I owe ya. All ya gotta do is play along because making this just vanish would alter stuff I just can't play with, okay?" He held out his fist, closed and facing Clyde, to seal the deal. "Let's blow it up, dude."

Clyde frowned at the angel's hand, bewildered.

Dizzy and weak with gratitude and relief, Delaney wiped yet more tears from her face and showed Clyde what Uriel meant when he offered his fist. "Like this," she said, knocking fists with Uriel, then spreading her fingers wide as she pulled back. "You know, to blow it up."

Uriel chuckled. "Yeah, like that. Ya know, you're one rad wahine, Delaney Markham. I owe you, too. 'Cause you saved Clyde's soul—a bunch of souls, in fact. If we had club presidents for mediums upstairs, you'd be my nominee."

Delaney reached out a hand to Uriel, letting her fingers find his, and squeezed with a weak grip, mouthing, "Thank you."

"Now who's glad I saved their life? I think you owe me a

banana Slurpee, medium," Clyde teased just before capturing her lips with a kiss. A kiss filled with promise—with the anticipation of things to come—with the thrill of discovery.

Her arms slipped under his, savoring this gift. The gift of opportunity. The gift of life.

Uriel's grin was wide. "Okay, then, we're coo'. Now you two knock it off and save that for tomorrow. Clyde—get back in that bed. I'll see ya both someday on the flipside."

Delaney helped a tired Clyde into the bed, tucking the blanket up under his chin, running a hand over his handsome face.

Before he did as Uriel commanded, Clyde held his hand out to Delaney and winked. She took it, clutching it with shaky fingers, pulling it up to her cheek.

"Close your eyes, man." Uriel let his free hand glide over Clyde's face. "Sweet dreams," he whispered.

Clyde obeyed, and in moments, his chest rose and fell with easy breaths. Her heart shifted, thumping against her rib cage. Seeing that he was settled, she had a couple of things to clear up. One a huge concern, and one a niggling worry. She turned to Uriel. "Two questions?"

"Shoot."

Delaney's heart throbbed with painful thumps. "My friend Marcella . . . I know it's a lot to ask after all this, but—I just need—I need to know she's okay. I know she's a demon, and that's way bad in your book—like no-going-back bad—but she risked everything to help us. Don't you guys have, like, a 'time served' program—something—anything . . ." Her gaze went to Satan's narrowed, angry eyes and fear seeped into her gut for her friend's well-being. Casting Uriel an imploring glance, she said, "He'll hurt her—"

Uriel held up a hand and leaned in to whisper, "You know I can't make promises like that, Delaney. She made a choice, wahine, and it so wasn't the right one, but she's the horned one's territory and I can't change that because it would screw up the balance of good and evil—or something like that. But I will promise you this—I'll try to hook her up, and you're gonna have to trust me enough not to ask anything else." His gaze was pointed when he added, "Try to rest easy where your BFF is concerned, okay?" Then he smiled at Lucifer. "Now ask me question number two so I can get this monkey off my back."

Delaney breathed a shuddered sigh of relief. Uriel's eyes said far more than his words and she'd cling to them in the hopes that Marcella would be safe from Satan's wrath. "Okay, question two. When he wakes up, is it going to be like all those stupid movies where he has no frickin' clue who I am? I saw that in some movie once, and the poor guy had to start all over again because his woman didn't know who he was. I have to tell you, I like him just like this. He gets that I have the gift of sight. No questions asked when some crazy ghost shows up in the middle of . . . well, you know. That would suck. He's broken in."

Uriel's face wore understanding, his eyes read warm. "That would be so bogus, huh? Nah. He'll remember. Promise. It's the least I can do for screwing this up. Chill, everything's good." Uriel gave her shoulder a gentle squeeze, preparing to leave.

"Wait, just one more thing. How did Clyde get up out of that bed? He was . . ."

"Dead? Yep, fo sho. Whew! It took me centuries upstairs and more levels than you have dogs to learn it, too. But it's a trade secret, ya feel me?"

Delaney's nod was grave, but her smile was warm. "Thank you. You have no idea how much . . ." She couldn't finish. This gift—this "get out of jail free" card—had overwhelmed her.

Uriel winked. "Oh, I think I do. And now, I'm out." He gave her the hang ten sign before sighing with displeasure in Lucifer's direction. "And you, Dr. Doom, you and me, we got plans. How do ya feel about *Dream Girls?* It was righteous. Or maybe because you're so bent all the time you might like something funny. You know, like ha-ha, Uriel stomped me again, funny?"

His voice trailed off, and then he and the devil were swallowed up by the velvety black of the night just outside Clyde's hospital room window.

Delaney shuddered a breath, closing her eyes and bowing her head. *Thank you, thank you, thank you,* she said in silent gratitude before putting down the bed rail and stretching out beside Clyde. Her head found the spot on his chest where his heart beat in strong, satisfying pumps. She sighed with a contentment she'd never known before.

As the sun pushed its way through the big window in Clyde's hospital room, the bright orange, settled among deep purple slashes, stirred Clyde.

Delaney sat up with a start, her heart jolting at first with fear, then fluttering to an even rhythm with relief when Clyde said, "So, ghost lady—does this mean I have to eat tofu while we listen to Michael Bublé?"

epilogue

"Hey, ghost guru—penny for them," Clyde whispered playfully in her ear when he kneeled beside her grandmother's newly upholstered chair upon his return from work. The reupholstery he'd paid for.

Delaney's lips instantly pursed for a kiss, her heart speeding up when his handsome face peered into hers. "I cost way more than that, Mr. Reincarnated, and don't call me ghost guru anymore, okay? It's still a raw nerve."

Clyde kissed her lips, tracing them with his finger, shooting her a smile of sympathy.

She couldn't see ghosts anymore. Nothing. Not a single flicker. The only time her chimes rang these days was when she had an actual customer.

So many things had changed since that night in the hospital room in North Dakota. Clyde's recuperation had indeed been deemed miraculous, and it was swift, but not totally painless. They'd gone to his neighbor's and collected Hypotenuse, who was as aloof as ever and forever meowing the indignity of sharing his new home with six dogs.

Clyde had a job now, working as a chemical consultant with a local research firm, and she was considering going back to school for her degree in veterinary medicine. A degree Clyde offered to fund one night when he'd wanted to soften the blow of taking her out for cheeseburgers and fries.

She was also considering dragging Clyde to the altar if he didn't drag her there first. Though they'd only known each other three months, she was all for having a short engagement.

"Maybe this was the universe's way of giving you a vacation— so we can hang out and, you know, be all carnal." Clyde wiggled his eyebrows at her, his deep blue eyes teasing, but sympathetic. No one understood better than Clyde how she'd mourned the loss of her gift and then in turns rejoiced in it. All those years, all those waffling souls needing guidance, messages delivered to people who just didn't believe and she'd spent a lot of time convincing, had taken a toll on her. Her life hadn't been hers totally for a long, long time. Some days she thought acceptance had finally come, yet others were still spent hoping Charles Bronson would offer up a *Death Wish* or Michael Landon would show up and want to play Name That *Little House on the Prairie* Episode.

The smile she returned was bittersweet. In this deal, she'd gotten Clyde. Brilliant, klutzy, sexy, sometimes too serious Clyde.

In this deal, she'd gotten a future.

And in this deal, she'd also lost the only close friend she'd had for ten years.

Marcella was gone.

At least in the physical sense.

Delaney couldn't bring herself to wade too far into the murky waters of her brain to reason where exactly her longtime friend was. When all was said and done, she had to trust in Uriel and what he said he'd do to help Marcella or she'd lose her mind. Though each time she thought of her closest friend, Delaney experienced a twinge of relief, a vibration that came as quickly as it went, and as sure as she was that miracles really did happen, she was sure Uriel was responsible for that otherworldly reassurance.

Though that didn't keep her from having a moment or two of selfish irritation with her BFF. If Marcella could have just kept her nose out of it. If she would have just listened, just once, instead of letting that damned temper of hers get the better of her. If she'd just not gotten involved, none of this would have happened. Delaney teetered between infuriated with her for never listening, and missing seeing her so much it hurt.

Clyde kissed the tip of her nose, tugging his glasses off to reveal the deep blue of the eyes she'd fallen in love with. "No Marcella either, I gather."

Delaney shook her head, her hair curtaining her face. "No, and I miss the hell out of her, but there's nothing I can do about it. If I can't see the spirits anymore, I can't ask around, but I have faith Uriel kept his word. And Kellen's just getting his feet wet with the medium thing, but maybe as he gets better at communicating with the dead, he'll find a way to check on her."

Because technically, Delaney had died the night of her showdown with Satan, the original contract with Vincent's father, and the clause that said the gift would be passed on to the next relative in line, lived on—in Kellen.

And he hadn't been too happy about the medium gift that kept on giving, but he'd picked up where she'd left off, and she'd been helping him to adjust to the sudden and abrupt turn his life had taken.

Clyde put his glasses back on and pulled her to her feet, enfolding her in his strong, secure arms. "I know you miss her, baby. I'm sorry I didn't have the chance to know her better. If it weren't for her, we'd have never known what had to be done that day."

They'd talked long into many nights about how lucky they were, how grateful they were to Marcella and Uriel.

Despite her anxiety and longing for certainty about Marcella's safety, she found herself letting Clyde's embrace soothe her. "And Darwin. Who's going to look after him and help him cross? He was such a stubborn shit I don't think there's another medium in the world that can do it. I'm worried about him."

Clyde never offered solutions when she grieved the loss of Darwin and Marcella. Instead, he quietly urged her to move forward by redirecting her thoughts, giving them focus on the here and now. Something neither of them would ever take for granted again. Today was no exception. "I think I might have found something to distract you," he said, kissing her forehead before pivoting on his heel and grinning as he headed for the storefront door. He popped it open, unhooking something from the doorknob.

"You didn't." She gave him a stern frown all while her lips turned upward in a smile.

Clyde gripped a pink leash in his hands. Attached was the muddiest, mangiest, most matted brown and white dog she'd seen in all her pet rescues. A black smudge circled one eye, and his alert ears stood high on his head.

And he had no right front paw.

"I found him outside the 7-Eleven, digging in the alleyway. I figured he'd match dog number six. They make one whole dog if you put them together," he said with a husky chuckle.

Delaney squealed when Clyde let the leash fall to the floor and their newest addition tackled her, lavishing her with smelly dog kisses. She couldn't stop the giggle of joy Clyde's bringing home a stray brought, or the swell of her heart as she made note of the fact that he totally and completely got it.

Lock, stock, and now seven dogs and counting.

Clyde dropped to the floor beside her, pressing a hand to the dog's backside to encourage him to sit. Clyde nuzzled her cheek with his nose, setting the butterflies in her belly free. "So tell me, fruit cup, how do you feel about actually naming this one?"

She shrugged her shoulders. "I dunno. How do you feel about a jealous canine uprising?"

"I was sorta thinking maybe something refined and classy like Tripod. How 'bout you?"

Her giggle tinkled in her ears while the new puppy buried his head in her hands, lapping at her fingers. "No go. That's like calling a pit bull Fluffy."

"Okay, then, what about Norville or Ned or Aloysius?"

Dogs one through six had sensed a new presence and began to bark. "I say you've had too much sugar today, Clyde the Reincarnated."

His eyes became serious when he cupped her chin and captured her gaze. "So, you in?"

"In?"

"Yeah, are we keeping him?"

"Definitely."

"No backsies?"

"Of course no backsies," she replied.

His sigh was big, and it held distinct relief. "So you *are* in. We're keeping him."

Delaney nodded with a wide smile, warming at the word *we* in the equation. "All the way." *All. The. Way.*

"Frank Sinatra was the first to record it, I think; 1957."

Delaney cocked her head at him. He was spewing music trivia— and that always meant he was stressed about something. It was probably the consumption-of-bad-preservatives kind of guilt. He'd better not have had a cheeseburger on the way home after she'd lovingly prepared a wheat germ salad and salmon burgers for their dinner—she'd have his ass on a platter. "Yeah, Frank. But whatever has you freaking has nothing to do with Frank. So spill, honey."

Clyde smiled, pushing his glasses up on his nose. "You just said yes—it geeked me out for a minute. Nerves about asking and all. It's over. I'm good."

The many facets of Clyde. "Now in English—for the non-Mensas of the world."

His grin was mysterious and playful. "I brought home a dog and asked if you were all in, and you said *yes*."

"Code for?"

"The dog is a symbol of my desire to mate with you, honey. He's my engagement gift to you. You know, like in foreign countries when the suitor brings his woman's family a wildebeest or whatever to declare his love?"

Though her heart raced, and her stomach danced a tango, she teased, "I thought that was goats, or a herd of sheep."

"Sorry—I couldn't find any sheep. So a dog it'll have to be. And you already said yes. That means no backsies."

Her giggles filled the store, startling the dog, who whined with impatience. That he'd brought her the one thing he knew she couldn't deny was what meant he could stay.

Forever.

"I did not either. Maybe I'd prefer a goat, Atwell. Goats make cheese. I like goat cheese—"

Tackling her to the floor, Clyde's rumble of laughter penetrated her chest—her heart. "Goats don't make cheese, honey," he corrected, shooting her a smile. "You make me batshit, Delaney Markham, and the sick thing is, I like it. Nay, I love it, and you. So, one more time: You all in?"

"All"—she punctuated the word with a kiss to his yummy lips and a breathy sigh—"in."

Clyde offered his fist to her.

She knocked it, and they blew it up.

Together.